AGAINST THE WIND

Cowgirls in Time Romance Series

A Chill Wind

Wind Beneath My Wings

Against the Wind

AGAINST THE WIND

Erica Einhorn

Ralston Store Publishing
P.O. Box 1684
Prescott, Arizona 86302

ISBN 978-1-938322-25-9

Professionally and lovingly edited by:
Jennifer Hope
www.MesaVerdeMediaServices.com

Printed in the USA.

Dedicated to the one I love

CHAPTER ONE

WHAT A GLORIOUS day to be alive on this earth! The sun streamed through the window, and Madison could see the brilliant blue sky with the mountains in the background. She stretched, yawned, and hugged herself in gratitude for how lucky she was. Walking around the different rooms in the big house, she marveled that it was all hers. Well, not exactly hers. The house still belonged to her Aunt Jenna who was now living happily ever after in the old Red Bluff. Jenna and her husband, Josiah, were content and settled in the nineteenth century. They only came back to the house occasionally, for dinner out or supplies—supplies they couldn't get back there—like batteries and Rocky Road ice cream.

Meanwhile, the house was all hers. She walked into the kitchen and started the coffee. Then she took the cinnamon roll out of the refrigerator. Putting it in the microwave, she glanced into the front room. Her mother would not approve. Kat, as everyone called her, was a nurse practitioner who kept a strict diet. No wheat, no sugar, no beef unless grass fed—Madison couldn't even remember all of her mother's diet restrictions. But she was not interested in following that regimen, so she removed the warm roll, inhaled the cinnamon-ness of it, took a bite, and closed her eyes. Best cinnamon rolls in town!

As she walked by the side of the refrigerator on her way to get a coffee cup, she frowned. It was almost Father's Day. Madison hated Father's Day. Her father, Billy, had died in the middle east when she was a baby. She never had the opportunity to call him "Daddy." Whenever her mother spoke of him, she spoke of "Billy," so that's how Madison thought of him. When she was a little girl, she'd ask her mother endless questions about him. So she thought she had the sense of him, the feel of him, in her head. But there was an empty place in her heart that would never be filled.

When she was in school, she dreaded all the Father's Days and the Father/Daughter dances. In art class, while everyone else made Father's Days gifts for their fathers, Madison would deliberately do something bad to get sent to the principal's office. Although she was a model student the rest of the time, no one ever figured out why she'd always misbehave right before Father's Day. Whatever punishment she received was always better than having to create a Father's Day card for a father who didn't exist. She suspected that her mother knew—although she had never said anything about it—and Madison never admitted it. Sure, there were other kids in school whose parents were divorced—plenty of them. But there was a drastic difference between an absentee father and no father at all. In the small elementary school that she had attended, there was one boy who had also lost his father. That didn't diminish the pain, though.

Madison tightened her lips and frowned. She hated that her mother didn't use Billy's last name. Kat said it was easier that way and eventually Madison would understand. But at twenty-one years old, Madison still did not understand. She used his last name with pride and walked tall. Madison always walked tall.

CHAPTER TWO

MOANING. SOMEONE WAS moaning, and it was keeping him awake. How could he fall back to sleep with that blasted noise? And he was freezing. His whole body shook with the chills. As Zack struggled to open his eyes, the morning light filtered through the curtains and the moaning stopped. Then he realized the moaning had been coming from him.

The room swirled around him. He closed his eyes and took a deep breath. It was morning, and he had a job to do. Opening his eyes again, he waited for the room to still. Cradling his arm, he swung his legs over the side of the bed. When the room swirled again, he swayed and fell backward onto the bed. This time he didn't fight it. The moaning started again, and the pain was intense. It had been getting steadily worse for the past few days, but this was the worst. How could he work when his arm hurt this bad? Zack didn't remember Sheriff Josiah complaining that his arm hurt this bad when he was shot.

He didn't know how much time had passed before he heard a knock at the door. "Zack? Zack!" More knocking. Zack tried to call out, but his voice came out as a squeak. Then the door opened.

Sarah rushed to the side of his bed, lightly brushing his arm as she put her hand on his forehead. He tried to focus his eyes on her. "Zack, are you all right? Oh, no! You're burning up! Is your arm all right?"

"Ow! Don't touch it! It hurts!" Although Sarah had barely touched his arm, it hurt too badly to let anyone near it.

"Zack, I need to put my hand on your arm," said Sarah.

"No, it hurts," said Zack, as he rolled away from her.

"Zack, I need to do this. Now please let me. I won't hurt it. I'll just put my palm on your arm. I need to touch it. Please."

Zack rolled back toward her and said, "Be gentle."

Sarah gently placed her hand on his arm, barely touching the skin. Then she put her hand on his forehead again. "Zack, you're burning up with fever, and your arm is hot." She pushed up his sleeve to look at the arm. "It's a good thing that there are no red streaks, so you don't have blood poisoning. Yet. You need to see a doctor. Now."

"No. All he'll do is bleed me. I don't want to be bled. I'll be fine."

"I'm going to get Matthew." Sarah disappeared out the door.

Zack tried to sit up, but couldn't. He wanted to use Sarah's toilet. It wasn't Sarah's anymore. Since she had married and moved in with Matthew, Zack had gotten her room and her toilet. Sarah called it a composting toilet. He didn't care what it was called. It was convenient, and he didn't have to go outside to the necessary.

But he was too weak to even sit up. He didn't dare try to walk across the room. Lost in his own thoughts, the sound of the door opening and Matthew bursting in, followed by Sarah, surprised Zack.

"Sarah says you're sick," said Matthew. "How do you feel?"

"I'm fine," said Zack, as he tried to sit up, failed, and fell backward onto the bed. "But can you help me use the toilet, please?"

"He needs a doctor, Matthew. It's serious."

"I don't want a doctor. He'll just bleed me again, and it didn't help before."

"Zack's right," said Matthew. "The doctor will just bleed him."

"Matthew, I want to take him to the *other* doctor," said Sarah.

"There is no other doctor, Sarah. Doc Mercer is the only doctor in town," said Matthew.

"No, Matthew, I mean the *other* doctor," said Sarah, as she raised her eyebrows. Zack had no idea what other doctor she meant or why she raised her eyebrows at Matthew. But he intended on staying right there until he felt better.

"Oh!" said Matthew, stepping away from the bed and looking from Zack to Sarah and back to Zack again. "We couldn't. Oh, no, that's not possible. I mean, he doesn't know."

"Could you two argue someplace else? Know what? What don't I know? Matthew, can you help me to the toilet?"

"His arm is *infected*, Matthew. Seriously infected. He needs to see a doctor. A *real* doctor. And I'm going to take him—no matter what you or Zack say. He's going!"

6

Sarah stomped out the door.

Matthew helped him up from the bed and asked, "Zack, why are you still in your clothes?"

"I didn't feel good enough last night to get 'em off."

When Matthew helped him back into bed after he used the toilet, Zack realized how weak he was. He could barely stand up without Matthew's help. Still, he didn't want to see any doctor. All Doc Mercer had done for him when he saw him last week was bleed him. It didn't help then, and it wouldn't help now. Zack knew he needed something else, but he didn't know what. He hoped that with a little more rest, he'd feel more like his old self.

The door opened, and Sarah walked in. "It's ready. Help me get him down the stairs."

"I'm not going anywhere, Sarah." Zack lay back down on the bed.

"He doesn't want to," said Matthew.

Sarah stomped back over to the bed and gently lifted Zack's arm. "Feel that arm, Matthew. Then put your hand on his forehead. He's hot! His arm is hot! The boy is sick and needs a doctor—a real doctor. He's not going to get that here. He needs to go *there*."

Zack didn't know where *there* was, but he wasn't going anywhere. He allowed Matthew to touch his arm, and then he pulled it back, cradled it, and turned his back on Matthew and Sarah. "I'm not going."

"But he doesn't know anything about, um, *there*," said Matthew.

"It doesn't matter. He needs to go. Besides, he would have found out eventually from Madison," said Sarah.

"Madison," said Zack, turning around. "You're taking me where Madison is?" Zack liked Madison. He had met her a time or two before and had enjoyed talking to her.

And she was pretty.

"Yes, Zack. Come with me, now, and you'll see Madison," said Sarah.

"Okay." Zack struggled to get up, and Matthew helped him.

"Let's get him downstairs," said Sarah. "Easy now."

As they started walking him through the door, Zack said, "Wait! My book! I want my book." Matthew propped him in the doorway and walked to get his book from the bedside table. He held it up so Sarah could see.

"*Purdon's Digest of Laws of Pennsylvania*? This isn't Pennsylvania. Why are you reading that?" asked Sarah.

"He wants to be a lawyer," said Matthew.

"I read everything I can about the law," said Zack.

With Sarah on one side of him and Matthew on the other, they helped him downstairs. He realized even more how weak he was. Without them, he would have toppled down the stairs. They helped him walk through the saloon and out the front doors. A horse and a narrow wagon waited outside.

"Help me get him in the back," said Sarah.

After a few attempts, they were able to get him into the back of the wagon. He lay down on the empty grain sacks, with a full bag for a pillow.

"See how nice Ezra made it for you, Zack?" asked Sarah. Ezra ran the livery stable where Sarah had rented the horse and wagon. Dancer, Sarah's horse, wouldn't pull a wagon if you paid him, thought Zack.

"Matthew, can you bring him a blanket?" asked Sarah.

While Matthew walked back into the saloon to get a blanket from upstairs, Zack relaxed onto the empty grain sacks. Walking down the stairs and climbing into the wagon had exhausted him. He had no idea how he would get out of the wagon. How far away did Madison live, anyway?

Matthew came back and wrapped Zack in the blanket. It felt good, but a little tight around his sore arm, so he pulled the arm out and put it on top of the blanket. "I'm ready," said Zack. "I guess." He closed his eyes and listened to the conversation between Matthew and Sarah, although he didn't understand it.

"Are you sure you want to do this, Sarah? We can find another way. Maybe have Kat come here," said Matthew.

"No, Matthew. I'm afraid it's really bad, and there's no time. I don't want him to lose his arm."

"Lose my arm?" asked Zack. "It's not going anywhere." He brought it back under the blanket, just in case.

"Okay, Sarah, if you have to. When will you come home?" asked Matthew.

"After I get him taken care of. I'll have to call Kat and see if he needs to go to a hospital."

"I love you, Sarah. Take care of Zack," said Matthew.

"Love you, too, Matthew," said Sarah.

Zack heard them kiss, and then he fell into a restless sleep.

CHAPTER THREE

ZACK AWOKE WITH a start. He realized he was riding in a wagon—he could feel the wheels rolling beneath him—but he didn't know why. When he touched his sore arm, he cried out in pain. It had gotten worse. Now he remembered. Sarah was taking him someplace to see a doctor—someplace where Madison was.

"Zack, are you okay?" asked Sarah.

"Not exactly okay, but I'm still here," said Zack.

"Zack, I need to talk to you about something important. Are you alert enough to listen to me?"

"Yeah, but where are we, Sarah? This looks like a cave."

"It *is* a cave, Zack. It is a cave that leads to the future. Jenna, Ryan, Granny, and I all come from the future."

"And Madison? Does she come from the future, too?" asked Zack.

"Yes, and Madison, too."

"The future? What do you mean?"

"What year is it, Zack?"

"1870."

"When we come out of the cave in another minute,

10

we will be in 2014."

"2014? How is that possible? I think you're trying to bamboozle me, Sarah."

"Bamboozle? You mean kid you? No. And to answer your question, none of us know how it's possible, but we have all been going back and forth for months now."

"Has Matthew been there?"

"Yes, Matthew has been there. He didn't want to go, but I convinced him that he needed to. You know when Matthew asks if you can handle the saloon for an evening or two? We come here to eat. Matthew likes Thai food," said Sarah and laughed.

"Tie? What do you mean?"

"Too complicated to explain. You'll be here for a while, so you'll find out soon enough."

"How long will I have to stay? I mean, how long can I stay? I might like this future of yours. Besides helping Matthew out, there's not a lot to keep me in Red Bluff."

"Oh, no, you don't, Zack. You will go to the doctor, and when you're well enough, you will return to the old Red Bluff."

They emerged from the cave into the bright sunlight. It hurt Zack's eyes, so he closed them. "Tell me more about the future, Sarah. I want to hear, but I need to rest now."

"We'll get you fixed up right away, Zack, and you'll feel much better."

"Tell me more, Sarah."

"Okay, well, remember Hilary Clinton, the rustler?"

"Sure. Sheriff Josiah caught him."

"Yes, but it was Jenna who figured out who he was. Do you know how she figured it out?"

"No," said Zack.

11

"Because Hillary Clinton is a former president's wife. She was also a senator and secretary of state."

"Secretary what?"

"Zack, are you okay? Do you want me to keep quiet now so you can sleep?"

"No, keep talking. I want to hear more about your future."

Sarah continued talking about cars, trucks, cell phones, skyscrapers, and airplanes. Zack fell asleep sometime after she described the machines that flew through the sky.

CHAPTER FOUR

AFTER MADISON FINISHED savoring her last sip of coffee, she looked out the window again at the mountains and the bright blue sky. Today might be a good day for a long ride into the mountains. She could pack a lunch and make a picnic out of it. Closing the front door behind her, she walked out to the barn. Since each stall had its own automatic hay feeder, besides a quick check to see if they were all functioning properly, she didn't need to spend much time in the barn. But she loved it—loved being around the horses and loved the "horse air"—the pleasant aromas that accompanied the horses' environment. Sometimes as she brushed her horse, she would stop, put her cheek against his neck, and just inhale the horsey perfume. There was nothing better.

There were only a couple of horses in the barn nowadays. Aunt Jenna took her horse when she moved to the old Red Bluff, and Uncle Ryan did as well, as did Sarah when she moved there, and Granny—who was Madison's great-grandmother, but everyone called her Granny—took Jenna's horse, Dolly, when she moved there. So the only horses in the barn now were her mother's horse, Paisley, and Madison's horse, Chaco. Paisley was a leopard appaloosa—an older and well-behaved mare that her mother had had for years and years.

Madison's horse, Chaco, had begun as a 4-H project. He had been a three-year old mustang, fresh off the range. Chaco was a brown and white pinto, with a bald face, three black socks, black mane and tail, and one blue eye. He had only been handled long enough to scare the dickens out of him when they forced him into a squeeze chamber to freeze-brand him and anesthetize him so they could geld him. It wasn't a great beginning between him and humans. When Madison first got him, she'd sit at the side of his corral with a handful of hay. It took patience—and hours—but eventually he would eat the hay from her hands. At first reluctantly, and later he'd take it from her with more enthusiasm.

From there, she would hold the hay in one hand and slowly bring her other hand toward the side of his face. It took more time and more patience, but after a while he relished her touches. She continued working with him every day, and their bond grew stronger. The real breakthrough came one day when Madison was lying out in the middle of the pasture after having a fight with her mother. Chaco came out of nowhere, sniffed her once or twice, and then lay down beside her with his head on her stomach. From then on, they were inseparable.

The rest of his training went slowly, because Madison didn't want to push him. First, she'd lean over his back until he was used to the feel of her weight on him. Then she'd push herself onto his back and immediately off again. Next, she'd stay up there for a few seconds and gradually increase the time. When she finally got around to riding him, he didn't buck even once. Well, except the time she put the saddle on him wrong, and it pinched him. She went flying that day, but Chaco didn't hold it against her. These days, both preferred to ride bareback, although Chaco would tolerate a saddle if it didn't pinch him.

Chaco and Paisley both nickered as she approached. Madison stroked Paisley's face and then walked into Chaco's stall to hug him. She moved her hand along his back and legs, getting some dust off.

"Chaco, would you like to go on a long ride today? We haven't done that for a while. It will be fun, huh?" In response, Chaco turned around, grabbed a mouthful of hay, and began munching. "Is that a no, then?" Madison patted the horse on his rump. She sighed. "Well, I guess I don't much feel like going either." After one last stroke on his neck, Madison locked up the stall and walked back to the house.

Chaco was usually as eager to go for a ride as she was, so when he acted like he didn't want to go, Madison listened. But she wasn't really disappointed. Lately riding alone had gotten her down. She enjoyed riding and had always cherished the time alone on the trail with Chaco, but it had begun to feel like something was missing. Like she was missing something essential to her.

Her whole life had started to feel like that. Although she loved college and loved what she was studying, something felt missing. During the three years she had spent in college so far, she had made a conscious effort not to get involved with any men. Her studies were important to her, and she didn't want anything to upset that delicate balance. Now she wondered if maybe she had been missing an important part of college life. A boyfriend.

Not that she had even met anyone with whom she

might consider a relationship. Well, except Zack. But he was from the old Red Bluff. Madison wasn't like Aunt Jenna or Sarah or Uncle Ryan, or even Granny for that matter. She had no desire to live in the nineteenth century. To use a cliche, it was a fun place to visit, but she wouldn't want to live there. Madison considered herself a woman of the twenty-first century. She came equipped with her iPhone, her iPad, her laptop computer—and she wasn't willing to give any of that up. No. She liked living in the "new" Red Bluff, and she knew she would stay here. So a relationship with Zack was not even worth considering.

Madison finished the vacuuming, cleaned up the kitchen, and started the dishwasher. She felt she had to keep the house really clean, because she never knew when anyone was going to drop in. It wasn't like Aunt Jenna or Sarah could call and let her know. They hadn't figured out yet how to communicate from one century to another—not that they ever would—but it was something to think about.

Walking back into the living room, she plopped down on the sofa. This house was so big. Although she did have people visit quite regularly, it still felt huge for just her. When her Aunt Jenna had first asked if she wanted to live in the house, she had jumped at the chance. At the time, she was sharing a two-bedroom apartment with two other women. Other people had "offered" to share the house, but since all Madison had to pay was utilities, she didn't need anyone. And after the cramped apartment, living alone for a while sounded great. Now, it was starting to feel lonely. It was a big house. She wanted someone to talk to.

As she sat there, pondering the possibilities and feeling

lonely, she propped her feet up on the coffee table. She leaned back and sighed. Madison needed a change in her life, a big change. She needed someone to talk to, someone to share her life with, someone to talk over her studies. But who would that be? Then the doorbell rang. And rang again and again. Six times in quick succession, like someone was in a hurry. Madison rushed to answer the door.

CHAPTER FIVE

"SARAH! WHAT'S GOING on? You know you can just walk in."

"Madison! Hurry! Help me get Zack into the house."

"Zack?" said Madison, concerned. She followed Sarah out to the horse and wagon parked in front of the house. Zack was lying in the back, under a blanket, with his head on a sack of grain, and looking pale. "Is he okay?"

Zack moaned, opened his eyes, and looked at Madison. "Mmmm. I'll be okay. Would you believe that Sarah's been telling me tall tales about coming to the future? I think she wanted to keep my mind occupied so the arm wouldn't hurt so much. How are you, Madison?"

He tried to sit up by himself, but couldn't do it with just his one good arm. Sarah and Madison helped him to sit up, and then helped him out of the wagon and into the house.

When they got him seated on the couch, Madison said, "What happened? Why did you bring him here?"

"You know he got shot, right? When all the men came to rescue me? Anyway, his arm is infected, *very* infected. I

18

wanted Kat to look at it. He might need to go to a hospital. I'll call her now." Sarah pulled the cell phone out of her pocket, while Madison stroked the hair out of Zack's face. Madison's cell phone rang.

"Hello?"

"Oh, Madison!" Sarah hung up the phone.

"Oh, we switched phones and numbers! Let me call her." As Madison moved her fingers across the iPhone, she looked up quickly and said, "Mom didn't like the iPhone, so we traded." Then she put the phone by her ear. "Hi, Mom. Listen, Sarah is here. She just brought Zack. . . . Yes, he's here now. Sarah says his arm is really infected and that he might need to go to the hospital. She wanted you to look at it. . . . Do what? . . . Oh, okay."

Madison turned her attention to Zack. "Mom says I need to look at your arm and feel it." When Zack held his arm protectively, Madison said, "I won't do anything to hurt you. I'll just put my hand on it gently and look."

"Oh, yeah, Mom, it's really hot," Madison said into the iPhone. "There is a lot of redness, but no streaks. . . . Yes, I'll tell her. . . . Okay, see you soon." Madison put the phone back into her pocket.

"What was that you were talking into?" asked Zack. Then, looking around the room and pointing to the television and the stereo, he asked, "And what's that? And that?"

Sarah and Madison both laughed. "Sarah, Mom said that you got him here just in time. Then she said some expletives about Doc Mercer, and said she might have to move back there just to take care of the people she loves!" Then, to Zack, she said, "Zack, Sarah wasn't kidding about bringing you to the future. The year is

2014. Welcome! I talked on my iPhone," she pointed across the room, "and that is called a television, I'll show it to you later, and that over there is a stereo that plays music. You'll like that. I think you'll like this future, Zack. I've been to your world, now welcome to mine! Oh! And wait until you see the kitchen! And the bathroom! You have all kinds of cool things in store for you in my world!"

"Can I see your iPhone thing?" asked Zack.

As Madison reached into her pocket to pull out her iPhone, Sarah put her hand on Zack's forehead and said, "Did she say how soon she'd be here?"

"Don't worry, Sarah. Mom knows that it's serious. She'll be here in fifteen minutes. She'll fix Zack right up!" Madison sat beside Zack on the couch, and when she leaned over to show him the phone, he screamed.

"Ow! My arm!"

"Oh, sorry, Zack. I'll sit on the other side of you." Madison moved to his other side. "Here. Let me show you how it works." A second later, Sarah's phone rang. "Sarah, will you go into the other room so Zack can talk to you?"

"He can talk to me here. I'm too worried about him to leave him alone."

"He's not alone. I'm with him, and Mom will be here in a minute. Come on, this will give you something to do so you won't worry so much."

Sarah sighed and walked into the other room, holding her cell phone to her ear. "Here, Zack," said Madison. "Hold it a little away from your ear, though. That's what my mom keeps telling me, anyway."

Zack held the phone close to his ear. "Sarah?" Then his face lit up, and he said, "I can hear you! I can hear you! What did you call this, Madison, cool? That's so cool!"

Madison laughed. "We'll make a twenty-first-century man out of you, yet, Zack!" She took the phone back from Zack. "Sarah, thank you." Then she held it up for Zack and showed him some of her favorite apps.

She was hoping to make him forget about the pain in his arm, and she hoped that her mother would arrive soon. Although she didn't show it, Madison felt as worried as Sarah was. The wound on Zack's arm looked terrible. She hoped her mother was right and that Zack wouldn't need to go to the hospital. And the arm looked so bad, swollen and all, that she hoped he wouldn't lose it. How would he get along in the nineteenth century with just one arm? Madison hoped that her mother could fix him up, and it wouldn't come to him losing an arm.

CHAPTER SIX

As SARAH PACED back and forth, looking at her watch every few steps, Zack tried to put *her* concern out of *his* mind. She was really worried—which worried Zack. Even Madison, who tried to hide it by showing him all the cool, new things in this century, looked worried. Whatever the challenge of his illness, Zack felt confident that he could handle it. That's the kind of man he was. He handled whatever was put before him, and he handled it well. What was the worst that could happen? Lose his arm? He could handle it. Have the illness kill him? He could see his father and mother again. Nothing was too much for him.

At the same time, he knew when to back down, and he wasn't afraid to do that, either. When those men in Matthew's saloon, where he worked, made fun of him for being Indian, he ignored it. What else could he do? Even if he could get them to stop, there would be more men coming in who called him the same names. No, better to just ignore it and not let it bother him. It did bother him on some level—he knew that. But if he let those men know that it bothered him, it would make it that much worse.

That reminded him of the time when Sarah had stood up for him. When the man started calling Zack names, Sarah had calmly walked over to him and poured a bottle of whiskey in the guy's lap. Zack felt good that Sarah had cared enough about him to do that. But he also felt guilty about it.

That man, who was dead now, turned out to be one of the scalawags who kidnapped Sarah. Then, several men, including Zack, accompanied Sheriff Josiah to rescue Sarah. That's how Zack had ended up with a gunshot wound in his arm. He had gone to defend Sarah, as she had defended him, and he was proud of that. Still, a part of him wondered if maybe those men never would have kidnapped Sarah if she hadn't stood up for Zack. Sarah and Matthew both told him it would have happened anyway, but Zack couldn't get it out of his mind. And it made him that much more grateful that Sarah worried about him now. She obviously wasn't wrathy at him about it.

"And check this out, Zack," said Madison, disturbing his thoughts. "This is the television. See, this is the remote control, and you can change channels from here."

Madison put the device in his hands and showed him what buttons to press. Zack was so engrossed with changing the channels and looking at all the different images on the screen, it surprised him when he found Madison's mother, Kat, standing in front of him with a medicine bag in her hand.

"Madison! Turn that thing off! I need to get to work!" said Kat.

Zack handed the remote to Madison and said, "Hallo." He had met Kat once or twice before, but had never talked with her.

When the room was quiet, Kat said, "Let me see your arm, Zack. I'll take care of you."

"Is he going to be all right, Kat?" asked Sarah.

"Give me a minute to examine him, Sarah. But I can tell you right now that he was lucky you brought him right in. See these red marks around the wound? Next step is blood poisoning." Kat reached into her medicine bag, retrieved a thermometer, and quickly ran it across Zack's forehead.

"What was that?" asked Zack.

"A thermometer. You have a high fever. One hundred two degrees. I bet you've had the chills all day."

"Yeah, I've been cold. How does that thing know that I have a fever?"

"It's called a temporal artery thermometer. It works very well. Okay, Zack, take off your pants and roll over." And to Sarah and Madison, she said, "Ladies, leave the room and give Zack a moment of privacy so I can give him a penicillin shot."

"What's a penicillin shot?" asked Zack.

"I'm going to stick a needle in your bum and put some medicine in it."

"No! It sounds worse than getting my blood let!"

"You'll feel a lot better afterward, Zack," said Kat. "I guarantee it. A few hours from now, you'll be thanking me. But it will hurt a little."

"Are you a doctor?"

"No. I'm what's called a nurse practitioner. I can do much of what a doctor does, but not all—I can't do surgeries or anything—and I don't have the extensive education that a doctor does. Although, I *do* have more education than that Doc Mercer of yours. Did he wash his hands before he worked on you?"

"No. Ow! That hurts!"

"It's over now. Pull up your pants and let me work on your wound."

"What does washing your hands have to do with anything?" asked Zack.

"Hold on, Zack." Louder, she said, "Madison! Bring me some clean towels!"

Madison, followed by Sarah, walked back into the room carrying two large towels. Kat put them under Zack's arm.

"Let's see now. Washing hands gets rid of something called germs, which cause disease. That won't be widely known in your time for a few more years. Zack, the swelling and the pain should go down when the penicillin kicks in. You'll feel better after that. This might hurt while I clean out the wound."

"Is he going to be all right?" asked Sarah. "Does he need to go to the hospital?"

"No, he'll be fine. I'll need to come by and check on him every day for a few days," said Kat. "To make sure everything is healing. If the penicillin doesn't work for some reason, there would be a chance he would have to go to a hospital. But since he has never had penicillin before, there should be no problem."

"When can he go back to his own time?" asked Sarah.

"Like I said, I have to check on him regularly for the next few days. I'd say a week would be safe—if everything is healing properly."

"A week, wow," said Sarah.

"You don't need to stay with him, Sarah. You can go back. Madison and I can take care of him. He'll be fine here."

"Oh, okay. I'll be back in a week to pick him up."

"You don't need to do that, Sarah. In a week when he can ride a horse, Madison or I can take him back."

Sarah walked up to Zack and put her hand on his shoulder. "You'll be taken good care of here, Zack. Are you okay with staying?"

Zack gave a quick glance in Madison's direction and smiled. "Sure. I'll be fine here."

Sarah kissed him on the forehead and turned to walk toward the front door. "Kat, thanks for coming right over. Madison, thanks for everything."

"No problem, Sarah," said Madison.

"No worries, Sarah," said Kat. "It just makes me think that I need to move back there so this doesn't happen again because of that inept doctor. You did exactly right by immediately bringing him here. He might have died if you hadn't. Another day or two, and this could have turned into sepsis. You saved his life, Sarah."

Sarah winked at Zack. "I guess that makes us even, Zack." To the others, she added, "He got that bullet wound from saving my life. Bye, everybody."

"Sarah! Wait! My book!" said Zack.

"Oh, yes. It's in the wagon. I have no idea why you'd be reading about Pennsylvania law, Zack, but I'll bring it in."

CHAPTER SEVEN

HAD MADISON HEARD right? Did Sarah say the book was a *law* book? Before she had a chance to absorb that, her mother interrupted her thoughts.

"Madison, I need you to pick up this prescription. Zack, what's your last name?"

"Murphy."

Kat finished scribbling out the prescription and handed the paper to Madison. "There you go."

"Be right back, Mom. See ya, Zack. Mom will take good care of you."

Madison skipped out through the door and closed it behind her. Her mind raced so fast, she couldn't keep up with the thoughts. Zack was into *the law*? If that were true, they could have long discussions about it. Maybe argue both sides of a case for practice and study together. Maybe he could even be her roommate!

Oh, wait. She realized she had gotten carried away. Zack didn't even live in her century. And why would he even want to with all the pollution and the crime and everything else that was wrong with the twenty-first century? Madison, having lived with it all her life, only focused on the good things about this century. But Zack, who had first-hand knowledge of the past—who lived in the past—would never want to live here in her world.

Madison sighed. It was a pleasant fantasy and would have made a wonderful reality. A man who she already felt attracted to and who was interested in the same subject she was *and* who would live with her and be her roommate. It was the kind of win-win situation that dreams were made of. She knew better than that. Madison prided herself on being grounded in reality.

She had learned about reality in a roundabout way from her mother. Although Madison's father, Billy, had died when she was a baby, her mother believed he was coming home. And it wasn't that he was missing in action—he had been *killed* in action. Granted, there was nothing identifiable in the casket when he "came home," but others had seen it happen and testified that the car bomb that exploded at his post had killed him. Still, her mother hoped it was all a mistake and that he would come home to her. She went on hoping for enough years that Madison had been old enough to remember. Even as young as she was, Madison knew he wasn't coming home. Billy had come to her in dreams and told her that he wasn't coming home, but he would always be with her.

Still, knowing that he was always with her, but not having him there with her, felt very different. As a girl, she longed for her mother to remarry so she could have a father. But even after her mother finally gave up hope of Billy returning from the dead, she had that go-nowhere-crush on Nick, who was her Uncle Ryan's best friend. Madison always thought Nick was a jerk and hoped nothing would happen. In her mind, Nick was *not* "Daddy" material. That crush faded, too, after a while, and her mother had become devoted to her work and reconciled to living alone.

It made Madison sad that her mother didn't have someone to love. And Madison didn't want that to happen to her as well, but she was only twenty-one years old and had plenty of time. Even if it didn't work out with Zack, she had plenty of time to find someone else. Wait! She had to get Zack out of her mind. She didn't even know if it was really a law book that he was reading. Maybe it was a novel *about* law—which would mean nothing. Plenty of people read novels about lawyers, but had no real interest in the law or in becoming lawyers.

Besides, she had only talked to him a couple of times. She knew hardly anything about him. What could they have in common, anyway? Madison shook her head and smiled to herself. Girl, you need to get out more. Meet people, find a boyfriend, stop being so isolated with your schoolwork. She would start her summer job in a few days, and that would be good exposure for her. Maybe she'd meet someone there. Someone perfect.

After she got the prescription filled, she stepped back into the car and headed home. Zack was a nice boy and all, but thinking about a relationship with him wasn't realistic. Well, at least not now, anyway. Her attraction to him was merely that he was cute, with his dark hair and dark eyes. And different. How could he not be different being a boy from more than a hundred years in the past? Of course he was different. That was part of her attraction to him. She realized that.

Now he would be staying at her home for at least a week while he recovered. That was her chance to get to know him, find out more about him, and discover if there was any reality to her fantasy. Of course, once she started her job, she couldn't spend that much time with him. And maybe he'd recover quickly enough that her mother would let him go home before the week was out. Whatever was in store for her and Zack, she knew that at least for now, it was out of her control.

CHAPTER EIGHT

ZACK LAY BACK and rested on the pillow. He had promised Kat that he would take it easy. She said that he couldn't work hard and expect his arm to heal. But he couldn't help it—at least not when he was back in his own time. It was his job to help Matthew, and he took that responsibility seriously. After all, Matthew had taken him in when nobody else would. After Zack's father died, Zack had no one in the world he could count on. Eliza and Samuel, who owned the hotel, had given him a room for a while. But it was harming their income, so he knew he couldn't stay there. Then Matthew moved to town and bought the saloon. He said that if Zack helped him out, he could have free room and board. That was five years ago, and he had been living in the same place as Matthew since then. Well, until Matthew married Sarah, and then Zack moved out and stayed in the room that Sarah had occupied before they were married.

But now, here in *this* century, he had no responsibilities. Kat had said the house belonged to her sister, to Jenna, and that Zack was welcome to stay as long as he needed to. Zack knew Jenna. She had moved

31

to Red Bluff several months before and had married Sheriff Josiah. Of course, Zack hadn't known that Jenna had moved from the future into the past to be with the man she loved. So had Sarah. And so had Granny.

Zack didn't understand that. Why would anyone leave *this* wonderful place of new inventions and opportunities for the limitations of his time? No, he didn't understand that at all. He had been in the future for less than a day, and he already didn't want to leave. Did he have to go back? Would it upset something in history if he stayed in the future? No, if that were true, then Jenna, Sarah, and Granny couldn't have moved to the past. Although, maybe it just went one way. Someone could move to the past, but they couldn't move to the future. That would make sense because they hadn't done anything in the past that wouldn't get done if they weren't there. But what if someone from the future did something in the past to change the past? It felt so confusing. He still hardly believed it himself. Another time, more than a century in the future. And here he was, lying in bed in the future. It hardly seemed possible.

If the thought crossed his mind that they were trying to hornswoggle him, it passed quickly. It was one thing for Sarah to tell him about this future time while he was riding in the back of a horse-drawn cart. It was something else to see the iPhone-thing and the television in action. Those were too remarkable to be products of his time.

Not to mention the bathroom that Kat had shown him before she left. There was a bathtub in it, but the room's primary purpose was to relieve yourself. It was even more convenient than the composting toilet that Sarah had brought into his life. He still couldn't get over how the water swirled around after you pushed on that little handle. After Kat had left him alone in the house, he had steadied himself with his hand on the wall and had gone back into the bathroom just to watch the water go down. He pressed the handle again and again so he could watch it. When he finally climbed back into bed, exhausted, he felt satisfied.

After Madison had left, Kat had carefully cleaned his wound, cursing Doc Mercer the whole time. She said the wound probably wouldn't have gotten infected if Doc Mercer had observed basic hygiene by washing his hands before touching the bandages and the wound. Although it hurt Zack when Kat cleaned the wound, he knew she was helping him and being as careful as she could, so he had turned away and bitten his lip to keep from crying out. Kat said the penicillin, which she called an antibiotic, would make Zack feel better. He didn't understand why, but he took her word for it.

Kat had also put his arm in a sling and said that should help with the swelling and the pain. Not having his arm hanging down had already made him feel better. He wished that Kat hadn't left him alone in the big house, though. She had put him in Sarah's bedroom, which had its own television and remote control, but he didn't turn the television on. Being in a strange house alone was skeery enough. But having that strange house be in another century was something else. What if something happened and Madison didn't come right back? What would he do? He couldn't even get back to his own time, because he had closed his eyes for most of the trip here. He had no idea which direction to go. Zack knew there was a cave, but apparently only a few people knew where it was.

Thinking about being alone in this future time, with no way to get home to the people he cared about, scared him. Maybe he wasn't ready to move here after all. Looking around the room, he shivered, though the room wasn't cold. The idea of being stuck in this century made him uncomfortable. Staying here because he chose to stay here was different from staying because he wasn't *able* to get home. That thought made him sigh and fight tears that wanted to come to his eyes. Zack was about to stand up, brace himself against the wall, and stumble to the front room to look out the window for Madison, when he heard her come in the front door. Relief swept over him, and he allowed himself to relax back against the pillow.

CHAPTER NINE

MADISON DIDN'T SAY a word when she came through the door. She had noticed that her mother's car was gone, so it meant that Zack was home alone. He might be sleeping, and she didn't want to disturb him. But although she couldn't call out to him and he hadn't called out to her, there was a certain comfort in knowing that someone was in the house waiting for her. It gave her a sense of purpose, a reason for being. Not that she needed that, but it felt good regardless.

"Madison? I'm back here," said Zack.

A feeling of warmth swept over her, and she liked it. It felt good having someone waiting at home for her—and when it was a man who was waiting for her, it was even better. When she lived with the two roommates, one of them was inevitably home when she got home, but the feeling wasn't the same. In that cramped apartment, her main feeling was wanting to be alone.

Zack's voice sounded like it came from Sarah's bedroom. Madison thought that her mother must have put him in that room because it had a television. She headed in that direction. When she walked into the room, she saw him lying in bed propped up with a pillow behind his head. His color seemed better.

She sat down on the side of the bed next to him and said, "Hi. How do you feel?"

"It still hurts, but not as much. I think this helps," he said, indicating the sling.

Madison held up the small sack in her hand. "I got your meds."

"What are meds?" asked Zack.

"Oh, sorry. That's twenty-first-century-speak for medicine. Your next dose is tomorrow morning."

Zack's eyes widened. "*You're* going to give me a shot?"

Madison laughed easily and patted his good arm. "Not to worry, Zack. There shouldn't be any more shots. These are pills."

"Oh, good," Zack said, as he relaxed and looked away embarrassed.

She noticed the book on the bed on the other side of him. "Can I see your book?" she asked.

Zack picked it up and put it on his chest. "Oh, it's just a book I'm reading, that's all."

"I know. Can I see it? Sarah said it was a law book. Did she mean a novel about law?"

"Ah, no. It's just, ah, well, here." Reluctantly, Zack handed her the book.

Madison read the title, *Purdon's Digest of Laws of Pennsylvania*. "Are you from Pennsylvania or something?"

"No, I read all the law books I can get. There aren't many, so I read whatever I can find."

She looked up into his face. "Are you interested in the law?"

Zack looked away and, without looking at her, said, "My dream is to become a lawyer. But before you tell me how crazy that is, I know that it's just a dream." He said it defensively.

"Zack, I don't think it's crazy at all. That's what I'm taking in college. Well, I'm in pre-law now and next year I'll start law school."

Zack's eyes sparkled when he turned to look at her. "*You're* going to be a lawyer? Really? I mean, girls can become lawyers, too?"

Madison tried not to laugh. "It's a different time, Zack. Women can do anything nowadays—at least in the United States and other progressive countries. You have a lot to learn about the twenty-first century!" She thought maybe she shouldn't have said that. Maybe he wasn't interested in learning about this century. Maybe he just wanted to go home and never see this future time again. But she could hope, couldn't she?

Zack leaned toward her. "I'd like to learn, Madison. I'd really like to learn. Will you teach me?"

She smiled at him. "Of course I will, Zack. I'll teach you and show you as much of this world as you're interested in. But for now, you need to rest. You've had a big day. Your body needs time to heal itself." Madison stood up. "Try to rest now. I'll be in later to check on you and make sure you're okay. Rest easy, Zack." She leaned over, kissed him on the forehead, and walked from the room.

It was all she could do as she left the room not to shout for joy. He wanted to be a lawyer! And he wanted to learn about this century. She forced her thoughts to slow down. Just because he wanted to be a lawyer and learn about her century, didn't mean he wanted to *be* a lawyer in *her* century. He was a bright guy. Perhaps he just wanted to accumulate all the knowledge he could about her century, but had no desire to stay. That would be reasonable. It would probably be easier to become a lawyer in his time, anyway.

Madison knew that she had to stop building on the Zack fantasy. Yes, it was a pleasant thought that he was the answer to all her wishes. Because she didn't just want a boyfriend. She wanted a boyfriend who was also a companion and could discuss with her the subject she was most interested in: the law. And hadn't she admitted today that she needed something more in her life? It was almost as if the universe had delivered Zack right to her. Maybe wishes really did come true. All you had to do was think about what you wanted, feel what it would feel like to have it already, and abracadabra, there it was in your life. She laughed at her own joke. It just didn't work that way in the real world.

Although—what if it did? Zack was a man who she was already attracted to, and he wanted to be a lawyer. So they could discuss the law together as she had wanted. And if he *did* decide to stay in her century, he would probably be comfortable staying with her in her house—everything seemed exactly perfect—if only it wasn't a fantasy.

CHAPTER TEN

ZACK WOKE UP in total darkness. Wow! What a crazy dream he'd had! Madison was in it. That wasn't the crazy part, though—he'd had dreams about her before. No, it was about the future! There was an object that you could hold in your hand and talk to people that was called an iPhone. And there was that other thing called a television that had moving pictures on it. Wait until he told Sarah and Matthew about the dream. And he wanted to remember to tell them about the bathroom, too. That was amazing.

Wait. He felt better, and he had felt so bad before. Not that he actually felt good. No, he still didn't feel good. His arm still hurt. But the pain was less, and he didn't feel as uncomfortable. Zack reached out and touched his sore arm. Something was over it. He felt all around. It was a sling! Like in the dream! Maybe Sarah had put it on him while he slept. He pulled the covers off himself and discovered they were different, too. His own blanket had been replaced by a thin blanket with little lumps spaced evenly apart. What was going on?

Zack's eyes had started to adjust to the darkness, and

he looked around. Nothing was clear, it was still too dark for that, but the room didn't look familiar. There was something sitting on the chest of drawers in front of the bed that looked vaguely like the television from the dream. Propping himself up with his good arm, he put his hand out to the bedside table and felt that it had a lamp on it. Feeling around the top of the table, he searched in the darkness for matches. None.

He relaxed back onto the bed. It was starting to dawn on him that it wasn't a fantastic dream after all. It had all been real. Going over everything in his head, he remembered waking up in the morning feeling especially bad, Sarah and Matthew putting him in a wagon, riding through a cave, arriving at Madison's house, and her mother, Kat, who was some kind of nurse, putting a needle in his bum. As he reached back, his bum still felt sore. It's all real, he thought. He was in the future!

His book lay beside him on the bed, and it reminded him of his conversation with Madison. *She* was going to be a lawyer! And she hadn't laughed at him when he said he wanted to become a lawyer. It wasn't like anyone in town had actually laughed at him. Matthew and Josiah would never do that. It was the way they looked at him when he mentioned it—almost like they felt sorry for him for wanting that. He didn't want people to laugh at him, and he didn't want people to feel sorry for him just because he wanted to be a lawyer.

He knew why they reacted like that, though. What were the chances of a poor boy like him going to law school? It was expensive, and he had no money. He didn't even have the money to get there, or money for books, or any of the many requirements that would be necessary for him to attend law school. Although he could probably find a lawyer in some town close by who might take him on as an apprentice—that wasn't the same. It wasn't a real education. Zack loved to read, and he loved to read about the law. Besides, since Josiah had told him that he had gone to school to become a lawyer, that's exactly what Zack wanted to do. It didn't matter that Josiah had given it all up to move out west and become the sheriff of Red Bluff. It only mattered that he had done it, and Zack wanted to do that, too.

Then his thoughts drifted to where he was. In the *future*. A future where even *girls* could go to law school. If girls could, then surely he could find a way. Could he stay in the future and leave behind everything and everyone that he cared about? If it meant becoming a lawyer, he could.

And the thought of maybe sharing that future with Madison made it an even better idea. Now that he knew the truth about Sarah, Jenna, and Granny—that they had moved to the past to be with the men they loved—it made his thoughts of maybe moving to the future for the same reason seem almost possible, almost realistic.

Then he remembered a quote that he had read from Ralph Waldo Emerson, one of his favorite authors: "Dare to live the life you have dreamed for yourself. Go forward and make your dreams come true." He had always considered his wish to be a lawyer just a dream. Now he had the chance to make that dream come true. But how would Madison feel about him moving to her century? Yes, she had said she would teach him about it. But teaching someone and sharing a life with that person were two different matters. He would absorb everything she had to say about life in this century and everything about becoming a lawyer before he even mentioned to her that he was considering moving here.

Was he considering moving here? Was he *truly* considering that? No, he wasn't considering. He had decided. This time, this twenty-first century—more than one hundred years in his future—would be his new home. He would make it work. And he would become a lawyer, just like he always wanted.

But another thought crept into his mind. Madison. With her long dark hair, and eyes so dark you could barely see the pupil—he loved looking at her, looking into her eyes. Although he had only spoken to her a couple of times before, he had always liked her. Now, being around her in her home, in her own environment, he liked her even more. Yes, he wanted to be a lawyer, but he also really wanted to be with Madison.

CHAPTER ELEVEN

MADISON THOUGHT SHE heard Zack stirring, but the light hadn't gone on, so she stayed in her room. She didn't want to disturb him if he was still sleeping. He didn't need any medication tonight, so she didn't have to worry about that.

Smiling to herself, she realized how much she liked having another person in the house. Not that she had ever been afraid living alone in the big house, but it was comforting having someone else there. Someone else who she could potentially really fall for. She had to be careful, though, falling for someone from another century without knowing what he thought. She didn't need heartache to disturb her life right now. But love—yes, she had time for love. Plenty of time for love—with the right person, of course. Was Zack the right person? Although she didn't know, it was looking more and more like he was.

After she had left Zack's room, she had spent most of the rest of the day studying for the LSAT—Law School Admission Test. Although she had signed up for an LSAT prep class for her first quarter in the fall, she wanted to make double sure that she was prepared. She had bought several books, had downloaded a sample test from the internet, and had been working with that. So far though, what she had seen were just basic reasoning questions that she had seen on those online IQ—intelligence quotient—tests.

If Pookie is a black bear who likes strawberries, and his wife, Puff, is a brown bear who likes blueberries, what color will their children be? Well, not exactly that bad, but the questions felt like that.

Madison heard Zack cough. She thought that he must be up, so she walked down the hall toward his bedroom, stood outside, and said softly, "Zack?"

"Yes, I'm awake, now, Madison."

She walked into the bedroom. "Did you sleep well?"

"Yeah, I didn't realize how much I needed more sleep. I'm feeling a little better now. Where are the matches for this light? I couldn't find them."

"Zack, it's the twenty-first century! No more matches! Here, let me show you. Put your hand here on the base of the lamp. Feel that little knob? Turn that."

Zack followed her instructions, and the light came on. "It's going to take awhile for me to figure out all these neat things in your time, Madison. But right now, I have to use the necessary—I mean the bathroom. I think I can make it on my own, though." He stood up shakily, and Madison helped him out the door and waited till he could brace himself on the wall to go into the bathroom.

She walked to the living room, bent over in front of the bookcase, and pulled a book from the shelf. Then she went back to Zack's room to wait for him. After hearing the toilet flush several times, she called out, "Zack, what are you doing in there?"

"Oh, this is so neat. I like to watch the water swirl down!"

"You need to stop, dude. Wash your hands and come back in here."

When Zack returned and lay back on the bed, Madison spoke, "You have to learn something about the twenty-first century, Zack. It's polluted."

"I know what polluted means, but I don't understand what you mean about this century being polluted."

"Because of cars and factories, we have put junk into the air. So the air we now breathe is not clean. Red Bluff's air is still pretty good, though. If you went to Los Angeles or another big city, the air is so bad that you can see a brown haze. It's disgusting. And because of the factories, we have polluted our water. So the clean water needs protecting. What I'm trying to say is that you can't waste water like that!"

"Oh! Sorry, I didn't know."

"I know. That's why I told you. You have a lot of catching up to do on the twenty-first century. Let's see, I told you about the lamp, you already know about the remote control for the television," she pointed to the remote on the bedside table, "and tomorrow I'll show you the kitchen and the rest of the house. There are some things that you are not going to believe! And I still have to give you a ride in the car!"

"What's a car?"

"It's like a stagecoach, but it goes without horses. You'll love it. That's tomorrow. Tonight, I brought you this." She handed him the book that she had retrieved from the living room.

He looked at the book she handed him and held it to his chest. "*A Time to Kill.* Is it some kind of law book?"

"It's a novel, but it's about lawyers. I think you'll like it. And the author, John Grisham, has a bunch of other books about lawyers. I'll show you where they're kept tomorrow. You can even take them back with you and return them later. You can come here any time to get more books. It will be like a library for you! Do you have a horse?"

Zack looked down, and Madison knew it was a bad question. "I used to. Echo is a black and white pinto horse, very gentle, great personality." Zack hesitated, and Madison didn't say anything, waiting for him to go on. "After my dad died and I had so little money, I couldn't afford to keep him anymore, so I sold him to Ezra at the livery stable. At first, I'd go visit him every day. Then I thought that it would be better for Echo and me not to see each other anymore. It was painful." Another hesitation, but Madison could tell that he wasn't finished talking. "I still see him around now and then, and although I know that Ezra at the livery stable treats him well, I can only hope the people who hire him out do the same. I know people have offered to buy him from Ezra—Echo is very pretty—Ezra hasn't sold him, as a favor to me, I guess, although I haven't visited him for years." Zack sighed.

"Why is he named Echo?"

Zack brightened. "Because when you talk to him, he 'talks' back. It's really neat. He'll nicker right back at you like he's answering. I loved that about him."

"Have you seen him lately?"

"A couple of weeks ago was the last time when I saw someone riding him back into the livery."

Madison thought for a minute. "How much does it cost to buy a horse in the nineteenth century?"

"I sold him to Ezra for seven dollars, why?"

"Do you have any money in your pocket?"

Zack shook his head. "I know what you're thinking, Madison, and even if I could afford to buy him back, I couldn't afford to board him at the livery. I have nowhere to keep him."

Madison put out her hand to Zack. "Do you have any money? Let me see it."

Zack reached into his pocket and pulled out one silver dollar, two half dollars, a quarter, and a penny. Madison turned over each coin inspecting it carefully.

"Why are you looking at my coins like that?"

"Times have changed, Zack. Some old coins are worth a lot of money. Money is made differently now, and old money—money from your time—is worth a lot more than face value. You could still spend any of this money here, but you can get more for it if you take it to a coin dealer. I know Aunt Jenna cashed in some gold coins for fifteen hundred dollars each!"

That got Zack interested. "Really? Do you think these are worth anything?"

"I don't know. They're all silver, and I don't think silver is worth as much. But we can check."

"How? When? Can we do it now?"

"Calm down, Zack. You need to get more sleep so you can heal."

"Oh, come on, Madison! I want to know!"

"Zack, you need to get some sleep." She put the coins on the bedside table and asked, "Do you need anything else?"

"Yeah. Why does this blanket have lumps in it?"

"Oh!" Madison laughed. "It's an electric blanket. If you get cold during the night, then flick this switch right here," she showed him the blanket control that sat on the bedside table, "and it will warm you right up. It has different heat levels, also, so you can turn it up or down to make yourself comfortable."

"Wow," said Zack. "Good night, Madison. Thank you for all your help."

"Good night, Zack. Sleep well, and I'll see you in the morning." Madison turned off the light, closed the door most of the way, and walked to her own room down the hall.

CHAPTER TWELVE

ZACK DIDN'T KNOW how he could possibly sleep. His first impulse normally would have been to turn the light back on and read the new book that Madison had just given him. That was before she had told him about the money. He reached out and felt the coins on the table. Could these coins really bring him enough money to buy back Echo and pay for his board without worry? Zack hoped so. That horse meant a lot to him, both personally, and as a connection to his dead parents. Getting Echo back was right up there with becoming a lawyer and being with the girl of his dreams—Madison. Could he possibly have it all? He hoped so.

Thinking about Echo, the new book, and all the experiences of the day tuckered him out. That, and the weakness he still felt from the wound in his arm, helped put him to sleep. He slept peacefully through the night and woke up refreshed. His arm didn't hurt as much, it wasn't as swollen, and he wasn't disoriented at all—he knew exactly where he was—the twenty-first century— with Madison.

Picking up his head and using his good arm, he

propped the pillow up behind him, so he could look around the room. The television sat on the chest of drawers directly in front of him. A heavy curtain over the window prevented much light from getting into the room, but he could still see clearly. There was a door on the side wall, but it didn't have a handle, only a little metal-lined hole. Besides the lamp on the bedside table, there was a light on the ceiling above his head. He wondered where the knob was for that. If it was on the side of it, then people in the twenty-first century would have to be very tall! There was no wood stove in the room— but Zack didn't remember seeing a wood stove in the living room, either. Since they had lights that didn't need matches, and the amazing bathroom, then there was probably some heat source that didn't require a wood stove.

Zack liked it here. He already knew that he didn't want to leave. Ever. He wanted to stay here with Madison, go to school to become a lawyer, and live happily ever after. Of course, Madison would have something to say about that. Allowing his mind to wander, he speculated whether they still had marriage in the twenty-first century. Yes, they did. Jenna had married Josiah, Sarah had married Matthew, and even Granny had married Edward. It wouldn't have happened that easily if marriage was foreign to them. That suited Zack. The idea of marriage suited him.

But before any of that could happen, he needed to get back to the nineteenth century, buy back Echo, and say good-bye to everyone in town. Especially Matthew and Sarah. Since Matthew had married Sarah, she helped around the saloon as much as Zack did. So he didn't need to feel bad about leaving. Besides, they didn't need an extra man around since they were new-married and all. No, his moving to the future would be good for everyone. He only hoped that Madison would agree.

The clock on the chest of drawers must be another of the twenty-first-century inventions. It didn't have a face on it, only numbers. It said 6:30, so it must mean half past six. Zack wondered what time Madison would wake up. He didn't want to disturb her. Then he saw the book on the bedside table. Oh, good! He could read until she woke up. When Zack looked up again to check the clock, an hour had passed. A noise coming from the other room sounded like a toilet flushing—but not the one by his bedroom. Would there be two bathrooms in one house? Why would anyone need more than one bathroom in a house? It didn't make sense to him. But he was from a time more than a hundred years ago. What did he know?

After putting the book down, Zack stretched and sat up in bed. No dizziness. He almost felt good. Standing up slowly, just in case, he walked slowly toward the bathroom without having to hold on to the wall. Although he did have his arm extended if he needed to catch himself. While he was in the bathroom, he inspected the bathtub. A movable glass door enclosed the tub, and there was a faucet high up on the wall. Why would there be two faucets for one bathtub? And the lower faucet had three handles. Hot, cold, and what? What would the third handle be for? More twenty-first-century puzzles. He'd have to ask Madison.

Returning to his room, he put his clothes on. He would have liked to change them, but no one—including him—thought to bring his other set of clothes. These weren't that dirty, though. He'd only worn them for a week. Although he had slept in them the night he didn't feel good. But they'd be fine for now.

Picking up the remote control from the bedside table, Zack sat on the end of the bed and switched on the television. Moving pictures came on, but they weren't real people—they were paintings or something. Clicking the remote control past several more channels, he came to one where they talked about the weather. They showed a map of the United States and talked about what weather was expected in each area. It amazed him. The future, and all the fascinating inventions in it, captivated him. It made him even more certain that he wanted to stay here. He clicked more times until he came back to the moving paintings. The people and animals did and said funny things, and it made him laugh.

"Cartoons? You're watching cartoons?" asked Madison from his doorway.

"Is that what they're called? They're funny!"

"Oh, you're already dressed. I thought you might want to shower first."

"What's 'shower'?"

"Come here, let me show you," said Madison.

Zack followed her into the bathroom. She stopped in front of the bathtub with the glass doors. Reaching in, she turned the handles by the bottom faucet and water came out the top faucet.

"Oh!" said Zack, surprised. "Why does it do that?"

"That's what a shower is. You stand under the water, so you don't have to fill the tub up. You wash and rinse as you're standing there. Want to try it?"

"Maybe later. I want to find out if my coins are worth any money first. Now that there's a chance to get Echo back, I can't think of anything else." Except you, Madison, but Zack didn't say that.

"Okay, we can do that, but I think you should eat first. Aren't you hungry? You didn't eat anything at all yesterday, did you?"

"I didn't feel good enough to eat, yesterday. But yes, I am hungry now."

"You have to take a pill this morning, too. Mom would be upset if I forget to give it to you." Madison walked back into Zack's bedroom and retrieved the bottle of pills. "Come on, let's go into the kitchen. More wonders await!"

CHAPTER THIRTEEN

As MADISON LED the way into the kitchen, she wondered if all the marvels of the twenty-first century would be enough to hold Zack here. Or would *she* be enough to hold Zack here? The more time she spent with him, the more she liked him. There was something about him that felt almost *familiar* to her. Although she didn't know him very well, it was almost like he already belonged here, belonged with her.

"And this is the kitchen. Wait until you see the cool things in here!" said Madison, as she motioned with her hand and opened the door. "This is the refrigerator. Put your hand inside."

"It's cold! How does it do that? Where's the ice?"

"Up here." Madison opened the freezer above the main part of the refrigerator and pulled out a single ice cube tray.

"That little bit of ice keeps this big thing cold?"

"No. Up here is where you keep food that needs to be frozen."

"What makes it cold, though?"

"I don't know the workings of a refrigerator, Zack.

You'll have to look it up online."

"Look it up where?"

"Online. Oh! Wait till you learn about the internet! But first, the rest of the kitchen." Madison walked over to the sink and the dishwasher beside it. "You've already seen running water in the bathroom, but look at this." She opened the door to the dishwasher. "This is the dishwasher. You put your dirty dishes in here, add soap, close the door, start it up, and voila! Clean dishes!"

"Do it now! Let me see!"

"Well, it's not exactly 'voila' . . . it takes an hour. But still, amazing, don't you think?"

Zack nodded. "No more washing glasses! Wouldn't Matthew love something like that!"

Madison walked over to the electric flat top stove. "This is the stove. You turn on these dials here, and the top of it gets hot. You can boil water on top here, or whatever. Inside," she opened the oven door, "is where you cook food. And step over here." She retrieved a cup from the cabinet, filled it with water, put it into the microwave, and turned it on. "This really is 'voila.' The water will be hot in a minute." The bell rang, and Madison removed the cup. "Feel it."

Zack stuck his finger in and pulled it out quickly. "It's hot! This is all cool, Madison. Now show me the internet!"

"Well, don't we look better today," said Kat from the doorway. "You must be feeling good today, young patient of mine."

"Much better, Kat. Thank you," said Zack.

Kat walked over to Zack and put her hand to his forehead. "You still have a fever, but not as bad as yesterday. Come. Sit at the table and let me examine your arm and take your temperature." Zack sat down at the table. "I hope you took your first pill this morning, Zack."

"Oh, sorry, Mom. I brought the pills in here to give him one, but we got sidetracked with the appliances. Here's the bottle. I'll get him a glass of water."

Kat reached into her medical kit and retrieved the thermometer. Then she ran it across his forehead. "Very good. It's gone down to one hundred degrees. You still don't feel very good, do you?"

"No, Ma'am."

"But I bet with these twenty-first-century wonders all around you, you're too excited to notice. Here, take the pill with the water Madison brought you." Kat opened the pill bottle and shook out one pill into the cap, then dropped it into Zack's open hand. After he swallowed the pill, Kat said, "Now let me look at your arm." Zack put his arm on the table, so she could see it. "Yes, much better. It's healing nicely. Less red. Not as hot. Not as swollen. It's all good, Zack. You're healing well."

"Is it all right if I take him to the coin dealer today?" asked Madison.

"Definitely no. He needs to rest. It would even be good if you could leave him alone for some time today, so he can rest." Turning to Zack, she said, "Zack, you need to take care of this. I know you're healing quickly, but you don't want it to get infected again. You need to take the pills twice a day and take it easy. No running around."

"When can I take him out, Mom?"

"I'll stop by tomorrow to check on him. But let's see how he is Monday. You'll be at your new job, right? I'll stop by before I go to work and check on him. I'll leave a note whether he can go out or not."

"You can just tell Zack. You don't need to leave a note," said Madison.

Kat smiled and looked at Zack. "It's not that I don't trust you, Zack. It's that I don't want any misinterpretations of what I say." Then, turning to Madison, she said, "If Zack needs anything in town, Madison, you can get it for him."

"I thought it would be more fun for Zack if he could go to the coin dealer himself."

"That's fine. He can. But not yet. I have to run now. Bye, sweetie." Kat leaned over and kissed Madison on the forehead. "Love you."

"Love you, too, Mom," said Madison.

Turning to Zack, Kat said, "Bye, Zack. I'll stop by tomorrow to see how you're doing. Take your pills and TAKE IT EASY!"

CHAPTER FOURTEEN

"Your Mom is so nice," said Zack. "It's so nice of her to do all this for me and check on me every day and everything."

"Yeah, for a mom, she's pretty cool," said Madison. "Okay, now that Mom's come to visit, and you've seen all the miraculous devices in the twenty-first century, how 'bout we eat? I'm starved!"

"I'm a little hungry, too."

"I'm not much of a cook. Are eggs and toast okay?"

"I'm a cook! I can cook something for us!" said Zack, standing up.

"Not today, Zack. You're still recovering. Wait till you're well, and I'll let you cook all you want."

"Okay," and he sat back in the chair. "Eggs and toast sound fine."

Madison fried some eggs and put two slices of bread in the toaster. She put the eggs in front of Zack and sat at the table next to him. "The toast will be up in a minute."

"Where did you put the bread?"

"Oh, I never thought to show you the toaster! You put

bread into it, and it comes out crispy."

"Why don't you use the microwave?"

"Microwaves heat food, but they don't get it crispy. Toasters work perfect for that. Oh! There it goes!"

Madison retrieved the toast and brought it over to the table. Zack took a piece, dabbed it in his eggs, and put it in his mouth.

"You're a better cook than you think. This is delicious, Madison."

"Thanks, Zack. It's only eggs. I'm not completely helpless."

"What are we going to do today?" asked Zack.

"*You* are going to rest today. But since we can't go to the coin dealer, we can at least look up the coins online and see what they're worth."

"How do we do that?"

"Wait until you see the computer, Zack. I think you'll love it. It's better than anything else you've seen so far!"

After they finished breakfast and Madison had put the dishes into the dishwasher, she said, "Zack, you get your coins, and I'll get my computer."

Zack walked back into his bedroom and picked up the coins from the bedside table. He wondered what kind of miraculous object a computer could be. Between the flushing toilet, the television, the dishwasher, the microwave, and the iPhone, it was hard to believe there was something even better. Returning to the living room, he saw Madison sitting on the couch looking at something in front of her. It didn't seem all that miraculous as he walked up and sat beside her.

"This is a laptop computer, Zack. I'll start you from the beginning, because you can use it when I'm at work."

"It's like a small television, except the pictures aren't

moving," said Zack.

"Oh, there's plenty of moving pictures, if you know where to find them. But first, Google. If you want to find information about any subject you could possibly think of, type it in here. Have you used a typewriter? The keys are still the same, even from your time."

"What's a typewriter?"

"Really? You don't know what a typewriter is? I thought they were invented already. Let's look it up on-line."

Zack watched as Madison typed in "when were type-writers invented" onto the Google page. "Don't you need a question mark?" he asked.

"With Google, it doesn't matter. Here. See all the different possibilities that come up? These links will all say something about when typewriters were invented. Let's click on this first one from Wikipedia. That's like an online encyclopedia. Ah, yes, here it is. Look at the second paragraph. See what it says?"

Zack read aloud from the screen, "After their invention in the 1860s—"

Madison interrupted him. "That's why you don't know what a typewriter is! It was barely invented in 1870! Well, anyway, you'll have to learn the keyboard. What else would you like to look up?"

"Like what?"

"Anything you could think of that you want to know."

"Let's look up the coins! I really want to know about that. Since you told me the coins might help me buy Echo back, I can't think of anything else." That was mostly true, because Zack wasn't going to tell Madison that he couldn't keep his mind off *her*.

"Okay, the coins," said Madison. Zack watched as

Madison typed "coin values from the 1800s" into the Google page. "Here we are. Let's start with the dollars. They're probably worth more. What date is your dollar?"

Zack looked at the silver dollar in his hand. "1859," he told her.

"Is there a letter by it? S, D, or something like that? I don't know much about coins, but I know most of them have a letter that represents where they were minted."

"S," said Zack. "1859 S."

"Here it is. Depending on what condition it's in, it's worth three hundred dollars, at least. There are several different categories of their condition, but I don't know enough about them to tell you what they mean. You can look it up later, if you want."

"Three hundred dollars? Really? I could buy Echo back and board him for more than a year with that!" As Zack said that, he thought that he didn't want to board Echo in the 1800s, he wanted him here. In the future. With him. With Madison. But he kept silent.

"Now let's look up your other coins," said Madison. "What dates are your half dollars?"

"1855 S and 1856 S."

"The 1855 is worth at least five hundred! You're worth a fortune, Zack!"

"Wow! It might be worth more than the dollar! That doesn't make sense to me, but not much of the twenty-first century does. What about the other one?"

"Oh, it's not worth as much, unfortunately. Maybe a hundred dollars."

"That's still a lot of money. What about the quarter? It's an 1869 S."

"It's worth maybe four hundred dollars. More than the half dollar!"

"And the penny is an 1867, with no letter."

"One hundred. Remember that it all depends on the condition of the coin. If it's in bad condition, the price will be less, but if it's in *really* good condition, the price could go up considerably. Since your coins are only ten or fifteen years old, they could be worth more. I think you're rich!"

Zack held the coins to his heart and smiled at Madison. He thought about how wonderful it would be to get Echo back and even more wonderful to live here in this century with Madison. But did she feel the same way? He didn't know enough about women to know, but he hoped she did.

Music started playing, and Madison reached for her iPhone. "Hello!" Then she turned to Zack and said, "Zack, I'll be right back. Go ahead. Try it. You can look up anything." Pointing to the keyboard, she added, "Click here to get back to Google. Press here to click. Be back in a few." Madison walked out of the room as she talked on the phone.

At first, Zack felt afraid to touch the laptop computer. It seemed so powerful that he wondered what would happen if he did something wrong. Then he decided that if he was determined to live in the twenty-first century, he had to learn to operate the different objects here. Starting with a laptop computer. Starting now.

He moved over in front of the computer, pressed the button, and clicked where Madison had showed him. The Google page came up. What should he look up? What did he want to know? Everything! He wanted to know everything about this wonderful century that he was now a part of. At least he hoped he was a part of it —that is, more than just staying long enough for his arm to heal. What did he want? Besides Madison, that is. To become a lawyer. Zack typed in "how do you become a lawyer." It was hard picking out the letters on the keyboard since they weren't in alphabetical order, and he could only use one hand. But he managed and clicked the search button.

The page changed, and Zack smiled at his success. He chose the second option: 5 Ways to Become a Lawyer in the United States. It talked about high school. Zack wondered what high school was. Did it mean college—a higher school than regular school? No, he didn't think so. Madison had mentioned college. So what was high school? He moved his fingers trying to see farther down the page. Finally, the page moved, although Zack wasn't sure what he had done to make it move. Attend a four-year college. What? A four-year college and *then* law school? Wow. That was a commitment. Did he really want to do that? He smiled to himself. Yes. Yes he did.

Zack thought he heard Madison coming. Since he didn't want her to know yet what he was thinking, he clicked back to the Google page and moved over so she could sit in front of the computer when she returned.

CHAPTER FIFTEEN

WHEN MADISON WALKED into the living room and saw Zack, she abruptly stopped. As he sat there, not yet aware of her presence, he gazed at the computer screen with an innocence that you might see on the face of a child. And he was beautiful. His hair, a little unkempt but still attractive, was jet black. Although she couldn't see his eyes from there, she knew they were large and dark brown. His long lashes would have been better suited for a woman, but they looked wonderful on him—they added to his innocence. Was she falling in love with him? She hardly knew him, how could that be possible? And yet, she thought that was exactly what was happening.

Zack turned to look at her and smiled. "Hi, Madison!"

Madison returned his smile and said, "Oh, just girl-talk. It was one of my old roommates." She sat down beside him. "Did you just sit there the whole time waiting for me? I wanted you to poke around some."

"Oh, I did. It took awhile to get the page to move down, but I somehow made it happen. I'm still not sure how, though!"

"Just do this." She showed him how to move his fingers on the trackpad. "See? Oh, I need to plug it in now."

"Plug it in? What do you mean?"

"I'll have to explain to you about electricity, Zack. I don't think your time gets it for a few more years. Come with me," said Madison, as she stood up and walked toward her bedroom. Once inside, she put the laptop on her desk and showed Zack how to plug it in. "Let's go out to see the horses now."

As they walked toward the barn, Zack noticed the cars parked on the other side of the house. "What are *those*?"

"Those are cars—like a stagecoach without horses, kind of. When Mom gives the okay for you to go out, I'll take you for a ride! We'll take the car when we go see the coin dealer."

When they reached the barn, Madison relaxed. Often, like now, she didn't even realize she was tense, but walking into the barn, with its horsey smells, always immediately relaxed her. Madison stroked Paisley's face as she walked by. "This is Mom's mare, Paisley. And this is my boy, Chaco. Isn't he handsome?"

"He's beautiful," said Zack, stroking the horse's face with his good arm. Chaco nickered at Zack and nuzzled him.

"He likes you! Maybe when your arm is better we can go riding. Mom doesn't ride very often, and Paisley could use some exercise."

Looking around, Zack said, "This is a nice barn."

"Aunt Jenna had it specially built. See the doors on the other side of the horses' stalls? They open out onto a paddock, and the horses can open the doors themselves."

"Why would they need to open the doors themselves?"

"Jenna's parents, my grandparents, died in a fire in the

65

old barn trying to get the horses out. So Jenna had this specially made."

"Oh, wow. That's a sad story. I'm sorry."

"It's been a few years now. I try not to think about it. But sometimes when I'm in here alone, I feel like my grandparents are talking to me. I like it." Zack nodded his head but didn't say anything. Madison didn't know if he believed her or not. She hoped that he did. It was early enough in the relationship that she wanted to continue thinking of him as perfect. Relationship! What was she thinking? She didn't even know if he liked her or not. Besides, he lived in another century! She told herself, get real, girl.

Zack interrupted her thoughts. "And they get hay automatically from that?"

"Yes, exactly. Most days, unless I close the gate, they can go out to the pasture themselves and eat all the grass they want. But they also have constant access to the hay. At first they gained weight, but after they got used to having it there all the time, they didn't eat as much. Come on, I'll show you the pasture."

Madison opened the gate to Chaco's stall and held it open for Zack to walk in. She noticed how he kept his hand on Chaco as he walked past him. He knew horses. She liked that. They walked out into the paddock, and Chaco followed them. Madison climbed onto the back fence that faced the pasture. She noticed that Zack climbed up with only his good arm, but didn't complain about it. He wasn't a complainer—she liked that, too.

"You have cows!"

"Yeah, they're Aunt Jenna's. I'm just taking care of them until she sells them. It won't be much longer, I don't think."

"Where are their horns?"

"They're called *polled* cattle. That means they don't have horns. Most ranchers don't have cattle with horns anymore because they're more trouble."

"So much has changed," said Zack, as he climbed back down from the fence.

"Let's go back in now," said Madison. As she walked by Chaco, she stopped and gave him a big hug. She walked toward the barn, but saw that Zack had stopped and given Chaco a hug, too. That made Madison smile.

CHAPTER SIXTEEN

As THEY WALKED back to the house, Zack asked, "What's high school?"

"They didn't have high school in the 1800s?"

"They might have, but not where I was. What is it? Do they mean college?"

"No. That's right, you probably went to the one-room schoolhouse, didn't you?"

"Yes, I did—when I was in school. Much of my childhood, I didn't go to school. But my father thought education was important, so he brought me books whenever he could."

"High school is the last school you go to *before* college —although some people never go to college, even now. Anyway, first you go to grammar school, then middle school or junior high, and last is high school. It's grades nine through twelve or ten through twelve—depending on where you live. But you need a high school diploma to get into college nowadays."

"Oh," said Zack, disappointed.

"Although for those who never finished high school, there's always the GED. That stands for General Equivalency Diploma. Then you would also need to take the SAT, Scholastic Aptitude Test, or the ACT test, American College Testing—probably both if you only have a GED. Why?"

"Ah, just wondering," said Zack. "I ran across the term 'high school' when I was on your computer."

When they stepped into the house, Madison walked toward the couch in the living room. "While we wait for the computer to recharge, let me show you some music videos. I think you'll like them."

"Sure," said Zack. Any time spent with Madison was time he enjoyed.

The afternoon and evening flew by, and before Zack realized, it was already time to go to sleep. "Zack, if you want to watch TV tonight, just close your door and keep the sound low. I can't hear it from my room."

"TV? Is that television?"

"Yeah. It's the abbreviation that everybody uses when they talk about televisions."

"Okay, thanks. I'll probably just read instead. Good night, Madison." He watched as she walked down the hall away from him, and he sighed. Although he didn't know when he would return to the past, he knew it would be too soon.

As he lay in bed and thought about the new wonders he had seen, like electricity, the internet, toasters, and cows without horns, it amazed him how easily he accepted it all. It was completely foreign to how he had lived the first twenty-two years of his life, and yet he took to it like a horse to grass. He thought about when electricity might reach the nineteenth century and realized he could look that up on the internet. But it didn't matter. What happened in the nineteenth century had no bearing on the Zack Murphy of today. Zack was starting to consider himself more and more as a man of the twenty-first century. He liked it here, and he didn't want to leave.

Then his thoughts drifted to the horses, Chaco and Paisley. It had been so long since he had touched a horse. Although he had ridden one when he and the other men rescued Sarah and again when they went after the men who had kidnapped her, Echo hadn't been available either time. Ezra, at the livery, had apologized, but Zack was secretly glad. It would have been awful to ride Echo and then have to leave him there, not knowing when he could ride him again. So when he did ride out those two times on the rented horse, he just got on and rode. There was more on his mind those two days with no time to stroke the horse or think about how wonderful a horse smells. Not everyone understood that. But Zack had seen Madison hug Chaco. He knew that she would understand. And that made him like her even more.

CHAPTER SEVENTEEN

MADISON COULDN'T BELIEVE how fast Sunday flew by. It started when her mother arrived in the morning to check on Zack. His infection was significantly improved, and he had no fever. She said that he could take a short walk, and Monday he could go to the coin dealer. After she left, Zack was so excited about riding in a car—to the coin dealer—that he could hardly contain himself. Madison had encouraged his excitement and said, "Go ahead! Celebrate!" Zack jumped up and down and waved his good arm in the air, making Madison laugh.

She enjoyed him. She enjoyed every minute with him. On their walk, after Madison pointed out the neighborhood, they talked and talked. It felt amazing that they had so much in common although more than a hundred years separated them. Madison liked everything about him: his looks, his intelligence, and the way his eyes got big when she showed him something new and miraculous from the twenty-first century. First he'd look at her like he didn't believe it. Then he'd get this huge smile on his face as he realized how cool it was. There was only one thing she didn't like about him—he wasn't from her time.

Of course, none of it even mattered if he didn't feel the same about her. And she had no idea. Judging by the way he sometimes looked at her, she was sure he felt the same way. Other times, he acted almost aloof, or as if he was deliberately trying to keep her away. It confused her. She didn't know if she should say anything about her feelings or not—she didn't want to scare him away. Except that she didn't want him to *get* away either. Maybe he felt the same way but didn't have the nerve to say anything. How much exposure could he have had to women in that small town? Madison didn't even think there were any women his age in the old Red Bluff. Should she say something? Or maybe put her hand on his leg? Or maybe she should really go for it and kiss him! Then she'd know!

The phone rang and interrupted her thoughts. "Law Office. Yes. I'll connect you." Madison put the phone down and continued with her typing. She didn't mind the job. Her Aunt Jenna had gotten her the job at the law office where she used to be a lawyer. Madison had worked there every summer since her first year in college. She was such a good worker that they had asked her back for a second summer, and again for the third summer. Since she wasn't technically a law student yet, almost all she did was typing and filing. Although last year she had done some go-fer work to the courthouse. That was fun.

She sighed. What was she going to do about Zack? Should she make the first move or wait for him? Madison knew she needed to talk to someone about it—someone more experienced than her friends. Her mother might be a good choice in a different situation. Since she had given birth to Madison while she was still a teenager, they were very close in age—only sixteen years apart. But Madison didn't know how her mother felt about Zack or about his being from the past. She had asked her advice before about some nameless man. But it was something altogether different asking her advice on someone that her mother actually knew. No, her mother was not a possibility. Maybe Granny. She may be old, but she was as sharp as they come.

That idea brought new thoughts to Madison, thoughts that had wanted to be acknowledged, but Madison hadn't brought them into her consciousness yet. She needed to go back to the past. Although she had intended on riding back with Zack, she could do it in one day. There and back wasn't a long trip at all—she had done that before. No, this time she'd stay overnight. Then she'd have a chance to talk it over with Granny. She lived in the past with a man from the past. If anyone would have good advice, it would be her. Madison smiled to herself and saved the file she was working on.

CHAPTER EIGHTEEN

ZACK DIDN'T KNOW where Sunday went, but he was glad it was Monday. When he was with Madison, a whole day could seem like a minute. He couldn't get enough of her. This morning, he had gotten up at seven so he could have breakfast with her before she left for work. She had sensed his uneasiness and guessed that he was nervous about staying alone. It wasn't exactly correct, but close enough. He was uneasy because he had been wanting to look up subjects on the internet, and he didn't want Madison to know. Namely, getting a GED, taking the SAT and ACT test, and enrolling in college. Zack knew he could do it. He was smart, and he was determined.

Madison had barely pulled out from the driveway when Zack was already sitting in front of the computer. First he typed in "how to study for the GED test." By clicking from one page to the next, he discovered a lot of information—much of which disappointed him. Although he knew he could do it, when he realized the test contained questions about science, math, history, geography, and more, it overwhelmed him. Most of what was on the test were events and discoveries that hadn't yet happened in his century. Studying for the test would feel like starting school from the beginning. He knew how to read, but the information he read would all be new to him. Zack set his jaw and decided that reading was enough. He could do it, and he *would* do it.

After clicking around more pages, he wrote down names of books that would help him learn the information. All he had to do was find a bookstore. There were no bookstores in the old Red Bluff except the occasional book that showed up at the Ralston General Store. But in the *new* Red Bluff, surely there were bookstores. Finding one was another matter.

Wait. Madison had said that you could find anything on the internet. Going back to the Google search page, Zack typed in "bookstores in Red Bluff." Reading through the listing, he realized there was more than one Red Bluff. He'd have to narrow it down. Back at the Google search page, he changed the search to "bookstores in Red Bluff, Colorado." Three bookstores came up, but he had no idea where the addresses were. In *his* Red Bluff, there was only Main Street, Back Street, and East Street.

Zack frowned, sighed, and decided to look up more information about coins. Everything hinged on making money with the coins. He knew the coins in his pocket would make him enough money to buy back and keep Echo. Although Zack had worked for Matthew the past few years for barely more than his room and board, he still considered himself an enterprising young fellow. And he had an idea; and he thought it was a good one.

Zack spent the rest of the day researching coins and taking careful notes—only some of which would serve him when he sold the initial coins to the coin dealer.

When Madison pulled up in front of the house at exactly five fifteen as she had told him, Zack was ready.

As he stepped into the car, Madison handed him the seat belt and showed him how to buckle it. "This is so cool, Madison! The seats are really comfortable—not like a stagecoach at all!"

"A car isn't much like a stagecoach at all, but it was the best comparison I could think of!"

As they pulled away, Zack asked, "Can you go faster?"

Madison laughed. "Just like a man! Wanting to drive faster and faster! If we have time after the coin dealer, I'll take you on the highway so you can see how fast we can go."

Zack nodded his head. "All right. How was work today?"

Madison didn't say anything for a minute. But when she stopped the car at a sign that said "STOP," she turned and looked at him with a wistful expression on her face. "Work was fine today, Zack. Thank you for asking. I appreciate that."

"Did you enjoy it?"

"Yes, it wasn't bad. It will be better when I get to do actual law work instead of just typing and filing, but it is a good start for me. How was your day?"

"I spent most of the day on the internet." He patted his shirt pocket. "I have lots of information here to help me at the coin shop."

Madison glanced at him, smiled, and kept driving. "You are the resourceful one, aren't you?"

Zack smiled and pushed forward against the seat belt like he wanted the car to go faster. A few minutes later, Madison parked the car in front of the coin dealer. They stepped out of the car, and Madison put a couple of coins into the parking meter.

"What's that? Why are you putting money in there?"

"It's a parking meter. We have to pay for parking. But we won't be long. It's not much." She turned and headed toward the door. "Come on. Let's go in."

CHAPTER NINETEEN

ZACK AND MADISON walked into the store and up to the counter. Reaching into his pocket, Zack plunked the coins down on the counter. "Would you be interested in buying these?"

The coin dealer looked at all of them before he picked the dollar up. "They all look in really good condition. Yes, I'm interested. Let's see," he turned the dollar over in his hands, "I'll give you five hundred for this one."

"Did you see the condition of the back?" asked Zack. "I think it's worth more."

The dealer looked up from the coin in his hands and smiled at Zack. "You drive a hard bargain, mister. How about seven hundred?"

"Done," said Zack.

Madison patted Zack on the back, and Zack smiled. They watched as the dealer picked up and turned each of the other coins over and over. He set the two half dollars aside, pointed to them, and said, "I'll give you eight hundred for these two coins."

Zack nodded his head. "That sounds fair."

The dealer picked up the penny and held it up, "I'll

give you a hundred fifty for this penny."

"It's in really good shape. Almost uncirculated," said Zack. "I think it's worth more."

"How 'bout two hundred?"

"Done," said Zack. "And what about this beauty?" He pointed to the 1869 S quarter—his last coin.

"This one *is* a beauty," the dealer said, as he looked up at Zack. "Better than uncirculated. Where did you get these coins?"

Without hesitation, Zack said, "In a box of my father's. My grandfather collected coins."

The dealer nodded and looked again at the quarter. "Twenty-five hundred dollars."

Madison gasped and covered her mouth with her hand.

"What? Was your boyfriend holding out on you? You didn't know these coins were worth this much?"

Madison stayed silent, and Zack said, "I couldn't part with that beauty for less than three thousand dollars."

"Yep, you drive a hard bargain. Fine. Do you have any more?"

"No, but I'd like to buy some from you. Do you have any 1840s or 1850s quarters?"

The dealer nodded and picked up the dollar tray from the counter, put it back, and placed another tray on the counter filled with quarters. "These are most of my quarters. I'm not sure of the dates."

Zack shuffled through his notes and then fingered through the coins in the tray. He'd pick them up, check the date, turn the coin over like he was checking its condition, and if it met with his approval, he'd set it to the side. When he finished he had twenty-five quarters stacked up beside the tray. He looked at Madison.

"This isn't enough," said Zack. Madison grimaced and nodded. To the dealer, Zack said, "Do you have any 1840s or 1850s half dollars?"

"I have plenty of those, some aren't in very good condition, though. Definitely not as good a condition as these that you had." He pulled out a large tray and laid it on the counter. "How about these?"

Zack looked at the coins without saying anything, while Madison watched. Before he picked any of them up, he pulled out his notes, shuffled through again glancing briefly at them. Then he looked through the tray setting coins aside. When he finished he had forty-one half dollars—most of what was in the tray—set aside on the counter next to the quarters.

"How much for these?"

The dealer carefully went through each coin and wrote an amount down. When he finished, he looked up at Zack, "I'll give you these for eighteen hundred dollars."

"You know, the condition of these coins isn't that great."

The dealer, an older fellow in his mid-fifties with close-cropped hair and blue eyes, said, "Let me make a buck here, will you?"

Zack looked at him, smiled, held out his hand, and shook hands with the dealer. "Done."

The dealer scratched out more figures on the piece of paper. "Okay. I owe you forty-seven hundred dollars, minus the eighteen hundred, that's a net to you of twenty-nine hundred dollars. Do you want a check?"

"Do you have cash?"

"Cash? That's a lot of money, I doubt it. Just a minute." The dealer disappeared in the back room, and came out counting a handful of bills. "I can give you fifteen hundred in cash. I can have the rest tomorrow, if you want to come back."

"A check is okay, Zack. I can cash it for you tomorrow," said Madison.

Zack nodded his head and said, "A check is fine," to the dealer.

The dealer wrote out a check and then counted out fifteen hundred dollars into Zack's hand. Then he held out his hand again to Zack. "Zack, nice doing business with you. My name is Stan."

"Nice to meet you, Stan. This is my friend, Madison."

"Nice to meet you, pretty lady," said Stan. As Zack and Madison turned to leave, "Come back and see me again."

When they got to the door, Zack turned around. "Stan? Are there any rare coins that you would be particularly interested in? I may be able to find them for you."

"Yes! I've been looking for months for an 1893 O silver dollar. Find that one and if it's in even decent condition, it could be worth a hundred thousand or two hundred thousand dollars."

"I don't have any resources for coins after 1870. Are there any older than 1870 that you're looking for?"

"Yes, the 1795 'Silver Plug' silver dollar is also difficult or impossible to find. That one is worth a fortune."

Zack nodded his head solemnly. "I'll see what I can do."

When they settled into the car, Madison turned to Zack. "Score! Where did you learn to do that? You were amazing! Wow! I can't believe what happened in there! You were awesome!"

Zack turned to her with a little smile on his face.

"Wouldn't you like to know, pretty lady?" Then he squeezed her hand. "Let's go home. I feel great!"

He wasn't sure if he should have squeezed her hand like that, but she had smiled and hadn't pulled away. Maybe he should have kissed her instead. That thought would have to wait for later. Right now, he couldn't be happier. Everything was going as he wanted. Now he had enough money to buy Echo back and to board him for a short time. But twenty-six dollars from his time would not last long and would not allow him to put the rest of his plan into motion. How could he get more of the old time money? Madison had said there was another coin shop in town. That might be the answer.

CHAPTER TWENTY

WHEN THEY ARRIVED home, Madison couldn't stop gushing over how magnificent Zack was. She thought maybe he was getting tired of hearing it, but he kept smiling. "You handled it so beautifully, Zack! You did everything right!"

"I did my research, and that made all the difference," said Zack. "It wouldn't have gone that way, if I hadn't known what they were worth."

"You were awesome! When you said that you wanted to be a lawyer, I honestly didn't think it was possible because you were so quiet and polite. But in there—you were—you were absolutely dynamic! You'd make a great lawyer!"

"I know I would," said Zack. "I know I would. But I need more nineteenth-century money. Can we go to the other coin store you mentioned—to see if they have more coins that I can buy?"

"That store closes at five o'clock, and I don't get off work until five o'clock."

"Can I walk there?"

"It's pretty far. We'll see what Mom says about walking that far. Or maybe she can drop you off or something. We'll work something out! You want to watch a movie tonight?"

They watched a movie, but Madison had to keep putting it on pause so she could tell him again how great he did. Zack smiled at her indulgently each time, and then pointed toward the TV, wanting the movie to continue. She wanted so much to hug him, but felt afraid she might scare him off. But he had squeezed her hand. Was that a friendly squeeze or a girlfriend squeeze? She didn't know.

The following morning her mother called to say that if Zack was feeling good, she would skip stopping by because she had an early client. Zack said he felt great and the arm felt great, so it was all good. When Madison asked her mom if Zack could walk all the way to town, Mom had said she'd prefer to check him again before he tried that long walk. Although Zack was disappointed, Madison thought he took the news well.

At work, Madison dreamed the day away. Although she was busy all day typing and filing, her mind and imagination ran free. Zack dominated her thoughts. At first going over every detail from the day before and remembering how incredibly he had handled himself, and second imagining them together, living together, studying together, and enjoying each other. She still couldn't get over the difference she had seen in him at the coin store. He had been subtle, but firm, naturally knowing when to back off and when to push forward. It was such a different view of the man she had known him to be, that it surprised her completely. In a pleasant way. A *very* pleasant way. As the day wore on and thoughts of Zack persisted, she realized the inevitable had happened.

She was in love with Zack Murphy. All her caution about falling for someone from the past had gone unheeded. There she was, hopelessly in love. And she still didn't know if he felt the same way.

Deciding she would be optimistic, she began to plan their future. First, she had to convince him to move to the future. There was no way she could live in the past. Of that she was certain. And Zack would do wonderfully here. He had already proven how easily he fit in. Imagine him in a court room! Madison sighed. She was jumping a little too far ahead here. Zack didn't even have a high school diploma. He'd have to go through four years of college and then law school. He had a lot of hard work in front of him if that's truly what he wanted. Maybe when he realized how much work it would be, he would change his mind. She wouldn't mind if he decided not to become a lawyer—although it would be nicer if he still wanted to.

But how could she approach Zack about staying in the future with her? Reminding herself that she still didn't know if he had the same feelings about her, she sighed again and leaned back in her chair. She would take it one step at a time. And the first step was to find out about Zack's feelings.

When she arrived home that evening, Madison felt strangely distant toward Zack. She had gone over and over it in her mind, and she didn't know what to do. "I like you, do you like me?" It sounded like something a first grader might say. Finding out if someone liked you was easier to think about than to put into motion. She wished Zack would just pull her into his arms and kiss her—or that she had the nerve to pull him into her arms and kiss him.

After spending the evening together watching another movie and talking, Madison turned off the television and sighed. "Time to go to sleep," she said.

"I'm tired," said Zack.

They walked into the hallway, and as they were about to part to go to their rooms, they turned toward each other. Did she have the nerve to just grab him and kiss him? Her eyes got wide, and she held her breath—but no. She didn't have the nerve. Had she seen Zack's arms move almost imperceptibly toward her? If they did, that's all the farther they got. Maybe he didn't have the nerve either. How would they ever get together if they were both too afraid to show their feelings?

CHAPTER TWENTY-ONE

THEY WERE SO close! They had both turned to face each other at the same time, and there was the opportunity, but he didn't have the confidence to just wrap his arms around her and kiss her. His arms wanted to—they had started moving in that direction, but he consciously made the effort to stop. He couldn't carry through. He could, he reminded himself, haggle with someone in another century, but he couldn't kiss the woman of his dreams. How did he ever expect to get anywhere in life, if he didn't have the nerve to move forward with Madison? As much as he wanted to be a lawyer, nothing else mattered if he couldn't be with her.

Because he felt so disappointed in himself for not kissing Madison, he slept fitfully that night and awoke feeling tired. At breakfast, Zack was about to take Madison's hand and tell her how he felt when Kat came through the doorway.

"How's my favorite patient this morning?"

Zack smiled at her. "I'm doing great, Kat, thank you."

She walked over and put her hand on his forehead. "Feels normal, let's check to be sure." She took the thermometer out of her bag and ran it across his forehead. "Yup, normal. Let's see the wound." Kat examined the wound, pressing her fingers on the surrounding area. "Any soreness?"

"Almost completely gone," said Zack.

"You're doing great," said Kat. "You have responded well to the penicillin, and your wound is now healing properly, no thanks to that quack you call a doctor. I think, Zack, that I'm going to give you a clean bill of health. You can return to the past anytime."

"I'll take him back Saturday, Mom. I've been wanting to visit Granny anyway."

"Sure. That sounds great, if you don't mind staying here another few days, Zack."

Zack smiled and gave a quick glance toward Madison. "No, I'm having a great time here. I don't mind staying."

"Sounds good. You're welcome to ride my horse back there, Zack. Madison can pony her home, and she'll be fine. She's a good horse. You can ride, can't you?"

"Yes, Ma'am. I used to have my own horse, and thanks to the coin dealer yesterday, I'm going to buy him back when I go home." Zack caught himself too late. He didn't want to call the past home.

"Oh, Mom, can you drop Zack off at the other coin dealer?"

"Sorry, Zack, I have another early appointment, and I have to hurry as it is. Why can't you drop him off, Madison?"

"It's on Pioneer—the other side of town," said Madison.

"Isn't there one on Sixth Street?" Kat asked. "You could walk to that one, Zack. Pioneer is way too far to walk to, though."

"We've already been to that one, Mom. Zack needs to get more 1800s money so he can board his horse, and he already bought all the coins he could from the one on Sixth."

"Well, you two kids work it out. I need to get to work. Bye, love." Kat waved as she hurried out the door.

"Sorry, Zack. Maybe I can hurry home tomorrow at lunch and give you a ride."

"Okay."

"I need to leave right now, though. Have a good day. See you soon." Madison put her hand on his shoulder as she walked by.

She liked him! He knew she did! Now he just needed the courage to either tell her how he felt, kiss her, or both. It all scared him. Zack knew why he was so skeery. He had never kissed a girl before. Sad truth was that he had never met one that he wanted to. It didn't matter now—he wanted to kiss Madison, and he had to find a way to make it happen.

After she left, he started a Google search on bookstores. He needed to buy books on studying for the GED test. That was his first step to moving to the future—although he didn't consider it the future anymore—he considered it his time. When he looked online how to get to one bookstore, it turned out to be close to the coin dealer they had been to, so he knew how to get there. Perfect. And Kat had said it was all right for him to walk there. Then he looked up where the other coin dealer was. According to the map, it was miles away from the first one. He hoped that he could get to it before he went back Saturday. If he couldn't, it would ruin his plans.

Zack spent the morning on the internet. At noon, he made himself a sandwich for lunch, then put a list of books in his pocket, and left the house. He had decided to bring his Pennsylvania law book with him. Although he didn't know if they bought old books at bookstores, he thought it was worth a try.

It only took him fifteen minutes to walk to the bookstore. When he walked in and saw all the books there, he gasped. He had never seen so many books in one place before. Walking up to the counter, he waited until the clerk had finished helping another person, and then he approached him. "Hallo, I was wondering if you would be interested in buying this book."

"We don't sell any used books here, but can I see it?" Zack handed him the book. "*Purdon's Digest of Laws of Pennsylvania*. It's old and in good condition. Wow, it was published in 1837. Dude! You could sell this on eBay and make a fortune! Would you mind if I looked at it while you look around?"

"No, go ahead. Where are the books on the GED test?"

"Straight down this aisle, turn left at the end and they're on the bottom shelf."

"Thanks," said Zack, as he walked down the aisle. He didn't want to ask the guy what eBay was—he could ask Madison when she got home, or look it up on the internet. The bottom shelf had many books on it, and before long, Zack had picked out seven books. He wanted to get a separate book for each subject he'd be tested on, a book that had *all* the subjects in it, a book that included test taking strategies, and a book of practice tests.

Before returning to the counter to pay for the books, he decided to walk up and down each aisle looking at the books. The sheer quantity of them amazed him. When he walked past the section on coin collecting, he looked through the books and picked out the one he wanted that he had seen mentioned on the internet. Since he couldn't look anything up on the computer while he was in the old Red Bluff, the book would be perfect. As he walked back to the front counter, he noticed a display with a book called *Sycamore Row* by John Grisham. Since he was enjoying *A Time to Kill* so much, he picked it up and was delighted to find that it was the sequel. Adding that to his stack, he plopped all the books on the front counter.

"I checked out this book for you. It could be worth a lot of money, just sayin'."

"Cool, thanks," said Zack.

The clerk rang up all the books and put them into two plastic sacks. "Someone's studying for the GED test," said the clerk, grinning. "When are they taking it?"

"When? What do you mean when?"

"Oh, it's only given at certain times of the year."

Zack's heart sank. What if he couldn't take the test in time to enroll in college? As Zack handed the clerk the money, he said, "Oh, I didn't realize that. Listen, I have a long way to walk, is there something besides a bag for me to carry the books in?"

"How about a backpack? You can pick up one at the thrift store down the street for a song."

Zack didn't know what he meant by song, but he asked, "Which way?" When the clerk pointed toward the right, Zack said, "Could you keep the books here for me while I walk down there?"

"Sure, dude. No problem."

Zack wasn't sure what a backpack was, but he thought that Madison might have mentioned it during one of their conversations. Walking down the street toward the thrift store, whatever that was, Zack looked around him and marveled at all the stores. One after another after another. He'd never seen anything like it. The mountains —the same mountains he could see surrounding the old Red Bluff—still guarded the town. Maybe that's why he felt so at home here—because it really was home. What's a hundred years? Meaningless.

He laughed and then found himself in front of the thrift store. Walking in, he looked around and noticed that most of the clothes he saw didn't look new. When he found the clerk, he asked her about backpacks, and she showed him where to look. He picked them all up and inspected each one carefully. One was too dirty, one too big, one had a broken zipper, and then he found the right one—perfect for what he needed. After looking over the rest of the store to see what they had, he paid the clerk and walked back to the bookstore.

After he put the books, including his Pennsylvania law book, into the backpack, he thanked the clerk, pulled the backpack on, and left the store. Smiling, he walked slowly back to the house, taking in all the newnesses of the century. The cars never ceased to amaze him, and he finally saw what Madison had described as an "eighteen-wheeler." He counted the wheels as it drove by, and sure enough, it had eighteen of them. Wow! No one in the old Red Bluff could ever imagine anything like that. There were so many amazing things to experience about the twenty-first century, and Zack had only just arrived. He loved this century and loved the idea of living in it.

As he walked back, he wondered what time it was. He hoped that he would get home before Madison, so he could greet her when she came through the door. She liked that, so Zack liked doing it for her. When he arrived back at the house, a surprise was waiting for him when he opened the door.

CHAPTER TWENTY-TWO

MADISON SPENT ALMOST the entire morning in court. At ten o'clock, Marcus, the owner of the law firm, had come in and asked her to take a special message to an attorney in court and wait for the answer. That didn't happen often, so Madison felt pleased that he had asked her. She always liked going into court—it made her feel like she was part of the legal system, and she liked that. After Madison gave the attorney the message, he nodded, and she walked to the back of the courtroom to sit and wait. The attorney knew it needed a response, but he was in the middle of a trial. She had to wait for the next recess. That was fine. Madison loved watching a good attorney work, and she knew this guy was good.

Two hours later, after one witness was brought to tears, and left the entire jury gasping, the judge finally called a recess. The attorney stood up, looked quickly around the room for her, spotted her, and quickly walked over. He scribbled a reply to the note and gave it to Madison. She thanked him and drove back to the office.

After handing the note personally to Marcus, she grabbed her lunch and hurried to the lunchroom. It was late, and she was starved. Several other women ate late lunches, too, so the talk in the room was animated. Between law office gossip, men, and speculations about law school, there was never a lack for conversation.

Madison hadn't mentioned her feelings about Zack to anyone. What she felt for him seemed more special than something shared with casual acquaintances over lunch. So she listened quietly, joining in the conversation only occasionally.

When she got back into her office and started typing, she realized that besides brief instances, she hadn't given Zack much thought all day. Not that she had time—but it made her realize how often she normally thought about him. *All* the time. She realized that she had thought about him long enough. It was time to do something about it! Whether he felt the same way about her or not, she needed to find out. In her heart, she felt strongly that he did feel the same way. But her head kept giving her reasons for doubt. Regardless, something had to be done. She had to find out one way or the other.

So what should she do? Should she speak to him about it, or just grab him, kiss him, and see if he kissed back? If she kissed him, and he didn't feel the same way, she would lose his friendship. And his friendship was important to her. She enjoyed his humor and both sides of his personality—his quiet demeanor and the enterprising side of him that she had seen at the coin store. Zack would make a wonderful study partner—bright and perceptive. That is, if he lived in her time and still wanted to become a lawyer. Maybe kissing him wasn't the way to proceed.

Deciding that talking to him would be better, Madison set about figuring out what to say. Again the first idea she came up with, "I like you, do you like me?" sounded way too first-grader for her. "I have feelings for you"? That sounded too heavy, it might scare him off. "I kinda like you"? Too wishy-washy. "I think you're handsome and smart, and I like you," could be something you'd say to a friend. Or maybe come at it from a different angle. "You said you wanted to be a lawyer—would you want to be one in this century?" But why would that mean that she liked him? It really didn't.

The first grader comment and question kept coming back to her. That must mean something. Maybe she could just tweak it a little. How about, "I like you, Zack. I mean I *really* like you." It sounded good. And she could touch his hand as she said it, and maybe raise her eyebrows. No. Nix on the eyebrows. That was too suggestive. A touch of the hand would be perfect.

That was it. She had decided. When she arrived home, after they had dinner and were sitting around talking—before she put on a movie—she would move closer to him on the couch, touch his hand, and just say it. Now that she had decided, she could hardly wait to get home. And get it over with, if she had to admit the truth.

Someone walking briskly into her office interrupted Madison's thoughts. It was Marcus, holding up hangers with suits on them.

"Madison, I need you to drop these off after work. Put a rush on them, and then pick them up first thing in the morning."

Madison glanced at the clock on the wall above the door. It was five minutes before five o'clock. "I'm sorry, Marcus. I need to go straight home tonight, so I can't do that. Someone is waiting for me."

Marcus blinked his eyes and rotated back on his heels. "You what?"

Madison didn't want to lose her job over this, but she didn't want to do it, either. She knew that Sarah used to take care of his cleaning all the time, but Sarah made a lot more money than she did. And Madison had no intention of becoming his dry cleaning go-to-girl. "I said I can't do it. I have someone waiting for me, and I need to get right home." Madison stood up, logged out of her computer, and grabbed her purse. "I need to leave right away, and I can't do it. Sorry, Marcus."

"Oh, well, okay then. I'll find somebody else. Sorry to have bothered you," said Marcus, practically stumbling over his words. Not many people said no to Marcus. Regardless, Madison wasn't going to say yes to this favor that would undoubtedly become a habit. She wanted none of it.

CHAPTER TWENTY-THREE

WHEN ZACK OPENED the door to the house, he heard the television. Turning, he looked out the front window to check if Madison's car was out there. It wasn't. Two dogs met him at the door. They looked like Jet and Bingo, Jenna's and Josiah's dogs. So when he walked into the living room, he wasn't surprised to see Josiah sitting on the couch, holding the remote, and watching television.

"Josiah! What are you doing here?"

Josiah adjusted the volume on the TV and turned to look at him. With a big grin on his face, Josiah said, "Looking for *you*, Zack! We thought you'd be in bed, recuperating. What are you doing up and around?"

"I healed fast. Kat gave me a clean bill of health this morning. I just walked to the bookstore and bought some books."

"Oh, that's good." Josiah moved his head toward the doorway. "Jenna! Zack's here! No need to worry!" Then to Zack, "You know women, Zack. She was worried about you."

"Where is Jenna?"

"She's in our room. Do you know which bedroom that

is? Go down the hallway and before you get to Madison's room, there's a door on the right. Go see her. It will make her feel better," said Josiah, as he adjusted the volume back up and turned back to the TV.

Zack walked through the doorway. He had never been down the hallway past his bathroom. He turned left and followed Josiah's instructions. The door was open. Jenna sat in front of a big screen that must be a big computer. Before this, he had only seen Madison's laptop computer. From the doorway, he said, "Hi, Jenna. I'm fine."

Jenna turned around with a big smile on her face. "Zack! So good to see you up and feeling better. Sarah and Matthew have been very worried about you. And since Josiah and I were coming to town anyway, today, I told her I'd check on you. It doesn't hurt that we're all in the same house, huh?" She laughed, and Zack joined her.

"I'm doing great. Kat gave me a clean bill of health this morning."

"Oh, good. We're riding back tomorrow. Would you like to come with us?"

"Oh, um, actually, Madison is going to take me Saturday. She wanted to see Granny." And then, to make sure Jenna understood, "I don't mind waiting for Saturday. I like it here."

"Okay," said Jenna, turning back to the computer. "Glad you're doing well, Zack."

Zack walked back to the living room and found Madison home and talking to Josiah. His first reaction was a sharp dose of jealousy—until he realized it was Josiah and Madison. Josiah, newly married and heels over head in love with Jenna, would never flirt with another woman. He wasn't that kind of man. And Madison would not flirt with her Aunt Jenna's husband. Although he didn't know Madison that well except for the past week, he knew she wasn't that kind of woman. Zack pushed aside the unreasonable feelings of jealousy and entered the living room.

"Hi, Madison!"

"Hi, Zack. Josiah just invited you and me to dinner with him and Jenna at the Thai restaurant. Would you like to go?"

"Sure. What's tie?"

"You'll find out! You'll love it! Honestly, you've been here all week, and I never even thought to take you out on the town." She looked at Josiah. "Poor Zack had to eat my cooking all week."

"I enjoy your cooking, Madison, and enjoy helping you."

"You're just saying that to be nice, Zack."

Jenna entered the room and said, "Hi, Madison. Josiah, did you ask them?"

"Yes, and they want to go. Shall we leave now?"

"Sure," said Jenna. "You guys ready to go?"

Zack and Madison both said yes. The two couples walked outside.

"I'll go get the truck," said Josiah.

"Josiah's going to drive?" asked Zack.

"I taught him," said Jenna. "He'd been wanting to learn. I finally broke down, took him to a parking lot, and showed him. He's a pretty good driver. You don't have to worry, Zack."

"I wasn't worried, just surprised."

When Josiah drove the truck up to them, Jenna said, "Zack, why don't you sit in the front with Josiah. Madison and I can sit in the back."

"Okay." Zack climbed into the front seat. He noticed that it was much higher than a car, which he could just step into. As they drove to town, Zack thought it felt different from riding in a car, too. Josiah impressed him by doing everything right. Zack wondered if maybe he could learn to drive, too. Maybe Madison would teach him after he moved to the future. *If* he moved to the future.

Josiah parked behind the Thai restaurant. They walked in, and Zack looked around at all the elephants in the room. There were pictures of elephants, stone statues of elephants, and elephants with sparkly things on their bodies. Pictures of people in clothing he didn't recognize and other statues adorned the room, also. Zack grinned. "This is awesome!"

Jenna and Madison laughed. Josiah didn't get it. "Awesome!" said Madison. "Zack, you're becoming absolutely twenty-first-century! Soon, we're not going to let you go back!"

They were seated in a corner and given water and menus. Zack had a seat where he could see everything. "This is so amazing. It's nothing like the restaurant at the hotel."

"That much is true," said Josiah. "Now you know why we come here once or twice a month!"

"You do? I can see why. This place is so cool. I love it," said Zack. He kept looking around and marveling at all the unfamiliar sights.

"Zack, look at the menu. I'm starved. We need to order. You can look around later!" said Jenna.

"Okay," said Zack. Looking at the menu, he read each item. Many words were not familiar. He decided that he would make the same choice as Madison, so he closed the menu.

"Oh, I know they have pineapple chicken, but I can't find it," said Madison.

"It's the third item from the bottom on the right-hand page," said Zack.

Madison looked up at Zack and then down at the menu. "Yep, there it is, thanks, Zack. Do they have any desserts?"

"Yes," Zack said. "Three items on the back."

While Madison turned the menu over to look at the dessert menu, Jenna tilted her head and looked at Zack. "Zack, what are the dessert items?"

"Fried bananas, Thai coconut custard, and mango pudding."

"Zack! Wow! You have a photographic memory!" said Jenna.

"What's that?" asked Zack.

"It means you look at something once and remember exactly what you saw."

"Can't everybody do that?" asked Zack.

"No! Not many people can," said Jenna.

Then the waitress walked up to their table and took their orders. Madison ordered the pineapple chicken, as did Zack, and Josiah and Jenna ordered something called Pad Thai. Zack didn't know what that was.

When the waitress left, Jenna said, "Zack, what have you been doing since you got here—besides recuperating?"

"I've been on the computer a lot, researching coins. Then Madison and I drove to the coin dealer, and I sold some coins and bought some more from the nineteenth century."

"You should have seen him at the coin dealer! You

know how quiet and polite Zack is? Well at the coin dealer, he was absolutely dynamic! You should have seen him."

"Oh, I wasn't really that brilliant," said Zack.

"Yes, you were! He was awesome!"

"So you made some money, Zack. What are you going to do with it?" asked Josiah.

"Buy back my horse," said Zack.

"I didn't know you had a horse," said Josiah.

"Yeah, I had to sell him before you came to town. But I need more money to board him."

"Zack needs to go to the other coin dealer, the one on Pioneer, so he can get more nineteenth-century money," said Madison. "We bought out all the coins that Zack wanted from the dealer on Sixth Street. And I haven't been able to take him to the other place."

"We can take you tomorrow, Zack, before we return. But you can ask the guy on Sixth to order more for you. That's what Sarah and I did. Maybe the other place can do that, too," said Jenna.

"You really should have seen him, though," said Madison. "He knew what each coin was worth. He sold his coins at the highest price, and then bought the cheapest nineteenth-century coins."

Josiah reached into his pocket, pulled out some coins, and put them on the table in front of Zack. "What about these, Zack?"

Zack looked over the coins and then picked up one quarter and turned it over. "1869 S. I sold one just like this for three thousand dollars. But this one is in better condition."

"Three thousand dollars for a quarter? And we've been getting only fifteen hundred for the gold dollars that we sell!" said Jenna. She picked up the quarter, looked at it, and handed it back to Zack. "Amazing."

Zack gathered up the coins and handed them all back to Josiah. Then Josiah looked through them and said, "Is this the quarter you mentioned?"

"Yes, that's the one. You can get more than three thousand for it, I'm sure," said Zack.

"No," said Josiah, as he handed it back to Zack. "*You* can."

"I can't take that from you. It's worth too much," said Zack.

"No, Zack. It's worth a quarter to me. That's all. I'm giving you a quarter."

"I can't accept it." Zack tried to hand the quarter back to Josiah.

"I'll tell you what, Zack. You give me a quarter for it. Then, we'll be even."

Jenna reached across the table and patted Zack's hand. "It's okay, Zack. You take it. Just give us a quarter. It's fine."

Madison said, "Zack. They want to trade you a quarter for a quarter. Do it!"

Reluctantly, Zack reached in his pocket, took out a shiny 2012 quarter, and handed it to Josiah. "Here."

"Thank you, Zack. Good deal," said Josiah, as he shook Zack's hand.

Zack still felt unsure about what had just happened. He looked at Josiah seriously. "Okay, Josiah, a quarter for a quarter, but I'm buying you supper." Smiling then, he said, "I have plenty of twenty-first-century money!"

Madison said, "He does! I still owe him more than a thousand dollars!"

The waitress came and placed the plates in front of

them. Zack thought the smells were intoxicating. He had never smelled anything like them. When he looked down at what he ordered, he didn't know what to do. "Madison?"

"You weren't expecting that, were you, Zack? It's a pineapple. Just use your fork and eat out of it like it was a bowl."

"What is it?" asked Zack. In front of Zack was a pineapple sliced down the middle. The inside of the fruit had been removed and replaced with chicken, chunks of pineapple, tiny ears of corn like he'd never seen before, and other items that tasted delicious but he didn't know what they were.

After they had finished eating and ordering dessert, Madison excused herself to go to the bathroom. When she walked away, Josiah said, "So how do you like it here in the future, Zack?"

"I love it here, Josiah. I don't want to leave."

"Does Madison know that?" Jenna dabbed her mouth with her napkin and looked at Zack.

"She's part of the reason I don't want to leave. But, no, she doesn't know."

"What would you do in this century?" asked Josiah.

"I want to be a lawyer."

"You know, I was a lawyer here, Zack. It takes a lot of schooling. Do you have a high school diploma?" asked Jenna.

"I didn't know you were a lawyer, Jenna. No, I don't have a diploma. But I can get a GED. Today, I bought a bunch of books so I can study for the test. But the guy at the bookstore said they only give the test at certain times."

"Late last year, I read something that in 2014, they

were starting on computerized testing, and you could take the tests any time," said Jenna. "You know there are several subjects. But you can take the different parts of the test at different times. There is probably more than one site in Red Bluff where you can take the tests."

"I bought a separate book for each subject," said Zack. "I like to be prepared, and I don't want to take any chance on not passing."

Jenna put her hand on Zack's. "Zack, if you have all these plans, I think you need to talk to Madison about them."

Zack nodded at her, as Madison returned from the bathroom and sat down.

"Jenna," said Madison, smiling, "you're not going to believe what happened today with Marcus! He asked me to take his dry cleaning, and I said no!"

Jenna laughed. "Sarah was stuck doing that job, and for a long time she liked it. She thought it meant that Marcus trusted her."

"I figured it would get to be a habit—him pawning off his laundry on me. And I wasn't going to let that get started. I'm not his maid!"

"Well, don't worry about him firing you or anything. He won't."

"Firing me?" Madison laughed. "It surprised him so much he didn't know what to say!"

Jenna reached across the table and patted Madison's hand. "Good show, Madison. Good job in standing up for yourself!"

"Thanks, Jenna!"

Zack looked at Madison with pride. He wanted to say, "You're awesome, Madison," but he just smiled at her instead.

CHAPTER TWENTY-FOUR

THE FOLLOWING MORNING, Zack was in the living room working on Madison's computer when he heard Josiah walk down the hallway and knock on Zack's partially closed bedroom door. "C'mon, Zack! Up and at 'em! We need to go back to Red Bluff early, so if you want to go to the coin dealer, better get up and ready now."

"Josiah!" Zack called out. "I'm in here. I'm dressed, and I've already eaten breakfast."

Josiah stepped through the doorway with a smile on his face. "Already hooked on the internet, Zack? You really *do* belong in the twenty-first century! Except for the Thai restaurant and the ice cream here, I can't wait to get home!" Josiah disappeared from Zack's view for an instant, then Zack heard him say, "He's already up, Jenna. C'mon. Let's go. I want to get home."

Seconds later, Josiah walked back out to the living room, followed by Jenna. "Good morning, Zack!" said Jenna. "I see that Madison already has you hooked on the internet."

"Morning, Jenna. I like to look stuff up. That's all. I'm learning a lot," said Zack.

"Would you like to have breakfast with us? I can fix you some eggs," said Jenna.

"Thank you, Jenna. Madison fixed some eggs, so I've already eaten."

Jenna smiled at him and walked to the kitchen with Josiah. While Zack worked on the computer, he could hear them in the kitchen, plugging in the coffee maker, using the toaster, and making eggs. Zack stopped what he was doing to listen to them. He wasn't eavesdropping. He enjoyed the easy way they were with each other—gentle conversation interspersed with laughter—it was the kind of relationship he hoped to have someday with Madison. Reluctantly, he returned his attention to the computer.

An hour later, Josiah and Jenna emerged from the kitchen. "Sorry it took us so long, Zack. We get carried away with our conversations like that," said Josiah.

Zack smiled. "I'm in no hurry, Josiah. But someday I hope to have the kind of relationship that you and Jenna have."

Josiah pulled Jenna into him. "If you do, boy, you'll be damn lucky." Then he kissed Jenna on her forehead. Looking at Zack, he said, "You ready?"

"Sure. Let me put the laptop back in Madison's room. I'll only be a second."

A few minutes later, the three of them walked outside. "Do you want to drive in the car or the truck today, Zack?" asked Josiah.

"I like the truck!" said Zack.

"I'll go get it," said Josiah.

A minute later, Josiah had driven up to them. Jenna let Zack sit in the front again, and she climbed into the back seat.

"Zack, if you want, maybe I can teach you how to drive," said Josiah.

"Josiah! You just learned to drive!" said Jenna.

"Yes, but I'm a good driver. *You* told me that."

"Okay, well, you are and I did, but I'm not sure if Zack is ready for that. He's only been in a car a few times."

"Oh, c'mon, Jenna. I'm a quick learner," said Zack.

"Maybe another time, Zack. Today we need to get back to town," said Jenna.

Josiah shrugged his shoulders. "Sorry, Zack, I tried." Then Zack and Josiah spoke about different vehicles, and Josiah suggested several for Zack to look at.

Jenna huffed playfully in the back seat. "Men and their vehicles!"

After several minutes of driving, during which Josiah talked Zack into buying a car after he moved to the new Red Bluff, they arrived at the other coin dealer. Josiah parked in the parking lot, and the three of them walked into the store together.

Zack walked up to the counter and pulled the quarter out of his pocket. "Are you interested in buying this coin? It's in really good shape."

An older woman, even older than Eliza, picked up the coin and held it under a lighted magnifier. "This is beautiful! I've never seen one in such good condition." She turned it over and kept looking. "Hardly any blemishes. It looks almost like it was just minted. It's not proof, but it's close." She looked up with a hint of a smile on her face. "Oh! I shouldn't have told you how wonderful it was. Now you'll want more for it."

Zack smiled back. "Whatever's fair, ma'am."

"Oh, such a polite boy. I'm going to like doing business with you." She patted his hand. "What would you think about forty-five hundred dollars?"

Zack blinked, gulped, and coughed out his reply. "Ah, yeah," he said with a smile. He heard Jenna gasp at the counter next to him, but Josiah stayed silent.

"Do you have any more that you'd like to sell?" asked the woman, cradling her new quarter to her chest.

"No, but I'm interested in buying some. Do you have any 1840s or 1850s quarters or half dollars?"

"Sure thing!" said the woman. She turned around and put two trays on the counter. "I don't think any of them are as good as the one you just sold me, though."

"That's okay," said Zack, as he examined the coins. "Poor condition is fine." He started picking out quarters and setting them aside. Then he picked out several half dollars. When he finished, he had found thirty-four half dollars and thirty-four quarters. "How much for these?" asked Zack, as he looked up at the woman.

"Let me see," she said, as she wrote some figures down on a pad of paper by the register. Nodding her head, she looked at the coins again, scratched out some more figures and looked up. She squinted her eyes at Zack. "Are you an Indian boy?" Before Zack could answer, she added, "Oh! I apologize. I know the politically correct term is now Native American, but in my day, it was Indian. Anyway, are you?"

Zack felt defensive and balled his hands into fists. He had enough of the name-calling in his time, but he didn't expect it in the twenty-first century. Madison had said things were different here. "Yes, ma'am, I am," he said as politely as he could manage.

The old woman nodded. "Yes, I thought so. Well, I'll tell you, boy, I would normally charge upwards of three thousand dollars for these coins, but since you're Indian —I mean Native American—I'll give them to you for twenty-five hundred."

Zack blinked and looked at her curiously. He had to blink his eyes repeatedly, because they were filling with tears. That was something he had never expected. He was getting something special *because* he was Indian. Zack nodded and held out his hand. "Yes, thank you, twenty-five hundred is fine. My name is Zack."

The woman shook his hand vigorously. "Hello, Zack. My name is Susan. Nice to make your acquaintance. I'm sorry about what we did to your people."

Zack couldn't look up at her, but he motioned toward Jenna and Josiah. "These are my friends, Jenna and Josiah." Zack's thoughts were swimming so fast in his head that he couldn't think a coherent thought. The room started to get blurry, and he blinked the tears from his eyes again. "Thank you very much, Susan. Good-bye."

"Zack, wait! I need to pay you," said Susan.

"You can pay my friends," said Zack, as he approached the door. As he walked out, he heard Jenna say to Susan, "It's okay. Where he's from, they make fun of him for being a Native American." And that's the last he heard before the door closed behind him.

Several minutes later, Jenna and Josiah came out to the truck where Zack was waiting outside. He had composed himself by then, and he looked up sheepishly. "Sorry."

Josiah put his hand on Zack's shoulder. "No need to be sorry, Zack. I've seen the way those men treat you in Matthew's saloon. You have nothing to be sorry about at all. It is good for a man to cry. It shows he has heart."

Josiah tapped him on the chest. "C'mon, get in. Jenna and I need to get back."

When they all got into the truck, Jenna said, "Zack, she gave us a check for two thousand dollars. Do you need it right away? We can stop at the bank on the way home if you want."

"No, Jenna, thank you. Whenever it is convenient for you. What I needed was more nineteenth-century money, and I got that. Oh, do you have it?"

"Yes, right here," said Jenna.

"I should give you back some money, anyway. I didn't expect her to pay me so much for that coin."

"We made a fair trade, Zack. I gave you a quarter, you gave me a quarter. We're even. The money belongs to you," said Josiah.

Zack nodded his head. "Okay."

"You did seem surprised when she said 'forty-five hundred dollars.'"

"That's more than the other guy would have paid me, I think. But she charged more for the old coins," said Zack.

"Then you know what you have to do, Zack," said Jenna.

Zack turned around and smiled into the back seat at Jenna. "Sell her my nineteenth-century coins, and buy more coins at the other place!"

"Exactly!" said Jenna.

"I really liked Stan—the guy at the first place. But I really like Susan, also. People here are so nice!"

"Not all of them, Zack. But most are."

"I belong here," said Zack. "Jenna, Josiah," as he said their names, he looked at them, "you know I do."

CHAPTER TWENTY-FIVE

Two DAYS FLEW by. Madison was busy at work doing special projects with no time to think about what she would do about Zack. She spent most of Thursday night on the phone with a friend whose boyfriend had just broken up with her. Friday night, she had dinner with that friend, so Madison still did not have a chance to talk to Zack.

Next she knew it was late Saturday afternoon, and she and Zack were getting ready to ride back to the old Red Bluff. She noticed that he had a backpack that was full of books. When she asked what he'd bought, he showed her a coin book and the latest John Grisham. But she thought he was trying to hide something from her. Books? What was there to hide? It didn't seem important enough to concern herself with. Her main focus now was to check into the hotel and find Granny to talk to her about Zack.

When they arrived at the cave, Madison noticed that Zack was getting antsy. "I want to get off and look around," he said.

"Not now, Zack. I really want to see Granny. Do you

mind?" Madison knew that the first time Zack came through the cave, he was in the wagon with his eyes closed, barely conscious. But she hoped he wouldn't mind. He could still see much of the cave from horseback as they walked through.

"No, it's okay," said Zack. "I'll see it another time."

Madison wondered what he meant. It sounded like he planned to return to the future. To her? With her? Now wasn't the time to talk to him about it.

When they emerged from the cave and trotted onto the main road, Zack smiled when he saw the sign that said Red Bluff, Colorado. "I recognize that sign!"

"We're almost there," said Madison. "Would you mind taking the horses to the livery while I check in?"

"No, not at all. That way I can buy Echo right away. I don't want another day to go by without him. Then I'll go to the saloon to see Matthew and Sarah. Will you meet me there later, or will you spend the whole evening with Granny, too?"

"I'll meet you over there sometime," said Madison. "Here we are." After dismounting, she handed the reins to Zack. "See you later, Zack."

"Bye, Madison!"

As Zack rode down the street leading Chaco, Madison stood in front of the hotel, watching. She smiled when he reached the end of the block and turned his head to look back at her and wave. Madison sighed. She was hopelessly in love with him and didn't know how he felt about her. What a miserable situation, she thought.

When she walked into the hotel, Eliza greeted her. "Hello, Madison! Nice to see you again. Have you come to return our young Zack?"

Eliza was warm and friendly, and Madison liked her a

lot. With her husband, Samuel, Eliza owned the hotel. And Granny and her new husband, Edward, lived here. Edward was Eliza's father. It was all one big happy family, and Madison was happy to be a part of it. Eliza always treated Madison like family, and Madison appreciated that.

"Yes, Zack is back, and I also wanted to spend some time with Granny."

"She's around here somewhere—maybe in her room, though—because my father is in the restaurant with Samuel."

"Okay, I'll find her," said Madison. Eliza gave her the key, and Madison walked upstairs to her room. Since Granny had married Edward, Eliza had stopped charging Madison when she stayed at the hotel. At first, Madison had protested. But when Eliza insisted, Madison gave in. After all, they were family now. Edward was officially her great-grandfather, which made Eliza her grandmother. Since Madison had lost her maternal grandparents in the barn fire and she never knew her paternal grandparents, she liked the idea of having Eliza and Samuel in her life. They were both such wonderful people.

She put her backpack in her room and walked down the hallway to Granny and Edward's room. When Granny opened the door, Madison hugged her. "Granny, I've missed you so much!"

"I've missed you, too, Madison. You never call, you never write," said Granny in her mock angry voice.

Madison laughed. "I would if I could, Granny. I would if I could."

"Come on in to my humble abode. Sit down there, make yourself as comfortable as you can with this crummy furniture."

"Granny, the furniture is fine, and you could get new furniture if you wanted!"

"Who needs new furniture? My butt won't get any younger sitting on newer furniture! So what have you been up to? You still working for those crooked attorneys?"

"Granny! They're not crooked. It's the same office that Jenna used to practice in."

"Madison. *All* attorneys are crooked in one way or another. That's why Jenna quit. Because she wasn't crooked, so she didn't fit in."

"Oh, Granny. I'm going to be a lawyer, and I'm not going to be crooked."

"Then you'll be the first!" said Granny.

Madison wanted to change the subject. Besides Granny's acerbic way of speaking, she could be intolerably stubborn. "How do you like living here—you know, in the past?"

"It's better than living in that old folks' home in the future!"

"Granny, you didn't live in an old folks' home. You had a nice apartment." Madison looked around the small room. It had a full-size bed, two chairs, two bedside tables, a chest of drawers, and a wooden sink with a pitcher of water on it, a wood stove in one corner and a chamber pot in the other (just like Madison's hotel room). "Your apartment was bigger than *this*, Granny. You don't even have a composting toilet."

"I don't mind peeing in that vase over there. I know, I know, its proper name is a chamber pot, but it looks like a vase to me. Living in the new Red Bluff was like being in an old folks' home. What did I do all day? Gab on the phone to those few friends who hadn't kicked the bucket yet, and then what did they talk about? All their ailments. I was sick of hearing about their ailments! No one here talks about that. They just live their life and enjoy every day. How do I like living here? I love it! It's paradise for me."

"And how do you like being married again? Grampy's been gone for a long time."

"Married life? With Edward? That rotten old coot!" Granny smiled at Madison. "I love it. He treats me well, and we get along wonderfully. The old coot." Granny wiped a tear from her eye. "Now look what you've made me do! Get all sentimental! I'll lose my grouchy reputation!" Granny stood up and straightened her long dress. She winked at Madison. "And I'll tell you something else, great-granddaughter. The sex is awesome!"

CHAPTER TWENTY-SIX

As ZACK LED Madison's horse down the street, he smiled when he thought about how she had still been looking at him when he turned around to see if she was still there. Although he didn't know for sure, in his heart, he believed that she felt the same way. At least he hoped so.

He rode into the livery stable. "Ezra! You here?"

The lanky man appeared from the back. "What do we have here, Zack? I heard you left town—and now you come back with two horses!"

"They aren't mine, Ezra. They need to be boarded for one night. But—do you by any chance still have Echo?"

"You want to see him? You haven't been to see him in a long time—years. And I never told you this, but when you walk by and he sees you—he still nickers. Yes, he's here. I'll go get him for you."

"Ezra, I don't want to see him. I want to buy him back. Will you sell him to me?"

"I knew you'd be back for him someday! Many people offered to buy him—such a pretty boy with a good temperament—and I always said no. Zack, I've seen people with horses before, but you and Echo had a bond that I hadn't seen before. And by the way, I only rented him out enough to pay his board—and then only to people who I knew would be kind to him."

Tears came to Zack's eyes. "Ezra, thank you. Thank you so much," he said, as he turned away.

"Let me take these two and get them settled before I bring Echo out. You two need some time alone." Ezra took the reins of the two horses and led them to stalls in the back.

A minute later, another stall opened and a black and white pinto stepped out. He turned toward Zack, nickered, and loped up to him, almost pushing him over. Zack stroked the horse, whispering to him how much he loved and missed him, and told him they'd never be apart again.

Several minutes later, Ezra walked up from the back with a bridle and handed it to Zack. "See, horses never forget. And I knew this horse would never forget you. Here's your bridle, Zack. I saved it for you. It's only been used on Echo."

"Thanks so much, Ezra—for everything. How much do you want for him?"

"Let's see, now. What did I give you for him? Seven dollars? Yes, I believe it was. Seven dollars it is, then."

"Shouldn't it be more?" asked Zack.

"I told you; I rented him out enough to pay his board. As far as I'm concerned, you've been boarding him all this time. Really, I shouldn't charge you anything."

Zack pulled some coins from his pocket. "Ezra, here's fifteen dollars. I'd appreciate it if you'd keep that. Everything you've done for him—and for me—you deserve more. I can't thank you enough."

"If it means that much to you, Zack. But as I told you,

the connection between you two was easy enough to see."

"Thanks so much, Ezra. I'll bring him back later. Here's ten more dollars for his board."

"He's welcome here anytime, Zack. Do you want a leg up? With one arm in a sling and that heavy thing on your back, I don't think you can swing up like you're used to."

Zack bent his leg, and Ezra boosted him up onto the horse. "See you later, Zack."

"Bye, Ezra, thanks."

It was a one minute ride from the livery to the saloon, but it was so good to be back on Echo's back, that Zack rode all around town. He loved the easy movement of the horse and the way Echo always answered when he talked to him. Looking down at his sore arm, Zack thought how lucky it was that it became infected. Otherwise he might never have known the pleasures of the twenty-first century, he might never have gotten Echo back, and he might never have had a chance to win Madison's heart. Not that it was exactly won yet, but he hoped it would be soon.

He slid off Echo's back and draped the reins over the hitching post. Zack knew he didn't need to tie the horse —Echo wasn't going anywhere. Looking over the top of the swinging doors into the saloon, Zack saw Matthew working at the bar and Sarah singing at the piano. This was the only home he'd known for the last four years, and he would miss it. But he knew he had to leave. Bringing beers and whiskeys to drunks and taking their insults, without saying a word, had grown old. He didn't need it anymore—not when he had the twenty-first century as an option.

Pushing open the swinging doors, he slowly walked in. Sarah saw him first. She left the piano and stopped singing in the middle of a song. "Zack! Zack! You're okay! I was so worried about you. I was afraid we'd never see you again!"

"Ouch! Not so tight, Sarah, my arm is still sore."

"Oh! Sorry, Zack."

When Matthew heard the commotion, he pushed between Sarah and Zack and made it a group hug. "We missed you, boy. Hope you're home to stay," said Matthew.

Zack smiled at the comment. Now was not the time to say anything—not with such a warm homecoming.

"We heard you'd be coming home today, so I cooked a special supper," said Matthew. "Rawlins is going to watch the bar, and we'll eat at a table—a regular family supper. It's so great to see you back and healthy again, Zack. Come on in. Can I bring your pack upstairs for you?"

"No, I can bring it upstairs. Thanks. When's supper?" Zack knew that Rawlins was the ex-drunk deputy sheriff, who still frequented the saloon, although he had stopped drinking after he assisted in rescuing Sarah.

"Whenever you're ready for it, Zack."

Zack considered asking if Madison could join them. But he thought with all the special treatment from Matthew and Sarah, he should just accept what it was. A family supper. And Madison wasn't family—yet. He hoped to have a chance to talk to Matthew about her. He needed some advice about women.

CHAPTER TWENTY-SEVEN

Matthew, Sarah, and Zack sat down for supper. Matthew had prepared fried chicken, mashed potatoes, and spiced beets. It used to be Zack's favorite before he had tried Thai food, but Zack didn't say anything about that.

"So how was it in the future, Zack?" asked Matthew.

"It was awesome!"

"Awesome?" asked Sarah. "I think you were there too long! You're starting to talk like you're from the twenty-first century!"

"I can't figure out the attraction to such a place," said Matthew. "Why would anyone want to live there, when this is a choice?"

"I was perfectly happy there until I found the old Red Bluff. And you." Sarah looked at Matthew lovingly.

Matthew patted her hand. "That's what I mean. Once you've been here, why would you want to go anywhere else?"

"I believe that's what you said about Missouri before you left," laughed Sarah.

Matthew and Zack laughed with her. "Well, darling,

that much is true! I guess I'm not much of an explorer."

"So you thought it was awesome, huh, Zack? And how about Madison? How did you get along with her?"

"Madison is great," said Zack. He liked Sarah and trusted her, but he felt he needed a man's opinion about what to do with Madison. So he didn't want to mention his feelings with her around.

"What was in that backpack you brought back? It looked heavy," said Matthew.

"Mostly books. I went to a bookstore and bought a bunch of them."

"Twenty-first-century books, I imagine?" asked Sarah.

Zack nodded. "Madison loaned me *A Time to Kill* by John Grisham, and I bought the sequel."

"Oh, yes, you would like books about lawyers. Did you get any more Pennsylvania law books?" Sarah joked.

Zack smiled. "No, I don't think I need those anymore. I'm thinking of selling that one on eBay."

"eBay? What's eBay?" asked Matthew.

"eBay is an online marketplace. You can buy or sell almost anything there," Sarah said to Matthew. "Zack, does that mean you will return to the future, or will you ask Madison to sell it for you?"

Zack put another bite of chicken in his mouth before he answered. Although he wasn't looking at them, he knew that Sarah and Matthew were looking straight at him. He thought it was as good a time as any to tell them what he had planned. And he didn't have to mention Madison in his plans—not now anyway. "Yes, Sarah. I want to return. I want to live there—permanently."

Matthew, who was sipping his beer, choked on it. "Permanently? You're not serious!"

"Yes, Matthew, it's what I want. To move there and

not return."

"You can't do that, Zack! I need you here!" said Matthew.

"You have Sarah now, Matthew. You don't need me," said Zack quietly.

"Is that what you think? Is that why you're leaving? Because you think I don't want you around anymore? Because I do! You're family!" said Matthew.

Zack noticed that Sarah sat quietly and didn't say anything. He supposed that she thought it was between him and Matthew. And it was. "No, Matthew. That's not why I'm leaving. You're family to me, also. I'm leaving because there is opportunity there. What would I do here? Always be your side-pal? Serving drinks to men who call me names? Never getting anywhere in life? Dreaming my life away reading old books and never getting what I want out of life? Matthew, I don't want to hurt you. You have been wonderful to me. You *are* family. But you need to let me go, make my own life."

Matthew dabbed at his mouth, put the napkin down, and pushed his chair from the table. He glared at Sarah. "I can't take this. I can't believe it! I knew this would happen if you took him there."

"Would you rather I had left him here to die?" asked Sarah.

"No, of course not. It's just that I like things as they are. I don't like change."

"And I *need* a change, Matthew. I can't be serving drinks my whole life. It's different for you. You own the place. I want to be a lawyer—I've always wanted to be a lawyer. If I move to the new Red Bluff, I *can* be."

"You need to go to school to become a lawyer," said Matthew.

"I know that. I've already started preparing. That's what was in the backpack—books to help me get into college."

"Do you have a high school diploma?" asked Sarah.

"No. I'm going to take the GED test," said Zack.

"Zack's right, Matthew. He's a man. He needs to make his own way," said Sarah, patting Matthew's hand.

Matthew pulled his hand away. "I don't have to like it, do I?"

"No. You don't have to like it. But you have to love him enough that you can set him free without making him feel guilty about going," said Sarah.

"Why do you always know the exact right thing to say!" said Matthew, as he stood up and walked briskly out of the room.

Sarah looked at Zack, her eyes soft with concern. "Don't worry, Zack. When he gets used to the idea, he'll be fine. I'll help him through it. I think it's a great idea. Since I found out that you were reading a law book from Pennsylvania, I've been thinking that moving to the future would be a good opportunity for you. You go for it, Zack. Follow your heart."

CHAPTER TWENTY-EIGHT

GRANNY STEPPED TO the door and opened it. "C'mon. It's almost time for supper. You'll eat with us."

Not will you, or would you like to, just "you will." That was Granny all right. She was a dear old woman, but she could get annoying, thought Madison, as she stood up and followed Granny out the door.

"You're staying here tonight, right?" asked Granny. "I don't want you riding back in the dark. Maybe if you go through that cave in the dark, you'll end up in another time."

"Yes, I'm staying here. I was hoping to talk to you alone, though, Granny."

"We were just alone in my room. Whatever you have to talk about, you can talk about in front of the family. They're your family now, too, you know."

"I know, Granny, I know." Madison thought about asking if Zack could come to dinner, too, but he wasn't family—yet. Although she still needed to talk to Granny about him, she wasn't comfortable doing that in front of everyone else. A girl needs some privacy.

They walked down the stairs and into Eliza's dining

area. Madison had never been in there. It had a homey feeling, and the table was already set for five—like they expected her to be there.

"Go ahead, sit down, Madison," said Granny. Edward was just coming out of the kitchen carrying a platter of food. Granny grabbed him before he returned to the kitchen and wrapped her arms around him. Madison couldn't hear what she said to him, but then Edward said, "Madison! Don't make my woman cry, or you'll make me cry, too!" Then he kissed Granny on the forehead and walked back into the kitchen.

Madison sat at the table facing the window. Looking across the street, she saw a pinto horse at the hitching post close to the saloon. That must be Zack's horse, she thought. Zack. She needed to talk to Granny. Alone. Interrupting her thoughts, Eliza and her husband, Samuel, sat down, and then Granny and Edward sat down. Supper was a blur of easy conversation and good food. Madison wasn't sure if Edward or Samuel knew about the twenty-first century, so she didn't say anything about it. She did know, though, that Eliza had gone with Jenna once to see it.

All Madison could think about was Zack. She didn't even remember what she ate. When supper was over, Granny said, "All right, Madison, what did you want to talk about?"

Feeling awkward, Madison looked down and only said, "Ummmm."

Edward stood up abruptly. "Old woman! Don't you know any better than that? Young girls don't want to talk in front of men! Come on, Samuel. Let's exit the premises and let them talk girl-talk." Edward grabbed everyone's empty plates and headed for the kitchen.

Samuel smiled, picked up the rest of what was on the table, and followed Edward out.

"Are you sufficiently embarrassed now?" Granny asked Madison. "It's good for you. Now what's up?"

Madison looked from Granny to Eliza. She would have rather talked to Granny in private, but since Eliza had known Zack for years, maybe this would be even better. "It's Zack. I don't know what to do about Zack."

Granny balled up her fists. "Has that boy done something to you, Madison?"

Madison pushed Granny's fists away and smiled. "Only made me fall in love with him."

Granny put her hands on her hips. "Well, how dare he do that to my great-granddaughter!" Madison and Eliza laughed. "What are you going to do about it?" asked Granny.

"That's what I need to talk about. Zack doesn't even know how I feel."

"So I suppose you'll be wanting to move here, into the past, like the rest of the family," said Granny.

Madison perked up her head. "No. Definitely no. I'm a twenty-first-century girl. I don't mind coming occasionally to visit, but I don't want to live here. And I have no idea if Zack would want to leave here—or even if he feels the same way about me."

"I don't know how he feels about you, dear, but I can tell you this," said Eliza. "Leaving here would be the best thing that could happen for Zack. He's needed a kick in the pants to start doing something, and maybe this is it. He's been wasting away at that saloon. His only joy in life is his books. It would be a good opportunity for him to move to the future and get an education."

"Do you really think that's what he wants?" asked

128

Madison.

"I don't know whether or not he wants it," said Eliza. "But I know it would be good for him. And I don't think it would take much persuading to convince him of that. Zack has wanted to be a lawyer since Josiah first told him that he had gone to school in Boston to be one."

"Really?" asked Madison. "Josiah is a lawyer, too, like Aunt Jenna?"

"No, Josiah quit law school to move out here to the west. He wanted to be a lawman, not a lawyer."

"Oh. But what can I do about Zack? How can I find out if he feels the same way?"

"I'd go right up to that boy and say, 'So you want to sleep with me or not?' That's what I think you should do!" said Granny.

Eliza laughed. "I'm hoping she's kidding, Madison. I still don't know half the time! No, honey, I don't think you should say that to Zack. I think you should spend time with him and see what develops between you. He's never had a girlfriend, you know, so he might be a little shy. Give him time."

"That does sound like a great idea except for one huge obstacle. He lives more than a hundred years in the past. How can we spend time together if he's here and I'm there?"

"Like I said," said Granny. "Ask him straight out how he feels and then you'll know. Problem solved."

"The hundred years does complicate matters," said Eliza. "If you want to know immediately, then asking him might be the way to go. But if you want to go slow and give him time to act on his own, then just start coming here every weekend to visit your Granny. She wouldn't mind. You know you're welcome here anytime.

And that would give you the time you need to find out."

"If I were you, girl, I'd stop talking to us old fogies and get your young butt across the street to talk to him now. Time's a wastin'! Get going!" Granny stood up. "I'm going to go help the men. I'd go over there if I were you. Go for it!"

Eliza, always mothering, squeezed Madison's hands. "It will work out the way it's meant to, Madison. Go on over and talk to him. Enjoy your time with him. Maybe the evening will unfold exactly how you would like it to."

CHAPTER TWENTY-NINE

After Zack helped Sarah clean up, he walked straight outside without looking at Matthew who was behind the bar. Zack stroked Echo's face and said, "There's my good boy, Echo. Just being around you makes me feel better. How did I get along without you for so long? We'll never be apart again, Echo. I promise." Then he whispered in the horse's ear, "I hope you like living in the twenty-first century, 'cause that's where we're going!"

He took the reins and led the horse into the street. With only one good arm, he couldn't swing up on the horse. Although he had enough "old" money to buy a saddle, he didn't think it would be that long before he could swing up again. Kat had not yet given him permission to take the sling off, but he thought it would be soon. Zack led the horse the long way around to the livery, stroking him the whole way. And with every word that Zack spoke to him, Echo nickered in reply.

After putting the horse back in his stall, Zack reluctantly walked back to the saloon. Matthew didn't want to talk to him at all. What was Zack going to do? He pushed open the swinging doors, strode inside and up the stairs to his room. He chose the new book by John Grisham and walked back downstairs to his usual table. Sarah was singing, Matthew was at the bar, and Zack was reading. Everything seemed back to normal except that Matthew was angry, and Zack was in love and planning to leave the old Red Bluff.

When Sarah finished her song, she walked over to the bar and said something to Matthew. Without looking up, Matthew nodded his head and put down the glass he was washing. Sarah returned to the piano, and Matthew walked over to Zack. Although Zack had watched the entire interaction, he pretended he was reading when Matthew sat down on the opposite side of the table.

"Sarah said I need to talk to you," said Matthew glumly.

Zack nodded his head but didn't say a word.

"I guess I should say I'm sorry for acting that way. I *am* sorry. But you're like a little brother to me, Zack, and I'll miss you so much!"

"You'll still see me, Matthew. It's not like I'm never coming back. I'm less than an hour away. You know that. I know you've been there."

"But I'm used to having you here every day. It won't be the same. Like I said, I don't like change."

"Sarah was a big change, and you liked that change."

"Sarah was an addition to my life. If you leave—well, when you leave—it will be a subtraction."

"I'm sorry, Matthew. I have to do it. There is no way for me to be a lawyer in the nineteenth century. But there *is* a way in the twenty-first. I wouldn't be true to myself if I stayed here and just dreamed about something that is within my grasp."

"You're right, Zack. I know you are. It will just take

me some time to get used to you being gone. I'll be okay," said Matthew, as he smiled a sad smile at Zack.

"Can I talk to you about something else?" Zack fidgeted in his seat.

"Sure, Zack, anything. I really apologize for how I acted. What do you want to talk about?"

"Madison."

"Madison? Is she the reason you want to move to the new Red Bluff?" Matthew asked, raising his voice.

"No. The main reason is that I want to be a lawyer. I want to make something of myself. But if I could be with Madison, too, then it would make everything that much more awesome."

"Awesome." Matthew shook his head. "You already talk like you belong there."

"So what should I do?"

"About what?"

"Madison! What should I do about Madison?"

"What do you mean?"

"Matthew, I don't know if she likes me or not. And I don't know how to find out or tell her that I like her."

"Oh. Oh." Matthew exhaled slowly. "Why don't you ask her out for supper? That would be a good start."

"You mean at the hotel?" Zack moved his head to indicate the hotel across the street from the saloon.

"No, Zack, I mean in the new Red Bluff. There's a Thai restaurant there that has delicious food. Sarah took me there."

"We ate there a few days ago. It was delicious."

"So invite her back there. Or someplace else. I know there's more than one restaurant there."

"Okay," said Zack slowly. "That is a good idea. But maybe she'd think it was to repay her for staying at her house for a week."

"I don't know, Zack! Then just kiss her! If she kisses you back, then she likes you, too. If she slaps your face, then she doesn't. Although that's not always true, either. When Edward first kissed Granny, at her birthday party, she slapped him and then kissed him back. I don't know, Zack. I guess the best advice would be to go with the moment. If it feels like you should ask her for supper, then ask. If it feels like you should kiss her, then kiss. All I can say is good luck. I have to get back to the bar now. I love ya, kid."

"Thanks, Matthew. I appreciate your help."

CHAPTER THIRTY

As MADISON OPENED the door of the hotel and stepped outside, she saw that Zack's horse wasn't in front of the saloon anymore. She wondered if he had returned the horse to the livery and if he was back yet. She looked at the saloon, the horses tied in front, and the dirt street, and she thought about what a different life it would have been growing up in this environment. How could someone who grew up like this, and she, who grew up in the twenty-first century, have anything in common? How could they form a life together? Could they overcome the differences? But Zack fit in so well in the twenty-first century. It really was like he belonged there. She wondered if he thought so.

Madison crossed the street, pushed through the swinging doors of the saloon, and saw Zack sitting at the back table reading a book. Sarah had just finished singing a song, so Madison walked up to her. "Hey, Sarah, how's it going?"

"Hi, Madison! Thank you for bringing Zack back."

Madison noticed that Zack had picked up his head, seemingly at the sound of her voice. He smiled at her, and she returned the smile. "Oh, you're welcome, Sarah. Talk to you later." She walked over to Zack's table and sat down.

"Hi, stranger," said Madison.

Zack laughed. "It does seem like we've been apart for ages, although it's only been a few hours." When he looked at her, his eyes twinkled. Did they always do that?

"I saw your horse outside before. He is beautiful. I bet it feels good to have him back."

Zack slowly shook his head back and forth. "I never thought he'd be mine again. It's like a miracle. Really, Madison, a miracle. Thank you."

"I didn't do anything," said Madison.

"You told me about the coins! And that's what allowed me to get him back."

"I'm just glad you have him again. I know what it's like to love your horse."

"Hey, chief! Get over here and gimme some whiskey!" called a voice from the poker table at the other side of the room.

"I'll be right back, Madison," said Zack, as he stood up, grabbed a bottle from the bar, and took it over to the poker table.

When he returned, Madison asked, "Why do they call you chief? Is that your nickname or something?"

Zack frowned. "I wouldn't exactly call it a nickname. They call me that because my mother was Indian." He looked at Madison, almost defiantly, through half closed eyes. "I'm half Indian. Does that bother you?"

"Bother me? That you're half Indian, as you call it?" Madison laughed.

"Why are you laughing?"

"Because I'm half Indian, too! Only they call it Native

American in the twenty-first century."

"You're half Indian? Really? No, you're trying to hornswoggle me!"

Madison held her right hand up. "Honest Injun, Zack! I'm half Native American!" She laughed again and shook her head. "I thought you knew. You've seen my last name, haven't you?"

"No," said Zack. "What does that have to do with anything?"

"My last name is Two Feathers," said Madsion.

Zack smiled at her again, and the twinkle returned to his eyes. "I can't believe it. Something else that we have in common. We both want to be lawyers, and we're both half Indian, er, Native American. It's going to take me awhile to get that one straight."

"That's okay, but you might offend some people in the meantime. Although, since you *are* Native American, too, it shouldn't bother them too much."

"Chief! Another round here! Now!" screamed someone from across the room.

Zack grimaced and stood up, but Rawlins appeared from the back and pushed him back down. "I'll take care of it, kid. You talk to your friend."

"Thanks, Rawlins."

As Zack sat down, Madison said, "Don't you ever think about standing up to them?"

"No," said Zack. "Never. Sarah stood up for me. She walked over there and poured whiskey in the guy's lap when he wouldn't stop calling me chief."

"Wow, that was cool of Sarah to do that."

"And she ended up getting kidnapped by the guy."

"That was just one guy. Not all jerks are kidnappers."

"There's something else," said Zack. "There's another

reason that I'll just take it and not say anything. My father got shot standing up for himself. In this saloon— just before Matthew and Josiah moved to town."

"Oh, Zack, I'm sorry. I understand now."

"It's been nearly four years."

"Chief! More whiskey!"

"I just brought you whiskey," said Rawlins.

"It tastes better when the chief pours it," said the man.

Matthew walked up to their table and looked at Zack. "Why don't you take Madison for a walk outside so this scalawag will forget about you? I think that's easier than throwing him out."

Zack stood up and handed Matthew his book to set behind the bar. Then he put out his hand to help Madison stand, and they walked out of the saloon together.

CHAPTER THIRTY-ONE

MADISON COULDN'T BELIEVE it. The one part of her identity that she had always felt strongest about was her Native American heritage. And now she finds out the man she has fallen in love with is also Native American. She wanted to scream out to the world how happy she was, but she stayed silent as she walked out the swinging doors beside Zack.

"Do you mind walking around town?" asked Zack.

"No, not at all," said Madison.

They walked in silence until they reached the end of the street. Zack turned left, past the Ralston General Store, and said, "Um, Madison, there's something I've been wanting to talk to you about."

Surely this was the moment that he would say how he felt. Madison felt the joy building inside her. She wasn't sure she could contain it. Instead, as calmly as she could, she said, "Sure, Zack. I'm listening."

"I've been thinking about this a lot, and I, um—"

When he hesitated, she said, "Yes," to encourage him. She smiled at him, but he was looking at the ground instead of at her.

"Um, I want to move to the future. I want to go to school there and become a lawyer."

Madison tried to conceal her disappointment, but she feared that her shaky voice gave her away. "Ah, I told you, Zack, that I thought you'd make a terrific lawyer."

"Do you really think so?" asked Zack, smiling at her and obviously not noticing the quiver in her voice. That annoyed Madison. But he was probably nervous about confessing this to her and more focused on himself.

Madison exhaled. "Yes, yes, I do. You'll have a lot of school in front of you, though. Four years of college before you even get into law school. And you'll have to take that GED test that we talked about."

"I already bought the books and study guides for the test," said Zack.

"You did? Wow, I didn't know that. You *are* serious." Madison chastised herself for being upset at his disclosure. She wanted him to live in the twenty-first century. Now he confirms it, and she's disappointed that he didn't declare his undying love to her. Give him time, she told herself. One confession at a time. Encourage his choice and be supportive. "I'll help you in any way I can, Zack."

"That would be awesome, Madison. I still don't know exactly what I need to do after I pass the GED."

"You need to apply to college. Sooner would be better than later, if you want a chance to get in this fall. You'll also need to take either the SAT or the ACT. When is the GED?"

"The guy at the bookstore asked me that and scared me. So I looked it up, and apparently this year they've changed it. It's computerized, and you can take the test almost any time. I figure I'll be ready in a week. Do you think that will give me enough time to apply for college?"

"A week! It's a long test, from what I understand. Several parts to it and all. And most of the information —has happened in the past one hundred years. How are you going to learn all that in one week?"

Zack smiled at her. "I'm a fast learner, Madison."

"Oh, that's right. You have a photographic memory! Well, that will definitely be an asset. There is one thing, though."

"What?"

"College is expensive."

"I have a plan for that. I'm not sure it's going to work, but I'll start on that after I get through the GED test."

"What's your plan? I hope you're not planning to rob the bank or anything!"

Zack laughed. "No, nothing like that. But I did buy a coin book at the bookstore. I know what coins are valuable and how to determine which coins are worth more. I'm hoping it won't be difficult to find the more valuable ones. And I'll be on the lookout for the 1795 silver dollar the coin guy wants. That would be a ton of money right there." They had circled the block and arrived back in front of the saloon again. Zack stopped in front of the saloon and said, "I don't want to take you back in there and expose you to that nonsense. Do you want to go into the hotel and talk?"

Madison, without a moment's hesitation, said, "No, Zack. I think I'm ready to go in for the night. It was nice talking to you. I'll probably see you in the morning before I ride home."

"Come on. I'll walk you over there." They walked across the street. Zack stepped in front of Madison so he could open the hotel door for her. But before he opened it, he leaned over and kissed Madison on the lips. "I like

141

you, Madison."

She leaned into him, and when he pulled away, she kissed him back. "I like you, too, Zack." Then she stepped through the door and ran up the stairs to her room.

CHAPTER THIRTY-TWO

MADISON COULDN'T SLEEP. She lay in bed thinking that she had acted like a first grader, after all. "I like you, too, Zack!" she had said. At least she had kissed him back, although it wasn't much of a kiss. But it was enough for a first kiss, she thought. Well, now she knew he had feelings for her, and she knew that he wanted to move to the twenty-first century. Where did that leave them? On the road to happiness or disaster? The real question was whether a man from the nineteenth century could find lasting happiness in the twenty-first century.

She knew that her Aunt Jenna, Sarah, and even her Uncle Ryan had successfully moved *from* the twenty-first century back to the nineteenth. They had all adjusted well and were happy—although they did make occasional trips to the future for various reasons. But could someone from the past be happy in the future? Zack was young enough to adjust. And it would be great for him to get away from those awful men who called him names. He did want to go to college and become a lawyer. It seemed like the future was a good fit for him. And he could return to the past any time he wanted to. With the cave, it didn't have to be an either/or choice.

Zack had already bought books to study for the GED test! He was serious about going to college. Was becoming a lawyer more important to him than she was? It was still early to be wondering about that. Maybe he just wanted to use her so he could go to school. Madison chided herself for thinking that about Zack. The one thing she felt certain of: there was nothing at all deceitful about Zack. What you saw was what you got. The men in her time were complicated, manipulating, and looking out for their own good. That's what she liked about Zack. He was innocent of all those confusing behaviors. He was just—Zack.

She closed her eyes again hoping to get some sleep. Five minutes later, she opened them. Too many thoughts —about Zack—swirled around in her mind. Madison reached for her backpack and fished out her iPhone. Midnight. How long had she been lying there unable to sleep? Too long. She touched the screen and all her music appeared. Moving her finger on the screen, she selected some soft music that she hoped would lull her to sleep.

It worked. Madison didn't wake until morning when she heard Granny pounding on her door and shouting, "Up and at 'em, great-granddaughter. You can't be sleeping the day away! It's time for breakfast! Come on! Get up!"

That was enough to rouse the dead, thought Madison. She stretched, dressed, and walked downstairs. No one was in the hotel lobby, so she went to the door that led to Eliza and Samuel's private quarters. Private, except they always kept the door open. She peeked in, and although no one was seated at the table, it was again set for five.

Like they were expecting her. Like she really *was* family. Madison liked the feeling.

A minute later, four people came bustling out of the kitchen carrying plates stacked with french toast, preserves, and a coffee pot. Everyone said hello to Madison, set down everything they were holding, sat down, and started eating.

"Glad to see you made it to breakfast, Madison. I thought you would sleep all day!" said Granny.

"Granny, it's only eight o'clock."

"We get up early in the nineteenth century! And I like it that way!" said Granny.

Everyone else mumbled their agreement and kept eating. When breakfast was over, Madison was grateful that neither Eliza nor Granny had brought up Zack or asked what had happened with him. And wanting to keep it that way, Madison helped carry the dishes into the kitchen, and then said her good-byes. She needed to say good-bye to Zack, though, so instead of going to her room, she walked across the street to the saloon.

The main door to the saloon was still closed, because they weren't open this early in the morning. Madison knocked on the door. A few seconds later, Zack opened the door with a big smile on his face.

"I knew it would be you!"

"Hi, Zack! I just wanted to say good-bye before I left to go home."

"You're leaving so early? I thought we could spend some time together before you left."

"I need to get back," said Madison, gauging his response.

"Oh, okay," said Zack, his smile fading.

"So, I'll see you in town when you come to take your

test, right? About a week?"

"Yeah, next Sunday is what I was thinking."

"You know you're welcome any time, Zack. Just come on in! You can't let me know, anyway."

"Okay," said Zack.

Madison looked around. It was morning, but although there was no one on the street, it didn't feel appropriate to kiss him out in the open like this. "Okay, bye." Madison started walking toward the livery stable, then turned around. "Oh, I forgot my stuff! Anyway, bye, Zack. I'm looking forward to seeing you next Sunday."

"Bye, Madison," said Zack.

Madison rushed up the steps of the hotel to the second floor where her room was. She packed, straightened the room, talked to Eliza for a few minutes at the front desk, and stepped outside to a surprise.

Zack was there in front of the hotel, bareback on his horse, and holding the reins on Chaco and Paisley, who were already saddled. "Hi, Madison. I thought I'd get the horses for you. And ride a ways with you—if you don't mind."

Madison's grin spread across her whole face. "Zack! Of course I don't mind. This was so sweet of you! But I owe you for the board on the horses."

"No, Madison. I stayed at your house for a week. It's the least I can do."

Madison hooked her backpack onto Paisley's saddle, pulled the reins over Chaco's head, and climbed up. "Let's go!"

CHAPTER THIRTY-THREE

ZACK FELT SO relieved when he saw Madison's wide smile. He hadn't been sure if he had done the right thing by getting the horses and offering to ride back with her. There was a chance, he thought, that she was just trying to get away from him. So when he saw her smile, his whole body relaxed.

"Have you—" said Madison.

"I started—" said Zack.

"Sorry," they said in unison.

"Go ahead," said Madison.

"I started studying for the GED last night and studied more this morning. I'm sure I can do it."

"I know you can, Zack! When did you say the test was again?"

"Oh, when I looked it up, I thought you could take it anytime."

"There are probably certain times, and you have to sign up for when you want to take it."

"I didn't realize that. When I discovered it wasn't just a few times a year, I stopped reading about it."

"It might be once or twice a week, or maybe once or

twice a month. And I'm sure you have to sign up for it."

"So if I come Sunday and want to take it Monday, that probably won't work, huh?"

"I doubt if it works that quickly." They turned off to the side trail, with Madison in the lead, Paisley following, and Zack at the rear. "See the cow pies pushed under the bushes? That's what the rustler did to hide the tracks of the cows that he stole. And here's the cave."

"I'll ride with you a little farther."

They entered the cave, and their conversation stopped. "Oh, look, here is the fence panel the rustler used to block the other entrance when he brought the cattle through here!"

"Why didn't we see it before?"

"He hid it in a good place. You either have to know where it is in the shadows, or have the light from the crack above exactly right."

They exited the cave, and Madison stopped her horse to let Zack catch up. "I should go back now, Madison. I don't want to ride all the way."

"Listen, Zack, if you want, I can sign you up and schedule a test for next week."

"That would be awesome! You wouldn't mind?"

"Not at all. I'd be happy to do it."

"Thanks, Madison." Zack leaned over and kissed Madison. "Then I'll see you Sunday!"

"I'm looking forward to it, Zack!" Madison leaned over and kissed him back. "Bye!"

Zack didn't move his horse. He watched as Madison and the two horses turned in front of the bush that hid the cave. As he was about to go back into the cave, he saw Madison's horse appear again.

"Zack! I'm glad you didn't go back yet. I need more

information about you so I can sign you up."

"Sure, what?"

"Your full name and your birthday. I know they'll ask for that."

"Zackary Allen Murphy. April 14, 1848."

"Oh, dear. That will never do. This may be more difficult than we had anticipated. Your new birthday will be . . . April 14, 1992. And I can use my address and the house phone number for you. We'll get it done, Zack. Don't worry. Oh, wait, spell your name for me."

"Z-a-c-k-a-r-y A-l-l-e-n M-u-r-p-h-y."

"Okay! Bye again!"

"Bye, Madison. Thank you so much!" Again he watched as she headed toward the bush. This time, she turned around, gave him a warm smile that sent his stomach into somersaults, and then disappeared down the trail.

Although he could no longer see her, he could still hear the two horses walking down the trail. When the sound of horse hooves faded, and all he could hear were birds and the sound of the wind through the trees, Zack smiled to himself and sighed as he turned his horse back toward the cave. He loved that girl. He was completely smitten, and it felt wonderful. She had kissed him back again. There was no mistaking it. She felt the same about him. He was going to be a lawyer, and he was going to be with the girl of his dreams. Life couldn't get any sweeter.

CHAPTER THIRTY-FOUR

EVEN AFTER MADISON had turned the corner and knew that Zack couldn't see her anymore, she felt his eyes on her. It was like he was still there, with her. A feeling of warmth ran through her. Oh, she did like that boy! Although she had just left him, she could hardly wait to see him again.

It was still morning, but the sound of the horses' hooves on the hard-packed trail and romantic thoughts about Zack lulled her into a peaceful, almost sleepy feeling. He was going to take the GED! That brought him one step closer to moving to the twenty-first century *and* to her.

Madison breathed in the scents of the pines and listened to the wind gently blowing through the trees. Soon, the back corral came into view. She walked the horses through the two gates, put them in their respective stalls, and walked dreamily into the house with a smile on her face. It felt like her feet weren't even touching the ground.

Immediately, she opened her laptop and googled, "GED test registration." When she clicked on the website where she thought Zack had found his information, she realized the first thing that Zack needed was an email account. After a quick visit to gmail to set up an account for Zack—using her name as the password, of course—she returned to the online GED site and signed him up.

Everything went smoothly until she came to the section that asked about the highest grade completed in school. What should she put for that? Reading over the possible answers, she chose, "I don't remember the highest grade I completed." Madison thought that would be the safest. The next tough question was, "In what year was the last year of schooling completed?" 1865-ish. That would never do! She'd have to ad-lib on that one! She continued to ad-lib more of the answers—work status, income, where did you study for the GED—the questions went on and on.

When she arrived at the page asking for a social security number, she felt relieved when it said "optional." If she hadn't been so hasty with her relief, she might have anticipated the problems yet to occur. Madison also neglected clicking the "testing policies" link. If she had, she would have discovered something unsettling. But as it was, she scheduled the "Reasoning through Language Arts" test for the following Tuesday, then closed her computer and called her mother.

"Hey, Mom."

"Hi, Madison. Did you get Zack settled back into the past?"

"Yes, he's back at the saloon now, safe, and feeling much better than when he left! Thank you!"

"Did he take off the sling?"

"You never told him to, Mom."

"Damn. I meant to and must have forgotten. He

doesn't really need it now—it's healed so quickly. Although he shouldn't be lifting anything heavy for a while longer."

"Mom, you ragged on Doctor Mercer so much, and here you've made a mistake, too. Granted, it's not a critical mistake, but he can only work with what he knows. And back then, doctors didn't know much."

"You sound like you're defending him, Madison. I didn't even realize you'd met him."

"I haven't. Just sayin'."

"Okay, point made. Maybe I need to give him a textbook on Louis Pasteur and basic hygiene."

"Might not be a bad idea," said Madison. "But then he'd know where you're from. I mean when."

"Practically half the town is from my 'when'! My own brother and sister live there now, for heaven's sake! What's this world coming to? Next, you'll be telling me that you're moving back there." Kat hesitated and then continued, "You're not, are you, Madison? You're not planning to move back there, are you?"

"No, Mom. I'm definitely not moving back there! No worries!"

"Oh, good, because I thought maybe— Well, I'm glad you're not. I don't know what I'd do if I was the only one left of the family to live here! I may not always show it, Madison, but I like having you around. You're important to me."

"Thanks, Mom. I need to run now," said Madison, uncomfortable with her mother's admission.

"Okay, Mad. I'll talk to you later. Love you."

"Love you, too, Mom. Bye."

CHAPTER THIRTY-FIVE

As ZACK AND Echo walked slowly through the cave, he noticed the fence panel again. He leaned down to feel it and tried to pick it up with his good arm. It surprised him how heavy it felt. Letting go, he continued through the cave into the bright sunshine on the other side. Closing his eyes, he inhaled the fresh aroma of his surroundings. Would he miss it here? Was he not giving enough credit to the value of living here—here in the nineteenth century? He would proceed with his plan to take the GED test, but he'd have to give it some thought. Maybe he was being too hasty in his decision to get out of the old Red Bluff—to leave everything that he knew behind.

Continuing at a slow pace, Zack and the horse approached town. He wasn't in any hurry to get there; he just wanted to enjoy the feeling of being on Echo's back again. But the dark thoughts of missing the old Red Bluff started to intrude on his happy thoughts of moving to the new Red Bluff. The new Red Bluff held everything he had ever wanted—being a lawyer and loving a good woman. And the old Red Bluff held everything that he had known and had once held dear.

When Zack had first decided to leave, he hadn't expected the internal struggle that he was now experiencing. Would it go away? Zack didn't know the answer to that, but he did know that he had to go forward with taking the GED test. If he had to acknowledge the corn, then maybe feeling unsure about passing the test made him insecure about the whole move. Study. He just had to study. That was the solution to that part of the problem, anyway.

Zack walked Echo into his stall, took off his bridle, and gave him a good brush down. Then he hugged him and walked to the saloon. As he walked inside, he looked around the room and realized that so much of his life in Red Bluff was his life in this saloon. He knew almost everyone. Matthew was like a brother to him.

When he heard Sarah tinkering with something in the back room, he smiled. Life was comfortable here. Not satisfying, but comfortable. Was he willing to give up a life that was comfortable and familiar for a life that was full of the unknown? Zack had security here. But in the twenty-first century, he had opportunity and possibility. And it wasn't like once he left he couldn't come back. Yet a part of him didn't want to leave. That part clung to the familiar and the security of what he had always known.

"Zack? You okay?" As Sarah bustled out of the kitchen, she saw him still standing and dreaming at the entrance to the saloon.

"Oh, yeah, Sarah, fine, thank you." Zack walked through the saloon to the stairs and jumped them two at a time all the way to the top. Stepping into his room, he gathered up his GED books. Which one should I start with, he wondered. Leafing through them, he picked up the one with sample questions.

Turning to the history section, Zack found this question:

Mussolini ruled Italy from 1922 to 1943. His type of government was called:
A. *Democracy*
B. *Oligarchy*
C. *Monarchy*
D. *Communism*
E. *Dictatorship*

1922. That was more than fifty years in Zack's future. Perhaps he should start with something easier and work up to history. Choosing the book on language arts, he put the rest back in the drawer and returned downstairs, sitting at his usual table in the back by the bar. He had just opened the book when Sarah sat down across from him with a sly smile on her face.

"Did you ride with Madison back to Red Bluff?"

"No, not all the way," said Zack hesitantly.

"Did you kiss her?"

Zack frowned, his hands involuntarily squeezed into fists, and he glanced at Matthew who was pouring a beer for someone at the bar. Sarah leaned across the table and patted one of Zack's fists.

"Oh, Zack, don't be mad at him. I forced it out of him. He honestly didn't tell me voluntarily."

Zack's fists relaxed, but he looked at Sarah with narrowed eyes. "That conversation should stay between us men."

Sarah put her head down. "I'm sorry, Zack. You're right. It's none of my business. But I was excited that my matchmaking efforts paid off."

"Matchmaking? What do you mean?"

"Do you remember the first time you met Madison? Eliza and Samuel were having a birthday party for Granny at their hotel?"

"Yes, and I was watching the saloon, while Matthew was at the party. Madison came over to give me a message."

"Who do you think sent her over here to give you the message?" Sarah cocked her head at him and smiled.

"You did?" Zack relaxed as a smile spread across his face.

Sarah nodded and stood up to leave. "Mission accomplished," she said, as she tapped Zack on the shoulder and walked away.

Zack smiled to himself and picked up the book that was in front of him. Opening it to the table of contents, he started reading but couldn't focus on the words. All he saw was Madison's face in front of him—the way she was that first time he saw her—when Sarah had sent her into the saloon.

He remembered looking up as someone came through the swinging doors. Madison. His heart leaped that first time he had seen her. She had just come to deliver a message, but they talked until the party across the street had ended. At that time, he didn't know if he'd ever see her again, but now, thinking back on that night, that moment, he realized that was when he started loving Madison. She had captured his heart the moment she walked through the door.

Thank you, Sarah, Zack said to himself.

CHAPTER THIRTY-SIX

LATER THAT AFTERNOON, when Zack's head had cleared and he could read again without thoughts of Madison intruding, he managed to get through half the book. Studying carefully and taking the sample test at the end of each chapter, he felt good about his progress. He had only missed one question after reading eight chapters; and when he missed that one, he read the chapter again. So he felt good about himself, and fortunately, he had been left alone because Rawlins was helping Matthew.

He had just started a new chapter, when suddenly a hand appeared in front of him and swept the book onto the floor. At the same time Zack heard raucous laughter, the man's foot stomped on the book bending its pages.

"How's that, chief? You shouldn't be reading when I need whiskey!"

Before the man could turn away, Zack had stood up, and with his good arm, he had planted a sockdologer on the man's face so hard that the man hit the floor. Zack bent over, and with his foot, pushed the man's arm away and picked up his book. Without looking around, he marched upstairs to his room without a second thought.

He was not going to put up with garbage like that anymore.

Walking into his room, he propped himself on the bed and kept reading. It didn't occur to him until he came to the end of the chapter that perhaps Matthew might be angry that Zack had punched one of his customers. The man had deserved it. Zack wasn't going to be sorry. But if Matthew was angry, then Zack would apologize to him. There were enough hurt feelings going around as it was. Zack didn't want to leave town with Matthew in a huff.

Before he had a chance to begin reading the next chapter, someone knocked on the door. Zack swung his legs over the bed so he was sitting up. "Come in."

Matthew and Sarah strode in carrying three glasses and a bottle. Zack didn't have to wonder if Matthew was angry—there was a huge smile on his face. Sarah held up one glass of the sparkly liquid. "To the winner and still champion!"

Matthew handed Zack a glass and said, "I know you don't like to drink, Zack, but this deserves a glass of champagne! It took you long enough!"

Zack, confused, said, "You're not mad?"

"Mad? Why should I be mad? You should have done that long ago—and it probably would have been the last time you had to do it. I don't think anyone will bother you anymore, Zack! Now maybe you can decide to stay here instead of leaving." Although Matthew still held up his glass in a toasting position, the smile had faded from his face.

Zack put down his glass of champagne and gave Matthew a big hug, spilling Matthew's champagne all over both of them. "I'm sorry, Matthew. I have to leave.

But you're awesome. You're the best brother anybody could ever have."

Matthew patted Zack's back and pulled away. "It's okay, Zack. I understand. I really do."

Zack nodded, picked up his glass of champagne, and clinked glasses with Matthew and Sarah. He took a sip and handed the glass back to Matthew. "I can't have any more right now, Matthew. I'm in the middle of studying for my test. *That's* what made me so mad. That guy smashed my *book*." Zack picked up his book and showed Matthew and Sarah the bent pages. "It's *my* book. No one has the right to do that. It's one thing to call me chief, but it's another altogether to hurt my book." Then he held the book to his chest.

Matthew and Sarah nodded, and Sarah encouraged Matthew toward the door. "We understand, Zack. Now we'll leave you to your studying. C'mon, Matthew."

After they left the room, Zack realized that Sarah had not mentioned that both he and Matthew had tears in their eyes from the interaction. Maybe Josiah was right. Tears just showed that Zack and Matthew both had heart. And it hadn't bothered Sarah at all. He wondered if it would bother Madison.

CHAPTER THIRTY-SEVEN

MADISON WAS COUNTING the days until Zack came back to the twenty-first century, but she had the feeling that counting just made the time go slower. She wanted to see him so much, maybe too much. She'd have to think about that one.

By the end of the day Wednesday, she had decided that as much as she wanted to see Zack, she shouldn't be alone with him until after his GED test. She could probably get a friend to spend the night one night, but probably not two. How could she get a message to Zack not to come until Monday—the day before his test?

Madison glanced at the clock. Four thirty. A half hour more. It had been a busy day, and she was eager to return home. Too bad there wasn't a legitimate way to get out of the last half hour of work. As she turned back to her computer, Marcus strode through the door, carrying more dry cleaning. She looked at him questioningly.

"Madison. I would like for you to take my clothes to the dry cleaners and pick them up in the morning. Just tell them they're mine, and they'll know how to handle them." He stopped and held his hand up, palm out.

"Now before you say no, I want to say that I know you're not on salary, so you can go ahead and leave *now*. That should give you plenty of time to drop it off. And come in a half hour later tomorrow. Is that fair?"

"More than fair, Marcus. It won't take me longer than fifteen extra minutes."

"That's okay, Madison. Go ahead and take the half hour, now and in the morning. Be sure to tell them they are mine. The last person used her own name and ordered extra starch. I *hate* extra starch. I'm counting on you to take care of this."

Madison bit her lip to keep from laughing. "Yes, Marcus. I'm sure I can handle that. No problem."

He handed her the clothes and rushed out of the room. Madison powered down her computer with a smile on her face. Ask and it shall be given. She wanted a way out of the last half hour of work, and she got it! Life was sweet.

She gathered her belongings, left the office, and stepped into her car. Five minutes later, she had arrived at the dry cleaners, given them the clothes and Marcus's name, and was back in her car. Several minutes after that, she was home. Jenna's truck had been moved. That was curious, thought Madison. Jenna and Josiah normally only came once a month. When she opened the door, the two dogs greeted her. And as she walked into the living room, there was Josiah in his usual spot: feet propped up on the coffee table and holding the remote.

"'Good afternoon, Josiah. Surprised to see you here today," said Madison.

"Jenna needed something in town. Couldn't do without it. You know how women are. Oh! Sorry, Madison!" He turned back to the television.

As Madison walked to her room and passed Jenna's bedroom, she had an idea. She knocked on Jenna's door and stepped in. "Hi, Jenna."

"Hi, Madison. Bet you're surprised to see us here today," said Jenna.

"Yes, I am. Listen, Jenna, any chance you have some time to talk? Girl-talk?" asked Madison.

"Sure, Madison. Come on in," said Jenna, as she turned her chair around and motioned for Madison to sit on the end of the bed. "What is it, girlfriend?" Jenna was officially her aunt—her mother's sister—but they were so close to the same age they were more like friends.

"It's Zack. I don't want him to come Sunday night as he's planned. I don't want to be alone with him."

Jenna looked concerned. "You're not afraid of Zack, are you, Madison? Because he really likes you. I don't think he'd do anything to hurt you."

"No, Jenna. I'm not afraid of Zack. I'm afraid of myself. I don't want to be alone with him until after he takes his GED test. I want him to have his whole concentration on the test. I don't want him to be thinking of other things. You know." Madison raised her eyebrows at Jenna.

Jenna, studying her fingernails as Madison talked, started to say, "No, what do you—" Then she looked at Madison and understood. "Oh! You mean—oh! Okay! But what do you want me to do?"

"If you could ask him not to come until Monday night, it would be awesome. And if you and Josiah could come back Monday night, it would even be awesome-er! Although Josiah probably wouldn't want to come back so soon, but if you could just tell Zack, I'd appreciate it."

"What? Did that ole boy tell you it was my idea to

come back this week?" Jenna laughed. "Josiah *insisted* we come back because he didn't get his ice cream last week. He *must* have Thai *and* ice cream, or his visit just isn't complete. That's why the truck was moved. We've already had ice cream and will probably have more tonight! You want us to come back next week? No problem! Since Rawlins has quit drinking, Josiah is free to leave anytime he wants!"

"Thanks so much, Jenna. I really appreciate it! Oh! Could you tell Zack something else from my mother? Tell him that he doesn't need his sling anymore, but he's still not supposed to lift anything heavy."

"No problem, Madison. I'll take care of it."

CHAPTER THIRTY-EIGHT

DAYS WENT BY, and Zack studied every day. Matthew had been correct. Since Zack had punched that man, no one had called him chief. Once, someone who hadn't been at the saloon on *that* day, started to call it out, and when Zack looked up, someone else had elbowed the man into silence. It made Zack wonder how much more peaceful his life would have been if he had punched someone years ago. But he didn't spend much time on those thoughts. Mostly, he studied and then studied some more.

By Thursday, he had finished language arts, history, and math. He had completed all the practice tests, and had passed all of them without issue. Science was the last book he had to study. But he also had to learn to write an essay. He wished that he had bought a book on it, but it was too late for that now. And if he already lived in the twenty-first century, he could look it up online. Laughing to himself, he thought he was already taking life there for granted. If he arrived Sunday, he should still have more time to study, regardless of when Madison scheduled him for the test. He should finish science sometime Friday, so he would still have Saturday to practice writing an essay. Although he had never written one—or written anything for that matter, except an occasional letter—he knew his grammar perfectly from all the study with the language arts book. Zack felt confident that he would do fine with the essay.

That afternoon, when the swinging doors opened, he watched as Jenna walked in. She looked around, waved to Sarah, but kept looking. Then she saw Zack sitting at the back table and walked over to him.

"Hi, Zack. I know you're studying, but can I sit down?" asked Jenna.

"Sure," said Zack, as he closed the book and smiled at her.

"I have a message from Madison."

Zack lit up, sat up straighter, and leaned forward. "Oh? What did she say?"

"She would rather have you come Monday instead of Sunday."

Devastated, Zack slumped in his chair. "Oh," he said, looking down at the table. "Would she rather me not come at all?"

Jenna reached across the table and put her hand on Zack's. "Oh, Zack, no. It's nothing like that. Nothing. She really wants to see you. A lot. Believe me on that. She *really* wants to see you. Just not Sunday. Okay?"

A smile slowly reappeared on Zack's face. "She really wants to see me? You're sure?"

"I am positive, Zack. I have no doubt in my mind at all." She patted his hand. "Okay? Are you okay riding up Monday instead of Sunday?"

"Yeah, sure. It will give me one more day to study."

"And my sister, Kat, said that it was okay to take off

your sling, but you still can't lift anything heavy—like those cases of bottles that you usually lift."

"Okay. I think I'll leave it on, though."

"Why? I'm sure Matthew wouldn't ask you to do that if you weren't supposed to."

"No, it's not Matthew I'm concerned about. He'd never ask me to do that. It's just that if cases needed to be lifted and I was around, I would do it automatically. I want to keep the sling on to remind myself!"

Jenna stood up to leave. "That makes perfect sense, Zack! See you Monday!" Jenna turned and walked away.

"Jenna, wait! What do you mean—you'll see me Monday?"

"Oh, I forgot to tell you. Josiah and I will be riding over there with you. Josiah needs more ice cream!"

"Oh, wow, okay. See you Monday," said Zack.

Zack picked up his book, opened it, and pretended to study. He couldn't concentrate, though. His head swam with this change of plans. He felt disappointed. An extra day to wait to see the woman he loved. And Jenna and Josiah would be there, too. He liked them. It wasn't that. But now he couldn't be alone with Madison. And he had hoped to be alone with Madison and maybe kiss her again. He'd like that.

Zack exhaled slowly and frowned. Going over the conversation again in his head, he remembered something that Jenna had said, and it made his smile return. She had said, "She *really* wants to see you," and Jenna had emphasized "really." Madison *really* wanted to see him! Wow! He wanted to get up and wave his arms and scream and shout at the top of his voice! Instead, he closed his eyes and took another deep breath. It would only be another few days and he'd see her. The woman he loved.

CHAPTER THIRTY-NINE

MONDAY MORNING, ZACK awoke early and packed everything he was taking with him, which consisted of his books, pajamas, and clean underwear. Then he walked downstairs, had breakfast with Matthew and Sarah, and parked himself at his normal seat at the edge of the bar. After an hour of wondering how soon Jenna and Josiah would come get him, he decided to take off his sling. When he returned to this century, his arm should be healed enough to help Matthew again—for the short duration of time that he figured he'd stay at the old Red Bluff.

Sarah came and sat down in the seat opposite him. "You're excited, aren't you?"

"Oh, Sarah. I can't wait! This is the beginning of my new life. If this all works out, I'll be at college in the fall."

Sarah reached out and squeezed his hand. "You'll do great, Zack. You'll make a great lawyer. Do you think, though, that Jenna and Josiah will leave this early? Don't they usually leave later in the afternoon?"

"Yes, but they must know how excited I am to be going. I thought maybe they'd adjust."

"Maybe they will," said Sarah, smiling. "Maybe they will." She gave his hand another squeeze and walked away.

Sarah was so sweet, thought Zack. She and Matthew were so perfect for each other. Zack wondered if he and Madison were perfect for each other. He thought so.

The hours dragged on. After sitting there for some time fidgeting, he finally dragged out the book he had bought on test-taking strategies, and he began reading it. It was difficult to keep his mind on the book when every time the wind jostled the front doors, his head sprang up to see if it was Jenna or Josiah walking in. So far, it wasn't.

Dinnertime came, and he shared dinner in the back room, prepared by Sarah. She finally got angry when he kept jumping up from the table to see if someone had come through the door. "You'll know when they come, Zack. I guarantee they won't leave without you. Guaranteed! And if they do, you know the way yourself."

"Okay, sorry, Sarah."

When he heard another sound and involuntarily jumped, Sarah said, "Oh, Zack! I'm sorry. I understand. Finish your lunch and go back out there. You'll feel more comfortable waiting out there."

"Thanks, Sarah." He stuffed the last bite in his mouth and hugged Sarah. Then he squeezed Matthew's shoulders and skipped out to the main room of the saloon to wait.

It was getting later and later, and still Josiah and Jenna hadn't come for him. Maybe, he thought, he was supposed to go to them. Leaving his backpack in the seat and his book on the table, he walked down toward Josiah's office. Looking through the window, he saw

Josiah talking to two ranchers. Jenna was nowhere around. Apparently they weren't waiting for him. Josiah was still working on sheriff's business.

Disappointed, he walked to the saloon and sat back down at his table. He put the book into the backpack and sat there trying to look patient, with his hands folded in front of him. When he thought about it logically, it made sense not to go until later in the afternoon. Madison had to work until five o'clock. But his shoulders slumped, and he tried to think of other things.

Another hour crawled by. Finally, he couldn't take it anymore. It was late afternoon. Surely they would be coming for him soon. He strode out the door and walked to the livery. He brushed and saddled Jenna's horse and Josiah's horse, put their bridles on, and led them out. When Ezra walked by, Zack asked him to hold the reins while he quickly brushed Echo. It didn't take much brushing because Zack had brushed him every day since he had gotten him back. He slipped the bridle on him and led him out of his stall.

"You want me to give you a leg up, Zack?"

"I think I can do it myself, if I go on the *Indian* side." When Zack had trained Echo so many years ago, his father had insisted that he teach the horse to accept a rider mounting from the left side—the white man's way —and the right side—the Indian's way. Zack always used to mount from the right until he moved to Red Bluff and saw everyone else mount from the left. So he started mounting from the left just so he wouldn't stand out. But shortly after that, he had to give up Echo and it didn't matter anyway.

Zack grabbed Echo's mane with his right hand and swung onto the horse's back, using his left arm for balance. "I might have been able to do it before, but I didn't want to take the chance of falling and hurting myself worse!"

"Good job, Zack! Here ya go," said Ezra, handing Zack the reins of the other two horses.

As he turned the corner and trotted toward the saloon, there were Jenna and Josiah waiting out in front. "Where you been, boy? We've been waiting for you for hours!" said Josiah.

Zack started to protest when he heard Jenna laugh and saw her give Josiah a shove. "Not funny, Josiah! Not funny!"

"Thanks for bringing our horses, Zack," said Josiah.

"You knew that Madison had to work today, right, Zack? That's why we didn't hurry to get over there," said Jenna.

"I figured it out after a while," said Zack.

"Come on, now," said Josiah, after swinging up onto his horse. "Let's go get some ice cream!"

"Wait just a minute, Josiah. I need to run in and get my backpack," said Zack, as he slid off the horse and raced into the saloon. Coming back out, he slipped the backpack onto his shoulders, and then used the hitching post to climb onto Echo's back. "Let's go!"

The three rode quietly out of town and turned onto the side trail that led to the cave. When they reached the fence panel inside the cave, Josiah said, "See this, Zack? This is one of the items that helped Jenna find out who was rustlin' the cattle."

"I've seen that. Definitely doesn't belong in the nineteenth century!" said Zack. "What were the other items?"

"One was a cigarette that I found—manufactured, not

171

hand-rolled. And the main thing is the rustler called himself Hilary Clinton—she is a female politician in the twenty-first century." They emerged from the cave.

"Oh, yeah. That sounds familiar. I think Sarah might have mentioned that when she brought me here the first time. But I was barely conscious that day."

"Word has it, young Zack, that you could have died if Sarah hadn't brought you," said Josiah. "Are you sorry that you got a taste of the future?"

"No, I still want to live there. This GED test is my first step in making that happen. I'm hoping to start college in the fall."

"Zack, I really admire you. First the GED, then en- rolling in college—in a world you never even knew exist- ed until a couple of weeks ago. You're awesome!" said Jenna.

"Let's not make the boy conceited!" said Josiah. The three of them laughed. "Although I do think it is a won- derful, courageous thing to do, Zack. You've got grit! I'm proud of you."

"Thank you. Both of you," said Zack.

CHAPTER FORTY

MADISON WAS BESIDE herself with worry. What if Josiah and Jenna couldn't make it? What if Zack rode over on his own and they had to be alone tonight? She tried to calm herself by thinking that Jenna must have given Zack the message, because he didn't arrive Sunday. And Jenna promised that she and Josiah would be back today. Jenna understood. She wouldn't let the wrong thing happen. Jenna wouldn't have said they would definitely be here if she thought there was any doubt they would be.

After Madison was at work for an hour, Marcus came in and asked her to take a message to court again. Although she knew it was a compliment that he trusted her —because if she couldn't do it, he would get a low level attorney to do it—today, she just wanted to do something that would take her mind off her thoughts. Sitting in a courtroom waiting for a reply could be monotonous unless it was an exciting trial. She didn't know the lawyer involved, so she had no idea what to expect.

After driving to the courthouse, she walked through the security station, then into the specified courtroom and handed the message to the attorney. He was a new attorney, but he was older, and he had a good reputation. He took the message from her, nodded, and went back to his paperwork. Madison sat down at the back of the courtroom to wait.

She had walked up during a witness change. After the witness was sworn in, the man she handed the message to began his questioning. The woman was accused of being a drug runner. Madison thought that she only looked thirteen, so she would be perfect for the job. But she denied it and said she had no idea the drugs were under the passenger seat of her car. She claimed she had picked up a hitchhiker, and that he had put them there.

It was all civilized until the prosecuting attorney began hammering at the girl. Although he made her cry, the woman held her head up the entire time and answered all his questions. When Marcus's attorney asked for a redirect, he revealed that the woman had worked with a police sketch artist and had correctly identified a known drug dealer. Then the prosecutor claimed that she had seen the man's poster in the post office, and that's how she identified him.

It was dirty business. Sometimes Madison wondered if her decision to become an attorney was a good one. When she had thoughts like that, which she did occasionally have, then she told herself that she would do something benevolent like working in the public defender's office or perhaps with the local Ute or Navajo tribe.

The trial continued and didn't break for recess until almost one o'clock. The attorney brought her the message to return to Marcus.

"Wow. Great trial," said Madison. "I hope you get her

off."

"So do I," said the attorney. "You're not an attorney, are you?" he asked.

"Not yet," said Madison.

"Why don't you stay and watch the trial? You'll learn more here than you will shuffling papers back at the office."

Before Madison could protest, the man had pulled his cell phone out of his pocket and called Marcus. She heard him say, "Marcus? This is Jimmy. Yes, it's going well so far. Listen, I have," he held the phone away from his face for a second and said to Madison, "What's your name?"

"Madison."

"I have Madison here with me. I think it would be a good learning experience for her to stay. It's going to be a tough trial, but I should win. What do you say? Yes, that's what I thought, too. Okay, bye." He put the cell phone back into his pocket and said to Madison, "He agrees. You'll stay. Be back in fifty minutes. Good-bye."

And then he walked away, leaving Madison flabbergasted. Just when she had recovered her senses enough to move, the attorney turned around and walked back toward her. "I forgot to tell you. Marcus thinks you have the makings of a fine attorney and says the experience will do you good. Bye." And he turned around and walked away again.

Madison chuckled to herself. She didn't expect such a great compliment today. What a perfect week this was turning out to be! Zack was coming today, he'd pass his test tomorrow, she'd be alone with him tomorrow night, and today she got a great compliment from Marcus, who never compliments anyone! Of course, if this "Jimmy" hadn't told her what Marcus had said, she'd probably never have known. Well, thank you, Jimmy!

Since her sack lunch was back at the office and she didn't want to go back there, she decided on the healthiest fast food she could get. After finishing, she was back in the courtroom with five minutes to spare. This time, she sat down closer to the front. She noticed that Jimmy was already at his table going over his notes. He was a thorough guy and a good attorney. Madison hoped that he did win the case.

After three more hours, the trial still wasn't completed, but another recess was called until the following day. She didn't want Jimmy to call Marcus again about tomorrow, so she hurried out while he was still working at the table. If Marcus wanted her to watch the rest of the trial, he would tell her in the morning. Tonight was dinner with Josiah and Jenna *and* Zack. That is, if Jenna and Josiah rode into town with him. She felt sure they did, though. And she was glad she had been busy all day so that she hadn't had time to worry about it.

CHAPTER FORTY-ONE

MADISON PARKED HER car. When she glanced over at Jenna's two vehicles, she noticed that neither of them had moved. Without going into the barn, there was no way she could tell if Jenna, Josiah, and Zack had arrived until she stepped into the house and saw them. She closed her eyes, took a deep breath, and said to herself, "They're here. They're here. They're here." She knew that it wouldn't magically make them appear, but she felt better when she did it, and that was enough.

Confident now, she opened the front door and strolled into the house. Jenna's and Josiah's two dogs met her at the door. She smiled as she walked in. "Hello, everybody!"

Josiah sat on the couch in his usual spot, watching television and clicking through the channels. Zack sat on the other end of the couch using Madison's laptop. He looked up as she walked in. "Hi, Madison!"

"Hey, Zack, Josiah. Jenna in her room?"

"Yup," said Josiah, without looking up.

Madison walked out of the room and into Jenna's bedroom. "Thank you," she whispered to Jenna.

"It was no problem at all," said Jenna. "I told you he'd want ice cream. You ready to go? It was a busy day and neither of us had lunch."

"Sure. Just give me a few minutes to change clothes and get ready. I'll be right out." Madison hurried into her room and five minutes later hurried out again. Then she walked out to the living room where Jenna sat between Josiah and Zack.

"Oh, good. You're ready. Okay, boys, let's go," said Jenna. She put her hands on Josiah's and Zack's legs and pushed herself up.

"Oh. I don't want to go," said Zack. "I need to study for my test tomorrow."

"C'mon, Zack. You have to eat." Jenna tried to pull him up, and he wouldn't budge.

Josiah walked over and stuck out his hand toward Zack, as if to shake hands. When Zack took his hand, Josiah pulled him up and put his arm around him. "Zack, my man, you need to eat. You'll perform better on the test if you have eaten and gotten a good night's sleep. I can't help you with the sleep part, that's up to you. But I can help you with the eating part. You're coming with us. Okay?"

Madison stayed silent and watched the interaction between the two men. She wasn't sure what Zack would do.

A second later, Zack's face broke out into a smile. "You're right, Josiah. I have to eat. Let me just put the laptop away."

Josiah nodded his head. "Good enough. We'll meet you in the truck."

Jenna, Josiah, and Madison walked outside. Jenna and Madison waited while Josiah got the truck and pulled it up beside them. Zack had come out by then, and he stepped into the front seat as the two women stepped into the back.

Josiah drove a few minutes and then looked at Zack. "How about a driving lesson?"

"Yeah!" Zack, excited, leaned forward straining against the seat belt.

"Oh, come on, Josiah. I'm starved," said Jenna.

"Food can wait," said Josiah. "The man needs to learn how to drive."

Madison didn't say anything, but in her heart she could not have been happier. If Zack learned to drive—she knew he would love it—and it would be one more reason he'd want to stay in the twenty-first century. Go, Zack!

"Okay, then go to the parking lot of a big box store. That should be safe," said Jenna. "You know, Josiah. Where I taught you to drive."

"I know just the place," said Josiah.

"On second thought, wouldn't it be better to teach him in the car? It's automatic. A stick shift just makes the learning more difficult," said Jenna.

"He's a man, and he's smart, Jenna. He'll do fine. Don't worry so much," said Josiah.

Madison noticed that Zack couldn't keep still in his seat, like a kid going to a candy factory. She patted his shoulder. "You'll do great, Zack!"

A few minutes later, Josiah pulled into the large parking lot and shut off the engine. "Out, girls. This is between me and my man, Zack. Come on, Zack, switch places with me."

Madison and Jenna got out of the truck and stood to the side. Josiah and Zack got out and switched places.

179

Madison heard Josiah say, "Is the seat in a comfortable position for you? Can you reach the pedals without stretching? Okay, put your hand under here and you'll feel a lever. Yes! That's it. Keep moving it until you feel comfortable. Okay, let's go. First put your left foot on that left pedal down there. Yes. Keep it there. Now, turn the key. Exactly."

Madison heard the truck start. But she was disappointed when the sound from its engine kept her from hearing Josiah's instructions. She wanted to be in the truck with Zack on his first ride—to share it with him—but she also realized that it would probably make him more nervous. That's why she hadn't argued when Josiah asked her to get out.

She watched as the truck inched forward and then stalled, inched forward and then stalled, and then inched forward and kept going for several feet. "He's getting it, Jenna! He's getting it!"

Jenna laughed. "I think you're more excited than he is."

The two women watched as the truck jerked across the parking lot. After a few minutes, it started running smoothly, and Madison silently cheered him on. Too bad, though, that he couldn't get past second gear in the parking lot, she thought.

The truck headed toward them and came to a smooth stop. The engine turned off, and Madison and Jenna started clapping. Zack jumped out of the truck and dashed toward Madison. He threw his arms around Madison and hugged her. "I did it! I did it!" He swung her around. "Now, let's eat! I'm hungry!" Putting Madison back on the ground, Zack walked to the other side of the truck and climbed into the front seat.

CHAPTER FORTY-TWO

ZACK COULDN'T STOP chattering about how awesome it felt to drive the truck and how he was somehow going to find the money to buy his own. Jenna and Josiah just laughed, but Madison felt thrilled. More and more events were occurring to keep Zack here—with her. Excellent. Zack had such an excited look on his face, Madison couldn't help herself.

"Zack," she said, interrupting him. When he turned to her, she snapped his picture with her cell phone. "Thank you." Then as if nothing had interrupted him, Zack continued on about buying his own truck. He didn't stop until they received their menus at the restaurant.

Josiah and Jenna ordered Pad Thai, and Zack and Madison ordered the pineapple chicken. When the food came, Zack looked at the Pad Thai carefully. "What are you looking for, Zack?" asked Josiah.

"Matthew recommended it to me, and I just wanted to see what it looked like. I almost ordered it tonight, but the last time I had the pineapple chicken, it was so good that I had to have it again," Zack said, as he dug into the pineapple.

"Zack, did Jenna tell you that your test is Tuesday, tomorrow?" asked Madison.

"Oops, forgot to tell him that. Sorry," said Jenna.

"No, I just knew it was this week. Did you schedule just one for me?" asked Zack.

"Yes. It's the longest one. Language arts. Tomorrow at one o'clock, so you still have the morning to study," said Madison.

"Oh, language arts," said Zack.

"You're prepared, aren't you?" asked Madison.

"Yes, but I've never written anything except a few letters, and I have to write an essay for the test to demonstrate my writing skills. I'm not sure if I have any writing skills."

Jenna reached over and put her hand on Zack's arm. "You'll do fine, Zack. Don't worry."

"I know all the grammar rules really well, so the paper will be technically perfect," said Zack. "But I'm not sure if I know how to put an essay together. I'll do my best, though."

"Oh, Jenna, you'll never guess what happened today. Marcus asked me to take a message to court, and—"

Jenna interrupted Madison. "Wait. Marcus asked you to take the message? He usually gets the lower ranked attorneys to do it. Most law offices aren't like that, but Marcus is funny that way."

"I know, but he's asked me a couple of times already. Anyway, I always deliver the message and wait in the back for the attorney to bring me a reply. When the judge called a recess, the attorney told me that I'd learn a lot more watching his trial than I would shuffling papers at the office. He pulled out his cell phone, called Marcus, and asked him if I could stay!"

182

"What was the trial about, Madison?" asked Zack.

"A woman accused of being a drug runner."

"What's a drug runner?" asked Zack.

"That's a discussion for another time, Zack," said Jenna.

"Okay. But Madison, do you think that sometime I can watch a trial?"

"Sure, Zack. Did you want to take another test this week? I think there's another test Thursday. If you were scheduled for a test Thursday, you could go to court Wednesday to watch. It would be a good experience for you."

"Yeah, that sounds great," said Zack.

"Madison, has Marcus asked you to take his laundry since you told him no?" asked Jenna.

"Yup. And he gave me a half hour to bring it in, and a half hour to pick it up. When I told him I only needed fifteen minutes, he said to go ahead and take the half hour!"

"Great job, Madison!" said Jenna.

The easy conversation went back and forth between twenty-first-century topics and nineteenth-century topics. When they had finished dinner, Zack excused himself to go to the bathroom. Josiah said, "Zack, have you ever gone in a public place before?"

"No," said Zack.

"Be sure to use the 'Men's' room—I didn't know there was a difference, and Jenna still won't let me forget it!" said Josiah.

"Got it," said Zack.

When Zack had walked away out of sight, Josiah said, "Madison, I did you a favor. While we were alone in the truck, I mentioned how wonderful it was to take a shower, and I encouraged Zack to try it. I think I have him convinced. I also suggested that maybe he could go back to the store where he got the backpack and buy more clothes. I explained to him that people in this century have more than two sets."

"Thanks, Josiah, I appreciate that!" said Madison.

When Zack came back from the bathroom, he said, "There are some weird things in that bathroom."

"Josiah will have to explain those things to you when you're alone," said Jenna. "Right now, are you ready for dessert? Josiah can't wait to get his ice cream!"

CHAPTER FORTY-THREE

ZACK WOKE UP early feeling confident and ready to take on the world. No one else was up yet, so he decided to try the shower. He loved it—what a cool feeling having that water rush down like that. After getting dressed, he walked into the kitchen to prepare breakfast for himself and Madison. He'd been letting her cook for him, but now that he had two hands again, he thought it would be a pleasant surprise for her. Because he didn't want to serve her a cold breakfast, after the food was prepared, he waited to cook it until he heard her get up.

When he heard her door open, he started everything cooking and put bread in the toaster. Madison walked into the kitchen and saw him. "Zack! You sweetheart! You're making me breakfast! Thank you! Today is your test day. I should be making you breakfast."

"I woke up early and took a shower. It's so cool! And now that I have both my hands back, I can cook for us—unless you want to."

"Zack, I don't mind at all that you like to cook. You are welcome to do the cooking any time you want!"

Madison poured herself some coffee and sat down at

the table watching him flip the eggs. Everything smelled delicious, and when he brought everything to her, she was overwhelmed. "This is awesome! You're awesome!"

When they finished, Madison stood up. "I'll clean up today."

"You always used to clean up because I could only use one hand. My turn. You go on to work. I have plenty of time before my test."

"Yeah, but you should study some more."

"Honestly, I feel really prepared. I'll go over it one last time right before the test. But otherwise, I feel good about it."

"Okay, you've convinced me. You shouldn't have any problem walking to the test site. It's closer than the bookstore, but on a different street."

Zack smiled. "I'll find it. I'm going to walk around town first—see what other wonders are in this twenty-first century of yours."

"Okay, I'm going to work now. I know you'll pass the test, but I can hardly wait to see just how wonderfully you do! See ya soon. Bye." She leaned over and gave him a quick kiss on the mouth.

Zack smiled and watched her walk out of the room. Life just couldn't get any better than this. His upcoming test would be his first step in moving into this future of magnificent experiences and incredible possibilities.

When Zack had finished cleaning up the kitchen, Josiah and Jenna were still not awake. Although he was eager to get going and do some exploring before his test, he also wanted to say good-bye to them. Finally, he decided that he would be seeing them again soon, anyway. So after looking over his language arts study book one final time and checking the address on how to get to the test center, he left the house.

He had studied the map that he found on the internet and decided to take a different route than he had taken when he walked to the bookstore before. There were lots of new stores that he hadn't seen on the streets where he walked.

The one that caught his interest, though, was a large market. Walking in, he couldn't get over how huge it was inside. He had never been inside anything so large in his entire life. It was amazing. Starting at one end of the store, he walked up and down every aisle. The sheer number of fruits and vegetables astounded him. And so many rows upon rows of food in boxes—he had never seen food in boxes before. It didn't look real. When he reached the freezer section, the volume and variety of ice cream and frozen pies surprised him. Frozen pies? Did you eat them cold? Zack didn't think that would appeal to him. One aisle had pencils and paper and other items that you might find on a desk. He'd return to the market after the test to get some supplies.

After he finished at the market and moseyed down more streets admiring more shops, it was getting closer to test time. He found a sandwich shop and walked inside. They had so many different sandwiches that he didn't know what to choose. He finally ordered a turkey sandwich, chips, and a soft drink. Sitting in a corner booth, he enjoyed eating everything. When he finished, he asked the clerk where the nearest ice cream shop was. Luckily, it wasn't too far.

The ice cream shop, different from the one that Josiah had taken them to the previous night, had many flavors to choose from. Zack chose a double-decker with chocolate mint ice cream on the bottom and chocolate brownie on the top. Nothing was more delicious than the ice cream! Although he was tempted to get another double-decker with two new flavors, it was time to find the testing site. He was supposed to be there a half hour early.

Zack walked to the corner and studied the street signs. Then he closed his eyes and visualized the map he saw on the internet. Turning left, he walked two blocks, turned right, and walked three blocks. The building was before him. Finally. He felt confident about the test and confident that this was the start of his new life in the twenty-first century.

CHAPTER FORTY-FOUR

THE FRONT OF the building was all glass. Zack looked inside and saw computers all over the room. He smiled, took a deep breath, and stepped through the door. It was thirty-five minutes until the test, so he was a little early.

The young man at the desk smiled at Zack. "Welcome! You're the first one here! What's your name?"

"Zackary Murphy."

The man tapped the keyboard. "Oh, yes, here you are. I need a picture ID, please." He held out his hand.

Zack, confused, said, "What?"

"You know, picture ID. Identification. You have a driver's license?"

"No."

"Learner's permit? School card?"

Zack shook his head. "No, none of those."

"Sorry, man, you need picture ID before I can let you take the test. Those are the rules. You should have seen that when you registered for the test."

"I didn't—" Zack started to say and then stopped.

"Why don't you go get an ID card at the DMV?"

Zack nodded his head. He didn't know what DMV was, but knew he could look it up on the internet.

"All you need is a birth certificate. Look. I can't return your money, but when you get an ID card, you can sign up again as a retake, and it won't cost as much. Okay? Next!"

Zack stepped backwards, but someone had come up behind him. He said, "Oh, sorry," to the girl behind him and somehow made it back out the door. He leaned against the building while his head swam. There was a feeling going on in his body that he had never felt before —a heaviness that was pulling him down. His legs felt wobbly, and he was afraid that he would fall. Instinctively, he started taking deep breaths until he felt more like himself.

More people had gone through the door right in front of him. People who had ID cards—people who were allowed to take the test when he wasn't. Zack felt devastated. He wanted to walk away from the building so he didn't have to see the people going inside, but he didn't feel steady enough on his feet to move. After a few more minutes, he moved slowly away. A birth certificate. He didn't have one, and even if he did, it would be from the nineteenth century which wouldn't help him out at all here.

His life was over. If he couldn't live in the twenty-first century, he certainly could never be happy again in the nineteenth—not after what he had seen and experienced here. Not after Madison. Madison. What would he tell her? He hadn't even been able to tell her he loved her yet, and now he was leaving. Zack stumbled and put a hand on the nearest building to catch himself before falling. He had never anticipated not being allowed to take the test. What would he do now?

He continued walking down the street, breathing deeply, and as he passed the sandwich shop, an idea came to him. Backtracking a few paces, he entered the shop and ordered two more sandwiches. Then he walked back toward Madison's house until he arrived at the market that he had explored earlier. He bought some canned goods, a can opener, pens and paper, and a pint of ice cream. Walking back toward the house, he felt so empty inside that he didn't think he could ever feel whole again.

As he stepped inside, he felt relieved that the dogs didn't greet him at the door. That meant Jenna and Josiah had already left. What he had to do, he had to do alone. Retrieving his backpack from his bedroom, he put the language arts book back into it, along with what he had bought at the market and the sandwich store. Except the ice cream. Sitting in front of the television, he flipped through the channels as he savored every bite of the ice cream. The last ice cream he would ever have. Taking a deep breath that caught in his throat, he wiped away a tear that slid down his face. He couldn't believe that his life was over just that quick.

When he finished the ice cream, he put the empty carton in the garbage, washed and dried the spoon, and put it back in the drawer. Then he went back into the room he had been sleeping in, pulled the sheets off the bed, and set them on top of the machine Madison had told him washed her clothes and her sheets.

He scribbled a quick note to Madison, grabbed his backpack, walked out the door to the barn, and put the bridle on Echo. He hung his backpack on the stall door, swung up onto Echo's back, and slipped the backpack over his shoulders. Through the back of the stall and through two gates, and he was on the trail that led to the cave.

His heart felt like it would wither with disappointment. Encouraging Echo to canter, they arrived at the cave in just a few minutes. The tears flowed freely now as Zack left the twenty-first century behind him. He took one last look at what was left of the future he had planned, and he disappeared into the cave.

CHAPTER FORTY-FIVE

MADISON FELT SO good when she went to work. Zack had prepared her a fantastic breakfast and had cleaned up, too. He was the perfect man! Everything about him was exactly the way she would like it to be. And the one hang-up—him being from the nineteenth century—was about to be gone forever. She knew he would do well on the test. He was smart and well prepared. And he was awesome! She could hardly wait to get home to see how well he had done. It wouldn't surprise her if he got every question right!

Madison had barely gotten her computer powered up when Marcus came into the room. "Madison?"

"Yes?"

"Are you still planning on becoming an attorney?"

"Yes, I am."

"Jimmy is right. You can learn more from him in court. Go back to court today for as long as it takes to finish his trial. You can catch up on your work when you return. Good-bye," he said. Before she could even respond, he had walked out the door.

She gathered up her belongings and retrieved her

lunch from the refrigerator in the lunchroom. It was in an insulated container, so she hoped it would last until lunch. Then she left the office and drove over to the courthouse.

Jimmy was already in his seat with all his papers in front of him. Not wanting to disturb him, she sat down close to the front. Jimmy turned around just at that instant, saw her, smiled, and motioned her over. He patted the seat at the table next to him. "Sit here."

Madison moved, but Jimmy didn't say a word to her after that. He just kept studying his paperwork. The trial started and proceeded like the day before. After he had finished with one witness and the opposing counsel finished, Jimmy said, "Redirect, your honor," and stood up. He asked the witness one quick question and then sat back down. "I reserve the right to recall this witness, your honor." Then he leaned over to Madison and said, "See? I asked one quick question—all that I needed at this time. But I reserved the right to recall the witness later if needed. Only ask what you need to." Madison nodded her head, but she didn't think Jimmy noticed because he had already returned his attention to the trial.

Court was recessed at twelve fifteen. Jimmy said, "See you in an hour, Madison!" and walked out of the courtroom. Madison drove her car to a park and had lunch sitting under a shade tree. It felt relaxing. She realized that she had been so involved in the court case that she hadn't had a minute to think about Zack all morning. Looking at her watch, she thought that Zack was probably just arriving at the testing center. If he had a cell phone, she could text him and say, "Good luck!" But Zack didn't have one yet. After he settled into the twenty-first century, he'd have to get one. They could talk about that later.

Court resumed in exactly one hour. Jimmy nodded when Madison came in and sat down beside him. Aside from an occasional comment now and then, Jimmy focused on the trial. When the jury went out to deliberate, Jimmy turned to her and said, "And now we wait. I feel that it went well, and I don't think it will take them long to decide. I would say go get coffee and a muffin, but honestly, I think they'll be back out here in fifteen minutes." Then he went back to studying his papers.

Madison sat there absorbing every detail of the courtroom. This is where she saw her future. The judge, jury, bailiff, the courtroom itself—all players in her future reality. She liked that. She liked how being in a courtroom made her feel. And she would especially like it when she was working on her own case.

Less than fifteen minutes later, the jury stamped back into the courtroom. Jimmy turned briefly and smiled at her. He was correct. Madison hoped that someday she could read a jury like that. When the announcement came and Jimmy had won, he turned to her again, said, "Good job, Madison," and turned away to congratulate the no-longer accused.

It was four forty-five, too late to drive back to work. Madison got into her car and wished for all green lights, so she could get home sooner and find out how Zack did. The test was only an hour and a half, so he would surely be home by now. She pulled into the parking area in front of the house and rushed inside.

"Zack? Zack? How'd you do?"

No response. Maybe he was out in the barn talking to Echo and telling him how great he did on the test. That's what I would do, thought Madison. She ran out to the barn and found that Zack wasn't there. And her heart sank. Echo wasn't there, either. Maybe something had happened to Matthew or Sarah, and Zack had to return to the nineteenth century. The possibility that Zack had failed the test never crossed her mind, because she felt certain he had been fully prepared for it.

Despondent, she returned to the house to look for a note. Surely he had left a note for her. He wouldn't have just left without saying anything—no matter how much of a hurry he had been in. Zack was too responsible to do something like that. Madison searched the house. Nothing on the coffee table or by the television. The kitchen had no note. She walked into Zack's bedroom and saw that he had stripped the bed. Why would he do that? It was almost like he didn't expect to come back.

Panic set in. "Zack! Why would you leave and do this? And no note! How could you leave me hanging like this?" She felt wetness come into her eyes, but she blinked it away and walked into her room to change. There, on her desk, sat her laptop with a note on top of it. From Zack.

CHAPTER FORTY-SIX

ZACK EMERGED FROM the cave, sniffled, and wiped his tears away. This is my future, now, and I'll do the best I can with it, he thought. When he came to the end of the trail, instead of turning right toward the old Red Bluff, he turned Echo to the left. Although he didn't know exactly what he was going to do, he couldn't return to Red Bluff. At least not now. Maybe never. It wasn't like he had failed the test or anything—what had happened was out of his control. Still, he felt catawamptiously chawed up, and he didn't like that feeling at all. He needed to be alone for a while and sort everything out in his mind.

He already missed Madison and wondered if he'd ever see her again. That was what he regretted most of all. If he couldn't be a lawyer, so be it, but losing Madison hurt him in ways that he had never felt before. He'd never ask her to live with him here. As much as she loved her iPhone, laptop computer, and the rest of the miraculous things in the twenty-first century, he would never ask that of her. Shrugging his shoulders, he thought that he hated to do that to himself. Zack loved all those things, as well.

197

He thought they were so close to becoming a part of his life, and now they were just a sad memory. The door to his future had just slammed shut. That bothered him.

A birth certificate. Who would have thought that a simple birth certificate would ruin his chances to move to the future? Maybe he left too soon. Maybe Madison could think of a way to get one for him. No. He'd never ask her to do anything dishonest. And since he didn't have one, how else could he get one? Not to mention that even if he did have one, it would have the "wrong" dates on it. No. There was nothing he could do, and his hopes and plans were now only dreams. Bad dreams. Nightmares. And the worst part was losing Madison. He'd never get over her. She had captured his heart, and although she lived more than a hundred years in the future, he would always love her.

Miles went by. As Echo moved down the trail, Zack felt the wind blowing in his face. Against the wind. He was not only riding against the wind, but he felt like his life had come up against the wind. There was no stopping the wind, and no stopping the new direction his life had now taken: back to where he had started. Zack's tears came and went. He thought about what Josiah had said—that crying meant he had heart. A lot of good heart did him now. His heart was broken. His spirit was broken. He honestly felt like he had nothing left. "Nothing!" he screamed aloud. "Nothing!" Echo nickered in reply, which made Zack smile. "You're right, Echo. I have you, now. So I do have something."

Echo nickered again, and Zack rubbed the horse's neck. "I guess I *will* return to the twenty-first century. I can find coins to trade in that will make enough money to board you. Or maybe I can find the right coin and have enough money to buy a place and raise a few cattle. It's not like being an attorney, but at least it's something. What would you think of that, Echo? Would you like to hang around some cows?" Echo nickered, and Zack rubbed his neck again.

A few miles later, Zack found the side trace that he had been looking for and turned the horse. Not long after that, they came to the old cabin. Zack had been here not too long ago when he and the other men had come to rescue Sarah. Years ago, after his mother died, Zack and his father used to camp out here sometimes. So the memories that clung to this place were not happy ones.

He swung off the horse and dropped the reins on the ground. The hitching post had fallen down, but he knew that Echo wouldn't leave him. Opening the door of the cabin, he looked inside. The cabin was twelve feet by fifteen feet. It had two single beds in the two corners away from the door. One mattress had been taken over by mice, but the other wasn't bad. And someone—probably those outlaws that kidnapped Sarah—had left a bedroll that was in good condition. Good. At least he'd have a decent place to sleep.

In the center of the cabin was a small wood stove with burners on top and a kitchen table, which had three chairs around it. Two of them had wooden frames with rawhide strips for the seat. The rawhide on one chair had come undone and hung down to the floor. The third chair was made completely from wood. A rocking chair that looked in decent condition sat in a front corner. A ratty old broom lay on the floor under the bed, and a couple of cupboards leaned against one wall. That was it. Where was the bathroom? Zack laughed to himself.

199

He had gotten used to the comforts of the twenty-first century, and he would miss them.

He dropped his backpack on the good bed and went out to take care of Echo. Woods surrounded the cabin, but Zack remembered a meadow with a small stream nearby. It's why he and his father used to stay here. Back then it felt like the sad old cabin had all the comforts of home. Zack slipped the bridle off Echo and walked toward where he remembered the meadow to be. Echo followed, but when they got close, he gently pushed past Zack and ran into the meadow, kicking up his heels. Oh, that's right, thought Zack. Echo had been here with him years ago and remembered where the meadow was. It was probably the first time poor Echo had grazed in a meadow for years. At least the twenty-first century had done one incredibly good thing for him. He had his horse back.

CHAPTER FORTY-SEVEN

MADISON READ THE note through bleary eyes.

Dearest Madison,
I bet you thought I failed the test.

"No, Zack, I never thought that," she said aloud, trying to blink the tears away.

I didn't. They wouldn't let me take the test! I needed an identification card. And I need a birth certificate to get the ID card. So, it's not happening for me. I guess I can't live in the twenty-first century after all. I'm disappointed about not becoming a lawyer, but I'm more disappointed about losing you. I love you, Madison. Good-bye, Zack.

"He loves me!" Madison said aloud. "He really loves me. And I love him, too, but now he's gone. Why did this happen? What can I do?"

Madison held the note to her heart while tears flowed down her face. She let them, although she moved the note so it wouldn't get wet. She had never imagined that it would end like this—before it had even begun. And she felt bad that she had put Zack through this. Madison realized that she should have known he would need to have a picture ID to take the test. How did that get past her? She knew how it got past her. She had been so excited about Zack moving here that she had lost her sense of reason.

Now what was she going to do? How could she fix this? How could Zack possibly get a picture ID? Madison had to think about that one. There had to be a way. But being a man from the past, he might as well be an illegal immigrant. He had no identity. If you have no identity, then how do you get one? There had to be a way!

Wait! Josiah had a driver's license. How did he get that? Madison would have to ask next time Jenna and Josiah visited. But they just left. They wouldn't return for at least a week, probably two.

No, she had to find out sooner than that. She'd have to go back to the old Red Bluff to talk to Jenna or Josiah now. And she wanted to see Zack anyway. To apologize. To beg him to come back and try again.

Try again? Try what again? Until she figured out how to get him an identification card, there was no trying. How was she to get him an identification card? The key had to be Josiah, and how he got his driver's license.

She would go right away and find out. After changing her clothes, she looked outside. It would be dark soon. There was no way she could ride over there today and return while it was still light. If she spent the night, she'd be late for work tomorrow. This was the time she always got home. Madison shook her head and frowned. The soonest she could go was Friday or Saturday. That was the plan then. She hoped that Jenna or Josiah would have the answer she needed.

CHAPTER FORTY-EIGHT

WHEN ZACK RETURNED from bringing Echo to the meadow, he glanced at the old broom under the bed and thought he should sweep the cabin. The dust and dirt was so thick that he would probably stir up more than he got out, and then he couldn't sleep in here. But he had to do something. And something physical, to get out some of this anxiety that he felt right now, would be best.

Rummaging through the cupboards in the cabin, he found a hammer, an ax, and some old rusty nails. Maybe they would work, maybe not, but he intended to try. Then he walked outside and around back to where the corral was. He thought he remembered seeing a shovel there at one time; maybe it was still there. It was. Zack picked it up and took it to the front. Then he pulled the rotten upright post out of the ground. It was the reason the hitching post had fallen over. He thought he could use it for wood in the wood stove, so he leaned it up against the cabin.

Grabbing the ax, he walked over to a stand of trees, picked out a good one, and started hacking away. It was difficult work, but exactly what he needed. He wanted to get his mind off what he had lost. He wanted to chop at that tree with all his might, and when it fell, he wanted the tree to hit the ground so hard that it shook all his lost hopes and dreams out of him.

Part of him wanted the tree to fall on him. A small part, but still Zack felt the wanting of it. What was his life worth now, anyway? He couldn't have anything that he wanted. His life was shattered, and maybe his body should be, too. It was a comforting feeling, knowing he wouldn't have to feel the disappointment anymore. The idea started to appeal to him. Just then, Echo, returning from the meadow, trotted up to him and gave him a shove with his nose.

It made Zack laugh. "Hmmm, old boy. I didn't think I'd ever laugh again. You know exactly what I need and when I need it, don't you? Okay, I guess I do have something to live for. You! Now get yourself back to the meadow before this tree falls on you! Go ahead! Back to the meadow with you." Zack slapped the horse on the rump. Echo jumped, nickered, and trotted back toward the meadow.

Zack kept chopping at the tree until it was ready to fall. He had cut it so it would fall away from the cabin. One more blow, and Zack backed away. It hit the ground with a satisfying thump. He took a deep breath and sat on the downed tree. He had more work to do before it would become the new upright for the hitching post, but for now, he just needed to sit down, put his face in his hands, and have himself another good cry. So he did.

And when every last tear was cried out of him, he stood up to prepare the tree by hacking off the small branches and removing the bark. Moving toward the top of the tree, he chopped it until it was the right length.

When he had finished, it was a straight post with a **Y** at the top where he had cut off two larger branches.

He carried the post over to the front of the cabin. Using the shovel to take out dirt and rotted wood from where the old post was, he continued digging until the hole was deep enough for the new post. He placed the post inside the hole, then packed in the extra dirt that he had removed. Realizing the old rusty nails wouldn't hold the post, he searched through the cabin for some long strands of rawhide. Although he found a long strip, it needed some work before it would hold up a post.

Zack walked outside and turned toward the meadow where Echo was. Passing through the meadow to the other side, he found the small stream that he remembered. Echo followed him over and splashed in the stream, getting Zack wet.

"Echo! You could have a drink any time. Why did you have to choose right now to do it? You got me all wet!" Echo gently pushed his head against him, and Zack hugged the big horse's head. "How did I do without you for so long?" When tears came into Zack's eyes again, he pushed the horse away. "Go back to your meadow now."

The horse turned around and raced into the meadow. Then he turned around and looked at Zack. The horse raced back, turned around, and raced away again. "You want me to play with you? Okay, give me a minute here." Zack leaned down and soaked the long strand of rawhide in the water. When it had softened, Zack put it in his back pocket and looked at the horse. "Okay, Echo. You ready?"

The horse nickered and ran farther into the meadow with Zack chasing behind him. When the horse had slowed, and Zack had caught up to him, Zack turned around and raced back toward the stream. Echo followed at a polite distance. The two of them ran up and back several times before Zack said, "Okay, Echo, enough playing. I have to go back to work." He stroked the horse's neck and walked back toward the cabin.

CHAPTER FORTY-NINE

BACK AT THE cabin, Zack picked up the horizontal log that had fallen down and propped it up on the **Y** part of the new post. Then he wrapped the wet rawhide around the two sections of wood several times until it held the horizontal log firmly in place. When the rawhide dried, it would hold the bar—for at least as long as Zack would be here.

How long would he be here? Zack couldn't answer that question. Zack didn't even know why he had come to the old cabin, except that he felt he couldn't face the old Red Bluff again. It wasn't like he had failed—he knew he hadn't. It was more like the world had failed him, and that bothered him. He didn't want to talk to his friends about how his dreams had been shattered. He didn't even want to think about that right now. Perhaps that was why he had come here. So he didn't have to think about it.

After chopping the tree down, running through the meadow with Echo, and repairing the hitching post, Zack felt hungry. Taking one sandwich out of his backpack, he unwrapped it and ate it. Then, from his backpack, he took out the other sandwich and the other food that he had bought at the market and set everything on the dusty table. He'd deal with the dust tomorrow. If he wanted this food to last, he needed to conserve it for as long as possible.

He knew that he shouldn't have eaten the second sandwich today. But after going through what he considered hell, he deserved the extra sandwich and the ice cream. How would he go on without ice cream? It was so delicious! No wonder Josiah insisted on going to the future every couple of weeks. Zack couldn't blame him for that. But there were more important things than ice cream for Zack to think about right now.

Reaching into his backpack, he pulled out the language arts book to go over it again. Opening the book, he began flipping through it and reading random parts. He knew it thoroughly and could practically recite it chapter by chapter and even word for word. Why was he even wasting time going over this material? Any possibility of life in the twenty-first century had evaporated along with the ID card that he didn't have and couldn't get. Angry with himself and his situation, he threw the book across the room, and tears came into his eyes.

"No!" he shouted as he rubbed the tears away. "No! I won't cry anymore over what I can't change!" Zack knew that if he was ever to find happiness he would either have to figure out how to change the outcome of what had happened or learn to accept it. Changing it didn't seem like an option. If it *was* an option, it was out of his realm of possibility. He didn't know enough about the future to understand all its subtleties and possibilities yet.

Maybe Madison could figure out a way to get him an ID card. Maybe Zack should have talked to Madison before he left. But he couldn't bear that. Exhaling slowly, he thought he still had a few days to give it all some thought. Seeing the food spread out across the table, he realized that it wouldn't last long—certainly not long enough to get him through the weekend, unless he was really, really careful. He nodded his head. Careful and hungry, that is. Careful and hungry.

After gathering the food and putting it into a cupboard so he didn't have to see it, he picked up the language arts book and brought it back to the kitchen table. He had had enough of that. Opening the backpack, he pulled out the rest of the books that were inside. Science, math, and social studies. What was this? The John Grisham novel! Zack hadn't had a chance to read much of it because he had been so busy studying for the GED test. Now, he had time to sit down, relax, and read a good novel. It was getting later in the day, and the sun was starting to go down. He had never thought to get candles while he was at that market. Did they even still use candles in the future?

If he was back in the twenty-first century, he could just flick on the light switch. He missed the conveniences there. More than that. He missed Madison. A lot. He missed her so much that his heart hurt. It was a longing deep inside him like a piece of himself was missing.

CHAPTER FIFTY

OUTSIDE, LEANING AGAINST a tall tree, Zack read the Grisham novel until it was too dark to see. Then he walked into the old cabin and fell asleep. In the dark—with no candles—what else could he do? Next morning, he lay in bed thinking about life in the cabin. No conveniences at all. Even the old Red Bluff had more conveniences than the cabin. The composting toilet in his room above the saloon wasn't as good as a regular bathroom in the twenty-first century, but it was better than going in the woods. Could he be happy living in the nineteenth century after experiencing the twenty-first? Granny, Jenna, Sarah, and Ryan had all moved from there and were perfectly happy. And they had grown up with all the conveniences.

So why did he feel so deprived when he thought about staying in the past? Because in a strange way, he didn't feel like he belonged here anymore. Truth of it was, he hadn't felt like he belonged here in a long time. He was the only Indian in town. Although his friends completely accepted him as just another man, it wasn't only the range cowboys who gave him a hard time. He had overheard some of the town's people referring to him as "chief" behind his back. Zack had always been an outsider and had always felt different.

The twenty-first century was different. When he was there, he felt accepted, comfortable, and free from the prejudice of the nineteenth century. While he was sure that some of that still existed in the twenty-first century, it wasn't as "acceptable" as it was in the nineteenth. That's where he wanted to make his life. That's where he wanted to get married and raise a family—in a place where his children could grow up proud of what they were and not ashamed of it.

Zack needed to go back and find a way to stay there. He wasn't ready to hang up his fiddle just yet. If it was not possible to stay there, he could still search for the valuable coins, trade them in, and somehow get enough money to go to college here in the nineteenth century. No, it would not be as satisfying and he would not be as happy. And most important, he would not have Madison, but at least he wouldn't be sitting around in a saloon, reading books, and dreaming of the good life. No, Zack was the kind of man who needed to do something about it. He had sat in that saloon for far too long already. Now —nineteenth century or twenty-first century—he would make something of himself.

He stretched, got out of bed, and regretted that he hadn't thought to buy some eggs so he could have a decent breakfast—not that they would have survived the long horseback trip over here—but they still would have made a good breakfast. Zack decided that although he had made his decision, he needed to "get back to the earth" and stay in the rustic cabin until his food ran out so he could overcome the bad feelings that had overcome him. Looking over his food supplies, he thought that if he really stretched and was really careful, he could make it last until Saturday. He'd be starving by then, but he'd have a little to eat every day.

So the decision was made. He would head back to the old Red Bluff Saturday. He imagined that Madison would be there. If she felt the same way about him as he felt about her, she would be there. And he didn't want her—or anyone—to worry about him. Because she had to work through Friday, she probably wouldn't arrive until Saturday. So he would ride in Saturday and see if she had come up with a way to get him a picture identification. Until then, he'd spend his days reading, studying, and contemplating life.

CHAPTER FIFTY-ONE

FRIDAY COULDN'T COME soon enough for Madison. After spending Monday and Tuesday in court all day with Jimmy, the rest of the week was busywork—typing, filing, and answering phones. It kept her mind occupied, though, so thoughts of Zack were minimal. Although every night when she arrived home and walked into the barn and saw where he had kept Echo, the pain of his absence all came rushing back to her.

Everything hinged on how Josiah got his driver's license. Her whole world depended on that information.

Madison rushed home from work, changed clothes, grabbed her already packed backpack, ran out to the barn, brushed Chaco, and was on his back and through the gates in record time. She had decided to go Friday night instead of waiting until Saturday morning for one reason: she couldn't wait to get there and make sure Zack was okay. So, now she was on her way, trotting down the trail toward the cave—and toward Zack.

Seeing the Red Bluff sign made her feel a little better. She was closer to seeing Zack and getting the information from Josiah. Everything would be fine. Although she knew that, she didn't feel very calm or very convinced. What if Zack couldn't do what Josiah did? What if whatever it was wouldn't work for Zack? What if what if what if? And all bad things. She thought maybe she should try what if happy statements. What if Zack could get a driver's license just like Josiah? What if Zack came to live with her? What if Zack attended the same college she did and they could talk about lawyerly stuff together? Yes, that was better. Madison took a deep breath and decided to take Chaco straight to the livery before checking in at the hotel.

After dropping off Chaco with Ezra, instead of going to the hotel, she walked directly to the saloon. She had to see Zack, and she couldn't wait. Madison pushed through the swinging doors with wide-eyed anticipation of seeing Zack. It was late enough that Sarah was already at the piano, but she had just finished a song and motioned Madison over to her.

"So how did our boy wonder do? Did he ace the test?"

Madison's smile drooped, and she felt all the blood rush out of her head. Grabbing the piano for support, she managed to wheeze out, "You mean he's not here?"

"What do you mean, 'here'? We thought he was with you!" Sarah stood up concerned and left Madison grasping the piano. Madison watched as she strode quickly across the saloon and behind the bar to talk to Matthew. He looked up at Madison and rushed over to her.

"Where's Zack?" he asked.

"I thought he was here," said Madison, feeling more stable on her feet now. "I came here to see him."

"What happened?" asked Sarah, who stood right behind Matthew. "We know Zack. There's no way he didn't pass the test."

215

"He never took the test," said Madison. "He needed a picture ID and didn't have any. That was my fault. I should have known that."

Sarah stepped forward. "Don't blame yourself, Madison. Coming from the future to the past is not a problem. But Zack's the first one who came from the past into the future. There's bound to be problems. You'll solve it. Don't worry." She patted Madison's hand.

"I hope so, Sarah. I hope so," said Madison.

"We need to go look for him," said Matthew. "Make sure he's all right."

Sarah turned Matthew around to face her. "Matthew, Zack is a man. He probably just needs some space. I know how much he wanted to move to the future, and this must have been terribly disappointing to him. I don't blame him for wanting to get away for a while. You need to leave him be, Matthew."

Matthew grunted, turned, and walked back behind the bar, sullen. Sarah and Madison watched him go. Then Sarah turned back to Madison. "Stay here tonight. You don't need to go to the hotel. You can stay in a room upstairs. It might make you feel better."

"I need to go see Josiah. Find out how he got his driver's license. If Zack could get a driver's license, everything would be fine."

"I don't know if he'd be there this late," said Sarah. "Now that Rawlins is always sober, Josiah has been leaving early to go home to Jenna. But you can try. You never know. Sometimes he stays late if something is going on."

"I have to try," said Madison.

"Here," said Sarah. "I'll take your backpack up to your room. You go ahead and check on Josiah." Sarah took the backpack, and Madison watched as she disappeared up the back stairs.

Madison walked slowly out of the saloon. She felt as if her whole life depended on Josiah's answer. As she glanced down the street, she saw Jenna heading into the sheriff's office. Oh, good, thought Madison. They're still here. I'll know in a minute.

Gathering speed and taking a deep breath to give her courage, she walked into the sheriff's office. Josiah was at his desk talking to a rancher, and Jenna was standing on the opposite side of the room looking at wanted posters. Jenna turned as Madison walked in.

"Hey, Madison," she said warmly. "How'd Zack do on the test? Knowing Zack, he probably got every question right!"

"Hi, Jenna, no. He never took the test. That's why I came here to talk to you. Zack couldn't take the test because he didn't have a picture ID."

Before Madison had a chance to say anything more, the rancher left the office, and Josiah walked over. "Hi, Madison! How'd Zack do?"

"He couldn't take the test, Josiah, because he didn't have a picture identification. How'd you get your driver's license? That's Zack's only chance," said Madison.

"Oops," said Jenna.

"I, uh, well, your auntie here convinced me, a man of the law, that I didn't need a driver's license as long as I didn't get caught. So I never got one. What would they do to me if they caught me? Not let me drive anymore? Fine, I'll go back to my horse. Or, let Jenna drive, of course."

"Oh," said Madison, disappointed. "That was my only hope—that if you had a driver's license, then Zack could get one, too. Then he could take the test."

"I never thought of that, Madison," said Jenna. "No, with all the new rules and regulations, I don't know how anyone from the past could get any kind of ID card. I'm sorry, honey." Jenna put her hand on Madison's face. "You'll figure something out. I know you will."

Madison turned to leave. "I don't have any idea what it would be, Jenna. This was my only hope."

CHAPTER FIFTY-TWO

MADISON HAD A horrible night's sleep. She was in the room next to Zack's room, and every time she heard the slightest noise, she woke up thinking it was him. But it was just old building noises, and then she had to struggle to get back to sleep. And sleeping came after spending hours in the saloon, jumping every time someone came through the door. But none of them had been Zack.

She had no idea where he could be and wondered why he had disappeared. There was no way he could feel ashamed at what had happened. It was beyond his control. More than likely, he was extremely disappointed and needed to be alone for a while. Madison understood that. She was disappointed, also. Now she also felt sick to her stomach, but she knew she wasn't sick. It was just that she felt hopeless—it didn't seem there was any way at all to get Zack a picture ID. And if he couldn't get an ID, then he couldn't take the test and couldn't get into college—which meant he wouldn't move to the twenty-first century and they couldn't be together.

She dragged herself out of bed and somehow managed to get dressed without weeping. When she heard

219

Sarah and Matthew walk by and head downstairs, she thought that eating something might settle her stomach and make her feel better. So she slowly walked downstairs, exhaling deeply, and feeling sorry for herself. And she knew she shouldn't. Zack had a lot more to feel sorry for himself about. He had just lost the future that he had planned. Still, that didn't make her feel any better, so she sighed, plastered a smile on her face, and walked into the back room where Matthew was cooking breakfast.

"Hi, Sarah. Hi, Matthew."

"Hi, Madison! Sleep well?" asked Sarah.

"I woke up every time I heard a noise that I thought might be Zack."

"He'll be back, don't worry," said Sarah.

"I hope you're right," said Matthew. "He's never disappeared like this before."

Madison sighed and looked down. "He's never lost a future that he had hoped for, before. But Zack is resilient. He'll come out of this okay. I know he will." She didn't know that, but she hoped he would.

The three of them heard the front doors open. It was too early for customers. Before anyone could stand up and investigate, Zack came bursting into the room. "Good morning, everybody! I'm starved!" He put his arm around Madison, kissed her on the mouth, and pulled up a chair beside her.

"Where have you been, young man?" asked Sarah sternly, making everyone laugh and breaking the tension.

"I rode out to the old cabin. You know the one," said Zack.

"You mean, *that* cabin?" asked Sarah.

"That's the one," said Zack.

"What'd you go out there for?" asked Matthew.

"I needed to get away, be by myself, think about my life. Madison told you what happened?"

"Yes, but none of us could figure out why you ran away. You had nothing to be ashamed of." Sarah put a plate of eggs in front of him and squeezed his shoulder.

Zack shook his head slowly from side to side. "No, it wasn't ashamed. I felt frustrated about what happened. It was a barrier to what I wanted: moving to the twenty-first century." He turned to Madison. "Is there a way I *can* get a picture identification?"

"Oh, I came here to talk to Josiah to find out how he got his driver's license. I thought that was the key," said Madison.

"He doesn't have a driver's license," said Zack. "He told me that when we were driving in the parking lot."

"Yeah, now I know that." She looked at Zack and frowned. "I'm all out of ideas, Zack. I'm sorry. I should have anticipated that you would need ID to take the tests and get into school. I just didn't think about it—I didn't want to think about it. I'm sorry."

Zack patted her hand. "It's okay, Madison. I'm not blaming you. What does a picture ID look like, anyway?"

Madison reached into her pocket and pulled out a bunch of cards. As she went through her school ID, library card, and credit cards, looking for her license, one card dropped out on the floor. Finding her license, she handed it to Zack and then stooped over to pick up the fallen card. As she was about to shove it into the pile with the rest, she held it out in front of her. "Zack! This is it! This is how you'll get an ID!"

Zack handed her back her license and took the card in her hand. He read the front of the card, "Madison Two Feathers is an official member of the Oglala Sioux Tribe.

Nice picture, Madison. But how will this ID do me any good. I don't look like you! And I'm Navajo."

"No, not *my* card! We'll get *you* a Navajo Nation ID card!"

"How are we going to do that?" asked Zack.

"There's an office not too far from Red Bluff," said Madison.

"How will they know that I'm really Navajo and not just saying that?" asked Zack.

"He's right, Madison. It will be the same problem there. No birth certificate," said Sarah.

"No! It's the twenty-first century! I bet they'll accept DNA testing!" said Madison.

"What's DNA? And how can I even take the test without ID?" asked Zack.

"Your DNA is part of you, Zack. Everyone has different DNA. They can test you with blood or saliva and I think hair, too. I know they can test dogs to find out their heritage, and this is the same thing. It has to work! It just has to!" said Madison. "Will you at least try it, Zack? Will you try?"

Zack smiled at Madison. "Sure, Madison. I'll try it. I have nothing to lose, right?"

"Great! You can come back with me tonight, and we'll go Tuesday afternoon. When I go to work Monday, I'll ask for Tuesday afternoon off. It won't be a problem. Then we'll go and take care of it! Get you an ID card!"

Zack took Madison's hand and looked into her eyes. "I'm not coming back with you, Madison. This is where I belong for now. Echo and I will ride over Tuesday and meet you at the house in the afternoon. Okay?"

Madison looked at Zack. She thought how this experience had changed him. He was more assertive now—

more sure of himself. The change bothered her in a way, but she thought she liked it. She nodded her head. "Okay, Zack, Tuesday afternoon then."

CHAPTER FIFTY-THREE

TUESDAY MORNING ARRIVED, and Zack felt relieved. He honestly didn't think anything would come of Madison's attempt to get him a tribal ID. DNA. He didn't know what kind of newfangled thing it was, but surely his traditional tribe would not accept it. But to please Madison, and to assure himself that it would not work, he said he'd try. Although to be honest, he had his own reasons for returning to the twenty-first century.

As he and Echo rode through the cave to the future, Zack wondered how many more times he'd come through that cave. At least once. He knew that. No matter what happened today at the tribal office, he needed to return at least one more time. Although Zack had planned to study his coin book Sunday and go to the bank Monday, Matthew had needed him both days. It made Zack feel good helping again. But he had thought that if he went through a bunch of coins at the bank, surely he would find some that were worth something. Maybe he'd even find the one that Stan, the coin guy, had requested. A 1795 silver dollar. It would mean a lot of money. And he needed a lot of money regardless of which direction his future lay.

He arrived at Madison's barn at midmorning. After removing Echo's bridle and making sure he had food and water, Zack walked into the house, which wasn't locked. Madison had said that most people always locked their houses, but she lived far enough out that she never locked the doors. Zack picked up Madison's laptop from her bedroom and carried it into the living room.

Opening a Google search screen, he googled "law schools in the 1800s." He didn't have much time for research, so it might not be complete, but he found four law colleges, all of them on the east coast. That disappointed him, but he'd do what he had to do. Zack wasn't sure he could count on the accuracy of something so long ago, but it said the first year tuition was eighty dollars! With the right coins, he could easily come up with that much. After scribbling down the addresses—he felt certain that even if they weren't exact, his letters would get there—he closed the laptop and returned it to Madison's room.

Then he grabbed the nearly empty backpack he had brought, slipped it over his shoulders, and walked into town. Madison shouldn't be home for more than an hour. If he hurried, he had plenty of time for the bookstore, the coin shop, and the thrift store. Fifteen minutes later, he arrived at his first stop, the bookstore. Although he didn't have much confidence in getting a tribal membership card—just in case—he wanted to be prepared for living in the twenty-first century. So he bought himself several vocabulary books. His nineteenth-century vocabulary was sorely lacking for a twenty-first-century education. And even if he ended up back in the nineteenth century, it didn't hurt to be more learned. He also bought a few more John Grisham novels.

Next stop was the thrift store, and they were having a sale. You could buy everything you could fit in a paper bag for only five dollars. Zack managed to stuff in five pairs of jeans and seven shirts, a belt, and a small backpack. All of that was put into his old backpack along with his new books.

Then he walked to the coin store and stepped in. "Hello, Stan," he said when he saw the man behind the counter.

"Hi, Zack. Are you buying or selling today? Or both? Did you find me that 1795 'Silver Plug' that I'm still looking for?"

"No, not yet. I haven't had a chance to do much research since the last time I saw you," said Zack. "Can you tell me if any of these are worth anything?" That morning, before leaving, he had gathered up all the coins in his room. He didn't recognize the dates on them, and he trusted Stan.

Stan took the coins and turned them over in his hands. "Most of them aren't worth much—especially if you're going to trade them back for quarters and half dollars. I'll give you five hundred for this one. And I ordered some more quarters and half dollars if you want more of those."

Zack picked out thirty-seven half dollars and nineteen quarters. "How much for these?"

"Well, with the five hundred for this one," he held up the coin that Zack had given him, "how about a thousand dollars?"

"That sounds good." Zack reached into his pocket and counted out the money for Stan.

"Do you always carry that much cash on you?" asked

Stan. "Red Bluff is usually a safe place, but there are people out there—"

"Not usually, but I knew I was coming here today," said Zack. "Stan, besides the 1795 silver dollar that you're looking for, are there any other coins that are worth a lot of money?"

"Most overdate coins are worth something."

"What's 'overdate'?" asked Zack.

"You're not really a coin collector, are you, son?"

"No, it was my grandfather," said Zack easily.

"You need to get yourself a good book on coins and look up overdate. That's when a coin was stamped with one date and then stamped with another date on top of it. Most coins like that are pretty valuable. Any time there is something 'different' about a coin—it's worth more."

"Thanks, Stan," said Zack. "I appreciate the help and the information. I'll come see you again—I hope with at least one of those special coins."

CHAPTER FIFTY-FOUR

ZACK STARTED WALKING back to Madison's house. As he walked through a residential neighborhood close to the house, a car pulled up beside him.

"Hey, handsome. Want a ride?"

"You bet, pretty lady!" said Zack, as he opened the door and sat beside Madison.

"Your backpack looks heavy! What's in it?" asked Madison.

"Some books and a bunch of new clothes."

"You can drop them at the house. I need to change before we go. Are you looking forward to this?"

"Sure! Let's find out if it's the answer."

"I hope it is," said Madison quietly. "I really hope it is."

After Zack dropped off his heavy backpack and Madison changed her clothes, they returned to the car. "It will take almost an hour to get there. You ready for a road trip?"

"Whatever it takes, Madison. It doesn't matter, though. I'm always happy when I'm with you." Zack looked at her lovingly, aware that this might be their last time together. But he didn't allow himself to think like that. He couldn't.

After a lively hour of listening to the radio and talking about the law, school, GED and SAT tests, picture identification, and the limitations of the nineteenth century, they were almost there. They had passed a sign that said, "Welcome to the Navajo Nation!" Just after that, Zack pointed out another sign that said "Diné Bikayah." Navajo Lands. He knew that Diné didn't mean Navajo. It meant "the people."

Madison pulled onto a narrow, paved road. Then Zack saw an incredible building with a sign in front that said "Diné Tribal Office." The building was made of red clay brick like he had seen when he was a kid traveling with his father. And it had wooden posts going through the top of the pillars in front to the main building. Although it was magnificent, Zack wondered why it wasn't in the shape of the traditional hogan, which he had lived in when he was very young.

When they stepped out of the car, Zack could tell that Madison felt nervous, but he didn't. Either it would work or it wouldn't. Although he wanted to stay in the twenty-first century with Madison and go to college here, he had come to the place where he could accept it either way. He thought that was a good place to be. So he smiled at Madison, grabbed her hand, and opened the big red door for her.

Following Madison in and looking around, Zack walked briskly up to the office window. A young woman with long, black braids and a shy smile was on the other side. She was Diné. He recognized the features. His people. Madison was Indian, but she was Sioux and looked different. He introduced himself to the woman in

Diné and explained what he needed.

"I'm sorry," she said. "I don't speak Navajo. My grandmother tried to teach me, but it didn't take." She shrugged her shoulders. "Speak English, please."

That confused Zack. She didn't speak Diné? More had changed than he had realized. "My name is Zack Murphy, born out of the Bitter Water Clan. My father, Isaac Murphy, is white. I'd like to get a Tribal Membership Card."

The young woman turned to her computer. "What's your mother's name?"

"Johona Benali."

The woman clicked away at her keyboard. "I'm not finding her, Zack. Was she a member of the tribe?"

"Yes," said Zack.

"Do you know if she was officially registered?"

"That I don't know," said Zack.

Madison stepped forward. "When did the official register begin?" she asked.

"1940," said the young woman.

"Oh, okay," said Zack, as he turned away from the window, disappointed.

"Wait," said Madison, stepping up to the window. "Do you do DNA testing?"

"DNA testing? Oh, no. Your mother or father has to be an enrolled member of the tribe before you can enroll. Sorry," she said, as she turned away from the keyboard and picked up the cell phone that was beside her.

Zack was out the door before Madison, taking big strides back to the car. Madison had to run to catch up to him. "I'm sorry, Zack. I'm so sorry. I was sure they would accept DNA testing. It's the newest thing."

"My people are traditional people, Madison. I didn't know what DNA testing was, but I didn't think it was something they would adopt so casually."

When Madison unlocked the car, he climbed into it. He looked out the side window, because he didn't want her to see the tears in his eyes. He thought he could handle it no matter what happened. But he couldn't. Again, he felt as if he had lost everything that was important to him—law school in the twenty-first century and Madison.

CHAPTER FIFTY-FIVE

ZACK WAS SO quiet on the way home that Madison had plenty of time to think. At first, she tried talking to him, but when he continued to stare out the side window and give her one or two word answers, she realized that he needed some time alone. So she didn't say anything more —just hoped that he wouldn't turn her way and see the tears falling silently down her face.

They stopped at a fast food place on the way home, and although he ate a lot, he was still reluctant to talk. A few more minutes down the road, however, he said, "I still can't believe that woman didn't know how to speak Diné. Is that what it's come to in the twenty-first century? Native people not knowing their own language, their own customs? That's horrible."

"A lot has happened in the last century, Zack. Many native people are ashamed of who they are. My own mother—she's not native, but her husband was— anyway, she won't use his last name. She says she's not ashamed, but it still bothers me."

Zack shook his head and then continued looking out the window. Madison didn't want to push him, but she was afraid of losing him, and she didn't want that to happen. And although something inside her gut was telling her to be silent and let it go, she couldn't help herself and had to speak. "Zack, I know this didn't work out, but there are other ways we can do this."

"You mean there's another way to get an ID card?" he asked, suddenly animated again.

"Well, no. But you know there are thousands of illegal aliens who have sneaked into this country, and they live perfectly normal lives here."

"Normal except they have to stay away from the law? Didn't we watch a movie where someone was deported when they caught him? Madison, I want to be a lawyer, not someone who runs from the law. If there's no way I can get an ID, then that's it. It's finished. I have to accept that, and you do, too."

Madison wanted him to ask her to move back to the nineteenth century with him. She wouldn't do that— couldn't do that. There was no possibility of her ever moving back there—even for Zack. But she really wanted him to ask—so she knew that he cared for her as much as she cared for him.

When they arrived home, it was almost dark. Madison followed when Zack walked into the house. She watched as he picked up his backpack and slid it on over his shoulders. Before he had a chance to turn around and head toward the door, Madison said, "Zack, it's getting dark. Just stay here tonight."

He turned toward her and looked into her eyes. "Madison, it's no use. I can't move here. As much as I want to be here with you and become a lawyer in the twenty-first century, it's not possible. Let's just let it go."

Zack took a step toward the door, and she put her

hand on his arm and turned him back toward her. "I don't want to let it go, Zack."

"We have no choice, Madison. We have no choice."

"Stay here tonight, Zack."

"No. I can still make it through the cave before dark."

"Spend the night with me, Zack."

Zack took a step backward and looked at her. "No. No, Madison, I can't do that."

She held onto his arm. "Stay with me tonight, Zack. I want you to."

Madison noticed that although he shook his head, no, his demeanor had softened—his body turned toward her instead of toward the door. "No, I shouldn't."

"Zack, please. For me."

Zack looked down. "Are you sure that's what you want? Are you sure, Madison?"

"Yes, I'm sure." She put more pressure on his arm and pulled him toward her. After they kissed, a long, satisfying kiss—their first—Zack followed her into the bedroom and closed the door.

CHAPTER FIFTY-SIX

MADISON LAY ON the bed crying hysterically—the kind of crying where you can barely catch your breath between sobs. It scared her, but she felt that she needed to cry it out, and that she would ultimately be okay.

After Zack left early in the morning, she had somehow managed to hold herself together long enough to call the office and say that she was sick. Never in her life had she called in sick before when she wasn't sick. Now wasn't any different. She was sick—at heart. It felt like she would never recover from the emptiness she now felt. She'd survive the violence of the sobbing, but she wasn't sure at all that she would survive the heartache.

Zack had been a gentleman, although he had insisted on leaving before breakfast. He said he couldn't handle the loss—that he almost had it all and now everything was lost to him. He had told her that he loved her, several times. And before he walked out the door and kissed her good-bye, he had put his hands on her shoulders, looked into her eyes, and said ardently, "I will love you, forever. *Forever*."

And now he was gone from her *forever*. There was

nothing she could do about it. No amount of wishing or hoping could get him a birth certificate or an ID card. A fake one? She had considered that. It would probably work to get him the GED test, but when it came around to show the ID for college, she didn't think it would work. If he could successfully take the GED test, then he would be even more frustrated that he couldn't get into college.

Zack, coming from the past with no traceable paperwork, was a nonentity. Although she loved him dearly, she felt she was too young to get married. Still, before she broke down completely that morning, she had done an internet search to see if he could become a citizen if she married him. The website she found, full of legal jargon, said that at some point in the process, he had to return to his "home country." Yeah, right. This *was* his home country! Just not his home time. No. She had gone over it and over it in her head. There was no feasible way to get him a legal birth certificate or an identification card. Which meant—there was no way for them to be together.

The thought of that sent her back into racking sobs. As much as she hated the thought, there was only one obvious solution to the problem. She had to go back to the nineteenth century to be with Zack. Losing her cell phone, her iPad, her laptop computer—as much as she loved her modern technological devices—they meant nothing to her without Zack in her life. It seemed the most logical solution; and yet, her electronics would not be all that she would lose. She wasn't positive, but she didn't think that law schools in the nineteenth century would even admit women for several more years. So what would she do in the nineteenth century? Zack could go to law school, and she would—what? Do the laundry and the cooking? It didn't matter. All that she was and all that she wanted meant nothing if she couldn't have him.

It was decided then. She would quit her job, give up everything she had been, everything she had known, to return to the nineteenth century to be with Zack. The thought was somewhere between comforting and disturbing. It made the sobs start all over again.

CHAPTER FIFTY-SEVEN

ZACK COULDN'T REMEMBER exactly when he made the decision. Was it before he reached the cave or on the old Red Bluff side of the cave? It didn't matter. The decision was made, and that was that. He couldn't let Madison move to the nineteenth century. And he knew that she would. He could see it in her eyes when he said good-bye to her. His desire to become a lawyer was always just a pipe dream anyway. Until he had found out about the cave and the twenty-first century, he never thought it would really happen. Yes, he had read and reread that silly Pennsylvania law book, but he didn't really believe he could become a lawyer.

The whole GED test and going to college in the future, it was something nice to hold onto, but it wasn't realistic. He was a nineteenth-century man and couldn't expect to go into the future, go to college, and become a lawyer.

But he could go to the future and *not* become a lawyer. If he didn't need the GED test, then maybe he could get away with not having a birth certificate and picture ID. He had to try. Zack laughed to himself. He wouldn't know where they'd deport him to if they caught him anyway! Regardless, he had made up his mind. He'd return to the twenty-first century to be with Madison. Half his dream would come true. He'd have Madison. That was more important than becoming a lawyer anyway. And he would immediately start putting his plan into motion.

Since he had left without breakfast, Zack was hungry when he walked into the saloon. He felt grateful that Sarah and Matthew had already finished—he didn't want to talk to either of them right now. After fixing himself some breakfast and eating it as fast as he could, he took two stairs at a time up to his room.

He unpacked his backpack and left the clothes that he had bought on the bed. There wasn't enough room in the chest of drawers for everything. No matter. He wouldn't be here that much longer. Taking out his pen and paper and picking up the coin book from the top of the chest of drawers, he sat down on the bed to work.

Two hours later, he had a long list of coins that were worth a lot of money—several thousand dollars up to fifty thousand dollars. One was worth more than eighty thousand. Another was worth a million—the one Stan had mentioned to him—but he didn't count on finding that one. Although maybe he'd get lucky and find one of those worth thousands. He stuck the paperwork in his pocket, gathered all the old coins that he had, and counted them. Only fifty dollars, but it should be enough to do what he needed.

He ran downstairs, eager to complete his "job." It may not be as satisfying as becoming a lawyer, but if he was successful at it, he and Madison could live like kings. And there were several coins coming out in the early 1870s that were worth a lot of money. If he could find those before they had too much wear on them, it would be a good profit for him and Madison.

Zack walked into the bank and up to the teller. After plunking twenty dollars on the counter, he said, "I'd like to have twenty dollars worth of pennies, please. And could I sit in a back room to look at them?"

The man behind the counter put the coins in a tray and handed it to Zack. "Look at them? What for?"

"Oh, sorry. I just need a table. Do you have one I could use?"

The man led Zack and his tray full of pennies to a room with a large table and several chairs set around it. "This is perfect," said Zack. "Thank you."

Zack sat down, hauled out his notes, and began going through the pennies. Most of them, he could look at the date on the front. But he needed to turn some coins over so he could examine them carefully. When he had finished, forty-five minutes later, he had one penny picked out that might be worth two thousand dollars. It wasn't exactly what he had hoped for. He replaced it with one of his own.

Carrying the tray back to the teller, he asked if he could have another twenty dollars of pennies. When the man looked at him as if he was nuts, Zack added, "Different pennies, please."

The man took the tray from him, shook his head, and started walking away. Then he turned back to Zack and said, "I'll bring them to you."

Zack walked back to the room and stuffed his paperwork in his pockets. While he waited, he mused on what he was doing: using a twenty-first-century coin book in a nineteenth-century bank to find coins that were valuable enough so he could live comfortably in the twenty-first century. It was crazy.

The world of coin collecting was a world unto itself. Coins were classified as to how sharp and unblemished the image on them was. If the rim of the coin was well defined and the image visible, it could be classified as very good. If the image was still shiny with no major flaws, then it could be classified as choice proof. Those were worth the most.

For a modern collector, choice proof would be almost impossible to find. But being in the nineteenth century had its advantages. He still might find some choice proof coins. At least ones from the last couple of years. Despite that he had only found one coin worth saving in the twenty dollars of pennies, Zack thought this method of looking for valuable coins could work.

The man brought Zack another tray of pennies and dropped it on the table in front of him. Some coins jumped but did not escape the tray. Zack looked at him and said, "Thank you." The man didn't reply and exited the room. Ignoring him, Zack began the long process of going through each coin.

CHAPTER FIFTY-EIGHT

MADISON DIDN'T KNOW how long she had lain there, sobbing, when her mother stepped into the room. Kat walked over, sat on the edge of the bed, and put her hand on Madison's forehead before saying anything. "Are you okay? Your temperature feels normal."

Madison pushed her hand away. "I don't have a fever."

"Then what's wrong? Why did you call in sick? Why are you in bed?"

"How did you know I called in sick?"

"I called you at work, and they told me. Now tell me, what's wrong?"

"It's Zack," said Madison.

Madison's mother, Kat, wasn't the most doting of parents, but she could act like a mother bear if provoked. Her hands balled into fists, and she slowly stood up. "Did that boy hurt you? If that boy hurt you after I was kind enough to nurse him back to health—"

"No, Mom. He didn't hurt me. I fell in love with him."

"And I suppose that he expects you to follow him back to the nineteenth century just like Jenna and Sarah did.

Is that it?"

"No, Mom. He was all excited about moving *here*. He wanted to go to school and become a lawyer."

"A lawyer? Oh," her mother said, a note of respect in her voice. "It sounds like a fine plan, Madison. So why are you crying?"

"He went to take the GED test—I had signed him up, and he had already studied for it—and he couldn't take it because he didn't have a picture ID." Tears came into Madison's eyes, and soon she was sobbing again.

"Oh. That is too bad. I'm sorry, honey." Kat climbed into the bed beside Madison and put her arms around her. She stroked her hair. "It will be all right."

"I know it will, because I'm going to move back there!" sobbed Madison.

"You're what?" Kat sat up in bed and said, "No! You can't do that!"

"Yes, Mom. It's exactly what I'm going to do. I'm quitting my job and moving to the nineteenth century to be with Zack."

"You're quitting your job? Madison, you can't be serious. What about your career?"

"None of it matters without Zack, Mom. I hate to do it, but Zack's more important to me."

"I knew nothing good would come of that damn cave! First Jenna, then Ryan and Granny, Sarah, and now you. You're throwing your life away for that boy, you know that, don't you?"

"I'm not throwing my life away. I'm living my life. With Zack."

They lay there for a long time like that, cuddled up, with Kat stroking Madison's hair. Madison couldn't remember the last time her mother had cuddled her like this. Maybe it was when she was ten years old, and some bully at school had pushed her down and skinned both of her knees. Instead of going back to class, Madison had run home from school, with her bloody knees dripping. And when she had stepped into the house, she called her mother. Kat had immediately left the office, came straight home to Madison, and cuddled her all night long.

That had been a long time ago. But Madison was an adult now. And as much as she liked the feeling, she knew it would probably be the last time it would ever happen. More likely would be that Madison would be cuddling her own child at some time in the future—or rather, in the past, in the old Red Bluff.

Madison must have fallen asleep in her mother's arms, because next she knew, when Kat stirred, Madison woke up. "I need to get back to work now. But I want you to promise me that you won't quit your job yet. Are you going to work tomorrow?"

"Yes."

"Promise me that you won't give your notice."

"I might as well get it over with, Mom. Nothing is going to change. There's no way for him to get an ID."

"Promise me, Madison. I have an idea. It might work. Promise me that you won't give your notice until I find out if this is feasible. It won't take long. Promise me."

Madison stretched. The short nap had made her feel a little better. "Okay, I promise. What's your idea?"

"I'll let you know if it works. When you get up, email me all the information you have on Zack. Everything you know. Do you have a picture?"

Madison brightened. "Yes! I took one the other night."

"Email me the pic, too. See you later, Sweetie. I'll try my best." Kat kissed Madison on the forehead and disappeared out the door, as silently as she had come in.

CHAPTER FIFTY-NINE

MADISON WORKED EXTRA hard at work Thursday and Friday, because she felt guilty about staying home Wednesday. She kept her word to her mother about not giving notice at her job, but she did start getting her personal belongings together for her move back to the nineteenth century. Although she appreciated her mother trying to help her, she didn't really believe anything could be done. Without breaking the law, getting Zack a birth certificate and an identification card needed a miracle. Madison didn't believe in miracles. She believed in the cold, hard facts. That's why she wanted to become an attorney. Oh well to that one, thought Madison, as she drove home Friday after work.

She parked her car and was surprised when her mother pulled in behind her. Madison waved, opened the door of the house, and waited there. Kat walked up to her with one hand behind her back and a funny expression on her face.

"Let's go in," Kat said.

"What's with you, Mom?" asked Madison.

Kat's eyes were bright with excitement. "I did it,

Madison, I did it!" Madison thought her eyes looked extra bright—like someone who was about to cry.

"Did what?"

Kat pulled her hand from behind her back and handed Madison a manila envelope. On the front it said "Katherine Leyton" and her mother's work address. No one called Kat by her full name, Katherine, unless it was the government. The envelope had a typed notice on it that said "Hand Deliver." Beneath that it said "Attention: Zackary Allen Murphy." It looked official and was time and date stamped in Washington, D.C. "What's this, Mom?"

Kat nodded her head and smiled. "Open it."

Madison opened the envelope and pulled out the contents. There was a birth certificate with Zack's name on it from 1992, with both his parents' names. There was a Diné Tribal Membership Card with his picture on it. And there was a "History Fact Sheet" with information about Zack—most of which was the information she had provided for her mother.

"You did it! How did you do this? Is it legal? Is it real?"

Kat nodded. "Very real. Very legal. I called in a favor from an old friend of your father's. Benny Roth was Billy's best friend in high school. Benny went to college when your father went to war. He was still around for your birth, and he was with me while I gave birth to you. Billy had asked him to do that. We were very close in the months after Billy died."

Madison raised her eyebrows. "How close?"

Kat looked down. "Not that close, Madison, not that it's any of your business! You're my daughter, for cryin' out loud. Anyway, he eventually left Red Bluff for a job in Washington, D.C. I knew he had something to do with the witness protection program, but I hadn't talked to him for years. When I tried to find him a couple of days ago, it turned out that he had been busy these last few years. He worked in the U.S. Marshal's office, and he was *in charge* of the witness protection program. He called in a few favors—especially from the Navajo tribe—and made me swear that Zack wasn't an illegal alien who was wanted in another country, and voila, Zack is now a legal citizen of the United States!"

"I can't believe it, Mom! I can't believe it! You did it! I can still become a lawyer now! And so can Zack! He will be so happy! Thanks so much!" Madison threw her arms around her mother and wouldn't let go.

"You have your paperwork now, and I have to go," said Kat, as she rubbed something out of her eye. "I'm glad it worked out for you. So you'll be heading out there tomorrow to tell Zack?"

"You bet I will," said Madison. "First thing in the morning!"

CHAPTER SIXTY

ZACK HAD SPENT the rest of Wednesday at the bank going through all their pennies, two-cent pieces, and half-dimes. He spent Thursday on dimes and quarters. Friday, he stayed until closing time again, going through all their dollars and half dollars. At the end of Friday, he had found fifty-nine coins that were all worth at least two thousand dollars each. Three or four of them could be worth more than ten thousand dollars.

It was not bad for three days work. If this was to be his job, it wasn't a bad one. He could help Madison with her homework, read the same books, test her—it wasn't exactly being a lawyer, but close. It would have to do until someone figured out a way for him to get a birth certificate legally. Maybe, if he believed long enough that it would happen, then it would. Until that time came, though, he'd have Madison. And for now, that was enough.

Friday, after the bank closed, he went around town and said good-bye to everyone he was close to, saving Matthew and Sarah until last. That one was a difficult and tearful good-bye, but he reassured Matthew by say-

249

ing that he would see him again—that he'd visit occasionally, and of course he would see them when Matthew
and Sarah came to the new Red Bluff to go to the Thai
restaurant. Clearly, Matthew was distraught over losing
Zack, but at least he had Sarah to help him through.
And Zack would be back soon enough. Madison would
come back to see Granny before too long, and Zack
would come with her. Matthew would be fine.

Zack slept well that night, after packing almost everything in his two backpacks. He was too tired to finish
cleaning out his chest of drawers, but he knew he could
do it quickly in the morning before he left. He wanted to
get out of the saloon before Matthew and Sarah awak-
ened. One teary good-bye was enough.

Early the next morning, as the first rays of light filtered through his curtains, Zack jumped out of bed. He
was ready to face the world, ready for his new life. But he
still had two drawers to go through. Before Zack had
bought the new clothes, he didn't have many possessions.
So one drawer was already almost empty. In the back
corner, though, was one coin, a half dollar, that must
have fallen out of Zack's pants. He picked it up, looked
at the date, looked at it again, and then smiled. It was an
1870 CC in excellent condition. Even the shine was still
on it. It was worth thousands—many, many thousands.
This coin was worth so much that he didn't even need to
look at any more for a year!

He put it into the pocket with the fifty-nine coins that
he had collected from the bank, and then he opened the
last drawer, the one on the bottom. It had some of his
father's things in it that Zack had never gone through
because it bothered him. His father's death had been
hard on him. Now was a good time to go through it since

it wasn't daylight yet, and Matthew and Sarah wouldn't be up for an hour or more.

He sat on the bed with a small cigar box filled with his father's belongings. There were only two things in the box: a handmade pipe of his father's that had fresh tobacco in it, as if his father had died before he had a chance to smoke it, and a leather pouch with a rawhide-pull top. Zack opened the pouch and turned it over in his hand. A small piece of quartz fell out along with three coins. Out of habit, Zack looked at the dates before putting them in his pocket.

The first one was a penny; the second one, a quarter; and the third one, a silver dollar. The dates of the first two weren't on his list. The third one, the dollar, was the 1795 silver dollar that Stan had wanted and had called the "Silver Plug." Zack held it to his chest. Stan had said it was "worth a fortune." When Zack had looked it up in his coin book, he found that it had recently been auctioned off for more than a million dollars. With this coin, Zack thought, with this coin, perhaps a million dollars would be enough to buy a legal birth certificate. It was a thought, anyway.

The light coming through the window was getting stronger. He needed to leave before Matthew or Sarah woke up. Zack put the Silver Plug, along with the other sixty coins, into the rawhide bag, closed it, and stuck it into his pocket. After putting the pipe into the outside pocket of the backpack, he quietly walked out the door, down the stairs, and out through the back door, which was closer to the livery. He had settled up with Ezra the day before, so he gave Echo a quick brushing, put on his bridle, hung the two backpacks over a post, and swung up onto Echo's back. Then, grabbing the backpacks, he managed to slip both of them on over his shoulders. He rode out of the livery to his new life.

CHAPTER SIXTY-ONE

EXCEPT FOR THE people who lived in town, Zack wasn't sad about saying good-bye to the old Red Bluff. When he came to the cave, he gave a quick glance over his shoulder, and that was enough. He'd be back. It wouldn't be gone to him forever. And he was so happy with his decision to move to the future even though he couldn't become a lawyer, that only good thoughts floated around in his head. But when he entered the cave and thought he heard the sound of hoofs coming toward him, he motioned for Echo to stop. Maybe someone wanted to steal his coins. That thought almost made him laugh out loud. Who, besides him, knew they were worth anything? But who could it be? Zack had Echo sidestep into the shadows of the cave.

When the person came to the center of the cave where light filtered down from above, Zack saw who it was and couldn't contain himself. "Madison!" he shouted. "Madison!"

"Hi, Zack," she said. "I've got good news for you."

Zack, thinking she was going to tell him that she had decided to move to the old Red Bluff to be with him, said, "And I've got good news for you! I'm moving to your time! I found sixty coins worth a lot of money—we can live in style for at least a year or two! Then, among my father's things, I found the silver dollar that Stan was looking for. He didn't say what it was worth, but it was auctioned last year for more than a million dollars! We're rich!"

Madison smiled and said quietly, "Save your money, Zack. You'll need it for college."

Zack didn't think he heard her right. "What?" he asked.

"I said that you'll need it for college."

"What do you mean?"

Madison reached into the pocket of her cowboy shirt, pulled out a card, and handed it to Zack. "Here. See for yourself."

Zack looked at the card. It had a picture of him on it, and it said "Zackary Allen Murphy, Diné Tribal Membership." "I don't understand," said Zack. He shrugged his shoulders. "This still isn't a birth certificate. Is it enough? Are you sure?"

"There's a whole lot more waiting for you at home— including a birth certificate saying you were born in 1992! Wait until you see it!"

Zack smiled, and although it was difficult hugging Madison with two backpacks pinning back his shoulders, he managed quite nicely. He even kissed her.

"Come on," said Madison. "Let's go home now. I'll tell you everything."

"Can I reschedule the GED test now?"

"As soon as we get home. Boyfriend, you're going to college!"

Zack kissed her again and followed her out the other

end of the cave. Then the two horses walked side by side on the trail, and the humans held hands as Madison told Zack everything that had happened since she saw him last. After Zack told her about his experiences at the bank and then finding the two coins in his chest of drawers, both of them had smiles so big that it hurt their faces.

And Zack, feeling Madison's hand in his own and feeling so grateful at his good fortune, started planning exactly what he was going to buy with all their money. First a laptop, then an iPhone, and of course a small truck would be nice, and . . .

THE END

If you liked this book, sign up on our mailing list to be notified of the next Cowgirls in Time book!
www.RalstonStorePublishing.com/cowgirls.html

In the next Cowgirls in Time romance, read how Kat and Doc discover they have more in common than just medicine.

Made in the USA
Charleston, SC
30 April 2015

GHANA:
End of an Illusion

GHANA:
End of an Illusion

GHANA:
End of an Illusion

by

BOB FITCH

and

MARY OPPENHEIMER

MONTHLY REVIEW PRESS

NEW YORK AND LONDON

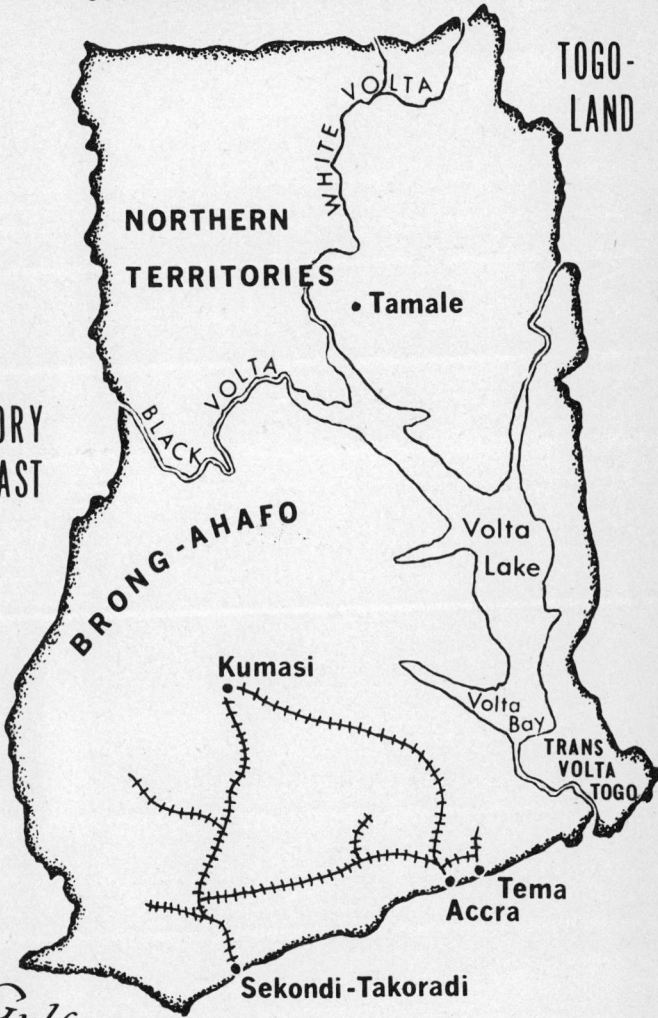

UPPER VOLTA

TOGO-
LAND

WHITE VOLTA

NORTHERN
TERRITORIES

• Tamale

IVORY
COAST

VOLTA

BLACK

BRONG-AHAFO

Volta
Lake

Kumasi

Volta
Bay

TRANS
VOLTA
TOGO

Tema
Accra

Sekondi-Takoradi

Gulf of Guinea

GHANA

CONTENTS

FOREWORD

Like many others on the Left, both here and abroad, we were shocked by the February coup which overthrew the Nkrumah government in Ghana. We had never been taken in by the myth of Ghanaian socialism—propagated by both friends and foes of the regime—but we knew that Ghana was the first black African colony to win its independence, that Kwame Nkrumah had an outstanding record as an opponent of colonialism and as a champion of African unity, that the Convention People's Party which he headed was a mass party, and that in some fields, such as education and health, notable progress had been made in the nearly ten years of independence. Against this background it seemed hard to believe that Nkrumah could be overthrown in an almost bloodless coup which, according to all press reports, was greeted with popular approval rather than resistance. How could one explain such an apparent anomaly?

One thing was immediately obvious: none of the "explanations" offered by the supposed experts really explained anything. One of the most popular, for example, put all the blame on the CIA. But if the CIA played a role (and we are prepared to believe that it did), it evidently acted through the army and the police. And this leaves us where we started, without any clue to the ease with which the coup succeeded and the apparent total absence of popular resistance then and later. Only one conclusion seemed possible: that the situation in Ghana was quite different from the appearance which we, along with many others, had all too uncritically accepted as reflecting the reality. Obviously the international revolutionary movement had a crying need—and responsibility—to reconsider the whole problem of Ghana, to make a serious historical and critical analysis of Ghanaian society, and to draw the necessary conclusions and lessons for the future.

On the morrow of the coup, and with these thoughts in mind, we received a manuscript which had been mailed in Berkeley, California, several days before the day the coup took place. An accompanying letter signed by the author, Bob Fitch, explained that he was a graduate student in African studies at the University of California and that the manuscript consisted of three chapters from a thesis in progress on the economic, social, and political development of Ghana during the decade preceding independence in 1957. Was there any possibility, he inquired, that Monthly Review Press might be interested in publishing a book on this subject?

The reader will understand both our surprise and increasing excitement as we read the manuscript and discovered that Mr. Fitch was engaged in carrying out precisely the kind of study of Ghana which the coup now made so necessary and important, and that he was doing so from the standpoint of historical materialism and with great insight and skill. We got in touch with him immediately and asked if he could drop everything else and concentrate on bringing the story up to date and compressing it into the compass of MONTHLY REVIEW's double summer issue. He accepted the challenge, enlisted the collaboration of Mary Oppenheimer, a fellow graduate student in political science at Berkeley, and together they produced the work which it is now our privilege to publish both as the July-August issue of the magazine and as a book which we hope and believe will reach a much wider readership both in the United States and abroad.

Leo Huberman
Paul M. Sweezy

New York
June 15, 1966

So let us look at history as history—men placed in actual con-texts which they have not chosen, and confronted by indivertible forces, with an overwhelming immediacy of relations and duties and with only a scanty opportunity for inserting their own agency—and not as a text for hectoring might-have-beens.

—E. P. Thompson

1

THE COUP

For if you think that you can manage a country without letting the people interfere, if you think that the people upset the game by their mere presence, whether they slow it down or whether by their natural ignorance they sabotage it, then you must have no hesitation: you must keep the people out.

—*Frantz Fanon*[1]

Within twenty-four hours the coup was over. It began at 5:00 A.M. when 20 tanks, under joint military and police command, surrounded Flagstaff House, the triple-walled residence of Dr. Nkrumah. By 10:00 A.M., members of Dr. Nkrumah's Soviet-led security guard were beginning to surrender. By 6:00 P.M., Radio Ghana was able to broadcast:

After Ghana's accession to independence, a new class was formed whose principal occupation consisted in emptying the Treasury and perpetrating crimes of all kinds under the pretext of creating a socialist state. Today Kwame Nkrumah and this new class have ceased to exist.

"Detention buses" began to work their way through the streets of Accra to Victoriaborg and the Cantonments, the former "colonial" sections of the city. Here they picked up the Ministers of State and other high party officials. In the center of the city, the buses were slowed by traffic. Crowds pressed in from all sides to identify the occupants. Howls of derision greeted the sight of Nathaniel A. Welbeck, the Minister of State for Party Propaganda. The jails, newly emptied of old political prisoners, began to fill up with new ones.

A crane was dispatched to the square outside Parliament House, where the famous statue of Dr. Nkrumah stood. The crane battered the statue to the ground, where it lay on its back

---

1. All epigraphs by Fanon are from *The Wretched of the Earth*, New York, 1964.

like a giant sarcophagus. Some ragged, barefoot children were
allowed to scamper on top of it briefly for photographers; then
it was smashed to bits and the pieces distributed as souvenirs
to the crowd.

In Accra and Kumasi, three days of demonstrations followed the coup. Thousands of students and market women ("mam-
mies") joined in street marches in support of the new rulers—
the policemen and military officers who now formed the "National Liberation Council." In houses, offices, and factories,
Dr. Nkrumah's picture was enthusiastically ripped from the
walls. Almost immediately, without waiting for more complete
information, Ghana's embassies from Peking to Paris began to
wire their support. Defections began to occur even within the
74-man delegation accompanying Dr. Nkrumah on his "peace
mission" to Peking. The outstanding international figure of the
regime, Alex Quaison-Sackey, was sent by Dr. Nkrumah from
Peking to Addis Ababa to protest the seating of the new
Ghanaian government's delegation at the Organization of African Unity meeting. Quaison-Sackey flew instead to Accra where
he pledged his loyalty to the police/military government. On
his arrival he announced: "The Army has taken power to
liberate the people from oppression. The Ghanaian people will
now have a free country and will not idolize a single man."

Loyalties shifted just as abruptly—if not actually in mid-
air—within the circle of government-appointed trade union
leaders. The Secretariat of the Trade Union Congress (which
had resisted wage demands for the last three years while food
prices increased as much as 400 percent) quickly swung into
line behind the police and the generals. "In the name of the
workers," the Secretariat greeted "with greatest satisfaction,
the deliverance of the country and the end of dictatorship and
economic chaos."[2]

The Convention People's Party (CPP), with its two million members and 500,000 militants, all pledged by oath to
support Dr. Nkrumah, organized no resistance at all. The CPP
had been founded in 1949 when Dr. Nkrumah, together with
communists and militant nationalists, decided that only a mass-
based party could carry out the struggle against British colonial-

2. *Jeune Afrique*, March 13, 1966.

ism. In 1950, it helped launch the first general strike in sub-Saharan Africa. The strike forced the concessions which brought Dr. Nkrumah from James Fort prison to the position of "Leader of Government Business" in the first popularly elected parliament in colonial Africa.[3] Now, after 15 years as Ghana's ruling party, the CPP allowed itself to be dissolved by a simple decree announced over the radio. The day after the coup, the generals wound up the affairs of the CPP by simply announcing over Radio Ghana: "All persons who find themselves in possession of vehicles belonging to the ex-party, the CPP, are requested to return them to the nearest police station."[4]

The scope of the collapse became even more obvious when General Joseph Arthur Ankrah, the junta head, announced that Dr. Nkrumah's personal security force, purged of its Soviet cadre, would be reintegrated without reprisals into the Ghanaian armed forces. Like the Deacon's wonderful one-horse shay, the Nkrumah regime had gone to pieces, "all at once and nothing first/Just as bubbles do when they burst."

But the totality of Dr. Nkrumah's collapse after 15 years of leadership, the speed of the coup, its relative bloodlessness, and the paucity of Nkrumah "loyalists" or diehards, surprised very few Ghanaians. Instead, it seemed more like a case of *déjà vu*. Rumors of an impending coup had been circulating in the capital for months. And it had been said that if Dr. Nkrumah again left the country on the eve of another unpopular budget message, he would never return again.

The Anglo-African Junta

Who were the generals and why did they strike? On the weekend of the coup, one Africanist wrote that "the first question many observers of the Ghanaian scene asked when they heard of the overthrow of Dr. Nkrumah was: How many

---

3. The progression from prison to parliament is a routine part of British colonial "devolution." After the successful experiences with De Valera, Gandhi, and Nehru, one can imagine that the handling of Nkrumah, Kenyatta, and Jagan was carried out according to some chapter on "Militant Nationalists—Countermeasures," in a *Manual of Standard Operating Procedure for Colonial Officials.*

4. *Jeune Afrique,* March 13, 1966.

Ashantis are at the head of the coup?"[5] It is clear now that no
form of "tribalism"—Ashanti or otherwise—motivated the
generals. They have not legalized any of the so-called "tribal"
parties which formed the CPP's only serious opposition from
1954 to 1958. "Tribal" politicians like Professor K. A. Busia
of Cambridge are still in exile.[6]

The generals and their police auxiliaries have an entirely
different frame of reference. General Ankrah, for instance, is
a Ga; but insofar as he shows any ethnic particularity, it is
Anglo-Saxon. Anglophilia permeates the Ghanaian officer corps.
This is partially explained by their service experience: most
Ghanaian officers were either trained in Great Britain or
trained in Ghana by British cadres. (Except for the personal
security forces trained in the Soviet Union, the rest of Ghana's
military training assistance has come from the United States
and Canada.) After returning from Great Britain, the Ghanaian
officers are isolated from Ghanaian society by the demands of
military life. As a result, they reflect, in exaggerated form, the
general tendency of African bureaucratic elites to imitate their
European counterparts.[7]

After their training, Ghanaian officers tend to judge their
daily African experience by the norms of British society and the
values of the British officer corps. Colonel A. A. Afrifa, an important coup leader, reflects this cultural outlook, in an interview in the London *Observer* (March 13). Explaining why he
and his fellow officers disliked the old regime, Afrifa said,
"We've lived in Britain before, and therefore didn't like this
dictatorship. There was no freedom of the press or of the in-

5. Ashanti, the populous central forest region of Ghana, has played
a notable role in the country's history. It is inhabited by tribes sharing the
Akan religion and language. These tribes, united in the militarily powerful
Ashanti Confederacy, successfully resisted the imposition of British colonial
rule throughout the nineteenth century.

6. Western observers of Ghanaian politics have greatly overemphasized
the "tribal" factor. Over 85 percent of the Ghanaian people are involved
in the money economy—the highest percentage in Africa. Yet professional
Africanists tend to conjure up pictures of political battles decided by painted
warriors with spears. Actually ethnic politics in New York City provide
a better model.

7. Three British Commonwealth nations now have leaders who were
trained as soldiers in Great Britain: President Ayub Khan of Pakistan,
General Aguiyi-Ironsi of Nigeria (who once served as Extra-Equerry to
the Queen), and General Ankrah.

dividual—things we know are fundamental human rights."
Afrifa went on: "Nkrumah introduced party politics into the
Army. He took a man with no training as an officer, a Mr.
Hassan, appointed him a brigadier, and put him in charge of
military intelligence. Hence we had a situation in which mess
corporals were watching commanding officers and reporting
them. What greater insult to our intelligence and patriotism."

The first indication of how dangerous this mixture of
military "professionalism" and Anglophilia was to prove for the
Nkrumah government had occurred during the 1961 UN Congo intervention. Ghana's UN contingent was commanded by
the British Major-General H. T. Alexander. Ankrah, then a
colonel, was second in command. Both opposed Dr. Nkrumah's
policy toward the Lumumba forces. Dr. Nkrumah followed an
essentially moderate course, between the nations of the Casa-
blanca group who withdrew their troops from the UN command, and the members of the Monrovia group which generally
supported the UN presence in the Congo. Dr. Nkrumah kept
his troops under UN command ("to his great credit," according
to General Alexander) but still sent weapons secretly to the
Lumumbaists. Even this middle course was criticized by Alexander and the Ghanaian officer corps. They opposed all aid
to the Lumumbaists on the grounds that it undermined the
UN mission and interfered with their "soldierly duty."[8] Alexander asserted that the main objectives for the UN forces were
to "stabilize" the Congo situation by bringing in as many non-
African troops as possible, while at the same time preventing
arms from reaching the Lumumbaists.[9]

In September 1961, after months of conflict with the
generals, Dr. Nkrumah decided to send cadets to the Soviet
Union for military training. Alexander naturally objected. He
observed that the Ghanaian officer corps would be split into
two camps if the plan were carried out. Complete ideological

---

8. Fikri Melika, "Ankrah: l'homme qui a su attendre," *Jeune Afrique*,
March 13, 1966.

9. Alexander complained that the African contingents were too friendly to the Congolese people: the climax of African "unreliability" came
when the Ghanaian 3rd Brigade mutinied and sent its officers fleeing into
the bushes. *African Tightrope*, London, 1965.

uniformity would be threatened. As he explained: "Whether the young men come back to Ghana as budding communists or not is not the point. They will certainly not come back like-minded to the present officer corps."[10]

Alexander's opposition became so strong that on September 22, 1961, Dr. Nkrumah dismissed him and the other British cadres assigned to the Ghanaian Army. The extent to which the Ghanaian officers supported Alexander against Dr. Nkrumah is now clear. For with the success of the coup, the "National Liberation Council" publicly revealed that they had been plotting Dr. Nkrumah's overthrow since 1961.[11]

The Anglo-Africans Take Charge

The strength of the police force and the power of the army are proportionate to the stagnation in which the rest of the nation is sunk.

—Frantz Fanon

The junta has been in power long enough to demonstrate that it understands completely the theory and practice of neo-colonialist economics. It accepts without question the double standard by which the Western countries guide themselves according to Keynes, while the underdeveloped countries are supposed to follow the wisdom of Malthus. "Cheap government," the policy of the nineteenth-century European bourgeoisie, has become the order of the day in an African country without a bourgeoisie. Thus Lieutenant General Ankrah (he promoted himself the day after the coup) has announced the abandonment of the Seven Year Plan; all "prestige" projects (e.g. factories) are being halted; the operation of the Ghana Airways will be restricted;[12] diplomatic representation is being

---

10. *Ibid.*, p. 92.

11. The generals are still inveighing against the 1961 act which sent the Ghanaian cadets to the Soviet Union. See Press Release No. 4, Ghana Information Service, March 1, 1966.

12. What bothered the British about the Ghana Airways was not its deficit, but the competition it gave over African routes to BOAC; in addition, Dr. Nkrumah antagonized the British aircraft industry when he bought United States and Soviet aircraft. See *Wall Street Journal*, March 10, 1966.

curtailed; and all salaries and wages will be reviewed with a view towards reducing expenditures. Ankrah, who became a director of Ghana's National Investment Bank in August 1965, has decided that the private sector of the economy will predominate: measures will be taken to "review" the scope of state corporations; private enterprise will no longer be forced to accept government participation; and the establishment of joint private/government enterprises will be on a voluntary basis.

The Anglo-Africans not only strive to coordinate theory and practice in neo-colonialist economics; they also show themselves careful students of the "wisdom of the West" in the administrative sphere. For them British colonial rule laid the foundation for Ghana's golden age: "A mere eighteen years ago," an official statement reminisces, "the United Kingdom which had ruled this country for over a century, began to release the strings of government to the people of Ghana. The country was then blessed, on the final attainment of political independence, with adequate funds in all our Departments which could successfully continue the intricate work of Government after the departure of the British."[13] Since then, the statement continues, Ghanaian self-rule has brought nothing but Debt, Dictatorship, and Declining cocoa prices.

In foreign affairs, the generals have been quick to follow the "opening to the Right" offered by the *Times* of London which suggested in a leading article the day after the coup that "if they [the generals] generate confidence, and want help, Ghana would be worth salvaging again."[14] Since then, the junta has resumed diplomatic relations with Great Britain, requested foreign aid, and affirmed its belief in the worldwide mission of the British Commonwealth which has "a vital role in the promotion and maintenance of world peace and security."[15] The only false step taken by the junta thus far was to exceed the bounds of Anglo-American anti-communism. The decision of March 2nd to expel 130 Soviet technicians was opposed by Western diplomats in Accra.[16] Except for this mis-

13. Ghana Press Release No. 4.
14. February 25, 1966.
15. Ghana Press Release No. 4.
16. *New York Times*, March 3, 1966.

step, the Western diplomats "could hardly contain their delight with the turn of events."[17]

The African Response

While the Ghanaian junta devoted itself to hammering Ghana into marketable salvage, and while Western diplomats rejoiced, the militant Left in Africa could hardly believe what was happening. Ousmane Ba, Mali Foreign Minister, spoke for many when he said, "President Nkrumah's revolutionary work cannot be replaced, and we do not accept that some musical comedy general, helped by policemen, should question the Ghanaian people's twenty years of struggle."[18] In Senegal, Egypt, Tanzania, and Mali, popular meetings were held to protest the coup. Even in Liberia and Ethiopia, official statements deplored the turn of events.

The most striking demonstration of support for Dr. Nkrumah came from Guinea. Strong ties had developed between the two countries in 1958, when Guinea cast her famous "No" vote against joining the French "Community." After their defeat by 1,136,000 votes to 57,500, the French pulled out of Guinea immediately, taking with them everything they could, and smashing everything they couldn't. Phones were ripped from the walls, administrative records burned, hospital supplies destroyed. Ghana quickly carried out what was probably the first concrete act of Pan-African solidarity. She lent Guinea £10,000,000 without interest or repayment schedule.[19] It was against this background and that of the late Ghana-Guinea-Mali union that President Sekou Touré conferred the Honorary Presidency of Guinea on Dr. Nkrumah. The gesture reflected the judgment that the Nkrumah regime was different from the five other African governments that had been overthrown since November 1965. It aimed at institutionalizing what should be clear: that Kwame Nkrumah was not a vulgar imperialist stooge like Upper Volta's Maurice Yameogo or Nigeria's Rt. Hon. Sir

---

17. *Ibid.*
18. The *Times* (London), March 8, 1966.
19. One Ghana pound = one pound sterling. Throughout this work the symbol £ is used for both currencies.

Abubakar Tafawa Balewa (O.B.E., K.B.E., C.B.E., P.C.), whose regimes had also been swept away without popular resistance.

What is the significance of the Ghanaian coup's failure to provoke any popular resistance? Did the fall of Nkrumah's fortified residence mark the end of the first socialist state in Africa? If socialism failed in Ghana, the richest of the sub-Saharan African states, what are the prospects for the rest of the continent? What forced the government into its obvious isolation? Does the Ghanaian experience have any wider implications for revolutionary movements elsewhere? Are the overturns in Ghana and Indonesia somehow related? Is the Ghanaian coup part of a world-wide counter-revolutionary trend?

The Ghanaian coup has given rise to these questions and many others which cry out for answers. So far, the analyses of the coup—both liberal and radical—have focused almost entirely on its obvious and superficial aspects. And the major emphasis has been on Nkrumah's personality. Liberals generally describe him as a romantic African Marxist whose megalomania grew as his charisma dwindled. They assert that he sank the whole economy under the weight of scores of grandiose but impractical schemes for industrial development. Radicals, on the other hand, portray him as the leader of the African revolutionary movement, a man who was close to his goal of creating a socialist state in Africa. But just as he was about to succeed, he was overthrown by an unholy alliance forged within a cabal of reactionary generals and "foreign plotters."

If the Ghanaian coup were an isolated phenomenon and had not followed a whole series of overturns in the under-developed world (Algeria, Nigeria, Indonesia, Brazil, Congo-(L), to name only a few), the two foregoing explanations might seem more plausible. But the pervasiveness of these coups, crossing continents without regard for world reputations or professed ideologies, demands a more sophisticated analysis.

The truth is that powerful social forces are systematically destroying the regimes established by the non-communist anti-colonial movements in Asia and Africa after the Second World War. If these forces are to be controlled or exploited, an analysis must be developed which places individual politicians, as well as "foreign plotters," in their proper socio-historical context. After the counter-revolution of 1849, Engels wrote:

> That the sudden movements of February and March 1849 were not the work of single individuals, but spontaneous, irresistible manifestations of national wants and necessities, more or less clearly understood, but very distinctly felt by numerous classes in every country, is a fact recognized everywhere; but when you inquire into the causes of the counter-revolutionary successes, there you are met on every hand with the ready reply that it was Mr. This or Citizen That who "betrayed" the people. Which reply may be very true or not, according to the circumstances, but under no circumstances does it explain anything—not even how it came to pass that the "people" allowed themselves to be thus betrayed. And what poor chance stands a political party whose entire stock-in-trade consists in a knowledge of the solitary fact that Citizen So-and-So is not to be trusted.[20]

No less than after the 1849 counter-revolution, a *political* analysis of the Ghanaian coup is now required. And this analysis must avoid both liberal psychoanalysis and "radical" hagiography. What is required is class analysis and historical analysis. Therefore, to understand how the Nkrumah state was destroyed, it is necessary to have some idea of how it was built. The character of the national states created in the underdeveloped world after the Second World War was shaped most decisively by the character of their national independence struggles. So it is to this period of Ghanaian history that we must now turn.

---

20. *Germany: Revolution and Counter-Revolution,* New York, 1933, p. 10.

2

THE GHANAIAN INDEPENDENCE MOVEMENT

We think there is something wrong with the simple interpretation of the national liberation movement as a revolutionary trend.
—*Amilcar Cabral, Secretary-General, Partido Africano da Independencia da Guiné é Cabo Verde*

Why did the British grant independence to Ghana in 1957? The Convention People's Party (CPP) Central Committee and the British Colonial Office answered this question quite differently. Convention People's Party spokesmen described how the nationalist movement, headed by Dr. Nkrumah, organized by K. A. Gbedemah, and assisted by Kofi Baako and Kojo Botsio, awoke the spirit of liberty in the towns, shook the villages into political awareness, and thus exerted continual pressure on the British authorities. Finally, with the entire nation massed behind the CPP, the British had no choice but to grant their demands for self-government.

The British, of course, tell another story. They deny that they were forced to leave at all. The British government, they say, has always been willing to grant independence to colonial peoples who are capable of managing their own affairs. Ghana was only another example of the British government's flexibility and desire to maximize "liberty" through an orderly process of constitutional devolution.

The British Colonial Office likes to claim that it constituted, if not the vanguard, at least the strong right wing of the Ghanaian independence movement. And if "independence" is defined in the very narrowest sense, the Colonial Office can hardly be denied its claim. Ghana, after all, has never experienced a Dienbienphu; nor did Accra fall to Nkrumah and his followers as Havana did to Castro's bearded *guerrilleros*. Ghana advanced to independence by carefully planned stages marked by periodic constitutional revisions which gradually placed more and more legislative responsibility in the hands of Nkrumah's party.

On Independence Day, March 4, 1957, the source of the new government's legitimacy could hardly have been made more clear. The Duchess of Kent, acting as Queen Elizabeth's official representative, announced at the ceremonies: "Henceforward all powers previously exercised by my government in the United Kingdom will be exercised by my ministers in Ghana." The presence of the Colonial Governor, dressed like the commander of an eighteenth century frigate; the display of all the mildewed symbols of British imperial authority; and the playing of "God Save the Queen" emphasized the tidiness of the transition.

The Duchess of Kent had spoken of "the powers previously exercised by my government." Were any of these powers so broad that they endangered Britain's vital economic interests in Ghana? Had the substance of power actually shifted from London to Accra?

Surely twenty years of bloody struggles on three continents —in Malaya, Kenya, Aden, and British Guiana—suggest the contrary. The colonial governments yield administrative powers to the "natives" only when vital British interests are reasonably secure. These natives must show themselves willing and able to serve as post-colonial sergeants of the guard over British property: rubber in Malaya, land in Kenya, oil in Aden, bauxite in British Guiana. When no cooperative stratum has yet emerged, "independence" is delayed. Meanwhile, elements hostile to British interests are liquidated, shoved aside, or co-opted.

The problem for the British in colonial Africa has been to shape a native ruling class strong enough to protect British interests, but still weak enough to be dominated. Sir Andrew Cohen, former head of the African Division of the Colonial Office, explains the process:

In the early stages, pressure of local opinion tends to be weak and unorganized and, if the official attitude is rigid, or negative, progress may be slow or non-existent. In such cases action by the government is often needed to induce movement forward by doing something which primes the political pump. Governors call this "Keeping one step ahead of public opinion." In the later stages of political advance, pressure by nationalist forces tends to be strong and here, if the government is rigid, there may be an explosion, or if the government is weak, progress may be too rapid in the wrong direction. In fact, where local political forces or movements are powerful, smooth progress depends on imagination as well as firmness on the part of governments, not only on strength but on flexibility.[1]

Thus the colonial governor serves as the midwife of the national independence movement—a midwife who always stands ready to strangle the baby in order to rescue and nourish the afterbirth. It is this afterbirth of the national independence movement which the colonial governor then treats as the soul of the independent state.

According to Amilcar Cabral, leader of the revolutionary movement in "Portuguese" Guinea, the national independence movements "induced" by the colonial regimes have as their objectives: (1) Preventing the enlargement of the socialist bloc; (2) Liberating the reactionary forces in Africa which were being stifled by colonialism; (3) Enabling these forces to ally themselves with the international bourgeoisie.[2]

In Ghana, the "liberation" of local reactionary forces had been dragging on for decades. British policy from the Guggisberg administration (1919-1927) through that of the hopelessly inept Sir Gerald Creasy (1948-1949) aimed at establishing some kind of coalition of "indirect rule" chiefs and Anglophile lawyers as a native ruling class. Within the Colonial Office, the liberals wanted to weight the coalition more heavily with lawyers, while the conservatives argued for the chiefs. Until 1947, Gold Coast "politics" consisted primarily of lobbying by various cliques of chiefs and lawyers for greater representation within the Gold Coast Legislative Council. And while the chiefs and lawyers tried to out-connive each other within the "sandbox" Legislative Council, the country continued to be run from the Governor's residence.

The possibility that the African masses would ever have anything to say about who would rule the Gold Coast never occurred to either the British, the chiefs, or the lawyers. As

---

1. Andrew Cohen, *British Policy in Changing Africa,* London, 1959, p. 37.

2. Amilcar Cabral, "The Struggle in Guinea," *International Socialist Journal,* August 1964, p. 441.

Cohen admits, even after the Second World War, British colonialists "based their attitudes and actions on the assumption that there was indefinite time ahead."[3] It seems fantastic, but the British actually believed that indirect rule could continue while railroads, mining, and construction industries developed; while an organized working class appeared; while the entire economy shifted its emphasis from subsistence to commodity production; and after 30,000 Africans had been sent off with modern weapons to fight the Japanese in Burma. After all these transformations, the Colonial Office thought it would still be able to rule through its favorite chiefs; continue to send District Officers into the "bush"; and generally carry on as in the days of Lugard. The February 1948 upheavals changed all that.

Even a few weeks before the riots, the colonial officials showed no sensitivity to the socio-economic changes that had taken place. "I shall give my fullest support to the chiefs and their councils," Sir Gerald Creasy announced on January 12th, 1948, on being sworn in as Governor. "The chiefs and their councils will become increasingly important."[4] And Lord Trefgarne, the newly appointed head of the Colonial Development Corporation described his view of the future a week later: "As I see it, it is a real beginning to the Colonial Century, the start of a new era of Colonial progress."[5]

By the first of March, however, the bright new colonial dawn could hardly be seen through the flames rising from the commercial district of Accra. The United Africa Company and the Union Trading Company stores had been sacked and burned; Africans were assaulting British and Syrian businessmen on the streets; 29 Africans were dead and 237 wounded. Anticolonial feeling spread from Accra to Kumasi and sparked strikes which closed down public utilities and transportation. By March 8, Nigerian reinforcements were in the country, additional British troops were convoyed from South Africa, and three troop carriers were sent to Gibraltar for possible deployment to the Gold Coast.

---

3. Cohen, *British Policy in Changing Africa*, p. 29.
4. *Ashanti Pioneer* (Kumasi), January 12, 1948.
5. *Ashanti Pioneer*, January 19, 1948.

The immediate cause of the uprising was the action of a British police officer who opened fire on an ex-servicemen's demonstration. But the incident was no mere spasm of hate quickly aroused and quickly abated. The violence reflected a general *prise de conscience* by the African masses. Transportation strikes, mining strikes, and a nation-wide boycott that even the indirect-rule chiefs were compelled to support had formed the immediate political background of the "Christianborg riots." Since the Second World War the working class had grown tremendously, and trade unions were being organized in every town. In the port cities of Sekondi-Takoradi, they were organized and led by Marxists like ex-locomotive driver Pobee Biney, Turkson Ocran, and Anthony Woode. And in addition to the trade union movement, a tremendous variety of organizations was springing up which contributed to the nationalist ferment: youth organizations, study groups, and veterans' organizations all played a role in the movement.

Nevertheless, despite the increasing militance and politicization of the African masses, the Christianborg riots were not "organized." None of the official nationalist organizations played a part—not even the United Gold Coast Convention (UGCC), the organization of wealthy lawyers and traders of which Kwame Nkrumah had become general secretary in 1947. At the time of the riots in Accra, Nkrumah was in Saltpond, sixty miles away, giving a speech on "The Ideological Battles of our Time." He acknowledges that he had no influence over the African participants in the struggle, but says that he was "certainly aware of their general dissatisfaction" and that "it had been my intention to organize them in due course as an arm of our movement."[6] This admission by Dr. Nkrumah deserves emphasis, for it is generally assumed that nationalist agitation in the Gold Coast somehow began with his arrival in December 1947. It is true that the form the nationalist movement took was decisively influenced by Nkrumah, but the existence of intense anti-British feeling and the determination of the African masses to engage in violent resistance to colonialism in no way depended on him.

---

6. Kwame Nkrumah, *Ghana*, New York, 1957, p. 77.

While neither Nkrumah nor the other members of the
UGCC, which at this time numbered some 1,800 members, led
or tried to organize the violent struggles of February 28th, they
nevertheless tried to gain some political advantage from them.
Both Dr. J. B. Danquah, Vice President of the UGCC, and
Nkrumah sent telegrams to the Secretary of State for Colonies on
the 29th. Danquah's lengthy telegram read in part:

Unless Colonial Government is changed and a new Government of the people and their chiefs installed at the centre immediately, the conduct of masses now completely out of control with
strikes threatened in Police quarters, and rank and file Police indifferent to orders of officers, will continue and result in worse violent
and irresponsible acts by uncontrolled people. Working Committee
United Gold Coast Convention declare they are prepared and ready
to take over interim government. . . . We speak in name of
inherent residual sovereignty in chiefs and people in free partnership with British Commonwealth for our country to be saved from
inept Government indifferent to sufferings of the governed. The
souls of Gold Coast people slaughtered in cold blood upon Castle
Road crying out loud for vindication in cause of freedom and
liberty. Firing by Police and military going on this morning. Let
King and Parliament act without delay in this direst hour of
Gold Coast people and their chiefs. God save the King and Floreat
United Gold Coast.[7]

Nkrumah's telegram, unlike Danquah's, did not suggest that
the UGCC should take over the country. He asked only that a
British Commission be sent to supervise elections for a "Con-
stituent Assembly." The inflammatory part of his telegram was
not the text but the people to whom he sent it. Seeking the
widest possible circulation for news of the uprising, Nkrumah
included not only the *New York Times* and the UN Secretary
General, but also Willy Gallacher, the Communist MP from
Glasgow, the London *Daily Worker,* and Moscow's *New Times*.

This, of course, constituted direct contact with "international Communism" and gave the bewildered and isolated Gold
Coast government a chance to stage a show trial and provide

---

7. Colonial Office, *Report of the Commission of Enquiry into Disturb-
ances in the Gold Coast* (Watson Report), HMSO, London, p. 95. "Floreat
United Gold Coast" is an adaptation of the Eton motto of "floreat
Etona"—may Eton flourish.

a badly needed scapegoat. Nkrumah, together with five other members of the UGCC, including Danquah, was duly arrested and detained. Sir Gerald Creasy appointed a Commission to investigate the "disturbances." The Commission discovered that Nkrumah was using some of the "legitimate economic grievances" of the Gold Coast people to stage a revolution which would establish a "Union of West African Soviet Socialist Republics." The Committee's Report, written in classic British colonialist style (filled with Dogberryisms, cold war effluvia, and unctuous paternalism masquerading as humanitarianism), included the following "analysis":

Mr. Nkrumah boldly proposes a programme which is all too familiar to those who have studied the techniques of countries which have fallen the victims of Communist enslavement. We cannot accept the naive statements of the members of the Working Committee [of the UGCC] that although this [programme] had been circulated, they did not read it. We are willing to believe they did. On the other hand we feel that the Working Committee, fired by Mr. Nkrumah's enthusiasm and drive, were eager to seize power and for the time being were indifferent to means adopted to attain it.[8]

The principle effect of the Government's efforts, as might have been expected, was to make the UGCC the leading nationalist organization, and turn Kwame Nkrumah "overnight" into the Gold Coast's outstanding nationalist hero.[9]

When Kwame Nkrumah arrived in the Gold Coast in December of 1947, he was 39 years old and had been out of the country for twelve years. In breadth and variety of experience, the decade Nkrumah spent as a young man in the United States recalls similar periods in the lives of Ho Chi Minh and Sun Yat-sen. Arriving in 1935, during the depression, Nkrumah studied at the University of Pennsylvania and Lincoln University, where he earned degrees in education, sociology, and theology. Nevertheless he was often forced to earn a precarious living at various odd jobs which included selling fish and working in a soap factory. He still found time to observe and take

---

8. *Ibid.*
9. Between March and May 1948, UGCC membership increased approximately twenty-five times.

part in political activity of every imaginable kind—from Republican to Trotskyist.

The two experiences that were probably most useful for his future career as a nationalist leader were the sermons he preached as a Baptist minister in Philadelphia and the Pan-African agitation he organized as a student at the University of Pennsylvania. From his regular sermonizing he developed the oratorical power that eventually helped carry him to the leadership of the Gold Coast independence movement. While organizing the African Students' Association, he met Ako Adjei, who later invited him to become the Secretary General of the UGCC.

In 1945 Nkrumah, now thirty-seven, left the United States for Great Britain to study logical positivism with A. J. Ayer in London, and to participate in the organization of the Sixth Pan-African Congress. But it was the problems of imperialism and political ideology rather than those of verification and meaning to which he began to devote his full attention. The Pan-African Congress, the men he met at it, the ideas generated there, the organizational commitments he made as a result, were critically important in his later life and in the history of the African independence movement. Before 1945, Pan-Africanism was just one of the eclectic and contradictory preoccupations in which he was actively involved. After 1945, his political focus narrowed greatly. His associates at the Congress were George Padmore, Peter Abrahams, C. L. R. James, and Jomo Kenyatta: men with radical and communist backgrounds, but whose politics were now influenced at least as much by anti-communism as by Pan-Africanism.

The principle resolutions of the Congress, some of them drafted by Nkrumah, reflected a combination of anti-imperialism and anti-communism which resolved itself into a desire for "economic democracy" and the hope that Gandhian tactics ("positive action") would always be viable. One resolution expressed the hope that "before long the peoples of Asia and Africa [would] have broken their centuries' old chains of colonialism. Then as free nations, they [would] stand united to consolidate and safeguard their liberties from the restoration

of Western imperialism, as well as the dangers of communism."[10]
Nowhere was the subject of socialism mentioned, although
"foreign monopolies of finance capital" were specifically
condemned.

The themes of the Sixth Pan-African Congress—non-
violence, "positive action," anti-communism, anti-imperialism,
non-alignment—became the core of Nkrumah's political approach. He has never significantly diverged from them. Those
who have labeled Nkrumahism the highest stage of opportun-
ism have missed the essential point about his political beliefs.
Had he been a simple opportunist—an African Hubert Hum-
phrey—his political path would have been much straighter and
easier to pursue (and the analysis of it much less rewarding).
But just as his political course was not simple, neither was his
political ideology. It embraced a series of contradictory positions: anti-communism and anti-imperialism; national liberation and abstract non-violence; non-alignment and economic
development through foreign investment. It was the clash between these contradictory principles and not his alleged "op-
portunism" that produced his erratic course in foreign and
domestic policy and led finally to his undoing. To see how he
tried to resolve these contradictions—for they inevitably posed
themselves within the context of the Gold Coast independence
movement—we must next observe how he responded to the
opportunity given him by the British authorities.

The Class Basis of the Movement

Nkrumah had come to the Gold Coast with very low expectations of the possibilities for radical political activity in his
new position as Secretary General of the UGCC. He regarded
the UGCC as a movement "backed almost entirely by reactionaries, middle class lawyers, and merchants." And consequently
he "prepared to come to loggerheads with the executive of the
UGCC" if it followed a "reactionary course."[11] The opportunity
to carry on Pan-African agitation in Africa was what really
attracted him to the Gold Coast. For up to this time, Nkrumah

---

10. Colin Legum, *Pan-Africanism,* London, 1965, p. 32.
11. Nkrumah, *Ghana,* p. 63.

had thought of himself primarily as a Pan-Africanist rather than a Gold Coast nationalist. (He implies that when he received the offer to become Secretary General of the UGCC, he had only a general idea of the political and social conditions in his native country.) His rise to the leadership of the national independence movement within six months is therefore all the more remarkable.

The response of the Colonial Government to Nkrumah's growing popularity was to try to isolate him from the independence movement while at the same time granting concessions to his UGCC comrades. A commission on constitutional reform (the Coussey Constitutional Committee) was formed in June 1948. All the leading Gold Coast politicians were invited to participate—all, that is, except Nkrumah. As Dennis Austin remarks: "This was a step of great importance, and one that the intelligentsia understood very well. They were at home with committees and schemes of political reform; and they had no hesitation in responding to the government's invitation."[12]

The Conventionists saw their chance for more power within a strengthened legislature and jumped at it. They made no effort to pressure the British into including their Secretary General on the Coussey Committee. (The Conventionists' later charge that Nkrumah betrayed them by forming another political party may be evaluated accordingly.) Nkrumah's exclusion from the Coussey Committee, however, had the opposite effect from that intended. Far from isolating him, it freed him to begin organizing his own political base. He was not a required participant in the constitutional negotiations and he had no obligations to the UGCC, although he retained his membership in the organization for several months more.

With an open political field, whom did Nkrumah seek to organize? Where did he seek to establish the class base of his movement? His terms of reference were not those of Marxist revolutionaries: he did not debate whether to go first to the peasantry or the organized working class, or puzzle over the relationship his party should have to the national bourgeoisie. In

---

12. Dennis Austin, *Politics in Ghana,* London, 1964, p. 80.

this period, he made no specific political approach to either the trade unionists, the unorganized agricultural workers, or the independent smallholders (Mao's "middle peasants"). Instead, he sought the support of the Gold Coast's "youngmen," forming the Committee on Youth Organization in August 1948. Who were the "youngmen"?

The youngmen were not necessarily young: the leaders—Nkrumah, Kojo Botsio, and K. A. Gbedemah—were 39, 36, and 33 respectively. The term was used to describe educated "commoners": storekeepers, petty traders, clerks, junior civil servants, and primary school teachers, all of whom were likely to be among the young generation. These youngmen, essentially a petty-bourgeois stratum, were engaged in conflict on three fronts: with the indirect-rule chiefs; with the colonial system; and finally with the wealthier commoner stratum—consisting of big cocoa brokers, lawyers, upper civil servants, and contractors —which was represented by the UGCC.

The youngmen clashed with the chiefs because they were no longer willing to obey laws, follow customs, or respect an authority which had become fossilized by changing economic circumstances and undermined morally by reliance on British support.[13] But as we shall see, only the petty traders, of all the strata within the petty bourgeoisie, were involved in direct *economic* conflict with the chiefs.

Since the early days of the cocoa industry, the chiefs, especially in Ashanti, had been able to assert control over tribal lands. The British authorities, constantly trying to create the basis for a "native" ruling class, also gave the chiefs trading monopolies. It was in this role that the chiefs were brought into conflict with the petty traders. They competed for access to capital and for trading concessions as well as for customers. The petty traders and big merchant chiefs were, however, also able to cooperate against their common enemy, the European

---

13. Reginald Saloway, Colonial Secretary in 1948, writes: "We had to make Chiefs who were liable to destoolment by their people into agents of an alien government. Such agents were powerless against the nationalist agitators who stirred up the militant young men among whom respect for traditional authority was already waning." "The New Gold Coast," *International Affairs,* October, 1955.

trading firms. And it was not the petty traders with whom the chiefs stood in sharpest contradiction. It was the landless agricultural laborers and sharecroppers who formed the Gold Coast's real oppressed class and who constituted the greatest potential threat to the colonial system.

The other strata of the petty bourgeoisie—teachers, clerks, independent artisans, et al—had no direct economic conflicts with the chiefs. They attacked only individual chiefs, and the basis of their attack was conservative: chiefs were criticised for violating "traditional" (pre-British) norms; chiefs were destooled for *abusing* their power, for flouting "customary" practices. The petty bourgeoisie attacked neither the legitimacy of the institution of chieftaincy nor the assumptions on which the politico-economic power of the chiefs was based.

The conflict between the petty traders and the wealthy UGCC supporters, including the big merchant chiefs, had an economic basis in competition for access to trading capital. But the main conflicts developed out of the wealthier commoner stratum's willingness to accommodate themselves to British political and economic power once token concessions had been granted. Dennis Austin describes how the conflicts between the two strata materialized in the small town of Bekwai in Ashanti:

> Relations between the youngmen and the [UGCC] Committee of Management grew more strained. . . . The more nationalist-minded youngmen in the Bekwai area looked on the members of the Committee of Management as "aristocrats" who were over-friendly with the District Commissioner and the local European manager of the United Africa Company. They were also suspicious of any alliance with those in authority.[14]

The youngmen's grievances against colonialism, like those expressed by petty bourgeois nationalists elsewhere in Africa, arose not so much out of the hardship and suffering they experienced as out of the contrast they perceived between their circumstances and those of the Europeans with whom they dealt. Amilcar Cabral cites himself as an example: "I was an agronomist working under a European who everybody knew was

---

14. Austin, *Politics in Ghana,* p. 100.

one of the biggest idiots in Guinea. I could have taught him his job with my eyes shut but he was the boss; this is something which counts a lot, this is the *confrontation* which really matters."[15]

Brought to this confrontation and fired with indignation, the young nationalist agronomist, whether in the Gold Coast or in "Portuguese" Guinea, has two choices: he can organize a political party which will win for himself and his petty bourgeois comrades particular redress for their particular grievances against the colonial system; or he can identify his particular injustice with the overall injustice of colonial society and organize to achieve total emancipation. This, however, requires a party not just of the petty bourgeoisie, but a party which includes all oppressed classes and strata within colonial society, one which makes the realization of the demands of the poorest and most oppressed strata of the working class the absolute moral imperative of the national independence movement.

Since the Second World War there have been numerous independence movements of the first type. When successful they have brought about a "partial political revolution." Movements of the second type have been rarer and have come to power in only two or three countries. In these latter countries the political revolution was not an end but a means to achieve universal human emancipation. Marx drew the distinction this way:

What is the basis of a partial, merely political revolution? Simply this: *a fraction of a civil society* emancipates itself and achieves a dominant position; a certain class undertakes, *from its particular situation,* a general emancipation of society. This class emancipates society as a whole, but only on condition that the whole of society is in the same situation as this class, for example, that it possesses or can acquire money or culture.[16]

After the partial, political revolution, the young agronomists become Ministers of Agriculture with Europeans as their subordinates. To bring about the second or "total" revolution, the

15. Cabral, *International Socialist Journal*, August 1964, p. 435.
16. Karl Marx, *Kritik des Hegelschen Staatsrechts,* tr. in *Karl Marx: Selected Writings,* edited by T. B. Bottomore, New York, 1964, p. 179.

agronomists first must become revolutionaries and guerrilla fighters.

Another characteristic of "total" revolution is that the class which forms the basis of the revolutionary movement must be one which has "radical chains" to break: the Cuban *campesino*, the Russian urban working class, the United States black ghetto-dweller. Marx says that it must be a class *in* but not *of* civil society:

> A sphere of society which has a universal character because its sufferings are universal, and which does not claim a particular redress because the wrong which is done to it is not a particular wrong but wrong in general. There must be formed a sphere of society which claims no traditional status but only human status, a sphere which is not opposed to particular consequences but is totally opposed to the assumptions of the . . . political system.[17]

The Gold Coast petty bourgeoisie was not such a class: it had no radical chains to break. To take just one example, it was not opposed to a society ruled by an economically privileged, all-powerful bureaucracy. It simply wanted that bureaucracy to be African. Consequently, the answer to the problem posed by bureaucracy was not democratic control—either now or in the future—but "Africanization."

In this respect Nkrumah was the perfect representative of the Gold Coast petty bourgeoisie. With admirable clarity he defined his position as one which opposed "particular consequences" but accepted the assumptions of the political system. We can get a vivid picture of the kind of political impact he tried to make during these early days of the movement from the report filed by a correspondent for the *Ashanti Pioneer* who covered Nkrumah's tour of the Northern Territories in March 1949. This is his account of a speech given in Tamale:

> In came Kwame Nkrumah dressed in rich and attractive NT [traditional] clothes and borne on the shoulders of six stalwart men wearing voluminous red turbans. The band—the Kumasi Rhythmic Brass Band—struck the high-life tune "Yenara yen asasi ni" (This is our own land). When Kwame was seated, it took some re-inforcements to keep the crowds back, while one robust Conventionist fanned him. . . .

---

17. *Ibid.,* p. 182.

[Finally Nkrumah speaks.] Mr. Chairman, chiefs, brothers and sisters, and friends. For me this is indeed a unique occasion. For me history is repeating itself today. The difference is that when I last came to you I was in chains.[18]

We have nothing to fear but fear itself. The time has come when the affairs of this country should be handed over to the chiefs and people of this country to manage or mismanage. . . .

This country is ours. This land is ours. It belongs to our chiefs and people. It does not belong to foreigners, but we don't say that all foreigners should pack up and go. They can stay as traders, and work with us not as masters and rulers. . . .

The age of politics of words is gone. This is the age of politics of action. We don't have guns. We don't have ammunition to fight anybody. We have a great spirit, a great national soul which is manifest in our unity.

If we get s.g. [self-government] we'll transform the Gold Coast into a paradise in ten years. Why should some people in the NTs go naked? I can find no reason for it. We can improve our native looms up here in the NTs in five years under a government of the people, by the people and for the people. . . .

Wherefore my advice is "Seek ye first the political kingdom, and all things will be added unto you.". . .[19]

The political kingdom Nkrumah speaks of here is the objective correlative of Marx's "partial political revolution." The "paradise" he holds out still maintains the traditional powers of the chiefs and the commercial powers of the British trading firms. Now, however, Ghanaians will wear pants while waiting in the political kingdom for "all things" to be added unto them. This was the vision. The agency was to be the Convention People's Party.

Storming the Political Kingdom

On June 12, 1949, Nkrumah founded the CPP in Accra. Sixty thousand people attended the ceremonies: the largest popular assembly in Gold Coast history. A year had passed since the British had created the Coussey Committee. The government had begun negotiating with what was ostensibly an embryonic native ruling class. But by this time their ne-

---

18. Nkrumah is referring to his arrest in March 1948, after the Christianborg riots. He had been detained in Tamale.
19. *Ashanti Pioneer,* March 5, 1949.

gotiating partners were merely African politicians with British titles but no Gold Coast constituencies. In 1949, Sir Gerald Creasy, after only a few months in the country, left the Gold Coast "for reasons of health." He was replaced by Sir Charles Arden-Clarke.

The new party was careful not to make itself appear to have broken completely with the past. It even kept the word "Convention" in the party title to emphasize its political lineage. How, then, did its leaders justify founding a new nationalist organization? Nkrumah tried to make it clear to those who remained in the UGCC that it was the leadership and not the rank and file which the new party opposed. The leaders of the UGCC were willing to fight only for "full self-government within the shortest possible time"; the CPP was organized to bring "self-government NOW." But even this distinction had less militant implications than might be expected. The reason why the CPP had to fight for "self-government NOW," according to Nkrumah, was because the Labor Party was now in power in Britain. "It would be more favorably disposed towards our demand. If the Conservatives were returned to power the following year, our struggle for independence might be suppressed."[20]

The operational differences between the CPP and the UGCC on the question of independence were actually narrow and turned on issues of low radical yield. These differences were not like those between Bolsheviks and Mensheviks (whether the revolution should be proletarian or bourgeois); or like those that divided the FLN from the Algerian Communist Party (whether to fight for independence or remain within the French "Community") Their differences were strikingly like those which separate the Congress of Racial Equality from the National Association for the Advancement of Colored People in the United States. The NAACP is wealthier, better established, and more solidly bourgeois. It aims at reforming certain aspects of a system whose assumptions it shares. It carries out its reformist attempts through the channels that the society provides: the ballot box, the court room, legislative lobbying, etc. The other group, while generally younger, more radical, and

---

20. Nkrumah, *Ghana*, p. 103.

less affluent, does not reject the assumptions of the society—although it sometimes questions them. Less affluent and less well-established, it is less able to utilize society's channels of reform: it attempts to use non-violence or direct action, exerting exogenous pressure on institutions it wishes to change or control. At a given point, after pressure from outside the system has been successful, it is possible for the less privileged reformist group to be allowed to work inside the system.

This was the situation in which the CPP found itself in 1949. To achieve its objectives, it had only to steer a course between two political extremes. The right extreme was conveniently defined by the position of the UGCC, which had tied itself to whatever concessions the Coussey Committee was willing to grant. Clearly, any position less militant than this would cost the CPP popular support and possibly cause a split.

The left extreme was any course which offered opposition not just to British rule, but to colonial society as a whole. This "adventurist" course could be avoided by frequent demonstrations of obeisance to the colonial "rules of the game," which were generally defined negatively: no preaching of class warfare, no resort to armed collective defense, no suggestion of independence outside the Commonwealth/Sterling area.

The programmatic reflection of the CPP's willingness to abide by these "rules of the game" can be seen in its first six-point manifesto:

(1) To fight relentlessly by all constitutional means for the achievement of full "self-government NOW" for the chiefs and people of the Gold Coast.

(2) To serve as the vigorous conscious political vanguard for removing all forms of oppression and for the establishment of a democratic government.

(3) To secure and maintain the complete unity of the chiefs and people of the Colony, Ashanti, Northern Territories and the Trans-Volta.

(4) To work in the interest of the trade union movement in the country for better conditions of employment.

(5) To work for a proper reconstruction of a better Gold Coast in which the people shall have the right to live and govern themselves as a free people.

(6) To assist and facilitate in any way possible the realization of a united and self-governing West Africa.[21]

Could the Labor government regard this program with anything less than unqualified approbation? As long as the CPP's "relentless fight" was carried out by "constitutional means" the party was still playing according to the rules; as long as the vanguard aimed only at such moderate and un-qualified goals as "democracy," "unity," and "a better Gold Coast"; as long as its perspective for the working class was no wider than "better conditions of employment," the CPP would no doubt become a useful partner in the Commonwealth/Sterling area.

The publication of the Coussey Commission's recommenda-tions in October, 1949, tested the party's ability to adhere to its middle course. The Report proposed a form of semi-responsible government: an executive council of three *ex-officio* and eight representative ministers and a nationally elected assembly. The assembly finally decided upon was a unicameral legislature, two thirds elected by popular franchise and one third elected by the territorial councils of chiefs. In addition, the Governor re-tained his "reserve powers."[22]

The CPP dilemma was this: the Report provided for a government which was far from sovereign. Should the party continue to abide by the colonial rules of the game—by entering the elections—or should it be guided by its program and fight relentlessly for "self-government NOW"? Characteristically, Nkrumah tried to split the difference. He attacked the Report as a "Trojan gift horse" and as "bogus and fraudulent," and spoke of the need for "positive action."[23] But at the same time,

---

21. *Ibid.,* p. 101.

22. The UGCC members opposed both the retention of reserve powers and the presence of ex officio members on the Executive. Their opposition expressed itself, not in resignation from the Committee, but in a minority report.

23. Nkrumah's definition of positive action was "the adoption of all legitimate and constitutional means by which we could attack the forces of imperialism in the country. The weapons were legitimate political agitation, newspaper and educational campaigns, and, as a last resort, the constitutional application of strikes, boycotts, and non-cooperation based on the principle of absolute non-violence as used by Gandhi." *Ghana,* pp. 111-112. Nkrumah's is a conservative interpretation of Gandhi, who never stipulated that non-violence must be "constitutional."

he entered into negotiations to liberalize the Constitution with Arden-Clarke and Reginald Saloway, the Colonial Secretary.

Just when it seemed as if an orderly process of colonial devolution would be worked out after all, the strongly anticolonial feelings of the Ghanaian people upset everything. Nkrumah himself was partially responsible for the militant temper of the masses. "Get ready, people of the Gold Coast," he told a huge rally in Accra on December 15, "the era of positive action draws nigh."[24] Nkrumah gave the government two weeks to accept the CPP demands. Everything was set for a confrontation. The Trade Union Congress began to prepare for a general strike; the people in cities readied themselves for a boycott of European stores.

Nkrumah, however, tried to postpone the conflict. Numerous meetings took place between Nkrumah, Arden-Clarke, and Saloway. The *Evening News*, the CPP newspaper, twice announced that positive action would be postponed. And once Nkrumah called it off altogether. Saloway's version is this: "Nkrumah publicly called off 'positive action' and tried hard to get the Trade Union Congress to call off the general strike, but the TUC no longer had any control over the wild men. [Moreover] Dr. Danquah taunted Nkrumah with having sold himself to the Colonial Secretary and thus infuriated the rank and file of the CPP who forced Nkrumah to retract."[25] According to Arden-Clarke's version:

The party leaders had been officially informed and were well aware that they had a perfectly constitutional way of achieving power and gaining their objective if their candidates at the forthcoming election were returned. I have good reason to believe that some at least of the party leaders would have preferred not to resort to "positive action" but to await the results of the general election, the outcome of which they were fairly confident. But they found themselves enmeshed in the coils of their own propaganda. The tail wagged the dog.[26]

Whether the CPP leaders did or did not want a positive action campaign became irrelevant on the 6th of January when

24. *Evening News* (Accra), December 16, 1949.
25. Saloway, *International Affairs*, October, 1955, p. 47.
26. Charles Arden-Clarke, "Eight Years in the Gold Coast," *African Affairs*, January 1958.

the TUC forced the issue by calling the general strike. Now the
CPP was left with a simpler choice: either side with the British
government (which warned that "the so-called 'general strike'
is illegal") or back the workers. After two days of negotiations
and conferences, Nkrumah announced his support for the
general strike. He agreed to begin positive action on January 8.
It would "take the form of a simple and fundamentally spiritual
exercise."[27]

The strike came off badly. Leadership was lacking and
there was little sense of working-class solidarity. The party newspaper was closed down, scabs were successfully introduced, and
"the extensive use of a new force of mobile police limited unrest
in the main towns to sporadic outbursts of violence."[28] During
the strike, Nkrumah appeared to one British correspondent as
"the most worried man in the Gold Coast." Mr. Nkrumah, he
wrote, "has been sincere in not wanting violence or a 'show-
down.' He seems not to have realized that his followers take
quite literally everything he says."[29] The *Times* also portrayed
Nkrumah as the unwilling victim of popular forces gone out of
control: "Against the better interests of his party and the
Gold Coast, Mr. Nkrumah allowed himself to be drawn into the
launching of a civil disobedience campaign accompanied by a
general strike."[30]

On the 21st of January, the government felt confident
enough of its command of the situation to arrest all important
TUC and CPP leaders. Charges ranged from sedition to
"coercing" the government and prompting an illegal strike. The
trials themselves produced no speeches in the manner of "History
Will Absolve Me." The spirit of courageous defiance was clearly
absent. Dzenkle Dzewu, a member of the CPP Central Committee, denied knowing what "positive action" was. Thomas
Hutton-Mills, one of the few lawyers in the party, admitted
that he knew what positive action was, but claimed that when
positive action was declared on January 8th he was "taken
aback." Hutton-Mills maintained that he disliked positive action

---

27. *Ashanti Pioneer,* January 7, 1950.
28. Austin, *Politics in Ghana,* p. 89.
29. *West Africa,* January 14. 1950.
30. *The Times* (London), January 23, 1950.

and made speeches against it. (He was eventually given the lightest sentence.) The CPP treasurer went even further in his denials. He claimed that he was not a member of the CPP and denied point blank that he had ever passed money into the bank on behalf of the CPP.

Only Nkrumah admitted having anything to do with the positive action campaign. Against the charge of promoting an illegal strike, however, Nkrumah defended himself vigorously. He denied having called on anybody to strike: he maintained that he even tried to stop the strike when he heard of it. Furthermore, Nkrumah said that he did not know of any section of the people which had struck because of the CPP. To the charge of "coercing" the government, Nkrumah replied that he had just called off the positive action campaign the day he was arrested.

This was undoubtedly the nadir of the Gold Coast independence movement. Reporters commented on the lack of nationalist fervor at the trials; the crowds themselves began to grow smaller; and in the working-class districts of Sekondi-Takoradi and the adjoining mining areas, there was considerable bitterness over the failure of the strike and the positive action campaign. Nkrumah was sentenced to three one-year terms to be served concurrently. Others were given sentences ranging down to Hutton-Mills' four months. By giving Nkrumah three one-year terms, however, the government had kept him legally eligible to run for office. As Nkrumah later remarked: "Few people realized that by our law, anyone who is convicted to a term of imprisonment not exceeding one year, is entitled to be registered on the electoral roll."[31]

With Nkrumah and the other party leaders in a British jail, the Gold Coast government was in an even more precarious position than with them out of jail. Support began to gather again for the CPP. The main organizers during this period were Gbedemah—who had been just released from jail when Nkrumah went in—and Mrs. Olabisi Renner, a lawyer whose husband was serving his sentence with the other trade unionists and party leaders.

---

31. Nkrumah, *Ghana,* p. 133.

Two months after the trial, municipal elections were held in Accra. Only the CPP organizers obtained complete voters lists and saw to it that their supporters got to the polls. The combination of efficient organization and live martyrs produced a notable victory: the CPP won every seat on the council, defeating the incumbent UGCC members by large margins. It was obvious that the CPP was the most powerful political force in the country. Arden-Clarke summarizes the position of his government in relation to the CPP at this time:

Nkrumah and his party had the mass of the people behind them and there was no other party with appreciable public support to which one could turn. Without Nkrumah, the Constitution would be stillborn and if nothing came of all the hopes, aspirations and concrete proposals for a greater measure of self-government, there would no longer be any faith in the good intentions of the British Government and the Gold Coast would be plunged into disorders, violence and bloodshed.[32]

From these premises only one conclusion could emerge: Nkrumah must be brought into the government. Arden-Clarke therefore allowed Nkrumah to run for office while in prison. The prison officials helped process Nkrumah's registration papers and enabled him to pay his election deposit. "My forms," Nkrumah recalls, "were completed and submitted to the authorities a few minutes before registration period closed and the campaign committee got to work on my behalf."[33] Under the election slogan, "Vote wisely and God will save Ghana from the Imperialists," the campaign committee began the tasks of electoral politics: fund raising, party caucuses, and vote drives, all of which have been well described by Dennis Austin.[34]

The 1951 manifesto, entitled "Towards the Goal," shows the CPP's mild reformist objectives:

(1) Constitutional: The Coussey Committee let the country down by prolonging white imperialism. The CPP will fight for self-government NOW.

---

32. Arden-Clarke, *African Affairs,* January, 1958. Cited in Austin, *Politics in Ghana,* p. 150.

33. Nkrumah, *Ghana,* p. 133.

34. Austin, *Politics in Ghana,* pp. 103-152.

(2) Political: An upper house of the Legislature, known as the Senate, shall be created for the Chiefs. Universal suffrage at the age of 21. Direct elections with no property or residential qualifications for candidates.

(3) Economic: A five year Economic Plan. . . .
   (i) Immediate materialization of the Volta hydroelectric scheme.
   (ii) Railway lines to be doubled and extended.
   (iii) Roads to be modernized and extended.
   (iv) Canals to join rivers.
   (v) Progressive mechanization of agriculture.
   (vi) Special attention will be given to the swollen shoot disease; farmers will be given control of the Cocoa Industry Board funds. . . .
   (ix) Industrialization will be carried out with all energy.

(4) Social: Education
   (i) A unified system of free compulsory elementary, secondary, and technical education up to 16 years of age.
   (ii) The University College to be brought up to University status.
   (iii) A planned campaign to abolish illiteracy.

(5) Family Assistance
   (i) A free national health service.
   (ii) A high standard housing programme. . . .
   (iii) A piped-water supply in all parts of the country. . . .
   (iv) A national insurance scheme.[35]

There was certainly nothing about these goals that could give offense to anyone. The economic platform of the manifesto, in fact, reflected the main provisions of Governor Arden-Clarke's "Ten-Year Plan" of 1951. Who could object to modern roads, or canals that join rivers, or mechanized agriculture? (And what political party would be *for* swollen shoot?) In contrast, the program failed even to mention agricultural workers or trade unions.

The trade unions began to play a smaller and smaller role in CPP activities. Militants within the TUC were divided on what relationship should be maintained with the CPP: should they continue to work within the CPP or should they form a separate party? Pobee Biney and Anthony Woode both ran

35. *Ibid.,* p. 130.

successfully under the CPP label. Within the Miners' Union, however, there were attempts to organize a "Labor Party," but nothing came of them.

How did the Ghanaian people as a whole react to the CPP programs for gradual reform? To what extent were they politically stimulated by "independence NOW"—which obviously meant later? On the basis of the 1951 election returns, two attitudes are reflected. The first is that the CPP was much more popular than its main opposition, the UGCC businessmen. Against the UGCC, the CPP won 34 out of 38 popularly contested seats, and its majority in some urban areas reached over ninety percent.

The second attitude shown by the 1951 elections is indifference on the part of the majority of the Ghanaian people to the CPP and its program. Despite intensive efforts by the British colonial administration to obtain a large number of registered votes, *less than a majority* of the adult population took the trouble to register. (See Table 1 below.) And when it came time to cast ballots in the municipalities, the major locus of CPP strength, the turnout was again less than a majority—47.2 percent of registered voters.[36] In comparison with other West African elections—e.g. Western Nigeria in 1956, Senegal in 1957, and especially Guinea in 1958—this is a very low figure.[37]

Table I
Number of Registered Voters, 1951[38]

Area	Estimated population	Eligible electorate	Registered Number	Per cent
Colony (incl. So. Togo)	2,153,310	1,095,190	350,525	32.0
Ashanti	784,210	398,590	220,658	55.4
Municipalities	290,230	141,480	90,275	64.1
TOTAL	3,227,750	1,635,260	661,458	40.5

36. As elections in rural areas were indirect, it is impossible to know what the turnout was. However, the registration figures show that city residents were much more interested in the election.

37. See Kenneth Robinson and W. J. M. Mackenzie, *Five African Elections,* Oxford, 1960, and Ruth Schachter-Morgenthau, *Political Parties in French-Speaking West Africa,* Oxford, 1964, for information on these elections.

38. Austin, *Politics in Ghana,* p. 113.

The mode of expression of Gold Coast nationalism was now completely altered—spontaneous mass demonstrations were replaced by Western-style elections and Western-style apathy. In the space of three years, the Gold Coast had reverted back to the status of a model colony. The Christianborg uprising had at first been commemorated as the beginning of resistance to British colonialism; now it symbolized a tragic communications breakdown which finally forced the British to recognize the need for constitutional reform.

After the 1951 election, the CPP turned to what it felt was the way to win independence for the Gold Coast—full cooperation with the colonial government in order to prove that the country was "ready" for self-government. The accommodation reached was so thorough-going that during the next six years the CPP never felt it necessary to leave the government.

All this had repercussions on independence movements throughout Africa, especially in British West Africa. Arden-Clarke's "act-of-grace" in freeing Nkrumah from prison began to take on the same significance for African nationalists that Dienbienphu would soon gain for Asian nationalists—both marked the end of European colonial power and indicated a specific means for achieving power.

3

KING COCOA

There was no alternative government to the CPP, none of whom had any training in public affairs. We had to build anew with what was then a crowd of agitators as our material.
     —Reginald Saloway, Colonial Secretary

On February 10, 1951, the Gold Coast government announced the electoral victory of the Convention People's Party. On the 12th Nkrumah was released from Fort James prison. At nine o'clock the next morning, he was invited to meet Arden-Clarke at the Governor's residence. Arden-Clarke describes the occasion:

That meeting was redolent of mutual suspicion and mistrust. We were like two dogs for the first time, sniffing around each other with hackles half raised, trying to decide whether to bite or wag our tails. Soon afterwards, Nkrumah came to see me alone and we were able to get to know each other. This time the hackles were down, and before the end the tails were wagging. . . . That was the beginning of a close, friendly, and, if I may say so, not unfruitful partnership.[1]

At this first press conference after release from prison, Nkrumah, now the "Leader of Government Business," announced that he was prepared to give the Coussey Constitution a chance to work, even though it had its "bogus" aspects. Nkrumah assured his listeners that he had no intention of nationalizing any Gold Coast industry. He added: "I would like to make it absolutely clear that I am a friend of Britain. . . . I want for the Gold Coast Dominion status within the British Commonwealth.

---

1. Sir Charles Arden-Clarke, "Eight Years of Transition in Ghana," *African Affairs*, January, 1958, p. 34.

I am no Communist and never have been, and I stand for no discrimination against any race or individual."[2]

The other newly elected party members prepared for their new roles as parliamentarians. King George V Memorial Hall in Accra was hastily transformed into a miniature House of Commons: during the three weeks between August 14 and September 6, the interiors were remodeled to resemble as closely as possible the Commons Chamber in London.[3]

Nkrumah called the post-election period, up to the development of the first serious internal opposition in 1954, the period of "tactical action." Tactical action was the method whereby the party leaders worked through the ordinary channels of British colonial government to bring about liberation from colonial rule. According to the imperatives of tactical action, Nkrumah would be drawn into what would *appear* to be collaboration with the British. No one, however, should have been fooled by appearances: "Kwame Nkrumah now sitting with the imperialists in power is forever vigilant. He knows he is there by the will of the people and his work is to see their welfare [sic]."[4]

While the CPP imagined themselves getting the better of the British through tactical action, the British prided themselves on their own subtleties. Arden-Clarke describes how he dealt with his CPP "partners":

> We learnt for example, how effective the device of changing names could be. It is, I suppose, true that "a rose by any other name would smell as sweet," but we learnt that if we changed the name of Leader of Government Business to Prime Minister and Executive Council to Cabinet, without in any way altering their functions and powers, or the name of Chief Commissioner to Regional Officer, or District Commissioner to Government Agent, they all seemed to smell much sweeter in the public nose. That device certainly helped us to get over some difficult periods.[5]

Tactical action and British nominalism enabled the "not unfruitful partnership" to continue. Meanwhile, the left-wing trade union agitators, such as Turkson Ocran, general-secretary

---

2. *West Africa,* February 17, 1951.
3. *West Africa,* September 15, 1951.
4. *Freedom,* CPP monthly, December 1952, no. 1.
5. Arden-Clarke, "Eight Years of Transition in Ghana," p. 36.

of the TUC, were expelled from the CPP for alleged communist connections. And the remaining agitators from the city squares and market places were remolded into practitioners of the Westminster parliamentary system.

Inside the scale-modeled replica of Westminster, however, there was little actual power to exercise. The "mother" country still controlled the police and army; the Colonial Governor retained his "reserve powers"; British bureaucrats held most of the senior positions in the civil service; British stockholders owned the gold mines; over 90 percent of the import-export trade was controlled by 13 foreign trading companies ("the firms"); the yearly budgets were prepared back in London by the Colonial Office.

Yet the most obvious instrument of foreign economic control—the one which had the most long-lasting and disruptive effects on the Ghanaian economy—was a government agency on which the CPP dutifully served. This was the Cocoa Marketing Board. But in order to understand and evaluate the effects of CMB policies on Ghana, it is first necessary to know something about who the Ghanaian cocoa producers are.

Agricultural Classes and Strata

The owners of Ghanaian cocoa farms are Ghanaian. How did this anomaly occur? Not because of the widely held British assumption that the plantation economy "is necessarily incompatible with the moral obligations to weaker peoples on which Native policy is professedly based."[6] Only the morality of the ledger sheet had brought the British to the conclusion that "they would be wiser to avoid competing with the Native cultivators." The United Africa Company tried unsuccessfully for 15 years to produce cocoa on a competitive basis with Ghanaian cocoa farmers.[7]

Unable to compete on the land with the African producers, the British plantation owners retired to the coastal areas. Africans not only cleared, planted, and plucked the cocoa; they also

6. W. K. Hancock, *Survey of British Commonwealth Affairs*, Vol. II, Part 2, p. 174.
7. *Ibid.*, p. 188.

organized the marketing system. The British trader, who, it is usually assumed, "taught the natives" the elementary facts of economic life, came in contact with the cocoa only after it had been produced, marketed, and transported. "He merely sat at (or near) the port receiving the produce and had no more knowledge than any other outsider as to how production was organized."[8]

Another widespread myth about Ghanaian cocoa production is that cocoa is farmed by independent smallholders. Polly Hill calls this "the myth of the peasant farmer, who, though unfamiliar with the cash economy, nonetheless succeeded in the space of twenty years in transforming the economy of Ghana."[9] The mythology specifies that this peasant farmer has only a small amount of land—one or two acres—and does all his work himself. But while the heterogeneity of the social organization of cocoa farming in Ghana almost defies generalization, it is clear that in both Ashanti and Southern Ghana the cocoa landowner is an employer of labor. Polly Hill's field investigations throughout Ghana showed that the proportion of independent smallholders (those who perform all their own labor) is probably less than 20 percent of the total.

That section of the owning class which is distinguished by its ability to employ labor can itself be broken down into two strata: the capitalist farmers who have been able to accumulate enough capital to set themselves up as creditors; and the small farmers who have fallen into debt and pledged their land.

The agricultural working class contains several strata which can be distinguished by the way they are remunerated. The so-called *abusa* gets one third of the value of the cocoa he plucks; other strata are paid on a daily or yearly basis. A survey carried out in 1959 established that for every landowner, six to eight caretakers and laborers were employed.[10]

The time-rate laborers appear to be the most oppressed strata of the agricultural working class. They have no tools, no

8. Polly Hill, *The Migrant Cocoa Farmers of Southern Ghana*, Cambridge, 1963, p. 173.

9. *Ibid.*, p. 11.

10. Tony Killick, "Cocoa," in *A Study of Contemporary Ghana*, Vol. I, ed. by Walter Birmingham, I. Neustadt, E. N. Omaboe; London, 1966, p. 239.

work clothes, and do not bring their wives and children to live with them on the cocoa farms. All strata of the agricultural working class are, however, relatively poorly paid, uneducated, and isolated from political life.

While this attempt to categorize the agricultural classes may do some violence to the complexity of actual land relations, consider the violence done by those analysts who have written about Nkrumah's dealings with "the farmers." An undifferentiated mass of "farmers" exists only in the pages of their books and articles. They write as if the day laborer who often owns not even the shirt he wears, and a rich capitalist farmer chief had identical economic interests.

The CPP politicians also like to speak in terms of "the farmers." As Hill points out, they "assume that all Ghanaian cocoa-farmers are wealthy."[11] As for the agricultural working class, it figured in the plans and programs of the party as did the helots in the Aristotelian *polis*. They were the obscene basis (about which polite discourse forbids discussion) on whose labor the whole superstructure of the state was built.

The Cocoa Marketing Board

In 1948 Britain's Labor government established the Cocoa Marketing Board as the Gold Coast's sole buyer, grader, seller, and exporter of cocoa. The ostensible purpose was to insulate the Ghana cocoa "farmer" from the uncertainties of the world cocoa market. The CMB would buy all domestically produced cocoa at a relatively stable price and resell it on the world market at an inevitably fluctuating price. By setting the domestic price lower than the world price, a reserve fund could be built up which would serve a number of important ends: it would provide savings which could be used to develop the country's economy; it would drain off excess purchasing power and thus prevent inflation; and it would provide a source from which the cocoa producer's income could be maintained in case of a collapse of world prices.

Table 2, giving prices paid to producers and export prices

---

11. Hill, *Migrant Cocoa Farmers*, p. 19.

from 1947 to 1961, shows that at least part of the theory behind the CMB was conscientiously put into practice. Throughout the entire decade of the 1950's the price paid to producers fluctuated within narrow limits (from a minimum of £131 to a maximum of £149 per ton), while the export price was consistently higher and usually very much higher (for the whole period 1947 to 1961, the producer price averaged only 54.7 percent of the export price). If we keep in mind that cocoa is far and away the most important export of Ghana, accounting for between half and three quarters of total exports, it is immediately apparent that during these crucially important formative years of Ghana's history, a very large part of the country's economic surplus was being collected and centralized by one institution, the Cocoa Marketing Board. And if we also keep

Table 2
Cocoa Producer Prices and Export Prices
1947-48 to 1960-61[12]

Crop year	Pounds per ton Producer price	Average export price	Producer price as percent of export price
1947-48	75	201	37.3
1948-49	121	137	88.3
1949-50	84	178	47.2
1950-51	131	269	48.7
1951-52	149	245	60.8
1952-53	131	231	56.7
1953-54	134	358	37.4
1954-55	134	353	38.0
1955-56	149	222	67.1
1956-57	149	189	78.8
1957-58	134	304	44.1
1958-59	134	280	48.0
1959-60	112	226	49.6
1960-61	112	175	64.0

in mind that the extent and direction of a country's development depend on how it uses its surplus, we can appreciate the importance of the question: *What did the Cocoa Marketing Board do with the hundreds of millions of pounds it accumulated*

12. Tony Killick, "The Economics of Cocoa," in *A Study of Contemporary Ghana,* p. 369.

*by selling cocoa on the world market at nearly twice the price
it paid to the African cocoa producer?*

The War, the Pound, and the Empire

To answer this question it is necessary to place the Gold
Coast, and later Ghana, in its proper historical and international
setting.

To finance her enormous import requirements during the
Second World War at a time when her capacity to export was
drastically curtailed, Great Britain was obliged to borrow heavily
abroad. Some of this debt was of course in foreign currencies
—and much more would have been if it hadn't been for Lend
Lease—but a very large part took the form of so-called blocked
sterling balances held by Britain's colonies and semi-colonies.
What happened was that these dependent countries sent their
goods to the United Kingdom in exchange for pounds sterling
which for the time being they were unable to spend. The total
of Britain's sterling liabilities increased in this way from under
£500 million before the war to over £3,000 million after the
war. Of this increase India (including what later became Pakistan) contributed £1,138, and Egypt and the Sudan contributed
£402 million.[13] These sterling balances represented a form of
forced saving for their owners and were far in excess of the
various countries' needs for monetary reserves. So as the war
drew to an end, "the voices of holders demanding payment
were becoming louder."[14]

The British tried to get countries like India and Egypt to
write off their balances as contributions to the war effort but for
obvious reasons were turned down. The balances therefore
remained as a source of constant pressure on the pound. Nor in
the conditions of the postwar world were they the only danger
to the pound. Britain needed imports of all kinds to make good
the losses and damage of war; export capacity was slow to
recover; military requirements, occasioned by unrest in the
empire and the incipient Cold War, continued at a high level.

---

13. Phillip W. Bell, *The Sterling Area in the Post-War World*, Oxford,
1958, p. 261.
14. *Ibid.*, p. 260.

The inevitable result of all these pressures and needs was a series of postwar financial and balance-of-payments crises which threatened Britain with international bankruptcy and reduction to the status of a second or third class power. It was in these circumstances that two things happened. First, the United States organized a huge rescue operation, culminating in the Marshall Plan, which poured nearly $7 billion of aid into the United Kingdom in the decade following the war. And second, the British government itself (under the control of the Labor Party, be it noted) took unprecedented steps to force its remaining colonies to transfer their surpluses to London to support the pound. The heart and core of this new imperial strategy was the establishment of a network of marketing boards, of which the Cocoa Marketing Board in the Gold Coast was just one.

Marketing boards were established in Malaya and East Africa as well as in West Africa. In West Africa there was a marketing board for every commodity from peanuts to mahogany. In Nigeria four marketing boards controlled 69 percent by value of all exports and 78 percent of all non-mineral imports.[15] In the Gold Coast the corresponding percentages were 69 percent and 90 percent. In Sierra Leone and Gambia the percentages were even higher. In these four colonies the marketing boards controlled practically 100 percent of all agricultural exports produced by Africans, including even the most insignificant commodities. In Nigeria, for example, the Groundnut (peanut) Marketing Board even controlled sunflower seeds, which were not listed on trade returns.[16]

By establishing the marketing boards throughout its colonies, Great Britain, once the free trade center of the world, carried out what was perhaps the most thorough-going attempt to control the marketplace since the Diocletian Code. From Accra to Mombasa and across the Indian Ocean to Kuala Lumpur, the marketing boards all operated in the same way. First, buying and selling monopolies were established; then producer

---

15. Minerals of course were owned by foreigners, generally the British themselves. And one can imagine the kind of reception the shareholder of a British owned gold mine would give to a proposal to give his company a percentage of the world price for its gold ore and withhold the remainder (so as to stabilize their income, prevent inflation, etc.).

16. P. T. Bauer, *West African Trade,* London, 1963, p. 276.

prices were set below the world market price; then the boards began to accumulate the difference.

What did the marketing boards do with the money? A large part of it, they simply sent off to London where it was held as sterling balances.[17] These sterling balances were generally invested in long-term British government securities. *In other words, the colonies were lending money to Great Britain.* Moreover, the interest rate on these securities was extremely low: 0.5 percent before 1950; from 2 to 4 percent after 1952.[18] Yet during the period from June 30, 1945, to June 30, 1956, sterling balances accumulated by the colonies showed a continual upward trend.

Table 3[19]
Colonial Sterling Balances
(Millions of Pounds)

June 30 1945	Dec. 31 1950	June 30 1951	June 30 1954	June 30 1956
670	735	908	1,183	1,301

Colonial Dollar and Capital Exports

During this postwar period the British Labor Party tried to distinguish itself from previous regimes by asserting that its colonial policy was based on "broader conceptions of development and welfare and a recognition that British funds must 'prime the pump.' "[20] But in reality it was the funds of the colonial peoples which were "priming the pump" of postwar British economic recovery. As one British financial expert pointed out in 1953, "the investment of £1,000 million in Britain does not accord well with commonly held ideas on the desirable direction of capital flow between countries at different levels of economic development."[21]

Ghana's contribution to the flow of colonial capital to-

17. The terms "sterling balance" and "sterling liability" are used interchangeably.

18. Phillip W. Bell, *The Sterling Area in the Post-War World*, p. 271.

19. W. M. Scammell, *International Monetary Policy*, New York, 1961, p. 262.

20. Cmd. 7433, *The Colonial Empire* (1947-1948), p. 2.

21. A. D. Hazelwood, "Colonial External Finance Since the War," *Review of Economic Studies*, December 1953, p. 49.

wards Britain, together with the role of the CMB in increasing it, are indicated by Table 4. Not only did Britain's colonies

Table 4
The Cocoa Marketing Board and Ghanaian Reserves[22]
(Millions of Pounds)

Year	Total CMB proceeds	Paid to cocoa producers	Total Ghanaian reserves
1948	41.5	15.4	n.a.
1949	37.5	21.2	n.a.
1950	45.1	21.2	113.3
1951	70.3	34.2	137.2
1952	51.6	31.4	145.1
1953	57.1	32.5	160.1
1954	74.7	28.0	197.4
1955	77.5	29.5	208.2
1956	52.3	35.0	189.8
1957	50.7	39.9	171.4

provide her with sterling, however; they also supplied the "mother" country with dollars which were in extremely short supply during the early postwar period. Britain needed dollars to import United States capital goods to rebuild her shattered industrial plant.[23] Much is made of the sacrifices made by British consumers during the period when the Labor Party reestablished British capitalism. Yet to a large extent it was the Asian and African peasant who played the decisive role and experienced the real "austerity."

Ghana's role in providing Britain with capital and specifically with dollars, was larger than that of any other colony with the exception of Malaya. As Arthur Creech Jones, former Colonial Secretary, remarked: "I think we should be conscious of the very considerable contribution which the Gold Coast has made to the Sterling Area."[24]

---

22. Adapted from Tony Killick, "The Economics of Cocoa," in *A Study of Contemporary Ghana,* pp. 360, 367.

23. After 1958, when sterling became freely convertible into dollars, this aspect of the Anglo-Ghanaian financial relationship disappeared. Similarly, after the 1957 sterling crisis which the British were able to overcome only by relying on United States loans, confidence in the British pound increased—at least for a while. The necessity for the colonies and other members of the sterling area to hold increasing amounts of sterling balances diminished accordingly.

24. *Daily Graphic* (Accra), December 20, 1955.

Ghana was able to make such a substantial "contribution" to the Sterling Area because she sold large amounts of cocoa to the United States. The United States of course paid in dollars, a percentage of which were then allocated to Ghana. Table 5 shows how much Ghana was able to retain of her dollar earnings during the pre-independence period of CPP rule.

Table 5
Ghanaian Dollar Allocations, 1951-1954[25]

Year	Value of Ghanaian exports to the Dollar Area (£)	Percent of dollar earnings allocated to Ghana
1951	30,047,000	17
1952	25,539,000	18
1953	25,407,000	21
1954	20,009,000	16

The dollar contribution that a member of the Sterling Area made was directly proportional to its weakness. Countries like Ghana turned over more than 80 percent; the powerful capitalist countries claimed whatever they wanted for themselves. As Sir Dennis Robertson explained, the disadvantages suffered by African members of the Sterling Area meant more than simply being unable to import goods costing dollars:

It meant that each country as a *country* agreed to hand over its surplus dollar earnings to Mother in exchange for sterling, and to go to Mother when it wanted extra dollars to spend. Naturally the degree of confidence with which it exercised or presented claims on the dollar pool depended partly on its political status: the little black children who were often the best earners could be smacked on the head if they showed too great a propensity to spend dollars, while the grown-up white daughters, who were often pretty extravagant, could only be quietly reasoned with.[26]

The British had a clear interest in the continuation of these CMB policies following the CPP's rise to power in 1951. Had Nkrumah broken the CMB's marketing monopoly and adjusted the domestic cocoa price to the world level, or used CMB profits within the Gold Coast, the British economy would have been seriously affected. But Nkrumah and the CPP did not choose

25. Source: Gold Coast Legislative Assembly, *Debates,* August 9, 1955.
26. *Britain in the World Economy,* London, 1954, p. 39.

to use their power as members of the CMB to strike out in directions that would have led to a confrontation with British power. The CMB under CPP control continued to levy what were in effect huge export taxes, send cocoa profits to Great Britain, and thus help Britain maintain the pound while renouncing, or at best postponing, attempts to start Ghana in the direction of economic independence and development.

The Cocoa Marketing Board and the policies it pursued both before and after the CPP acquired representation on it, go far to explain what appears to be a strange paradox of Ghanaian development. In a country as productive as Ghana, with Africans growing hundreds of millions of dollars worth of cocoa annually on African-owned soil, one would naturally expect the emergence of a powerful class of African capitalists. We can now see that owing to the channeling of the profits of African cocoa production via the CMB to the "mother" country, growth of the Ghanaian capitalist class was stunted. There were some wealthy men like George Grant in timber and the Ocansey family, which had made a fortune from moving pictures. But a class of African businessmen, supplied with African capital, producing commodities for domestic consumption or for export, did not exist.

Instead what did develop in Ghana was a stratum of small businessmen, small contractors, wholesalers, capitalist farmers, cocoa brokers, etc., *who wanted to become* full-fledged African capitalists. At the same time, there had arisen the large petty bourgeois stratum composed of the elementary school graduates. It was this latter stratum which was able to step into the power vacuum caused by the absence of a true African capitalist class.

The "Atomic Bomb"

It would be a mistake to think of the CPP leaders who were the representatives and spokesmen for this petty bourgeois stratum as simply agents of the British: they were never stooges like the "direct-rule" chiefs of French West Africa. The CPP had its basis of support among the youngmen, and within certain limits prescribed by their relation to British power, they tried to advance the interests of their constituents. The primary instrument through which the CPP sought to secure its political base without infringing on British financial prerogatives was the Cocoa Purchasing Company, founded in 1952 as a subsidiary of the CMB. But while the CPC's activities strengthened the CPP's base among both debtor and creditor farmers of southern Ghana, they alienated the native cocoa brokers and the capitalist farmers of Ashanti. Thus the policies of the CPP continued the process of fission within the nationalist movement that had begun at the time of the Coussey Committee.

When the Cocoa Purchasing Company was organized in 1952, there was no question that the CPP controlled it. As Krobo Edusei explained to members of the Legislative Assembly:

The CPC is the product of a master brain, Dr. Kwame Nkrumah, and it is the atomic bomb of the Convention People's Party. As honourable members are aware, the Prime Minister in his statements to the CPP told his party members that organization decided everything and the CPC is part of the organization of the Convention People's Party.[27]

The purpose of the CPC, according to George Padmore, who now served as official advisor to the Prime Minister, was to "assist the Marketing Board to buy cocoa directly from the farmers instead of through the middleman brokers." According to Padmore, the CPC represented "the highest percentage of Africanization." He said that as a result of the formation of the CPC, the buying monopoly once held by the big trading firms had been smashed.[28]

Since the cocoa middlemen, or brokers, were themselves Africans, and since the big trading firms were in no way excluded from their positions as licensed brokers of the CMB, the Cocoa Purchasing Company cannot truly be said to have represented "the highest percentage of Africanization." What the CPC did represent—as the evidence before the Jibowu Commission, later formed to investigate its activities, showed—was an attempt by CPP leaders to seek the greatest financial self-aggrandizement possible.[29]

---

27. Gold Coast Legislative Assembly, *Debates,* March 3, 1954.
28. George Padmore, *The Gold Coast Revolution,* London, 1953, pp. 204-205.
29. Gold Coast, Commission of Inquiry into the Affairs of the Cocoa Purchasing Company, Ltd. (Jibowu Commission), *Report,* 1956, *passim.*

The objectives of the CPC, according to one of its own memoranda, were:

(1) . . . furthering or promoting the interests and objects of the Gold Coast Marketing Board, to purchase, store, export, sell or otherwise deal in cocoa. . . .

(2) To purchase cocoa, make advances or loans to assist persons to purchase cocoa, and to do all things necessary for and in connection with the purchase of cocoa in the Gold Coast.[30]

The first objective of the CPC turned the CPP into a super cocoa broker. In this new role, the party entered into competition with the African cocoa brokers, many of whom had been supporters of the CPP. The political reaction of the brokers was quick and predictable. Those who had been active in the CPP quit the party or were expelled for opposing the formation of the CPC. Later, many of them became important financial backers of the opposition.

The second objective of the CPC was to put the government into large-scale loan activity.[31] This role adversely affected the very important stratum of rich capitalist farmers who were the major source of agricultural credit in the country. The CPC had, through the CMB, a large supply of credit. By granting loans at low interest (or, as the Jibowu report showed, by granting loans to politically certified farmers without interest and without attempts to collect principal) they could bring interest rates down to a level at which the rich farmers could not afford to compete. In addition, by enabling small farmers to pay off their debts, the CPC undoubtedly antagonized some creditors who would have preferred to continue collecting interest payments.

The political effects of the CPC loan policy were more striking than they might otherwise have been because of the blatantly corrupt and partisan way in which it was administered. The CPP/CPC did not simply advance money to needy farmers. CPP organizational affiliation was required before any farmer could receive a loan. Without membership in the CPP-sponsored United Ghana Farmers' Council, farmers were not

30. *Ibid.*, p. 17.
31. Bauer, *West African Trade,* p. 262.

entitled to sell their cocoa to the CPC or to receive loans from
that body. In this way, the CPP took advantage of the small
farmers' financial predicament to build a patronage machine.[32]
Politically screened farmers not only were given instant credit,
but if their loans fell into arrears, no penalties accrued. Loans
were given in excess of statutory limitations.

Vote buying was channeled through the CPC. During the
1954 elections, the CPP greatly expanded the number of cash
advances it made to the farmers. For the six-week period which
preceded the election, advances rose over 450 percent above
normal. This total amounted to £317,000.[33] "Bearing in mind,"
the Jibowu Report says, "that Mr. Dennis, then Loan Manager,
stated in a letter to Mr. Djin [Acting Managing Director] that
they depended on the farming community for votes, we are led
to the inference that this excess of £317,000 over the cost of
cocoa was largely used for securing votes."[34]

Personal enrichment took place at all levels of administration of the CPC. In the highest echelons, Djin lent Nkrumah
£1,800 to pay for the importation of a Cadillac.[35] The Commission found that

Mr. Djin's case does not, in our view, reflect any credit on the
Government. . . . It has been suggested that [the Prime Minister]
was indebted to Mr. Djin. This is denied, but he failed to erase from
our mind the impression that he had unfortunately placed himself
in such an embarrassing position in relation to Mr. Djin that he
could not take or cause to be taken steps which might displease
or be unpleasant to Mr. Djin.[36]

Djin himself, according to the Jibowu Commission, "con-
nived at irregularities committed by certain employees . . . took
advantage of his position as Managing Director to reduce freight

---

32. Before a farmer could be considered for a loan, according to the
CPP minute book, the officer dealing with the application had to be
satisfied that the applicant was "a bona fide cocoa farmer and that he
was a member of the UGFC." Jibowu *Report*, p. 30. Martin Appiah
Danquah, General Secretary of the UGFC, also made a statement to this
effect before the Jibowu Commission.
33. Jibowu Commission, *Report*, p. 41.
34. *Ibid.*, p. 41.
35. Gold Coast Korsah Commission, *Report*, paras. 89-93.
36. Jibowu Commission, *Report*, para. 209.

charges made by the Company for transporting goods of his firm . . . managed his personal business while full-time Managing Director contrary to his agreement," and "made full use of CPC staff to sell wares of his private firm." The Commission concluded that

in view of our findings on the allegations of irregularities made against Mr. Djin, we do not consider him to have been a fit and proper person to have been in what was virtually sole control of the affairs of a quasi-public concern whose assets and those of the Loans Agency at 30th September, 1955, totalled over £6,000,000.[37]

In addition to vote buying, speculation, and bribery, the CPC leadership also gave a good account of themselves as bureaucratic empire-builders. From a paper organization in 1952, the CPC expanded to an agency which employed, by 1956, a staff of about 700 for its produce and loan operations alone. This did not include the so-called "receivers," who were paid on a commission basis, and who numbered around 1,800. By 1956, the CPC operated 38 districts which had administrative control of 1,960 buying centers.[38]

The forces of "good government"—the lawyers, brokers, and respectable businessmen of the UGCC—were outraged at the crude political methodology employed by the CPP. But, with only two seats in the legislature, they were in no position to launch a crusade. They were disorganized and politically impotent. The Ghana Congress Party (GCP), the new organization formed after their 1951 defeat, was only a fossilized remnant of the UGCC, once the vehicle of the entire nationalist movement. The accents of outraged and impotent virtue are audible in the statement issued at the time of the GCP's founding in May 1952:

Congress . . . will show the country the right way. It will meet the CPP squarely and defeat it. . . . We cannot sit down and allow our country to be so run and ruined by men who think of themselves only and who compromise principles without the least compunction. . . . Of course the Congress means business. We cannot allow this fooling and thieving to go on any longer or else we are all doomed. The great array of intellectual giants behind

37. *Ibid.*
38. *Ibid.*, para. 19.

the party, the response of the chiefs and farmers and the joy and support of the thinking man at the birth of Congress give evidence of the strength of the new party. This Ghana must be saved from a one-party evil, the evil of dictatorship.[39]

The professional stratum by itself was powerless to do any more than perhaps harass the CPP. But CPP cooperation with the British policy of piling up sterling reserves through the CMB had its inevitable political backlash. Ghana's capitalist farmers became increasingly antagonized by the operations of the CMB. Their income, they soon saw, was not being "stabilized" as the British and the CPP claimed: it was being reduced. The professional stratum now discovered a base of support for its attacks against "dictatorship"—the capitalist farmers and Ghana's traditional leaders.

---

39. *Daily Echo* (Accra), May 6, 1952. Cited in Austin, *Politics in Ghana*, p. 182.

4

THE RIGHT OPPOSITION: "TRIBALISM"

The Ghana Congress Party's 1952 Manifesto, with its charges of corruption and dictatorship, seems to foreshadow the 1966 coup. Actually, the generals have used only the political *vocabulary* of the old Right Opposition. The political organizations of the Right—regional, religious, and "tribal"—have been specifically and categorically proscribed. Most probably, however, the generals imposed this ban more for reasons of administrative convenience than of political necessity. Any political growth on the part of the agro-mercantile strata which formed the Right Opposition would be like hair growing on a corpse. Ghanaian capitalism is dead.

It died from a combination of wounds inflicted by British capital and CPP politicians. These two antagonists prevented the agro-mercantile strata from making the transition from landowners and traders to factory owners and bankers which is the *sine qua non* of national capitalism. The role played by British mercantile capital and "the City" in the destruction of Ghanaian capitalism has been partially described; the CPP's role in the process was to turn back the political counterattack of the agro-mercantile strata whose economic bases had already been thoroughly undermined.

The period of open political struggle between the CPP and the Right Opposition was 1954-1958. It began with the agro-mercantile strata—goaded into political activity by the CPP's heavy export taxes on cocoa—challenging the CPP for state control; it ended with the incarceration of their parliamentary delegates and the exile of K. A. Busia, their party chairman. In early 1954, the CPP found itself without any serious organized opposition. By 1958, the struggle with the Right Opposition had transformed the CPP and the Ghanaian state apparatus: the latter had been absorbed by the former. And in the process,

Dr. Nkrumah and his colleagues found that they had no room left for the liberal residues of British rule.

Who spoke for the Right Opposition? No single voice or party, not even a single class. In the chorus of voices raised against the CPP, many accents could be detected. There was the Ashanti chief, typically a landlord or capitalist farmer, whose social philosophy and political program found a close analogy in the seventeenth century *Frondeurs;* there was the Kumasi businessman who articulated the political philosophy of John Locke, but whose desired economic instrumentalities were those of the Gosplan; there were the desperate voices of the jobless, homeless "Tokyo Joes" of Accra, who were still sleeping on the verandahs of the rich and whose accents were those of the city lumpenproletariat everywhere; there were the separatist demands of the Ewe cocoa farmer of Trans-Volta Togoland. This Gold Coast Ewe, if he could unite with his brother Ewes in French Togoland, could reunify the entire Ewe nation, and triple his income at the same time.

With such a heterogeneous movement, it is understandable that no ideological unity was achieved and that the cry of protest was the only one uttered in perfect harmony. Neither of the forces which might have polarized and deepened the political struggle (the Ghanaian working class[1] and the British owning class) was an open participant. The political organizations formed by the Right factions reflected the absence of the two decisive forces. Each opposition tendency formed its own party with its own leaders and program. They merged to form the "United Party" only when, in November 1957, the CPP itself imposed unity by making "tribal," religious, and regional parties illegal. The various tendencies, tacitly accepting the government's definition of themselves, finally joined forces. But it was a unity imposed from without rather than a unity which resulted from recognition of the necessity to carry on opposition at a higher level of discipline.

As late as 1954 the CPP position appeared very strong. There was nothing to suggest the political turmoil of succeeding years. Nkrumah was maintaining the "not unfruitful partner-

---

1. Agricultural as well as urban proletarians.

ship" with the colonial Governor; cocoa prices had reached record highs; and in June the party received a mandate at the polls. In the Legislative Assembly elections, the CPP won 72 out of 104 seats, with 60 percent of those registered to vote casting ballots. The remaining 32 seats were won by independent and local candidates. The Ghana Congress Party—the party of the commercial and professional strata—won only one seat. It appeared to most observers that the CPP would be able to strengthen further its "political kingdom" without any serious challenge, and that Britain would grant independence within a few months. The formation of the National Liberation Movement in Kumasi in September, 1954, therefore came as a complete surprise to everyone.

The NLM, which became the most powerful element within the opposition, was formed as a direct result of the CPP's August decision to freeze the price paid to cocoa producers at a time when world market prices were setting records. From £290 per ton in 1953, the world price had risen to over £500 per ton.[2] Predictably, the main backers of the NLM were cocoa farmers and chiefs who owned cocoa land. They were joined almost immediately by the Ghana Congress Party members. Description of the long-range strategy of the NLM can be reduced to one word—federalism. The cocoa farmers and traders wanted to escape the confiscatory levies on cocoa and to avoid the consequences of the government's partiality to foreign business. In a sense, Ashanti, which produced the majority of the country's cocoa, had become, like Katanga and the old Ivory Coast, the prime source of tax revenue for a larger political entity. Like these other areas, its owning classes claimed to be tired of the milch-cow role.

The other rich cocoa-producing area, the Trans-Volta Togoland region, shared the same political goal—escape from the taxing authority of the central government in Accra. The solution of its party, the Togoland Congress, was to join French Togoland, whose cocoa was being subsidized at *above* the world market price by the French government. Both movements had the same class components and shared the rhetoric of "tribal-

2. For average yearly prices, see Table 6, p. 85.

ism"; but while the NLM's goal was federation, the Togoland
Congress demanded complete separation.[3]

Cocoa and the Togoland Question

The clearest expression of the Trans-Volta Togoland farmers' position towards price-fixing comes from a Legislative Assembly speech by M. K. Apaloo. Apaloo charged that the CPP
government had decided to move against the capitalist farmers
and that the government's fiscal policy aimed at getting its
revenue entirely from the cocoa export tax and not from "the
firms" or from loans from abroad. This policy, he argued,
"places the burden of our development entirely, almost entirely,
on the shoulders of our cocoa farmers." He said that the bill
would deprive the farmer

of all the monies he will be entitled to, in excess of 72s. a load for
his cocoa, which works out at £134 a ton, although the world
price now is hovering around £500 a ton or 268s. a load. . . . Even
our own native customs have a more humane system of sharing produce between the landlord and the tenant. Under the "abusa"
system a tenant works on the land and the landlord takes only
one third, but in our system even though the land belongs to the
farmer and the government is, as it were, a trustee of the farmer,
we are calling upon him to surrender two thirds of what is due
him every year.[4]

Apaloo said that the government was creating a peasant
slave system and that the development schemes benefited only
the cities and the bureaucracy. The people in the rural areas,
he said, lived "in the same old mud houses" roofed with iron
sheets. What the farmers really needed was not CPC loans but
higher cocoa prices:

These people want the money and instead of our giving their
money to them we have taken the money and we tell them "we
will give you loans." . . . I am saying: do not give them loans, give

---

3. A third element which arose during this period and which was
included in the opposition was the Northern People's Party. The NPP
was a loose alliance of chiefs which served more as a lobby for specific
"welfare" projects than as a modern political party. The most important
of the chiefs in this area, the Tolon Na, a firm believer in Moral Rearma-
ment, eventually became Nkrumah's Ambassador to Nigeria.
4. Gold Coast, Legislative Assembly, *Debates*, August 12, 1955, p. 342.

them their money so that they can buy building materials for their own buildings with their own money.[5]

Kodzo Ayeke, another member of the Legislative Assembly from TVT, pointed out that while the cocoa-growing area of Trans-Volta Togoland comprised less than 5 percent of the population of Ghana, it contributed nearly 30 percent of all the cocoa revenue. He added that, after forty years of British administration as part of the Gold Coast, and after contributing millions of pounds in cocoa revenue to the CMB, "not one mile of road has been tarred" in Togoland, although there were, at that time, 4,000 miles of tarred road in the Gold Coast.[6]

While TVT politicians spoke against price-fixing, TVT farmers opposed the tax in their own way. Extensive smuggling operations were organized. While the price of cocoa was set at 72s. per load in British Togo, just across the border it sold for over 200s. per load. Smugglers on the French side were willing to pay as much as 120s. per load, and a single truckload successfully negotiating the mandate line could bring a gross profit of £400-500. It should not be surprising that the TVT farmers' party, the Togoland Congress, had only one real plank in its platform—unification with French Togoland.

Naturally, the CPP did not suggest in its propaganda that increased revenue was the reason for keeping the Ewe of TVT in Ghana. Instead, they argued that they were true Ewe nationalists. The aims of the Togoland Congress could be achieved, they said, by remaining in Ghana: with independence from Great Britain achieved, the first stage in the struggle to "liberate" French Togoland would have been completed. Later, French Togoland could be united with Ghana. This was the way to bring unity to the divided Ewe nation.[7]

This playing on the theme of unity versus "tribalism" is characteristic of the way CPP politicians dealt with the various elements within the Right opposition. "Unity" was good and "tribalism" bad. Support for the CPP and its aims meant support for "unity"; opposition to CPP aims meant support for

---

5. *Ibid.*
6. Gold Coast, Legislative Assembly, *Debates*, March 1, 1955.
7. Austin, *Politics in Ghana*, p. 192.

"tribalism"—which became a criminal offense under the "Avoid-ance of Discrimination Bill" of November 1957.

"Tribe-baiting" in Ghana, like "red-baiting" in the United States, became an effective mode of discrediting diverse forms of opposition. Both "red-baiting" and "tribe-baiting" exploit the same fears: that the "communist" or "tribalist" *claims* to stand for certain principles, but "in reality" owes allegiance to some foreign entity. The communist, it is argued, will use his position as union leader, not to fight for the working class, but to advance the aims of the "international communist conspiracy" or of "Russia"; the "tribalist" politician, if given a national posi-tion of trust, will not carry out the program he argued for, but will use his office to benefit his own lineage, family, or tribe. Once the definition of "tribalist" as someone who only "seems" to be interested in national welfare (just as the communist only "seems" to be interested in fighting for the working class) was accepted, it became possible to proscribe any political party or individual.

The Founding of the NLM

Besides the Ewe, in Trans-Volta Togoland, the other source of "tribal" opposition was beginning to gather strength in Ashanti. On September 19, 1954, the National Liberation Move-ment held its first meeting in Kumasi. It was a foreshadowing of the contradictory tendencies within the movement that the first meeting was held "amidst the beating of drums, the firing of muskets, the singing of Ashanti war songs, and loud cries of *Mate me ho!*" and that the scene of all this ethnicity should be a place called Prince of Wales Park.[8]

Bafour Osie Akoto, a wealthy cocoa farmer[9] and the Asan-tehene's senior linguist,[10] was elected chairman; a ritual sheep was slaughtered. At the same time, party membership cards

8. Austin, *Politics in Ghana*, p. 262.

9. According to Austin, Bafour Akoto employed some two dozen laborers on his cocoa farms, which produced between 500 and 700 loads of cocoa per year. *Politics in Ghana*, p. 261.

10. "Linguist" is misleading, although it is the usual English transla-tion. More accurately, an *okyeame* is the chief's spokesman. The Asantehene is the paramount chief of the Ashanti nation.

were sold, on which was printed the motto of the NLM—"good government." This mixture of middle-class uplift with the symbols of traditional Ashanti authority was an accurate reflection of the class composition of the NLM leadership and its ideological requirements: the inherently contradictory plea for both mass support and respect for the privileges of the Ashanti land-owning classes, whose members were typically chiefs or chiefs' relatives.[11]

It would have been politically impossible to organize a popular movement whose announced objective was simply to enable the absentee landlord chiefs of Ashanti to regain from the CPP the profits that had originally come from the labor of the agricultural proletariat. An "ideological" approach was necessary. The NLM said that the policies of the Cocoa Marketing Board and the Cocoa Purchasing Company were not its main targets: "The cocoa issue is only a facet of a larger problem." Instead, the NLM was appealing to the Asanteman Council "for help in the campaign against the larger issue, namely the stamping out of dictatorship and communistic practices. . . ."[12]

This attempt to red-bait the CPP served as part of the counterattack against the CPP's "tribe-baiting." The NLM tried hard to popularize anti-communism. The *Ashanti Pioneer* carried a comic strip called "Animal Farm" which was designed to make vivid the alleged horrors of "communist" society through pictorial dramatization of the Orwell fable. At rallies, the dangers of communism were described in great detail, while evidence of its imminent approach was cited. NLM spokesman Joe Appiah, for instance, said at a rally beside Lake Bosumtwe, an Ashanti shrine, that the erection of a statue of Nkrumah in front of the Accra post office was evidence of "what happened in some of the Iron Curtain countries. . . ." "We know these things," he went on, "because many of us in the opposition have been fortunate to travel around Europe and that is why we can discern Communism as soon as we see the slightest evidence of it."[13]

---

11. See below, pp. 64-65.
12. NLM memorandum, October 19, 1954. Cited in Austin, *Politics*, p. 264.
13. *Daily Graphic,* June 11, 1957.

The NLM and the People

A permanent wish for identification with the bourgeois representatives of the mother country is to be found among the native intellectuals and merchants.

—Frantz Fanon

In order to gain support from the Ashanti peasants, the NLM used traditional Ashanti symbols as well as an anti-communist campaign. But the NLM considered itself above "party politics." It never made serious attempts to organize at the grass-roots level. Despite passing out membership cards and using popular symbols of Ashanti national tradition, its leaders constantly emphasized their aversion to party organization. They took the position that it was the patriotic duty of every Ashanti to support the party.[14]

Many leaders of the NLM actually distrusted and hated the Ghanaian masses. Cobina Kessie, for instance, felt that the people must be firmly held in check by tradition and authority:

When the masses act on their own, they do so only in one way, for they have no other: they lynch. It is not altogether by chance that Mr. Nkrumah himself preached "direct action" or "positive action" against a previous government. For lynch law comes from America, the paradise of the masses, and Nkrumah was educated in America.[15]

An interview that Richard Wright had with Dr. Danquah further illustrates the elitist attitude which permeated the NLM:

Wright: Do you think [Nkrumah will] keep power for long?
Danquah: Yes, until the illiterate masses wake up.
Wright: Why don't *you* try to win the masses to your side?
Danquah: Masses? I don't like this thing of masses. There are only individuals for me.
Wright: But masses form the basis of political power in the modern world today.
Danquah: You believe that? I know you fellows dote on this thing of the masses. . . . I've read that you claim that this mass unrest comes from the industrialization of the Western world.

14. *Ashanti Pioneer,* January 24, 1955.
15. *Ashanti Pioneer,* January 26, 1955. Kessie was later the Ghanaian government's ambassador to the People's Republic of China.

Wright: Why is it that you cannot appeal to the masses on the basis of their daily needs? You're a lawyer; you're used to *representing*. . . . Well, represent them. As we say in America: be a mouthpiece for them.

Danquah: I can't do things like that.

Wright: It's the only road to power in modern society. No matter how deeply you reject it, it's true.

Danquah: It's emotion.[16]

Wright concluded, "He was shaking his head. . . . It was no use. He was of the old school. One did not speak *for* the masses; one told them what to do."[17]

By tradition, class position, and personal inclination, the NLM leadership seemed unable to ally itself with Ghana's working class. These inclinations were probably correct from the standpoint of long-term political survival. Any attempt to democratize the movement by going to the masses would have required giving them something to fight for, and it is quite possible that, once stirred politically, the landless workers would have wanted to fight against the semi-feudal land relations which were their most immediate source of oppression.

Cut off from the masses, the NLM had its only solid strength among the capitalist farmers (including the chiefs) and in business and commercial circles. This provided insufficient political leverage to overthrow Nkrumah. Support was required from somewhere else. Where could it be obtained?

The NLM and the British

The NLM's strategy was to win federal powers by appealing to British imperial proclivities. The road to a federal assembly in Kumasi would have to pass through the London Colonial Office. But the NLM recognized that Nkrumah was able to count on British support. As John Tsiboe, editor of the *Ashanti Pioneer,* said: "The British are . . . using the CPP in the same manner that they once used the chiefs. The present government is for British interests; it's the same situation with

---

16. Wright, *Black Power*, p. 221.

17. *Ibid.* One of the first acts of the National Liberation Council was to hold a memorial service for Danquah, who died while held in preventive detention.

62 GHANA: THE END OF AN ILLUSION

the chiefs in reverse."[18] Consequently, British power had to be neutralized.

Nevertheless, the NLM really had very little to offer the British. In fact, if the proposed Ashanti Federal Assembly were to lift the export tax on cocoa, it would stop the flow of dollars and pounds which were used to stave off the always imminent collapse of the pound. And as far as Ghana was concerned, it was this flow that concerned the British above all else. The NLM leaders were conscious of this. As K. A. Busia, the leader of the Parliamentary Opposition, told Sir Charles Arden-Clarke: "The British here care nothing for our people; they are concerned with their political power which enables them to defend their financial interests. They sided with the CPP in order to protect those interests. It's that simple."[19]

As they were not able to make substantive concessions to the British, the leaders of the NLM were forced to make superficial appeals to British power and susceptibilities. They sought to retain "God Save the Queen" as the national anthem; they tried to have Queen Elizabeth's head placed on the national currency; they loudly deplored the ouster of "the Queen's representative in Ghana," the Governor-General, from Christianborg Castle in Nkrumah's favor; they protested that Queen Elizabeth's head rightfully belonged on the new postage stamps instead of Nkrumah's; and they consistently accused opponents of these measures of fomenting "sedition and treason against Her Majesty the Queen."[20] The willingness of the NLM to offer Great Britain the shadow and not the substance of power was to have its counterpart in British willingness to see that the NLM received only paper guarantees of federal power.

The NLM and "Tribalism"

Oxford has made me what I am today. I have had eleven years contact with it and now consider it my second home. Most of my friends are here.

—K. A. Busia, 1950

18. Wright, *Black Power*, p. 275.
19. *Ibid.*, p. 229.
20. The *Times* (London), June 11, 1957.

"The name of the Asantehene," the Golden Stool, Ashanti interests, Ashanti history, and Ashanti rights formed the stock of the symbols and slogans by which the NLM sought to win mass support. At more advanced ideological levels, the NLM separatist demands became pleas for pluralistic democracy. They included arguments that might have been advanced by a Madisonian structure-functionalist:

The peoples of these territories, belonging as they do to different tribes, have different structures of society, and are at different stages of adaptation and adoption of Western culture. . . . There is not enough consciousness of national identity to make possible easy and at the same time democratic unitary government. In the absence of this consciousness, the safest course is to ensure that not all the powers of government are concentrated at the center but that a substantial part of them is retained in the component territories where people have learnt the habits and attitudes of living together for some time.[21]

There is in this statement a kind of sophisticated, self-conscious "tribalism" that would be impossible for truly traditionally oriented people to maintain. The NLM "tribalism" owed more to Margery Perham and to Radcliffe-Brown than to the Mau-Mau rebellion.

Despite these self-conscious attempts on the part of the NLM to be "tribal," many of its leaders, like K. A. Busia,[22] actually despised tribal life, as this interview between Busia and Richard Wright shows:

Wright: What is the significance of the oath-taking and libation pouring at the CPP's rallies?
Busia: It's to bind the masses to the party. . . . Tribal life is religious through and through. An oath is a great thing to an African. An oath links him with the past, allies him with his ancestors. That's the deepest form of loyalty that the tribal man knows. The libation pouring means the same thing. Now, these things, when employed at a political meeting, insure with rough authority, that the masses will follow and accept leadership. That

21. "Preamble of Proposals for a Federal Constitution for an Independent Gold Coast and Togoland by Movements and Parties other than the Convention People's Party," Kumasi, n.d. Cited in Austin, *Politics in Ghana*, p. 277.
22. Busia was related to the important stool at Wenchi.

is what so-called mass parties need. . . . The leaders of the CPP use tribal methods to enforce their ends.

  Wright: I take it that *you* wouldn't use such methods?

  Busia: "I'm a Westerner," he said, sucking in his breath, "I was educated in the West."[23]

Wright remarked of the interview, "I had the feeling that he was speaking sincerely, that he could not conceivably touch such methods, that he regarded them with loathing, and that he did not even relish thinking that anybody else would."[24]

Nevertheless, while for many NLM intellectual leaders the tribal values of their people were of no personal significance, they were able to cooperate with the Asantehene (the Paramount Chief of the Ashanti nation) and with other "traditional" leaders. In order to understand the basis for this cooperation, it is necessary to understand the functions of the chieftaincy and its socio-economic basis in rapidly changing Ghanaian society.

The NLM and the Chiefs

The modern chief, in addition to his traditional roles, is often both landowner and trader. Important chiefs may have several hundred *abusa* laborers working for them and be land developers and commercial investors as well. The Asantehene himself demonstrates this tendency to acquire non-traditional sources of power through a combination of feudal and capitalistic devices. On one hand, he was the biggest landowner in Ashanti; on the other, he was a major stockholder in the Kumasi Race Track Club. Through the Asantehene's Land Department, he invested in new housing developments and carried out town-and-country planning and investment. The whole process of uneven socio-economic development in Ghana and the part played by the chief in this process are symbolized by a photograph in the *Daily Graphic* of June 26, 1957. It shows the Asantehene, wearing his traditional robes and ceremonial slippers, and holding a golden key "weighing twelve ounces." With his golden key, he is unlocking the new £60,000 Kumasi branch of Barclays' Bank.

---

23. Wright, *Black Power*, p. 228.
24. *Ibid.*, p. 228.

The Asantehene's great wealth and the scope of his business interests reflect the changing class position of the Ashanti capitalist farmer-chiefs as a whole. More Anglican than Akan, they were no longer leaders of a religio-military hierarchy, but leading citizens and employers in rural capitalist communities. It was precisely their *lack* of traditional orientation that made it possible for an Oxford-trained sociologist like Busia to form a political alliance with them. Had the chiefs maintained their traditional roles, Busia might have studied them, but he would never have served as head of their parliamentary party.

Because of the chiefs' changing roles, it was possible for them to gain political allies among the intellectuals. But how were they able to gain the support of the "commoner" businessmen as well?

5

THE RIGHT OPPOSITION: BUSINESSMEN

The national consciousness of the Ghanaian commercial-professional strata before the postwar independence movement was shaped by two primary factors. The first was their symbiotic relationship with the British colonial government: successively, the commercial-professional strata conceived of themselves as political and cultural mediators between the British and their own traditional rulers; as competitors with the traditional rulers for British favor; and as heirs-apparent to British colonial rule. Insofar as members of the commercial-professional strata accepted these roles, they fitted the Fanonist model of national bourgeois consciousness: "Seen through its eyes, its mission has nothing to do with transforming the nation; it consists prosaically of being the transmission line between the nation . . . and neo-colonialism."[1]

Those who rejected the role of mediators tended to develop a self-conscious neo-traditionalism with anti-colonial overtones. One of the first written reflections of this form of national consciousness is the work of Attoh Ahuma who hoped in 1911 for "an era of Backward Movement" among all cultured West Africans. He maintained that "Intelligent Retrogression is the only Progression which will save our beloved country," and urged the need "to rid ourselves of foreign accretions and excrescences" as an indispensable condition of "National Resurrection and National Prosperity."[2]

The national consciousness of the commercial-professional strata was generally a mixture of these conflicting symbiotic and neo-traditional tendencies. Dr. Danquah was perhaps the most articulate example of this typically bifurcated consciousness,

---

1. *Wretched of the Earth*, p. 124.
2. Cited in David Kimble, *A Political History of Ghana, 1850-1928*, Oxford, 1963, pp. 499-501.

which in his case embraced traditional Akan religion, chieftaincy, Anglophilia, and anti-colonialism.

The second factor shaping the national consciousness of the commercial-professional strata was the struggle with the British import-export oligopoly. Thirteen British firms, led by the United Africa Company (a subsidiary of Unilever and the world's largest trading company) controlled prices, import licenses, and wholesale credit. Only the economic activity that seemed too arduous or too small to be worthwhile for the larger concerns became a source of unrestricted opportunity for the Ghanaian trader.[3] Because the British cocoa magnate, William Cadbury, found it more profitable to wait at the port to collect the accumulated cocoa harvest, there was an opportunity for Ghanaian middlemen to penetrate the rural hinterland, finance the landowners, organize transportation, and collect the produce.

But the African middlemen were often dependent on the big British firms for capital, and the firms were their chief customers. In the 1930's, the middlemen had attempted to by-pass the British trading firms by selling cocoa directly to agents in Europe and the United States. These attempts were largely unsuccessful. Consequently the African trader was torn between opposition to British oligopolistic control and the need to maintain his source of capital and his trading outlets. Contradictory economic pressures thus reinforced the division already present in the national consciousness between anti-colonialism and accommodation, neo-traditionalism and all-out assimilation.

The professional stratum formed the elite *par excellence* of Gold Coast society. Numerically insignificant—in 1948 there were only 57 lawyers and 47 doctors in the Gold Coast[4]—the professional stratum dominated every nationalist and proto-nationalist organization from the Aborigines Rights Protection Society (1897) to the UGCC. Members of the professional stratum typically sprang from the wealthiest of the coastal

---

3. The Ghanaian traders were also forced to compete with the usually better-financed Levantine traders, who formed an intermediate commercial stratum between the British and the Africans. As a result of their greater visibility, the Levantines often absorbed much of the antagonism which would ordinarily have been directed at British enterprise.

4. Gail Margaret Kelly, *The Ghanaian Intelligentsia,* unpublished Ph.D. dissertation, University of Chicago, 1959, p. 57.

merchant families; their wealth combined with their foreign education enabled them to occupy the highest positions open to Africans in Gold Coast society. The nationalist movement of CPP youngmen threatened this position, but it was inconceivable to the professionals that the British would ever turn the Gold Coast over to those whom they liked to describe as "the hooligans."

In 1951, however, when Arden-Clarke performed his famous "act of grace," the political expectations of the African commercial-professional strata were dissipated. They no longer had any position to protect as colonial heirs-apparent. They now developed feelings of bitterness and betrayal which found their most unambiguous reflection in the accusations Busia directed against Governor Arden-Clarke.[5] While some members of the commercial-professional strata still clung to the vain hope that the British would help their party work out federal and separatist compromises with the Nkrumah government, others began to attack British colonialism openly for the first time.

Between 1954 and 1958, the commercial-professional strata found themselves in the unaccustomed position of defending the national interest against Anglo-American business. They were antagonized especially by the way the CPP served as broker for these foreign interests. They demanded that the government bring the British banks in Ghana under the control of the central banking system; they opposed Nkrumah's policy of allowing United States control over the Volta power complex; they fought for increased outlays for industrial development projects; they ridiculed the "colonialist mentality" which produced annual budget surpluses despite increased national revenues.[6] In making these nationalist charges and demands, the commercial-professional strata exposed the developing neo-colonialist tendencies within the CPP regime early in its history. Neither the CPP nor the commercial-professional strata within the United Party were capable of the great national tasks of the democratic revolution: industrialization, elimination of

---

5. See p. 62 above.
6. Budgetary surpluses prevailed until 1954-55. In that year the surplus amounted to approximately 10 percent of the Gross Domestic Product.

foreign financial control, and elimination of semi-feudalism. But the commercial-professional strata at least had the brief opportunity to act the role of "conscience of the Republic"—before Nkrumah shoved them off the national stage.

Banks, Credit, and African Business

Ghanaian businessmen, whether building contractors, timber merchants, cocoa buyers, or small manufacturers, all faced the same problem—inadequate credit facilities. The timber merchants complained that they lost out to foreign competition because they were unable to get loans to buy timber-cutting equipment; the building contractors charged that lack of capital prevented them from hiring enough labor to bid on big government projects; small manufacturers claimed that insufficient credit prevented them from expanding their operations. A parliamentary spokesman for the National Liberation Movement analyzed the situation this way:

We all know that foreign traders are dominating the commercial field in this country, and are gradually displacing African traders because the financial position of the African traders is weak. In the timber industry, for instance, Syrian, Lebanese, and other commercial firms have been able to come together and have succeeded in raising loans from the foreign commercial banks with which to start business operations as their working capital. On the contrary, even though small African traders may come together for the purpose of trading, they usually do not succeed in getting credit facilities from the foreign commercial banks.[7]

Why couldn't the Ghanaian businessmen get credit? There were actually several reasons. First, the Cocoa Marketing Board was draining Ghana of its capital.[8] Second, the United Africa Company, the largest single source of credit in Ghana (and in British West Africa as a whole), had no interest in financing potential competitors. Along with the twelve other import-export firms operating in Ghana, the UAC advanced money to buyers

---

7. Gold Coast, Legislative Assembly, *Debates,* February 14, 1957.
8. The authoritative work on African colonial banking states: "It is probable that the policies of the Marketing Boards in accumulating large stabilization funds have further reduced the finance available to Africans." W. T. Newlyn and D. C. Rowan, *Money and Banking in British Colonial Africa,* Oxford, 1954, p. 217.

during the crop seasons and advanced goods to retailers. But this credit was given only to Ghanaians operating on the lower trading echelons. The system made it practically impossible for a Ghanaian to become an important cocoa broker, i.e., an agent of the marketing board, or to enter into the wholesale import trade.[9]

The third reason was perhaps the most critical. The banks, the source from which one would ordinarily expect credit to come, were completely closed to Ghanaians. There were only two important banks in Ghana at the time of independence: the Bank of British West Africa and Barclays' Bank DCO.[10] Both gave numerous reasons for not lending to Africans. They claimed that the complexity of African family relationships and land tenure made it impossible to trust even an apparently prosperous African. Moreover, they preferred, they said, to deal with customers who passed all their transactions through their bank accounts. With Africans, the bankers maintained, it was impossible to know with any certainty just what their actual financial position was: these complications did not arise with Europeans or Levantines.[11]

The basis for the refusal to lend lay deeper than discrimination: the banks were not really in Ghana to lend money. Their main source of income came from banking services, e.g., transferring money, discounting bills, and drafts. The charges by British banks for banking services in West Africa are thought to be the highest in the Commonwealth.[12] Their lending activities were minor. Since they refused to lend to Africans and weren't able to lend to the big import-export firms, which had their own sources of capital, their loan activity was confined to small import-export firms. This meant that the banks had considerable surplus funds which were sent to London and put to work there.

---

9. *Ibid.*, p. 139.
10. Barclays' Bank DCO is a subsidiary of the British Barclays' Bank Ltd. The shareholders of the Bank of West Africa include the other major British commercial banks—Lloyds, Westminster, the National Provincial, and the Midlands. In 1963, the Bank of British West Africa had 115 branches, of which 41 were in Ghana. Barclays' Bank DCO had 1,364, of which only 60 were in Ghana.
11. P. T. Bauer, *West African Trade,* p. 183.
12. *Ibid.*, p. 181.

This was another instance of how the British operating in Ghana were able to institutionalize capital export back to the "mother" country.

The British banks were able to do this even after independence, for Ghana did not have a real central bank or her own currency authority. The Ghanaian pound was really still just the British pound printed on different colored paper. The British banks could take Ghanaian pounds out of the country and change them into British pounds with impunity. This loss of money deflated the economy and compounded the difficulties facing the African businessman.[13]

With the foreign banks acting like gilded vacuum cleaners, sucking up local capital without any feedback in the form of loans, it is understandable that the commercial-professional strata would press for regulatory legislation. This they did when the 1957 Central Bank bill was under consideration in the Legislative Assembly. They argued that, unless foreign banks were brought under firm control, there would be no justification for having a central bank—except for national pride. "If we are going to have a Central Bank," one Opposition Member said, "we must have a Central Bank with 'teeth' and not a Central Bank which is only a channel for controlling the financial assets of this country by a foreign power."[14]

The Opposition demanded further that Ghana's banking legislation contain a provision enabling it to break parity with the pound sterling. This was especially important in case the British pound had to be devalued, as had happened in 1949. As long as parity remained, devaluation of the British pound would automatically lower the value of the Ghanaian pound.

The official CPP attitude to the Opposition proposals, and to all other proposals which involved greater fiscal and monetary independence from Great Britain, the pound sterling, and the foreign banks, is revealed in the following highly significant exchange between Joe Appiah, an NLM floor leader, and the Minister of Finance, K. A. Gbedemah:

---

13. See Tony Killick, "The Monetary and Financial System," in *A Study of Contemporary Ghana* (especially pp. 312-326) for a discussion of the operations of the Ghanaian banking system.

14. Gold Coast, Legislative Assembly, *Debates,* February 5, 1957.

Gbedemah: It may be that some future Government of Ghana will wish to break away . . . [from the pound] to set forth on uncharted and unpredictable financial seas.

Appiah: Is the honourable Minister afraid that honesty and integrity will have to be imported in?

Gbedemah: But this present Government will not expose the new ship of State to such hazards. That is why we introduce Clause 18 as a vital provision in this Bill—"The parity of the Ghana pound shall be one Ghana pound to one pound sterling"—(Interruption) Honorable Members opposite are making rude political jokes which do not disturb me. We shall maintain the parity of the Ghana pound to the pound sterling. That is our anchor of safety.[15]

The same measures which tied the CPP government to the pound sterling, provided its "anchor of safety," and kept it from "uncharted and unpredictable financial seas" served to destroy the Ghanaian businessman. All that could possibly save him was a steady increase in the availability of credit. But this would have involved a restructuring of Ghana's fiscal and monetary system, which was, at this time, completely inadmissible to the CPP. The CPP's anchor of safety had become the African businessman's millstone.[16]

The CPP Response

Within the Legislative Assembly, the commercial-professional strata were in their chosen political arena. Generally better educated and more polished, their representatives were consistently able to embarrass the CPP by exposing concessions made to the requirements of the Sterling Area. Outside the Legislative Assembly, however, they were on less sure ground. Their party had no more to offer the urban working class than the CPP; and in the rural areas, because of their alliance with the chiefs and capitalist farmers, the NLM represented essen-

---

15. *Ibid.*
16. Later, in the 1960's, the Ghanaian government's banking system began a tremendous expansion of its lending activities—not, however, to African businessmen, but to the government itself. In 1961, the banks owed £157,000 to the government. By the end of June 1963, the government was a net debtor to the banking system to the tune of £33 million. Bank of Ghana, *Annual Report* 1962-63, Table XLIII.

tially what the landlord means to any tenant. The NLM consequently attempted to fight for their federal cause at the higher diplomatic levels: they preferred to use the formal mechanisms of appeal and quiet negotiations rather than mass rallies and popular demonstrations.

How did the CPP try to cope with these tactics? One would suppose that the leaders of the 1950 Positive Action campaign would have welcomed an open popular contest with an elitist party like the NLM. But this was not the case. As early as 1956, it could be seen that the CPP had become skeptical of its popular appeal. The tactics used in the struggle with the Right Opposition provide an opportunity to determine the strength of the CPP and its relations to the Ghanaian masses.

The most obvious change from the 1950 Positive Action days was that the CPP no longer behaved like a mass political party. Instead it combined a preference for "summit" conferences with the style of a United States political machine. The CPP did not work through the trade unions or involve the masses in its battles in any way; it did not attack the elitist NLM from a class point of view. Rather than organization, agitation, and political education aimed at generating power from below, the CPP preferred or felt forced to try to exert influence from the top down by negotiation. And when negotiation failed, it resorted to administrative repression. The CPP's behavior during and after the third and last general election in 1956 illustrates its increasing isolation from its popular base.

In mid-1955, the Togoland Congress and the NLM were gaining momentum, especially among the capitalist farmers in their regions. In a July by-election, in Ashanti, the NLM candidate won 70 percent of the vote. The CPP response was not to "parachute" organizers into the rural areas to organize the landless agricultural workers, who would have been natural allies in any fight against the capitalist farmers and rentier chiefs. Instead, Nkrumah tried to negotiate the differences through a series of conferences with NLM leaders.

When both the NLM and the TC insisted that their demands were "non-negotiable," Nkrumah turned to the British. He requested that the Colonial Secretary of State appoint a "Constitutional Advisor" to study the problem of "devolu-

tion." Sir Frederick Bourne drafted a report which favored CPP
"centralism" as opposed to NLM "federalism." The British, at
this time, would tolerate no plan for federation that allowed
Ghanaian cocoa revenue to be diverted from its normal British channels. Instead of federation, the Bourne Report offered
dissident elements another chance at the ballot box.

The CPP violently opposed this feature of the report.
According to Nkrumah, the "members of my party executive
were almost unanimous in voting against a general election and
even to mention the subject was like waving a red flag before a
bull."[17] Nor was an election favored by the NLM. Several
months of negotiations between the political parties dragged on
until the British government finally forced the issue: the Colonial
Secretary ordered that an election take place in July 1956.

In view of the close cooperation between the CPP and the
colonial government, together with the CPP's desire to avoid an
election, what made the British finally insist on a vote? Their
advocacy of an election appears to conflict with their stand
against the NLM's federalism. Why did they give the NLM any
chance at all?

First, the British were anxious to head off any action that
might lead to Ashanti's secession from the Gold Coast. Ashanti's
cocoa wealth provided both revenue for the Gold Coast government and sterling balances for Britain. It was the "Katanga"
of Ghana; it could not be allowed to fall into the hands of its
capitalist cocoa farmers.[18] By forcing the NLM into an election
which it would very likely lose, the British could indirectly dispose
of the federal plan and at the same time reduce the chance that
the constitutionalist NLM would attempt to secede.

Second, if the NLM were to pull an upset and win the
plebiscite, the British had effectively hedged their bets. The
Secretary of State for Colonies intimated that "the British
Government would hesitate to grant independence to the Gold
Coast until a *substantial majority* of the people had . . . agreed
upon a workable constitution for the country."[19] (Emphasis

---

17. *Ghana,* p. 244.

18. The *Report of the Constitutional Adviser* stated that the NLM
proposal would "slow down development and introduce an intolerable
handicap to the administration of the country."

19. Kwame Nkrumah, *Ghana,* p. 245.

added.) The British of course would determine what a "substantial majority" was. In other words, if the NLM lost, that meant the end of the federal plan; if it won, the British could always claim that the "substantial majority" had not been achieved.

This was apparently the conclusion drawn by the NLM leadership also. Early in the campaign, they felt that even if they won the election, the British might not let them form a government. Dr. Busia wrote an open letter to Governor Arden-Clarke reminding him that in accordance "with constitutional practice in the United Kingdom, the National Liberation Movement and its allies will expect Your Excellency to call upon Dr. K. A. Busia, their Parliamentary Leader, to form a Government should they (together with the independents supporting them) win more than 52 seats at the election."[20]

The final results of the election justified the skepticism both parties had entertained about their mass appeal. Although the CPP won 55 percent of the votes cast, this represented only 32 percent of the registered electorate and only 16.5 percent of the eligible electorate. In other words, on the eve of independence, only one out of six Ghanaians eligible to vote supported the CPP.[21]

To carry the municipalities, the CPP relied on Nkrumah's personality, pan-Africanist sentiments, and gratitude for previous welfare benefits. A leaflet used in Accra and published in the party paper three days before the election shows this approach. Here are some of its points:

Why You Should Vote for Nkrumah

(1) Because Nkrumah is a man of the Common People. . . .
(3) Because Nkrumah is honest, straightforward, hardworking, vigilant, stainless. . . .

---

20. *Daily Graphic,* July 15, 1956. (Cited by Austin, *Politics in Ghana,* p. 319). That the British do not feel bound to act "in accordance with constitutional practice in the United Kingdom" in the case of parties which are unacceptable to them, has been demonstrated again in the 1965 elections in British Guiana. The leading party in the election, the Progressive People's Party, was not permitted to form a government.

21. Harold S. Jacobs, *The Myth of the Missing Opposition: Ghana, A Case Study,* unpublished manuscript, University of California, 1965, p. 20.

(8) Because through Nkrumah's instrumentality Africanisation, free education have been encouraged, building of hospitals, clinics, roads, bridges, harbours, Achiasi-Kotoku railway, the formation of IDC, ADC, CPC, Bank of the Gold Coast, the Volta Project, Tema Development Corporation and many others. . . .

(9) Because . . . on June 12th, 1949, the CPP was conceived and born and Nkrumah chosen by us to lead us for independence.

(10) Because it was Nkrumah who asked the youth of Ghana . . . to make the Gold Coast a paradise so that when the gates of Heaven are opened by Peter we shall sit in heaven and see our children driving their aeroplanes, commanding their own armies.

(11) Because in Africa today the sun is rising not in East but in West all through Kwame Nkrumah.

(12) Because Nkrumah is talked about with surprise in Johannesburg, in Nairobi, Uganda, Alabama. . . .

(13) Because if Nkrumah fails, a great hope will die in Africa. . . .[22]

In the countryside, the main tactic used by the party was exploitation of rivalries between chiefdoms, lineages, and localities. The CPP, which liked to talk about its opposition to "tribalism" and "tribal reactionaries," and its allegiance to "unity," nevertheless concluded an alliance with a group of dissident Brong chiefs in Ashanti. The Brongs, the largest cocoa landowners in Ghana, agreed to give the CPP electoral support and were in turn rewarded with the creation of a separate Brong state (presently the Brong-Ahafo region) carved out of Ashanti territory.

The following extract from the journal of two CPP party workers campaigning in the villages of the Northern Territories vividly illustrates the CPP's methods:

We made it an issue that it was a fight between the Chianas and the Pagas. We will not like the Chianas to be paramount over us. We would have to walk to Chiana for court cases and pay our levies to them; we made it known that if we allowed the Chianas to win, that means Chianapio [the chief] would be paramount and would dictate to our chief in Paga.

---

22. *Evening News,* July 13, 1956, cited in Austin, *Politics in Ghana,* p. 334.

Owing to this news the whole of Paga went haywire. Enthusiastic representatives from all sections volunteered to help Paga win the election so that we might not become servants to the Chianas but masters of our own.[23]

In addition to battening on the numerous local and tribal disputes which beset Ghanaian society, the CPP was not averse to American-style "pork-barrel" campaigning. The party would often hold out to a local council the promise of a generous development grant or threaten its withdrawal.[24] In rural areas the CPP campaigners worked primarily through the chiefs or their emissaries. Outright bribes played a major role:

We slept in the town for two days and at night called on the Headman and explained what [the CPP candidate] was trying to do, tipped them heavily, gave out Kola and drinks, i.e., spirits, and clothes, etc. Before leaving ...., we left two of our men and a native who helped us a great deal, we gave them about 5 pounds each for canvassing, i.e., buy [sic] kola and tipping them, etc. We spent heavily in this constituency. The other side also spent heavily. In one case, a headman who was supporting us turned later to be our enemy. We understood the other side gave him about £40 cash as he was a popular man in this area and having many subjects under his command.[25]

In 1949, the CPP had relied on the youngmen as the class basis of the party. But because the party was trying to form as broad a coalition as possible against British colonialism, it had not felt able to organize an attack on chieftaincy. By 1956 the CPP had regressed to the point where it no longer based itself on the youngmen in the rural areas: it simply attempted to outbribe the Opposition for the favor of the chiefs. Yet it was the power of the chiefs that had to be broken if the democratic (to say nothing of the socialist) revolution were ever to take place in Ghana.

Consolidation and Repression

Although the CPP had only won the elections by a relatively narrow margin, the stage was now set for the formal

---

23. Austin, *Politics in Ghana*, p. 360.
24. See *ibid.*, p. 335, for examples.
25. *Ibid.*, p. 361.

grant of independence. Less than a month after the elections, Nkrumah introduced a resolution in the Legislative Assembly calling for independence. The CPP had won a national plebiscite and had strong British backing: the Right Opposition could do nothing but walk out. Now the NLM and its allies not only were reduced to regional support, but were forced to take the anti-nationalist position of trying to delay independence until their federal plan was adopted.

As late as November 1956, only a few months before independence, the NLM announced that it would declare a separate independence and proposed that "a partition commission to divide the assets and liabilities of the Gold Coast among its four component parts" be established.[26] The Opposition's demands were, of course, rejected by the Colonial Office; and its leaders shrank from organizing popular violence.[27] They therefore promised to set aside their plans for separate independence, and in return the CPP promised to establish the popularly elected regional bodies desired by the Opposition.

In the Trans-Volta Togoland area, the combination of "pan-Eweism," low cocoa prices, and a leadership uncommitted to the principles of non-violence produced rebellion. Two days before independence, on March 4, 1957, "disturbances" broke out. The new government moved troops and police into the area, and by March 18th more than 20 people had been killed or injured and nearly one hundred Ewes had been seized, tried, and sentenced to imprisonment. The top leaders of the Togoland Congress, MP's S. G. Antor and Kodzo Ayeke, were later arrested and convicted of organizing "the plot."

Only a few weeks later, in the capital itself, there sprang up an anti-CPP movement of the unemployed Ga workers and petty-bourgeoisie, which called itself the *Ga Shifimo Kpee* (Ga Standfast Organization). They demanded jobs, better housing, and lower food prices. Their rallies and marches, which often

---

26. *The Times* (London), November 21, 1956.
27. Busia, Joe Appiah, and J. B. Danquah issued a statement disavowing violence in 1957. They said: "Violence against established authority is practically unknown in the country. Except for the ugly and untraditional incident of positive action, led by Dr. Nkrumah in 1950, the country won its independence without any form of planned violence against the imperial power." *The Times* (London), November 4, 1957.

numbered in the tens of thousands, forced CPP ministers to drive their limousines down the side streets of Accra. But the really permanent effect of the GSK was to spur the passage of the Avoidance of Discrimination Bill. Henceforth, all "tribal, religious, and regional" parties were illegal.

In Ashanti, the leaders of the NLM could only bring themselves to support the *aims* of the new anti-CPP militants in Accra and Togo. The men and the methods still offended their special predilections. No organizational synthesis occurred until November 1957, and even after this date formal rather than organic unity joined the opposition forces. The Opposition in Ashanti and the Opposition in TVT continued to exist side by side, always approaching each other, yet never joined in practice.

In these circumstances, the CPP, shaken by the mass rallies in Accra and the armed revolt in Togo, but still in command of all the levers of power, began to use the state apparatus to prevent further erosion of its narrow popular base.

The following year, 1958, became the Year of Repression —relatively bloodless, but nevertheless effective. In January the newly-granted State of Emergency powers were used in Kumasi to make arrests and carry out deportations without trial; in February the NLM-dominated Kumasi State Council and the Asanteman Council were subjected to official investigation; in March Antor and Ayeke were sentenced to six years hard labor; in May the most important pro-NLM chief outside Ashanti, Nana Ofori Atta II, was destooled for "improper conduct."

In July, Dr. Nkrumah personally moved the first reading of the Preventive Detention Bill; in August, the 1957 compromise Constitution was tacitly rescinded by the reduction of the regional assemblies to advisory bodies.[28] In September, as a result of the February inquiries, the Kumasi and Asanteman Councils were deprived of their treasuries, and all lands and properties possessed by the Asantehene were taken from him. In November, the arrest and incarceration of 43 opposition members of the National Assembly was carried out. And in December the CPP closed out the year by making strikes illegal.

Thus by the end of 1958 not only had an important weap-

---

28. The Regional Assemblies were abolished in March 1959.

on of the organized working class been declared illegal, but the
Ga urban movement, the cocoa farmers in Ashanti and Trans-
Volta Togoland, the rentier chiefs, and the commercial strata
had all been utterly defeated or disorganized. If the CPP could
not achieve the power that flows from the organized allegiance
of the Ghanaian people, it still controlled the administrative
organs of the state. How did the CPP use them?

6

ECONOMICS IN THE POLITICAL KINGDOM, 1957-1961

As Charles Bettelheim has pointed out, the "poor" nations of the world are not underdeveloped: they are oppressed. Their problem is not lack of development but morbid development. This is no mere terminological quibble. It is the key to understanding the problem of economic backwardness. When a morphological study is made of the two types, it becomes clear that the industrial nation is not simply the enlarged "mature" form of the poor nation or its "logical" outgrowth:

Today's industrialized countries are not economically dependent. The structure of their production does not correspond to that of "underdeveloped" countries in which a few hypertrophied sectors are narrowly tied to a few foreign markets, deeply penetrated by foreign capital. These economies do not develop or stagnate according to the evolution of the world market for this or that mineral or agricultural raw material. They are not forced to support the cost of heavy foreign financial obligations (interest, dividends, royalties paid to foreign capitalists). Their infant industries do not have to face the competition of powerful, already established industries dominated by the same big capital which already dominates their own natural resources. These economies do not depend for their enlarged reproduction on imports of equipment coming from abroad. Even when they were not fully industrialized, they were not deformed and disequilibrated but, on the contrary, integrated and self-centered.[1]

According to Bettelheim, it is incorrect to say that the poor countries have not developed. They have. But their development has been skewed by their relationship with the West.[2] Consequently, the problem of economic growth is not solved by

---

1. *Planification et croissance accélérée*, Paris, 1965, pp. 28-29.

2. Bettelheim admits that there *are* some countries that could properly be called underdeveloped, i.e., have maintained the same socio-economic structures for centuries. But these countries—Yemen and Nepal are two examples he gives—have been cut off from contact with the "developed" countries and do not present the same characteristics as the majority of oppressed nations.

evolution, i.e., by stimulating growth within the old economic structures and by intensifying the existing relationships. Growth can only be attained by the opposite means—by smashing the old structures and severing the old relationships. Only then is it possible to achieve rational, democratic, collective control over economic inputs and outputs—that is, socialist planning.

The Two Ghanas: 1957-1966

Ghana's morbid development—the hypertrophy of her foreign-dominated export sectors, the rudimentary growth of her internal productive sectors—typifies the dualism characteristic of oppressed nations. We have seen thus far that during the early years of its rule, the CPP made no effort whatsoever to restructure Ghanaian society: the leaders did not see the institutions left behind by the British colonialists as barriers to national economic development. The CPP, at this time, believed that in order to achieve rapid economic growth the institutions of colonialism needed only to be administered by Africans.

At this point one might ask: "If Nkrumah simply maintained all the old colonial institutions, what made the 'free world' attack him so bitterly? Why did the Soviet Union consistently single him out for special praise? How did Ghana become known as a center of African socialism?" The answer is that there was not one Ghana, but two—a pro-Western Ghana from approximately 1957 to 1961, and a pro-socialist Ghana from 1961 to February 1966. The first Ghana operated as an ordinary neo-colony stagnating within the British sphere of influence. It looked to the British pound as its "anchor of safety," kept its external reserves in London instead of Accra, and allowed the British banks to systematically deflate the economy. Post-1961 Ghana attempted to adopt socialist planning techniques, tried to build up the state industrial sector, and finally brought the British banks under some measure of control.

Pre-1961 Ghana had been guided by a development strategy formulated by W. Arthur Lewis.[3] This strategy, which emphas-

---

3. W. Arthur Lewis is an eminent West Indian economist who has taught at Manchester University and Princeton. He is the author of the much praised book *The Theory of Economic Growth*, London, 1955. He has also written a series of articles in *Encounter* magazine about politics in West Africa.

ized total dependence on foreign capital to industrialize the country, brought nearly complete disaster. During the "Lewis era," Ghana experienced rapid deterioration of her balance of payments position, loss of huge amounts of external reserves, and failure to attract anywhere near the amount of foreign capital which Lewis counted on to assure Ghana's industrial future.

Then during the depth of Ghana's 1961 balance of payments debacle, Nkrumah introduced the "Seven Year Plan for Work and Happiness." This plan forms a real watershed in post-independence Ghanaian history. The plan declared socialism to be the national objective and sought to achieve self-sustaining industrial growth by 1967. Contrary to the Lewis strategy, the state was to have the major role in economic development.

Historical accuracy is not the only reason for emphasizing the existence of two stages of Ghanaian history and attempting to describe how one stage led to the next. There are also important political reasons. By telescoping Ghanaian history into one horrendous "socialistic-communistic dictatorship," the NATO intellectuals are able to ignore the neo-colonial background from which Ghana tried to escape; they are not required to defend the embarrassing Lewis period. This period provides an obvious case study of how the most "affluent" of the oppressed nations carefully followed the orthodox teachings of a respected NATO intellectual and achieved rapid progress—to the brink of economic disaster.

By treating Ghanaian history as a monolith, it is possible to ignore entirely the reasons why Nkrumah at last tried to take a non-capitalist path. Instead, his increasingly bitter attacks on neo-colonialism can be discussed in psycho-pathological terms: "paranoia," "love-hate relationship," "increasing megalomania," "transference," etc. Finally, if all of Ghana's post-independence history was an experiment in socialism, and if that experiment failed, then it can be argued that socialism is really unworkable in Africa.

As we will try to show, the failure of the socialist experiment in Ghana did not lie in the peculiarity of African circumstances, and still less in the psychology of a single man. It failed because the attempt to break with Ghana's colonial past was not made soon enough, and because when it was made, it was not complete enough. In order to understand the failure of the post-1961 socialist experiment, as well as the earlier failure of the Lewis strategy, it is necessary now to analyze more precisely the neo-colonial mode of production in Ghana and the barriers it presented to balanced, integrated economic growth. Three major sectors of the economy will be touched upon: cocoa, mining, and manufacturing.

Cocoa and Economic Control

Everyone knows how important cocoa is to the Ghanaian economy: from 1950 to 1962, it formed anywhere from 56 to 75 percent of Ghana's total exports. Many also know about the post-1960 fall in cocoa prices. And it has been widely suggested that this fall in cocoa prices was responsible for Ghana's economic difficulties. A few writers have even asserted that a conspiracy by London chocolate manufacturers was responsible for the drop in prices. The truth is both less simple and more intractable.

All cocoa manufacturers have an interest in keeping prices low—just as cocoa-producing nations have an interest in keeping them high. But neither group has been able to get a corner on the market. It is the interaction between world supply and world demand that actually determines the price of Ghanaian cocoa. The world supply of cocoa is increasing rapidly, but in recent years the world demand for cocoa has been relatively inelastic. That is, the more Ghanaian cocoa that hits the market, the less willing its foreign consumers are to buy it at the same price. Thus the world cocoa price drops as production increases.

Looking at Table 6, we see that after 1958, Ghana's cocoa income reached a kind of plateau, fluctuating within a narrow range. At the same time, production and exports expanded rapidly, with exports more than doubling between 1958 and 1962.

Assuming that demand remains relatively inelastic, as it has since 1957, some have suggested that Ghana ought to try to increase her share of the world cocoa market as against the other African producers. Actually, it is doubtful that Ghana will even be able to hold her own. Cocoa production is highest on virgin

Table 6
Prices and Volumes of Cocoa Exports, 1950-1962[4]

Year	World price £ per ton	World production in thousands of tons	Ghanaian exports in thousands of tons	Ghanaian cocoa earnings £ million
1950	208	752	267	54.6
1951	285	801	230	60.3
1952	301	642	212	52.5
1953	237	796	237	56.1
1954	467	774	214	84.6
1955	302	798	206	65.6
1956	221	840	234	51.1
1957	247	893	260	50.9
1958	352	767	197	62.3
1959	285	905	250	68.8
1960	226	1041	303	66.4
1961	180	1157	405	69.3
1962	170	1216	421	67.0

forest land, which in Ghana is in perilously short supply. The Ivory Coast and Nigeria, on the other hand, are said to have large amounts of suitable unexploited land. Ghana's competitive position is further undermined by the higher productivity elsewhere in Africa: Nigerian producers grow over twice as much cocoa per acre as their Ghanaian counterparts.[5] Thus Ghana may have to make considerable efforts to cut costs, rationalize, and intensify production just to hold her own against the other cocoa-producing nations.

But what about withholding the cocoa or storing it? An attempt to construct refrigerated cocoa storage facilities was actually begun in 1965. But while storage may conceivably enable Ghana to take advantage of seasonal price fluctuations, a long-range program could only be successful if all cocoa producers participated. The history of such ventures leaves little room for optimism: in the past, attempts to withhold cocoa on an international basis have been defeated by one or more nations giving in to the lure of higher prices, and thus destroying the

4. Adapted from Tony Killick, "External Trade," in *A Study of Contemporary Ghana,* pp. 345, 348.
5. *West Africa,* December 14, 1963.

withholding scheme. Thus, in the long run, given the present political situation, cocoa storage would probably not change the price level appreciably. Consequently, neither increasing cocoa production nor decreasing it, neither storing cocoa nor burning it, can solve the dilemma of cocoa monoculture.

The problem of cocoa monoculture can be discussed superficially in terms of decisions about comparative advantage, marginal costs, sectoral stability, etc. The piecemeal social engineers of the World Bank and the Agency for International Development encourage this type of discussion. Yet the obvious alternative to monoculture is diversification.

Diversification, however, cannot come about as long as semi-feudal land relationships are maintained and as long as investment and savings decisions are uncoordinated. It can only be achieved through new social and economic structures: large-scale farming, central planning, and domestic production of agricultural capital goods. But the prerequisite for building these new structures must be made clear—a social revolution. Those socialists who try to conceal this prerequisite become increasingly hard to distinguish from the technocrats of the World Bank. The structures of the new Ghana cannot be adaptations or outgrowths of the old. This can be further seen from the way the mining industry has skewed the development of nearly every sector of the economy.

Mining and Infrastructure

Ghana has been famous for its gold mines for centuries. As early as 1471, there is a record of Portuguese traders dealing in gold near the mouth of the Pra River. But it was only in the late 19th and 20th centuries that European mining with modern technology was begun.

The long-run significance of the foreign-owned mines lay not only in the loss of Ghana's gold, manganese, and diamonds without adequate compensation.[6] It was of equal importance that as a result of the mineowners' requirements, the internal

---

6. The "rent" paid during the early part of the twentieth century by foreign mine owners as a result of negotiations with Gold Coast chiefs, who were generally illiterate, was derisory.

Ghanaian economy was forced to adjust to an artificial infrastructure. As H. S. Frankel explains: "The history of . . . [foreign] investments in Africa and elsewhere affords many examples of railway lines, roads, ports, irrigation works, etc. in the 'wrong places' which not only failed to lead to income generating development, but actually inhibited more economic developments which might have otherwise taken place."[7] All over Africa—and Asia and Latin America as well—wherever British mining industry and trading interests gained a foothold, the railroads became inland continuations of British steamship lines.

Another decisive effect of the British mining industry on the Ghanaian economy has been felt on the national wage structure. Superficially, it would seem improbable that the mining industry could exert any considerable influence. It contributes only a relatively small proportion of gross value added (5.3 percent in 1960) and employs only a relatively small percent of the total Ghanaian labor force (2.9 percent in 1960). Nevertheless, mine workers occupy a strategic position: 15 percent of all those employed in the private sector work in the mines. Mine workers also account for an especially large percentage of employed skilled workers. The gold mining industry alone employs 32 percent of skilled workers in both the private and public sectors.[8]

Further, while miners have been among the best organized strata of the Ghanaian working class—as early as 1948 the mine workers' union numbered over 15,000—they are divided into skilled and unskilled categories and geographically scattered according to their place of work. The mine owners, on the other hand, all have identical interests in wage policy and are able to concentrate their economic power to a much greater degree.

The catalyst which makes these factors influence the wage structure so decisively is a peculiarity of the market for gold. Goldmining, which is by far the largest of all Ghanaian mining activities, is especially vulnerable to rising labor costs, because

7. *Some Aspects of International Economic Development of Underdeveloped Countries,* Princeton, 1952, p. 14.

8. Tony Killick, "Mining," in *A Study of Contemporary Ghana,* p. 131; also Table 11.5, p. 264.

the price of gold on the world market is set at $35.00 an ounce, the price at which the United States Treasury is obligated to buy. Practically speaking, the world price can go no higher and no lower than this unless there are sweeping changes in United States monetary policy.

Obviously, if wages rise beyond a certain level, profits will be squeezed to the point where mining operations must be curtailed. Consequently, the mineowners must lobby constantly to prevent the minimum wage—which is set by the government—from "getting out of hand." Their success has been noteworthy: while the real wages of workers have not risen since 1938, Ashanti Gold Fields Ltd. consistently shows an annual profit of anywhere from 35 percent to 50 percent.[9]

The failure of real wages to show a significant rise since 1938 has had implications far beyond the mining industry. Low wages have prevented the growth of demand for consumer goods and thus retarded the development of manufacturing industry and contributed to maintaining Ghana's export orientation.

Merchant Capital and Manufacturing

The Ghanaian manufacturing sector is minuscule. In 1958, it accounted for only 1.8 percent of Gross Domestic Product.[10] And since Ghanaian industrial statistics reflect the output of all kinds of independent artisans (92 percent of all "manufacturing" establishments had no paid employees at all), the modern manufacturing sector is even smaller. What modern manufacturing does exist is almost entirely foreign owned.

But what is really significant about foreign capital in Ghana is not its control of modern manufacturing. Even more important is the insignificance of the total investment. The foreign investor has made no serious attempt to exploit the possibilities of the Ghanaian consumer market, much less provide risk capital or sink money into capital-goods-producing industries. The foreign capitalist today is not inundating the oppressed nations with his capital: his investment, particularly in manufacturing, is trifling.

---

9. *Ibid.*, p. 141.
10. Robert Szereszewski, "Performance of the Economy, 1955-1962," in *A Study of Contemporary Ghana*, p. 62.

In Ghana, the entrenchment of huge amounts of foreign merchant capital poses a formidable barrier to foreign manufacturing investment. Firms like UAC, which itself accumulates yearly net profits higher than the tax revenues of most African nations, effectively control the channels of exchange not only in Ghana, but in several other countries in East and West Africa. The basis of these firms' business is the import of manufactured goods from Great Britain. Any growth of consumer goods industries—whether established by Ghanaian socialists or by Ghanaian capitalists—would constitute a direct threat to their import lines.

Whenever manufacturing activity "threatens" to break out, the UAC attempts to contain it or take it over for itself. This speech by a CPP backbench businessman illustrates the process:

The government told us some time ago that the Industrial Development Corporation [a government agency] was going to establish a soap factory. All that the Corporation did was to buy somebody's soap factory at Korle Gonno for about £10,000. Now we learn that a certain engineer is coming to establish a £1 million soap factory for the UAC at Tema. Are we to allow foreigners to set up industries which we have the facilities to establish ourselves? Whenever we suggest that certain industries should be set up in the country, some expatriate [foreign] higher-ups [in the civil service] cleverly turn them down. They do so on the ground that the industries would not be economic simply because they want their friends overseas to come and establish them.[11]

UAC "manufacturing" activity is confined to cheapening the cost of imported commodities through processing, assembling, or packaging them in Ghana.[12] This saves the UAC the cost of shipping certain commodities in bulk, but it does not begin the process of developing an integrated manufacturing sector in Ghana. Merchant capital remains one of the most formidable enemies of the socialist revolution because it is the most formidable enemy of the industrial revolution.

---

11. Gold Coast, Legislative Assembly, *Debates,* January 21, 1957.
12. The UAC's investment criteria are presented in the company's journal, *Statistical and Economic Review,* April, 1964.

The 1959 Plan

We have already noted that up to 1961, Ghana's economic policies followed the lines laid down in W. Arthur Lewis's 1953 *Report on Industrialization and the Gold Coast*. For two years after independence, the Lewis strategy of governmental passivity and reliance on foreign capital was so influential that Ghana actually had no economic development plan at all. The 1951 Development Plan (the Arden-Clarke Plan) which had concentrated on expanding Ghana's infrastructure, was completed; the country had entered a "period of consolidation." And when the second Five Year Development Plan was introduced in 1959, both its targets and its economic instrumentalities showed the influence of the Lewis strategy for economic development.

The Plan had been drawn up with a "shopping list" technique. Since the state had no control over the means of production, the question of how to generate the maximum surplus for development purposes could not even be raised. Instead, the various ministries simply suggested lists of whatever projects they thought might be both useful and economically feasible. The planners were then limited to dropping or modifying proposals in order to keep within the total budget: considering the interrelationships between projects in different sectors of the economy was not part of the planner's job.[13] In this respect, the Second Development Plan resembled the colonial Gold Coast's earlier development plans.

Although the 1959 Plan also shared the "welfare state" orientation of the colonial plans, it appeared to be a considerably more ambitious effort. Over £350 million was allocated for a five year period, while the 1951 plan had spent only £117.5 million in six years. But this apparent break with the colonial past was wholly illusory.

Within the 1959 plan there were actually two separate plans. One, providing for expenditures of £132 million, was for implementation. The other, which was to remain on paper only, amounted to £250 million. The £132 million figure was called the "small coat" plan, while the £250 million paper

---

13. See E. N. Omaboe, "The Process of Planning," in *A Study of Contemporary Ghana.*

plan was referred to as the "big coat" plan. The small coat plan was private but operational; the big coat plan was public but only inspirational. E. N. Omaboe asserted that:

The small coat plan was based on a realistic appraisal of the country's resources and potential. The projects listed under this plan were those which could be implemented without much difficulty during the course of the following five years. The large coat plan on the other hand, contained in addition to the projects in the small coat plan, a number of projects which the planners themselves knew could not be carried through during the plan period for a number of reasons.[14]

The 1961 Crisis

In 1961, the Second Development Plan was publicly abandoned. Increasing balance of payments deficits, dwindling reserves, and failure to attract foreign investment forced Ghana to search for a new development strategy. Not "flirtation" with socialist planning, not hostility to British entrepreneurs operating in Ghana, but complete reliance on the conventional wisdom reflected in the Lewis approach had led Ghana into this predicament.

A series of increasing balance of payments deficits interrupted in only one year since 1956, culminated in a 1961 deficit of almost £53 million—approximately 12 percent of the national product. In order to appreciate the significance of such a deficit in an economy the size of Ghana's, we can compare this figure to the balance of payments deficits that preoccupy the United States government. The United States government institutes "voluntary" controls on private overseas investment and considers curtailing tourism by American private citizens, as a result of deficits of around $2 billion—or less than half of one percent of the national product. What factors were involved in this terrible Ghanaian economic blood-letting?

The largest sources of outflow were greatly increased expenditures for non-durable consumer goods (chiefly food and clothing), rising costs of invisibles (chiefly shipping costs and

_____
14. *Ibid.*, pp. 446-447.

freight insurance), and *disinvestment* by private capital. In addition, the foreign banks were steadily increasing their external assets. These were the main channels through which the leakage occurred.

What prevented the Ghanaian government from closing them off by instituting import and exchange controls? The answer is that imposing controls would have brought the government into direct conflict with the two largest blocs of capital in Ghana—the banks and "the firms." To discommode them would reduce "business confidence" and discourage foreign investment. And, according to the Lewis prescription, Ghana could not industrialize without the foreign investor.

The Wasted Reserves

In the 1953 *Report,* Lewis had suggested that industrial investment of about £2 million yearly was necessary in order to achieve a "take-off." In 1954, however, the Gold Coast government had well over 200 million pounds locked up in long-term, low-interest British securities. In order to meet the Lewis target, it would seem that foreign capital investment was totally unnecessary: all that was really needed was transfer of capital assets. The Government could have disinvested in Britain and begun to put the capital to work building factories at home. But such a course of action would have violated the guidelines established by the Lewis report. The 1954 *Economic Survey* explained why the Gold Coast had to continue holding its reserves in London as follows:

> If the Gold Coast is to be able to stand on its own feet as an independent country, then it is essential that it should be able to demonstrate its ability and will to meet its commitments and so inspire the confidence without which foreign assistance whether in the form of private investment, managerial ability, or financial assistance, will not be forthcoming.[15]

According to this through-the-looking-glass logic, the way to obtain capital imports was to increase capital exports!

---

15. Gold Coast, *1954 Economic Survey,* para. 43.

In the event, however, it turned out that Ghana's reserves could neither "inspire confidence" nor build Ghanaian factories. They had to be used to meet the balance of payments deficits. In other words, Ghana did not use up her reserves in an orgy of spending on so-called "prestige" projects: she used them to meet the obligations imposed on her by the "crackpot realism" of the Lewis strategy.

In Search of the Foreign Capitalist

The crowning irony of the whole pre-1961 period lay in the inability to attract foreign capital despite every conceivable inducement and concession. From 1957 to 1961 there was a net *outflow* of private capital amounting to about £6.5 million. Yet Ghana had followed Lewis's conventional recommendations to the letter. The constitution contained a pledge to compensate foreign capitalists in case of nationalization. The 1959 "Pioneer Industries and Companies Act" eliminated the maximum of five years' tax holiday and instead provided tax relief for as long as it took a company to recover its initial investment. And an Import Duties Act gave private companies remission of import duties on their raw materials.[16]

But despite fiscal and monetary policies which were conservative by any standards, generous guarantees to private investors, and special bureaus set up to attract foreign investment, the effort failed completely. It would appear that factors other than "business confidence" shape the investment decisions made by foreign capitalists. After all, if friendliness to foreign business could attract capital to the manufacturing sector, Liberia would be the Pittsburgh of Africa. The Lewis strategy for Ghana's industrialization failed because its main preoccupation—establishing the government's conservative credentials—was only ancillary to the foreign capitalists' investment criteria. The foreign capitalists most interested in Ghana were merchant capitalists who were primarily concerned to maintain the existing import-export pattern. They had no desire to see countries like Ghana outgrow their services.

---

16. "Promoting Private Investment in Less Developed Countries," in *Financing African Development,* ed. by Tom J. Farer. Cambridge, 1965, p. 134.

In the attempt to establish a conservative "image," Ghana had opened the way for the balance of payments difficulties of the 1959-1961 period and lost the greater share of her reserves without any tangible benefits. After 1961, the policies of the Nkrumah government changed: they included large government outlays for consumer- and capital-goods factories, Soviet-inspired planning techniques, stringent import controls, and expanded fiscal and monetary powers. All these policies were part of Ghana's natural reaction against the failures of the neocolonial period.

7

POLITICIANS AND "LABOR ARISTOCRATS"

On September 4, 1961, a general strike broke out simultaneously in Sekondi-Takoradi and Kumasi. Quickly it spread to Accra: by September 6th, economic activity in Ghana's three largest cities had come to a halt. It was the first general strike since the Positive Action campaign of 1950. And while Nkrumah's attitude towards that strike had been ambiguous, his position towards the 1961 strike was clear as could be. During the early days of the strike, he had been attending the Conference of Nonaligned Nations in Belgrade. Apparently hoping local leaders would be able to handle the situation, Nkrumah traveled to the Soviet Union, where he began what was supposed to be a long vacation on the Black Sea. Finally, however, after two weeks of the strike, Nkrumah felt compelled to leave the Soviet Union and confront the workers himself. Threats, ultimatums, and administrative measures finally forced the workers back to their jobs.

Both CPP Ministers and Trades Union Congress officials denounced the strike as "counter-revolutionary." The government's duty, they said, was to assure the welfare of the country as a whole: it could not allow national economic planning to be sabotaged by the demands of workers, who already enjoyed a higher standard of living than the majority of the population. In 1950, however, the workers had also been better paid than agricultural laborers—yet they had been the vanguard of the CPP's Positive Action campaign. What had occurred to split the workers from the CPP? What had they contributed to the independence movement, and what had they gained from it?

One indication of their working conditions comes from Richard Wright's 1954 description of stevedores in Accra:

Coming toward me was an army of men, naked save for ragged strips of cloth about their hips, dripping wet, their black skins glistening in the pitiless sun, their heads holding pieces of freight —parts of machines, wooden crates, sacks of cement—some of which were so heavy that as many as four men had to put their heads under them to carry them forward. . . .

The wet and glistening black robots would beach their canoes filled with merchandise and, without pausing, heave out the freight and hoist it upon their heads: then, at breakneck speed, rush out of the sea, tamping through soft, wet sand toward a warehouse. They ran in single file, one behind the other, barely glancing at me as they pushed forward, their naked feet leaving prints in the soft sand which the next sea wave would wash away. On the horizon of the sea, about two miles away, were anchored the European freighters and between the shore and those ships were scores of black dots—canoes filled with rowing men—bobbing and dancing on the heaving water.[1]

The goods Wright described could have been unloaded on the Sekondi-Takoradi docks. But this would have required shipment by rail to Accra—and a lowering of the importers' profits. And so men and canoes did the work of docks and cranes, for a wage of fourteen cents per trip. In one day, a man could make seven trips maximum—98 cents.[2]

In terms of real wages, 1954 (when Wright visited Ghana) was a relatively good year—one of the best since the peak year of 1939. As Table 7 shows, it was not until 1958, seven years after Nkrumah became Prime Minister, that real wages rose above prewar levels. Independence brought a temporary increase in real wages, but by 1963 they had again fallen below the 1939 level. While official figures for 1964 and 1965 real wages are not available, they have obviously deteriorated still further. Minimum wages remain at 6s./6d., and the most conservative estimates of price increases since 1963 put the figure at 20 percent.

Workers were forced to take jobs like those Wright described for such low wages because of widespread and continuous unemployment and severe disguised unemployment. The unemployment figures in Table 8 do not come from a slump year:

---

1. Wright, *Black Power*, pp. 120-121.
2. *Ibid.*, pp. 121-122.

Table 7

Wages of Unskilled Workers in Accra, 1939-1963[3]
(May 1939 = 100)

Date	Daily wage rate	Money-wage index	Cost-of-living index	Real-wage index
May 1939	1/6	100	100	100
Dec. 1941	1/10	122	151	81
Nov. 1943	1/10	122	168	73
Nov. 1945	1/10	122	186	66
Nov. 1946	2/1	139	198	70
Nov. 1947	2/9	183	212	86
Dec. 1948	2/9	183	227	81
Sept. 1949	3/2	211	243	87
Dec. 1950	3/3	217	285	76
Dec. 1951	3/3	217	333	65
Dec. 1952	4/6	300	326	92
Dec. 1953	4/6	300	324	93
Dec. 1954	4/6	300	324	93
Dec. 1955	4/6	300	344	87
April 1956	5/2	344	351	98
Dec. 1957	5/2	344	351	98
Dec. 1958	5/6	367	354	104
Dec. 1959	5/6	367	364	101
July 1960	6/6	433	364	119
Dec. 1961	6/6	433	410	106
Dec. 1962	6/6	433	426	102
Dec. 1963	6/6	433	486	89

in 1960, real wages and Gross Domestic Product per capita were both at record heights. It is necessary to emphasize these figures, for it is frequently denied that serious unemployment exists in Ghana.[4] But as P. T. Bauer noted from personal experience:

Notices of "no vacancies" are ubiquitous. A constant stream of applications for employment reaches the mercantile firms, and this increases several times over when it becomes known that a definite vacancy has occurred or that an extension of activities can be expected. The inclination to trade even when only a few pence a day can be earned, the large internal migrations in both Nigeria

---

3. *A Study of Contemporary Ghana*, pp. 141, 155.
4. See, for example, W. A. Lewis, *Report on Industrialization in the Gold Coast, 1953.*

and the Gold Coast (which are only partly seasonal), . . . all these point in the same direction and suggest a widespread lack of opportunities for unskilled or poorly skilled peoples seeking employment at current wages.[5]

Bad working conditions, low wages, and high unemployment all undermine the theory that the Ghanaian worker is part of a labor aristocracy. So too does the history of the early trade union movement.

Table 8
Unemployment, 1960[6]

Age	Sex	Labor force	Wage-labor force	Unemployed	Unemployed as percentage of: Labor force	Unemployed as percentage of: Wage-labor force
All ages	M	1,682,730	567,760	109,560	6.5	19.3
	F	1,042,120	89,910	54,250	5.2	60.3
15-29	M	685,340	n.a.	82,670	12.2	—
	F	467,190	n.a.	43,330	9.3	—
30-49	M	709,770	n.a.	21,530	3.0	—
	F	404,480	n.a.	7,180	1.8	—
Over 50	M	287,620	n.a.	5,360	1.9	—
	F	170,450	n.a.	3,770	2.2	—

Unions and Politics

With the growth of an urban working class in the 1940's, the British took measures to prevent workers' organizations from expressing radical or nationalist aims. As Sidney Webb had explained when he was Labor Secretary of State for the Colonies:

There is a danger that without sympathetic supervision and guidance, organizations and labourers without experience of combination for any social or economic purposes may fall under the

5. *West African Trade*, p. 19. Bauer recalls that he asked the manager of a British-owned tobacco factory in Ibadan whether he could expand his labor force without raising wages if he wished to do so. The manager replied that his only problem would be to control the mob of applicants.

6. *A Study of Contemporary Ghana*, p. 149. The "wage-labor force" is defined as the number of employees (generally wage or salary earners) plus the number of unemployed. The "labor force" includes non-salaried (generally agricultural) workers.

domination of disaffected persons by whom their activities may be diverted to improper and mischievous ends.[7]

Thus, when unions were legalized in the Gold Coast in 1941, they were also required to submit their accounts, rules, and membership to colonial officials each year. British trade union bureaucrats were imported: they advised emulation of British organizational models and stressed the dangers of "political" involvement. The Gold Coast's first Trades Union Congress, headed by Sir Charles Tachie-Menson, C.B.E., was formed under their guidance.[8]

The British policy of de-politicization was unsuccessful. Richard Wright noted that every union meeting he attended was devoted to political questions: "Their standard of living could not be thought of as being separate from their colonial status and nobody could ever fool them on that fundamental point."[9] The clear-headedness of trade unionists on this point enabled them to form the real vanguard of the independence movement; the CPP youngmen often followed reluctantly. In 1950, it had been the trade unions' declaration of a general strike which had finally pushed Nkrumah into opening the Positive Action campaign.[10]

Trade unionists played leading roles in the early CPP: H. P. Nyemitei held positions of both assistant general secretary of the CPP and president of the Meteorological Workers' Union. Anthony Woode, Pobee Biney, and Turkson Ocran also doubled as both trade union leaders and CPP spokesmen. Biney and Woode, both Marxists, were elected to the Legislative Assembly in 1951. Biney was an especially versatile trade union leader. He began as a locomotive driver and became vice-chairman of the Gold Coast Trade Union Congress. Then he became a rural organizer for the CPP. Biney established one of the first solid rural political bases for the party in the Denkyira area, and, in the parliamentary election in that district, de-

---

7. Walter Bowen, *Colonial Trade Unions,* London, p. 4.
8. Sir Tachie later became the first Ghanaian appointed to Barclays Bank's Ghana Board.
9. Wright, *Black Power,* p. 328.
10. See above, pp. 29-30.

feated the local "indirect rule" chief, Sir Tsibu Darku, O.B.E., by a margin of four to one.

After the 1950 Positive Action Campaign, however, with Biney, Woode, and other working-class leaders imprisoned, the Gold Coast government had pushed the Gold Coast Trade Union Congress (GCTUC) to reorganize. New leaders were appointed and affiliated the Congress to the International Confederation of Free Trade Unions (ICFTU), the "free world" trade union organization. This was the apogee of the continual British effort to de-politicize the trade union movement. On the release of the militants from jail in 1951, however, they organized a rival Trade Union Congress, the Ghana Trade Union Congress (GTUC). This new group was pro-CPP, anti-ICFTU, and took a stronger position than the GCTUC on both wage and political matters.

But while the radical trade unionists helped to form a pro-CPP Trade Union Congress, they often took an independent line: GTUC leaders were especially critical of the "tactical action" period. Anthony Woode warned of the dangers involved in foreign capital controlling the Volta project. He and Ocran (then president and general secretary of the GTUC, respectively) attacked the party leaders in August 1952 for having compromised on the issue of immediate self-government.

This critical left-wing position was only tolerated for a short time. In 1953, the rival trade union organizations merged. Shortly thereafter, both Woode and Ocran were suspended from the CPP. One of the charges brought against Woode was attendance at a meeting of the World Federation of Trade Unions (WFTU), the international communist trade union organization. Ocran was removed from his post as general secretary of the Trade Union Congress and replaced by John Tettegah, a young clerk of moderate views. In 1954, the CPP refused to renominate Woode and Biney for their parliamentary seats. During the same period, with the militants purged, the Trade Union Congress moved towards a formal alliance with the "free world" trade unions: in 1954 membership in ICFTU was renewed.

The CPP Takes Over

Originally, the trade union movement had supported the

CPP voluntarily. Following independence, steps were taken to ensure that the unions would be unable to oppose it. After dumping the militant leaders, the trade unions were reorganized and integrated into the state apparatus. The major instrument of change was the 1958 Industrial Relations Act, the most visible effect of which was to create 24 big unions with large operating budgets and full-time staffs. Like most militant trade unions in underdeveloped countries, Ghanaian unions had been short on strike funds and relied on unpaid or poorly paid union leaders. Even the largest union, the Mines Employees, had started a hundred-day strike in 1955 with reserves of only £571.

The newly strengthened unions were subordinated to the Trades Union Congress (TUC). The TUC received 45 percent of the compulsory 2s per month union dues. Half of this sum, a quarter of the workers' dues, went for the TUC's "administrative expenses," i.e., headquarters buildings, officials' cars, and salaries. In addition, the administrative expenses of both local and national unions had to be met. As a result, only 15 percent of the dues went into social benefits, insurance, and strike funds. Furthermore, the TUC exercised disciplinary powers over member unions. Its Executive Board could investigate union activities, direct unions to discontinue any action, and suspend or expel disobedient officials.

The Trade Union Congress was, in turn, subordinated to the state and party. The Minister of Labor could arbitrarily dissolve any union—no rights of appeal existed. Similarly, the President of the Republic could freeze the funds of the TUC in response to any action which he thought "not conducive to the public good." Most important of all, strikes were, for all practical purposes, prohibited.[11]

Substantial trade union resistance to this reorganization developed. The 1958 act was opposed by two of the oldest and best organized unions in the country: the United Africa Company Workers' Union and the Sekondi-Takoradi Railway Workers, the union in which Biney, Ocran, and Woode had been

---

11. For further details on the Industrial Relations Acts, see Tony Killick, "Labor: A General Survey," in *A Study of Contemporary Ghana*, pp. 142-147. See also Douglas Rimmer, "The New Industrial Relations in Ghana," *Industrial and Labor Relations Review*, January, 1961, pp. 206-226.

active. This resistance led the TUC to request a new law
making unions outside the TUC illegal. The request was
granted: the Industrial Relations Amendment Act of 1959 gave
unions two months to amalgamate with the twenty-four ap-
proved unions or be dissolved by decree.

The leadership of the new unions served the interests of
state and party rather than the interests of the rank and file.
In 1961 indirect taxes on coffee, tea, and tobacco, as well as on
such staples as cloth, vegetables, and fish, were raised 50 to
100 percent. Real wages dropped 15 percent. In July, the
government imposed a five percent compulsory savings deduc-
tion on all wage-earners receiving over £150 per year. Though
these measures bore especially heavily on workers, the trade
union leadership made no protest.

The General Strike

On September 4, 1961, workers received the first pay
packets from which the five percent compulsory savings had
been deducted. The general strike broke out the same day.
Transport workers in Accra and Kumasi participated, but the
real heart of the strike was Sekondi-Takoradi. There, railway-
men, dock workers, commercial employees, civil servants, and
market women joined to protest the wage deductions.

The first day of the strike, Krobo Edusei, Minister of
Communications and Transport, addressed a meeting of railway workers, ordering them to return to their jobs and accept
the compulsory wage deductions. From no other man in Ghana
would a speech on austerity have been more inappropriate.
Edusei, the owner of a £70,000 house in Kumasi, also gained
notoriety as the importer of the first solid gold bed in Ghana.
He once pointed out that "Socialism doesn't mean that if you've
made a lot of money, you can't keep it."[12]

Trade Union Congress officials reflected Edusei's position:
they ordered the strikers to return to work. It was, as one Accra
labor official commented, "a demonstration where the workers
are leading their leaders."[13] On September 9, John Tettegah, the
general secretary of the TUC, returned from Yugoslavia, where

12. Conor Cruse O'Brien, *London Observer*, March 17, 1966.
13. *Ashanti Pioneer*, September 6, 1961.

he had been attending the Belgrade Conference. Instead of supporting the trade unionists, he joined Krobo Edusei in calls for crushing the strike. A limited state of emergency was declared in Sekondi-Takoradi on September 9 and extended two days later. Then a dusk-to-dawn curfew was imposed. But the strike continued.

On September 17, Nkrumah returned from Sochi, repealed the emergency measures, and gave the strikers two days to return to work. On the 19th, the workers were still out. Nkrumah made a further appeal. This time he equated the strike with treason: "Those who do not [return to work] will have given clear indication that they and their instigators behind them are determined to bring about the overthrow of the constitution by illegal means."[14] He also suggested that the workers present their grievances to their "spokesman"—the TUC.

The strike had been based on serious economic grievances: falling real wages, rising prices, and salary deductions imposed without consulting the workers. The CPP never even acknowledged these specific grievances. Nevertheless, on September 23rd, with their funds totally exhausted, the workers returned to their jobs. A few weeks later, the government began its clean-up campaign: the railway workers who had emerged as leaders were arrested; the market women who had organized provisioning of food supplies to the workers were detained; union officials who had supported the rank and file were expelled from their posts.

The CPP's Rationale

The CPP government rationalized its police measures against the organized working class by equating independence with socialism. According to John Tettegah, colonial trade unions are primarily concerned with improving the wages and working conditions of their members. Under colonial conditions this is acceptable, for any economic victories won by the union are simultaneously blows against the power of the foreigner.

But with independence, all this changes. Though the work-

---

14. *Ibid.,* September 22, 1961.

er is still employed by the same foreign-owned companies, he is now his own master and must devote his energies to increasing output. The "consumptionist" orientation of the trade unions becomes harmful, for wage demands on the foreign firms slow down the rate of economic growth. Thus, after independence the trade unions must take on new functions. Their role is not to agitate for higher wages: these will be determined by the government in the light of overall plans for development. Nor are they allowed to concern themselves with the content of economic planning, to aid in industrial management, or even to articulate workers' demands. Instead, they provide bone and sinew which supports the ideological "vanguard"—the CPP. Tettegah described the relationship as follows:

> The first task of our revolutionary Trades Union Congress is to strengthen our Party continuously. Under the leadership of Osagyefo, the CPP is the vanguard of those who are grappling with the problems of today and tomorrow. In order to realise this, it is necessary that the aims of the Party are clearly explained to the workers so that they will see for themselves how they coincide with their own interests and they will consequently defend them against every kind of opposition.
>
> Unless the workers are made familiar with the Party's goal, one cannot properly expect them to exert their fullest energies towards the realisation of these aims. Besides there is the danger that they may deviate to a course which would be harmful to their own interests.[15]

Paternalism is the keynote of the theory: it is the CPP which leads the workers, acquaints them with the party's plans, and protects them from themselves. The party's aim, according to Tettegah, was achieving economic independence. But economic independece was to be achieved by increased output, not by changing economic structures or property relations. Productivity, not revolution, was the key to development. Tettegah explained that "We will bring about our economic independence by the transformation of our entire national economy by raising the productivity of every worker at his place of work and in our entire national economy."[16]

---

15. John Tettegah, *Towards Nkrumahism*, Accra, 1962, p. 15.
16. *Ibid.*, p. 24.

Increased productivity brought increased output; increased output brought increased profits to Ghana's foreign-owned business. But while CPP "austerity" legislation enjoined party officials to be content with no more than two automobiles and two mansions, ordinary laborers in Accra were told for nearly six years to be content with their daily rate of 6 shillings 6 pence—as food prices rose and unemployment increased. Essentially the CPP solved the problem of moral vs. material incentives by denying both: the workers were ordered to become Stakhanovites to defend a revolution that had never really begun.

8

PEACEFUL COEXISTENCE IN ONE COUNTRY

A country is socialist or capitalist not because of the ideas or intentions of its government, but because of the social structure which characterizes it, and the nature of the classes which play the decisive role in ruling it.

—*Charles Bettelheim*

We have tried to show how a combination of stagnating cocoa revenue and government permissiveness in dealing with British banks and import-export firms produced a severe balance of payments crisis which could only be resolved by drawing dangerously on Ghana's reserves. We have also discussed the erosion of the Convention People's Party's popular base within the organized working class. Now we must try to analyze the interrelation between these two pressures.

The task of defending the economy against the unregulated power of foreign business units operating in Ghana had to be undertaken or economic collapse would result. But constantly circumscribing any effort to reduce the powers of the British firms, banks, and mines was the CPP's lack of a popular base.

The structure of CPP support had been formed in the early and mid-1950's by appealing to local, sectional, and ethnic interests in the countryside, and by building patronage machines in the urban areas. The CPP ran main roads through pro-CPP towns instead of through neighboring anti-CPP towns, backed Brongs against Ashantis, and provided ambitious school teachers and petty clerks with well paid quasi-political jobs. But the tactics which won the elections of 1954 and 1956 were inapplicable when it came to the arduous and dangerous job of confronting British economic power and building a strong national economy.

Yet considerable economic growth would be required merely to maintain Ghana's relative "affluence," as population pressure increased in the cities and as the new political and administrative elites became accustomed to their recently acquired consumption standards. Thus the new period required a break with the techniques of log-rolling, patronage wielding, and high-level negotiation. New methods of organization, mobilization, control, and communication were needed.

The six-year period of stewardship the Party leadership had served under the administration of Governor Arden-Clarke was a poor preparation for learning new political skills. The new situation required, above all, that the leadership make the demands of the most oppressed strata of the working class the moral imperative of the Party organization. The CPP, however, as the Ga Shifimo Kpee and the 1961 General Strike had shown, had grown steadily more and more isolated from Ghana's masses.

Although the CPP constantly referred to itself as a mass political party—one which supposedly first brought the techniques of Western political organization to Africa—this identification was quite misleading. The CPP was a mass party only in the sense that it had a large membership. It was not a mass party in the sense of mobilizing large numbers of people and bringing them into the political arena as active and politically conscious participants. Many of the men and women who bought membership cards in the CPP did so for the same reasons that citizens in the United States buy tickets to a policemen's ball. In both cases, the sale involves a tax levied on the vulnerable by the powerful. We have seen that membership in the CPP was required if the debtor-farmer was to be eligible for a loan from the CPP-administered Cocoa Purchasing Company. This principle was systematically extended to nearly every government agency. The "mass" membership that it generated could provide very little of the leadership and self-sacrifice required for the CPP to meet the challenges it now faced.

The CPP leadership, it must be said, recognized that a break with the past was required. It tried to develop new strategies and new approaches. Part of this awareness was reflected in the scrapping of the Second Development Plan and the substitution of a new Seven Year Plan which held out socialism as a goal. The CPP also formulated a new party program, which was formally adopted in April 1962. Entitled the "Program of the Convention People's Party for Work and Happiness," it tried to define the Party's approach to socialism.

In trying to break with the past, however, the CPP showed how securely it was still bound by it. One of the critical tests of the solidity of mass support for any party is its ability to conduct open self-criticism. If it is not afraid of its constituents, it can afford to admit its mistakes, explain what errors produced untenable positions, and suggest how a new course can be taken. But if the party no longer has the confidence of the masses, it builds up a web of mystifications about its past and seeks to show that every new course of action is somehow related to, or the logical result of, an old victorious action. Thus the party has never made a mistake and, as long as it is guided by its present leaders, never will make a mistake. Even as the party abruptly changes its political direction by 180 degrees, the leaders announce, over their shoulders as it were, that the course of the party has never changed. And so we learn from the CPP program:

The Party has always had a consistent theory for enlarging the country's prosperity as the outline of our history included in this program will make clear. This theory has been tried out in practise during the difficult circumstances of the last ten years. The progress that has been made is indisputable proof of the practicability and correctness of the Party's line.[1]

Since the party's line was both consistent and correct, and since it had led to success after success, it was clear that whatever problems still existed in the country must be the result of vestiges of the past. According to the CPP program, therefore, it was not the present-day property system or productive relations that constituted a barrier to change—the legitimacy of existing owners, managers, and leaders is never questioned—but the remaining influences of colonialism.

The Program for Work and Happiness states as one of its "pivotal" points that it is because of the "heritage of imperial-

---

1. "Program of the Convention People's Party for Work and Happiness," paragraph 6. The program is reprinted in David Apter, *Ghana in Transition,* New York, 1963, pp. 393-421.

ism and colonialism" that socialism must be adopted.² Socialism, for the CPP, is seen as a superior institutional means for coping with colonialism. It is not explicitly viewed as a vehicle for the betterment of a specific class, or as a system which offers a more rational or ethical way to organize society. It is forced on the leadership by outside circumstances and the need for rapid economic growth. As the Program for Work and Happiness states, socialism was adopted because the colonial heritage militated against choosing any other method of economic growth: "Owing to the absence of facilities for capital formation, it was clear from the very beginning that this prodigious task could only be accomplished successfully by the institution of socialism."³

Here we have the key to the CPP concept of socialism: it is a set of techniques and institutions which enable rapid economic progress and economic independence in the face of a colonial heritage, rather than the mode of operation characteristic of a workers' and peasants' state. The whole theory and practice of CPP socialism flow from this basic distinction.

The Theory of CPP Socialism

Although one of the aims of the Program for Work and Happiness was the achievement of economic independence, the Ghanaian government thought that foreign investment could still play a positive role in the economy. In the Lewis era, foreign capital was to be the engine of industrialization; now the state was to be the engine, while foreign investors provided the fuel, i.e., the capital and foreign exchange.⁴ Foreign capital was assigned a major role in the Seven Year Plan: of the £1,000 million capital expenditure foreseen, no less than 40 percent was to come from foreign sources. But how did the CPP think it could protect the economy against the effects of such large-scale foreign enterprise? And why, in view of the failures of the Lewis period, did it think foreign capital would be attracted to Ghana —especially now that it had proclaimed socialism as its goal?

The CPP's answer was to deny that there was any fun-

2. *Ibid.*, paragraph 7.
3. *Ibid.*, paragraph 33.
4. *Ibid.*, paragraphs 105-106.

damental conflict between foreign investment and economic independence. This denial was clearly expressed in Nkrumah's speech at the dedication of the Volta Dam, one month before the coup: "[The United States] is the leading capitalist power in the world today. Like Britain in the heyday of its imperial power, the United States is, and rightly so, adopting a conception of dual mandate in its relations with the developing world."[5] "This dual mandate," Nkrumah said, "if properly applied, could enable the United States to increase its own prosperity and at the same time assist in increasing the prosperity of the developing countries."[6] He pointed to the Volta Project as "living proof that nations and people can cooperate and coexist peacefully with mutual advantage to themselves despite differences of economic and political opinions."[7] State enterprises and private enterprises, foreign capital and underdeveloped nations—all could work together to their common benefit.

The most ambitious attempt to explain how this peaceful coexistence between different social systems could contribute to socialism was made by J. H. Mensah, Chairman of the National Economic Planning Commission, in his presidential address to the Economic Society of Ghana. In a speech on "The Relevance of Marxian Economics to Development Planning in Ghana," Mensah argued that it was impossible to apply a theory dealing with European experience directly to the Ghanaian situation. Traditional Marxist theory, he said, is aimed "at the reorganization of the ownership of existing property."[8] But in a developing country this is not a central issue, for "by and large, the means of production do not exist."[9] The real problem to which socialists in developing areas should address themselves

---

5. Cited in *Africa Report,* April 1966, p. 22. "Dual mandate" was the theoretical rationalization for the policy of "indirect rule," a scheme which enabled British colonialists to rule large areas cheaply by co-opting indigenous chiefs as British agents. Credit for this theory belongs to Lord Lugard, acclaimed as the "conqueror" of Uganda and Northern Nigeria. After serving as military governor of the latter territory, he wrote the notorious *Dual Mandate in British Tropical Africa,* London, 1923. The book presents the last serious defense of slavery by a 20th-century author.
6. *Africa Report,* April 1966, p. 22.
7. *Ibid.*
8. *The Economic Bulletin of Ghana,* Vol. IX, No. 1, p. 4.
9. *Ibid.,* p. 14.

"is not the rearrangement of the ownership of the means of production. The central concern must be with the building up of the nation's stock of productive assets."[10]

Because increasing the nation's capital stock is the primary problem, there is "a necessity for encouraging private investment, making tax concessions, and extending state guarantees to private investment as an integral part of the economic policy of a developing country despite its socialist ambitions."[11] Socialist ambitions, however, do have an important role to play: the rate of growth of the state sector must always exceed that of the private sector. But, Mensah warned, citing the *Guide to the Implementation of the Seven Year Plan,* "This should not be done by hindering the growth of the private sector, but by maximizing the growth of the public sector. Private enterprise will not be killed; it will be surpassed."[12]

Mensah also maintained that there are no classes and no class conflict in Ghana. Operationally speaking, there are really just citizens. And since class conflict does not exist, there is no need for a socialist party to mobilize poor peasants and landless laborers to transform the countryside. Instead, Mensah noted, "We are using the chiefs and other leaders of village society in laudable programmes of community development. Our political theory should not be based on the assumption that the chiefly class is an antagonistic class."[13]

Mensah, it must be stressed, did not hold views that were radically different from those of the rest of the CPP. Take, for instance, the description of socialism offered by Kofi Baako,

---

10. *Ibid.,* p. 14.

11. *Ibid.,* p. 14.

12. *Ibid.,* p. 14. Léopold Senghor of Senegal has propounded almost the same theory. Compare, for example, the following statement: "And yet we have not legally suppressed private capitalism which is foreign to our country; we have not even nationalized anything. . . . Why? Because we began by analyzing our situation as an underdeveloped and colonized country. The essential task was to win back our national independence. Next we had to eliminate the flaws of colonial rule while preserving its positive contributions. . . . Where private capitalism comes into peaceful competition with socialism, the latter must, I feel sure, emerge triumphant. . . . In the meantime, we need capital, even from private sources." Cited in *West Africa,* May 12, 1962, p. 507.

13. Mensah, "The Relevance of Marxian Economics to Development Planning in Ghana," p. 15.

one of the founders of the CPP and a man who was often closer than anyone else to Nkrumah:

In an Nkrumahist-Socialist state, the farmer will not lose his farm; the landlord will not lose his house, but will not be allowed to exploit the tenant; the employer will not be allowed to exploit the worker, nor will the worker be allowed to cheat the employer by idling about; the car owner will still have his car. . . . [Nor will] the property or wealth which some one has acquired or earned through hard labour and through honest use of his mental and physical energies be taken away from him and shared among lazy, unscrupulous, indisciplined but able-bodied citizens.[14]

Neither landlords nor capitalists will be abolished—they will simply be regulated.

This is one of the remarkable things about the CPP: despite the wide differences in professed ideology between the Marxists like Mensah and the Nkrumahists like Baako, all seemed to mean the same thing when they talked about "socialism." None of them thought that socialism required sweeping changes in the social relations of production. Was Krobo Edusei really so far from the mainstream of CPP thought when he defined "socialism" as a system in which "if you have a lot of money you can still keep it"?

The CPP theory of socialist development is not, as one might suppose, an idiosyncratic deviation or innovation in the history of socialist thought. The main elements of CPP strategy can also be found in the programs of numerous social democratic, socialist, and communist parties, not only in Africa but throughout the world. The doctrine of peaceful coexistence between private and state sectors in one country is especially popular. It not only forms the basis of political strategy in such oppressed countries as Léopold Senghor's Senegal, but is advocated by Soviet "third world" specialists.[15]

It is not surprising, therefore, that many view the coup not as a product of the Nkrumah regime's failures, but as a direct result of its successes. For them, Nkrumah's Ghana has already become a socialist Atlantis which other oppressed coun-

14. *West Africa*, May 13, 1961, p. 505.
15. See especially the collection entitled *The Third World in Soviet Perspective*, ed. by R. Thornton, Princeton, 1964.

tries are urged to emulate. For example, we read in *Political Affairs,* the theoretical organ of the Communist Party of the United States, that:

This military coup is not the ordinary one. It is a desperate effort to reverse the path Ghana has chosen to secure its economic independence—the path of non-capitalist development; the path toward socialism. For the path of Ghana symbolized for all the new emerging nations how to break out from dead-end dependence on the imperialist ravagers of their natural wealth and resources.[16]

According to this view, "Ghana would have weathered the economic storm" she faced, and this was precisely why the coup was organized. "Time was running out for the imperialists to sabotage and retard the advance of the new system. They decided to strike."[17]

Was the "advance of the new system," along with its two million CPP supporters really stopped by a few hundred military "saboteurs"? Or was there something inherently wrong with the theory and practice of CPP socialism? This is the problem we must now examine.

CPP Socialism in Practice

CPP thinking about the transition to socialism is based on three assumptions. The first assumption is that state ownership of certain of the means of production necessarily leads to socialism. The second is that the state sector can overcome the private sector without engaging it in a life-and-death struggle. The third assumption is derived from the second but must be discussed separately: it is that foreign private capital will let itself be used to build socialism. What did CPP practice show about the validity of these assumptions?

(1) State Ownership and Socialism

The CPP's main interventions into the private sector of the economy were not in manufacturing, agriculture, or mining, but

---

16. "Ghana" (editorial), April 1966, pp. 1-2.
17. *Ibid.,* p. 4.

rather in trade and marketing.[18] The CPP was never able to achieve as much state ownership as the country described in the following passage:

> The government owns and operates the railroads. There are a not inconsiderable number of industrial enterprises owned and operated by the government. . . . There are a number of mixed public-private enterprises. Public utilities, the radio, the telegraph, telephone, local transportation systems, municipal savings banks, etc., are publicly owned.[19]

The public budget in this country is 35 percent of the total national income, and the government is responsible for 25 percent of capital formation. Which country is it—Sweden? Finland? Burma? No, it is the West German Federal Republic. The example illustrates that it is not the size of the state sector that determines whether the society as a whole is capitalist or socialist, but the use to which the state sector is put. Does it exist primarily to serve the interests of private capital (as, for example, in the cases of Italian oil and British coal), or does it operate to serve the interests of the people as a whole?

In Ghana, there has been a state sector—railroads and utilities—for many years. It was established by the Guggisberg Ten Year Plan, which was drawn up in 1919. Twenty-four million pounds were spent in order to provide the Gold Coast with a modern, state-owned infrastructure.[20] The function of this state sector was, of course, to provide transportation and harbor facilities to assist the operations of the mineowners and the import-export firms. Merely by expanding this inheritance quantitatively, the CPP did not necessarily change its function. Since neither size nor growth in the state sector indicates whether or not a country is undergoing a transition toward socialism, we

---

18. CPP "nationalization" of several exhausted British gold mines was carried out because the owners had abandoned and threatened to flood them if compensation were not paid. The Nkrumah government paid off the British mine owners and worked the mines at a considerable loss because it needed the foreign exchange and could not find other work for the unskilled labor in the mines. See Tony Killick, "Mining," in *A Study of Contemporary Ghana*, pp. 257-262.

19. Alvin H. Hansen, *The American Economy*, New York, 1957, p. 14.

20. E. N. Omaboe, "The Process of Planning," in *A Study of Contemporary Ghana*, p. 440.

must further examine the relation between the state sector and the private sector, both in theory and in the actual Ghanaian context.

(2) Peaceful Coexistence between Sectors

The first major intervention into the trading sector since the disbandment of the corrupt Cocoa Purchasing Company was announced in December, 1961. The CPP began to regulate import licenses and to exercise quantitative control over imports. The Ghana National Trading Corporation (GNTC) was also set up, with 43 branches scattered throughout the country. The GNTC was later expanded by the £6-million purchase of the A.G. Leventis chain, and eventually received a monopoly of the import of "essential" goods.

These measures were desperately needed to gain control of the balance of payments situation. If the firms were allowed to continue to import freely, not only would deficits be threatened, but coordinated economic planning and collection of tax revenues would be impossible. As Tony Killick writes:

Ghana has been criticized for resorting to a regime of import restrictions and exchange controls. The truth may be that she delayed too long before imposing them. Thus the Seven Year Plan came into operation with . . . [the reserves] exhausted and it depended entirely for its success on an inflow of foreign capital on a scale completely without precedent in the recent history of the country.[21]

Simply from the standpoint of preserving national economic integrity, an agency with the functions of the GNTC was justified. As the chairman, E. N. Nortey, explained, "The idea is to end a situation in which 95 percent of our retail and wholesale trade is in foreign hands."[22] Yet in 1961, Nortey felt compelled to minimize the extent of this CPP intervention in the trade sector. "We are competing," he said, "in a small way at first, on absolutely equal terms, with private firms." Nortey denied at the time that the CPP had any immediate plans to take over the means of distribution within the country, but

---

21. Tony Killick, "External Trade," in *ibid.*, p. 359.
22. This, and the following Nortey quotes, are cited in *West Africa*, March 17, 1962, p. 296.

acknowledged that it might happen "if the logic of the situation should take us there." "Our concern now," Nortey said, "is to build up our business and efficiency in order to compete freely without the benefit of any favoritism." Nortey explained that the GNTC would have to pay the same duties as other import agencies and would have to stay within the same import quotas. Similarly, the GNTC had to raise money from the commercial banks "in the same way as everyone else." The grants which it received from the government were for initial administrative expenses only.

But the GNTC, even though it eventually received "monopoly" powers, soon became the plaything of the private trading sector and a burden on the public. The Abraham Commission, formed in 1965 to investigate the activities of the GNTC, reflected in its report the fact that the GNTC actually intensified the role of the big import-export firms. Small retailers were driven out of business, while big retail interests were often able to bribe and extort rights and privileges with respect to practically any commodity. Goods destined for the Northern Territories were diverted to the Kumasi market; special commodities were allocated to favored traders; "corruption, prevarication, the diversion of stocks and the black market came to stay."[23]

The Abraham Commission's recommendations for ending the situation, however, would have increased the big firms' power still more. It suggested curtailing the number of importers by cutting out small importers on the basis of "poor performance"; requiring bank certification of importers; and granting licenses only to those importers with wholesale or retail facilities.[24] All these measures would have hurt the remaining Ghanaian commercial entrepeneurs, without affecting the big firms in the least. A few weeks before the coup, the government did rescind the licenses of all importers who had no retail or wholesale facilities, i.e., small Ghanaian businessmen and suc-

---

23. The words are those of Frantz Fanon, written in 1961 and undoubtedly with the experience of Ghana in mind. *The Wretched of the Earth*, p. 145.
24. *Daily Graphic, January* 31, 1966. Both the firms and small Ghanaian importers were still allowed to import "nonessential" commodities.

cessful market women. It also ended the GNTC's monopoly over the import of essential commodities.[25]

The collapse and scandal of the GNTC was not an anomaly: it was a mirror of nearly all Ghanaian attempts to enter the marketplace in competition with private business. Early agricultural experiments with state farming, carried out in the mid-50's on unoccupied land, proved a complete failure. An official report on these experiments, known as the Gonja Development scheme, evaluated it as follows: "The fundamental lesson is, without doubt, that the new ways cannot at present compete with traditional methods of agriculture as practiced in that region."[26] And the experiments of the 60's, according to the Abraham Report, were no more successful: the Ghanaian state farms had not, by 1966, produced enough foodstuffs to justify the amount of capital tied up in them.[27]

Nor was CPP intervention into manufacturing any more successful. According to the Minister of Finance's 1965 budget statement, the government had invested £40 million in 32 state enterprises, whose total losses up to the end of 1963 amounted to over £15 million.[28]

In studies of labor productivity, state-owned establishments tended to be well below the average. In electricity there was one privately owned establishment while the rest were public: the private concern had the highest productivity. There were four publicly owned printing concerns, all of which ranked low in terms of labor productivity, with an average half that of the private concerns. In logging and sawmilling there was one public enterprise: it had the lowest productivity recorded for the industry. In construction, there were 14 publicly owned concerns, 71 privately owned concerns, and two "unknowns." Almost all of the publicly owned concerns were well down in the bottom half

25. *Daily Graphic*, February 10, 1966.

26. Gold Coast Agricultural Development Corporation, *First Report and Accounts*, 1955-1956, Accra, 1957, p. 9. Cited in Tony Killick, "Agriculture and Forestry," in *A Study of Contemporary Ghana*, p. 232.

27. *Daily Graphic*, January 31, 1966.

28. *West Africa*, April 17, 1965, p. 419.

of the rankings, and they had an average productivity of about half that of private enterprises in the industry.[29]

While the Abraham Report blamed the failures of state-run enterprise on corruption and lack of Ghanaian administrative ability, the real cause for the consistent failures lay not in the Ghanaian character but in CPP theory and practice. The CPP at first imagined that it could compete on an equal basis with the import-export firms; later, when it granted the GNTC a monopoly on import licenses, it thought that legal advantage was sufficient to guarantee the GNTC a competitive position. The assumption that private and state sectors can co-exist prevented the CPP from realizing the power the big firms could generate even against a legal "monopoly."

What is the appropriate method of bringing the capitalist sector under effective control? On the basis of his experience in Algeria and Ghana, Frantz Fanon wrote:

If the government wants to bring the country out of its stagnation and set it well on the road towards development and progress, it must first and foremost nationalize the middleman's trading sector. . . . Nationalizing the intermediary sector means organizing wholesale and retail cooperatives on a democratic basis; it also means decentralizing these cooperatives by getting the mass of the people interested in the ordering of public affairs.[30]

The correctness of this view is borne out by the experience of the Chinese Revolution. When the state began to intervene in the capitalist sector to control the means of exchange and coordinate industrial planning, the private sector resisted by the same methods that were later used in Ghana—bribery of government workers, theft of government property, etc. A government counter-attack was launched: in 1952 the *san fan* movement was organized among government workers against the "three evils" of corruption, waste, and bureaucracy. It was followed by the *wu fan* movement against the "five evils": bribery of government workers, tax evasion, theft of government property, cheating on government contracts, and stealing economic in-

---

29. Tony Killick, "Labour: Industrial Productivity," in *A Study of Contemporary Ghana*, p. 170.
30. *The Wretched of the Earth*, pp. 144-145.

formation from government sources. According to Hsueh Mu-chiao: "The latter movement scored a victory as a result of the exposures made by the workers and other employees in the capitalist enterprises and the legal actions taken by the state. This struggle again shows that it would have been impossible to score successes in the economic struggle without relying on the strength of the masses and the proletarian dictatorship."[31]

But not even political mobilization is enough to protect the state sector. Full *economic* mobilization is also necessary. As the Soviet economist Preobrazhensky pointed out in 1926, the newly formed individual state enterprise is in a completely different position from the typical capitalist enterprise. It is much weaker. Therefore, it cannot be supposed that the socialist factory will outproduce the capitalist factory in competitive struggle in the same way that the capitalist factory conquered the crafts. This analogy, according to Preobrazhensky, is a "crude, superficial, uncritical analogy with the past."[32]

Like Mensah, Preobrazhensky recognized that the means of production in his country were undeveloped. The USSR, he said, lacked "the material prerequisites needed for reconstructing [socialism's] technical bases."[33] But his response was very different from Mensah's. He argued that "for the state economy of the proletariat it would be utterly (and most stupidly) self-destructive to try to defeat capitalism in the arena of free competition at the present state of development of socialist economy. The latter would be disintegrated and eventually beaten in the struggle."[34] Instead, Preobrazhensky argued:

The state economy goes into action, and cannot but go into action, only as a unified whole. An individual state enterprise detached from the whole . . . would probably not survive but would be crushed. But the same enterprise forming part of the unified complex of state economy has behind it all the power of this complex, and for this reason, it is now not at all an isolated enterprise or trust of the old capitalist type.[35]

---

31. *The Socialist Transformation of the Nationalist Economy in China*, Peking, 1960, p. 52.
32. *The New Economics*, Oxford, 1965, p. 127.
33. *Ibid.*
34. *Ibid.*
35. *Ibid.*, p. 128.

During the period in which individual state enterprises accumulate material resources, they will inevitably be weaker than private enterprises. Consequently, the superiority of a socialist enterprise only makes itself felt as a result of very large-scale cooperation and coordination.

The CPP lacked both the mass base and the economic control needed to establish the hegemony of the state sector. Lacking this strength, it nevertheless expected to compete according to the capitalist rules of the game. When a state-run industry exposed its inevitable weakness, however, this was a sign to the CPP that the enterprise should be abandoned as impractical. Unable to capitalize on the initiative of the organized working class, and increasingly disappointed by the "failures" of state enterprises, the CPP not surprisingly became more and more convinced of the correctness of its third major assumption—the ability of the state sector to attract and control foreign capital while building socialism.

(3) Foreign Capital and CPP Socialism

There is a seeming anomaly in the pattern of foreign investment in Ghana. During the Lewis era of laissez-faire and state inactivity in industrialization, foreign investment was unimpressive; in the post-1961 period, foreign capital poured in, comparatively speaking. If the foreign capital involved in the Volta Project is temporarily excluded from consideration, we find that, although long-term investment was negligible, short-term investment totals exceeded anything achieved during the Lewis period. According to the 1964 *Economic Survey,* Ghana had received £168 million worth of medium- and short-term credits. Practically the entire sum had been received since 1961. How had Ghana been able to draw so large a sum? What were the conditions under which the money came? And what specific advantages did it bring to the Ghanaian people?

If we break down the figure of £168 million somewhat further, we find that £157 million consisted of "suppliers' credits" with the bulk of repayments concentrated within four to six years.[36] The system of suppliers' credits is one in which

---

36. *West Africa,* October 9, 1965, p. 1123.

individual foreign firms undertake to complete a "development" project under an agreement guaranteed by the firm's government. The firm then advances the credit for the cost of the project to the African government, generally at terms above the prevailing bank rates, with the principal to be repaid within four to six years. The debt is in turn guaranteed by the African government. Consequently, one of the main points about these foreign "investors" is that they do not invest. They neither risk any of their own money nor wait for the project to pay before they take their profit.[37]

This system proved to be highly beneficial to lagging industries in Great Britain and West Germany. To take one example, British shipbuilders were able to get a guarantee from the official British Export Guarantee Department for a £5 million submarine chaser for the Ghanaian government. Leaving aside the question of Ghana's vulnerability to submarine attack, this guarantee was reportedly given simply to boost British exports and help solve unemployment in British shipyards.

Another project financed by the suppliers' credit system involved a new road between Tema and Accra. Civil servants advised a modest project costing £1.9 million. However a £3.9 million contract for a full-scale motorway complete with telephones at regular intervals, was given to Parkinson Howard, the British contractors, and covered by the U.K. Export Guarantee Department.

Similarly, the West German government guaranteed a £9.5 million contract for a German firm to improve Accra's water and sewage system. Yet before the contract had been let, an expert study carried out by consultants appointed by the World Health Organization and the UN Special Fund had recommended a plan costing only £6.5 million.

The leader among all the firms providing suppliers' credits to Ghana is believed to be the Drevici group, also of West Germany. Ghana owes Drevici approximately £60 million in credits, all of which were guaranteed by the West German government. One of the projects planned but never built by

---

37. *West Africa*, March 26, 1966, p. 341. The examples following are also taken from this article.

Drevici was a giant tower topped by a revolving restaurant for the International Trade Fair in Accra.

As suppliers' credits increased, it soon became apparent that Ghana could not possibly finance the debt she had accumulated. Nevertheless, various Western countries, anxious to increase their export earnings, continued to cooperate with their firms, regardless of Ghana's ability to pay. As one observer noted in 1965: "Ghana has been sold a massive shipyard (how Ghana can provide credits to finance the sale of ships is a mystery) by a contractor from one of the several countries where the shipbuilding industry is notably 'depressed.' Perhaps this is one explanation for the contract?"[38]

Even in 1964, the mounting debts owed to Ghana's "investors" abroad were beginning to disrupt the economy. Total revenue for that year was £120 million, and total government expenditure amounted to £144 million.[39] Of this sum, it was necessary to spend approximately £26 million for debt service payments.[40]

In 1964, as it happens, the budget was more nearly balanced than in either of the two previous years. Beginning in 1960, with Ghana's reserves sinking, deficit financing had been required, and severe inflation followed. For example, between March, 1963 and December, 1964, the price of locally grown food rose by as much as 400 percent in some parts of Ghana. The average rise in food prices was 36 percent and the average rise in all prices was 17 percent.[41] But inflation, instead of stimulating the economy, was accompanied by growing unemployment.[42] This resulted in part from the kind of projects Ghana's Ministers had been persuaded to buy on suppliers' credits. They did not invest in projects that would be produc-

---

38. Douglas A. Scott, "External Debt-Management in a Developing Country," in *Financing African Development*, ed. by Tom J. Farer, Cambridge, 1965, p. 55. The country referred to is Great Britain and the contractor is Parkinson Howard.

39. *West Africa*, October 9, 1965.

40. Scott, "External Debt-Management in a Developing Country," p. 57.

41. *West Africa*, February 19, 1966.

42. Robert W. Norris, "On Inflation in Ghana," in *Financing African Development*, p. 104.

tive in a relatively short period: only 16 percent of the total spending involved industrial projects; agriculture accounted for only three percent, but infrastructural loans amounted to 72 percent.[43] Many of Ghana's investments would yield a return only after many years—if ever.

As Ghana's total external obligation soared—in 1964 it reached £349.2 million—confidence in her ability to pay decreased proportionately. In addition, import restrictions were imposed more tightly; the black market thrived; foreign exchange became the most valuable asset in the country; foreign-owned banks grumbled at requirements forcing them to hold government securities against their deposits; and there were growing complaints about the difficulty of getting payment from Ghana. Meanwhile, Ghana's Ministers continued to negotiate suppliers' credits—until the coup brought the process to a halt. As the *Wall Street Journal* noted the day after the coup, "Ghana is bankrupt, but you can't liquidate a country." Ghana was not liquidated after the coup: she was placed in receivership. And her Generals are now negotiating with the "creditors."

The Volta Project

Despite the mounting burden of suppliers' credits, many like to point to the Volta Project—the dam and aluminum smelter complex financed by the World Bank and the Kaiser Company—as proof that the CPP's faith in foreign capital was not totally misplaced. *Political Affairs* described it as the most important accomplishment of the Nkrumah period: through it, "Ghana became the first former colony in Africa to establish a power base of electrical energy for the all-sided development of the country."[44] Nkrumah himself, in his dedication speech referred to it as "a concrete symbol of the type of international cooperation which can, to quote my friend Edgar Kaiser, help to 'forge world peace.' "[45]

Whatever the Volta Project may have meant in the international context, it certainly was a monument to the CPP's faith

---

43. *Ibid.*
44. "Ghana," April 1966, p. 3.
45. *Africa Report,* April 1966, p. 22.

in foreign capital. What exactly is it that the Volta Project is supposed to do for Ghana that calls forth such profuse praise?

Preliminary analysis indicates that many of the expectations raised by the dam will be disappointed. In 1961, when Eugene R. Black, then head of the World Bank, was negotiating the loan for the project, he noted:

In the long run, these projects may well be the foundation on which an industrial Africa rises. But now the major benefit to the new African nations is simply the rent or royalty or taxes that accrue to the government. I am the first to admit that, desirable as these projects are, they do not by and large provide great numbers of new jobs, particularly skilled jobs for Africans; they do not produce goods for the local market and thereby encourage the learning and spread of modern business practices; they have not succeeded in stimulating local African enterprises.[46]

Since 1961, there has been no major change in the nature of the Volta Project that might cause a re-evaluation of this appraisal. The project, now completed, consists of a dam at Akosombo capable of generating 833,000 kilowatts. Behind the dam is a lake 250 miles long, providing possibilities for inland fishing.[47] The power from the dam runs a smelter—not an aluminum factory—at Tema. As we shall see, this is one of the most important aspects of the project. As Black indicated, the project does not require much labor: the preparatory commission estimated a maximum manpower requirement of 145 for the operation of the power project. This works out to £400,000 worth of capital per man.[48]

According to Nkrumah's dedication speech, "The Kaiser Company's re-examination of the project enabled us to lower substantially the cost of the entire project."[49] The reason why Kaiser was able to cut costs below original estimates is because

46. Eugene R. Black, *Tales of Two Continents,* New York, 1961, p. 9.
47. Flooding the lake involved moving 78,285 people. Because farms have not been made available, the displaced persons have been quartered in camps and fed by the UN Food and Agricultural Organization. It has been estimated that it will take five years for many of the "settlers" to be provided with land. The "settlers" have been accused of developing a "refugee mentality." See *West Africa,* February 5, 1966.
48. Tony Killick, "Volta River Project," in *A Study of Contemporary Ghana,* p. 394. Our analysis is drawn largely from Killick's article.
49. *Africa Report,* April 1966, p. 21.

the project originally included an aluminum factory, not just a smelter. The British government, together with British aluminum companies, was going to enter into a contract to build an integrated aluminum industry, using hydroelectric power from a dam across the Volta at Ajena to refine Ghanaian bauxite. Projects to irrigate the Accra Plains and to develop a fishing industry were also included. This was before 1956, however; at that time dollars and aluminum were still scarce, and Britain wished to gain a certain independence from United States suppliers. But after 1956, neither aluminum nor dollars were so scarce, and the British lost interest in the project.[50]

The project seemed to have fallen through when, in 1958, Nkrumah made contact with Edgar Kaiser who agreed to participate. Kaiser, however, was in a position to drive a very hard bargain, for no other aluminum company was interested. By any standards, Ghana got a much worse deal from Kaiser in 1958 than she would have received from the British in 1955. Among other things, the Kaiser project did not provide for irrigation or fishing, and the public utilities aspect of the project was separated from the aluminum industry. Most important of all, Ghana no longer got an integrated aluminum industry—only a smelter. The smelter *imports* alumina, mined in Jamaica and processed in the United States; while the development of Ghana's own mines is "deferred." Now Ghana will get only about half the revenue that an integrated industry would have brought.

But why should Kaiser ship alumina from abroad to Ghana, when bauxite deposits lie so close to the source of power? The answer is that the price of power which Kaiser has contracted to buy from Ghana is so low that transhipment is more profitable than utilizing local sources.[51] Ghana, in fact, is furnishing power to Kaiser virtually at cost. Had the price been higher, Kaiser might have had to develop the local bauxite resources. The agreement however, runs for 30 years, so it will be a long time before Ghana gets an integrated aluminum industry.

Since Ghana is providing power to Kaiser at nearly cost,

---

50. Killick, "Volta River Project," p. 392.
51. *Ibid.*, p. 398. The price (2.625 mills per kwh) is said to be one of the lowest in the world.

the key to the project's financial success is ability to find other customers for the power. Use of the power has been offered to surrounding countries, but they are reluctant to give Ghana, or any foreign nation, control over their power. So far the only prospective foreign customer has been the United States Embassy in Togoland.[52] Thus it is likely that Ghana will have to find the needed customers within her own territory. And ability to find customers depends, in the final analysis, on the rate of industrialization in Ghana.

Meanwhile, the maximum amount of power that Kaiser is obligated to buy is £2.5 million per year. Interest and principal, which begin to fall due in 1967, amount to £3 million per year. How will the government meet the remaining costs? One suggestion is irrigating the Accra Plains. But this would cost nearly £28 million—a sum Ghana is not likely to be able to raise in the near future. A plan to stock the lake with fish faces the same financial problem. Perhaps the new government will adopt Nkrumah's suggestion that the dam be turned into a tourist attraction like Niagara Falls. ("At night the fountain can be lit by thousands of multi-colored lights.") No matter what is decided, it is safe to say that, whatever the Volta Project did to "forge world peace," it has not guaranteed Ghana's economic future. Now Ghana has power—its factories remain to be built.

Mediation and Revolution

The setting in which Nkrumah stood, on January 22, 1966, to deliver his last important speech, accepting the American "dual mandate," was indeed appropriate. Before him lay a gigantic dam, built with foreign capital, blocking off a mighty African river. African resources and United States capital combined—to provide cheap power for Henry Kaiser's smelter, stoked with raw material mined in another neo-colony. The finished ingots would be shipped back to the land of the mandatory power to be sold for industrial purposes. The leaders of the mandatees would be given, as Eugene Black pointed out, "simply the rent or royalty or taxes."

---

52. See *West Africa*, January 29, 1966.

Thus it is that the doctrine of peaceful coexistence between sectors in one country leads back inexorably to the colonial mode of production. In the colonial era, the African chief granted mining rights or use of the land to the foreigner for a few pounds yearly; now, in the post-independence era, the African president grants use of the rivers for a somewhat larger sum. The whole process operates on a much more sophisticated level, but the essential relationship remains unchanged—as do the living standards of the people of the mandated country. The question to be answered is: where did the Ghanaian national independence movement begin to double back toward the past?

The first indication was the CPP's behavior during the Positive Action campaign in 1950. Arden-Clarke's announcement that the CPP could achieve power under certain narrowly prescribed conditions split the movement in two. At the Positive Action trial, the entire party leadership denounced the General Strike. The stage was set for the CPP to begin its parliamentary career.

The CPP was then, it should be remembered, less than a year old: it had not had the years of experience which teach a party which alliances can be accepted as tactical devices and which must be rejected on principle. Within the CPP, those who accepted Arden-Clarke's temptation—and his conditions—prevailed. In a sense, therefore, the CPP's first mistake was its last —for clearly a coalition with colonialism is fatal to any party which seeks to base itself on the strength and aspirations of the colonized.

As parliamentarians, the CPP members were forced to take over duties that had hitherto been exercised only by the colonialists. It was the nationalist party which now served on the Cocoa Marketing Board and sent the country's economic surplus back to Britain. It was the nationalist party that was forced to hold the line on wages in order to protect the mine owners' profit margins. It was the nationalist party which came to believe that its "anchor of safety" was the British pound.

During the pre-independence period, the CPP naturally developed group interests which were neither those of the colonialists nor yet those of the colonized; and the granting of independence failed to reduce the fundamental divergence of interests. Ideologies appeared which sought to mask the conflict: they asserted that foreign capital and African socialism could coexist, while the party and masses worked to overcome the colonial heritage. But ultimately the CPP could not overcome the contradictions generated by its position as mediator between the former colonialists and the erstwhile colonized.

In any country, the political elite can derive its income only from tapping the economic surplus. But in an oppressed country like Ghana, there is no inherent tendency for self-sustaining economic growth. How, then, is the elite to derive its sustenance without starving its subjects? In the food-farming sector, a subsistence economy prevails; cash crops like cocoa have been subject to deteriorating terms of trade; mining is dominated by foreign firms with varying profit margins. Taxing the foreign-owned intermediary sectors—the banks and import-export firms—is as politically hazardous as trying to tax the mines. This leaves only one sector—manufacturing. In order to increase, or even maintain, its standard of living and its political machine, the political elite *must* increase manufacturing.

But, as we have seen, this cannot be accomplished without the complete mobilization of the organized working class, the same working class that the political elite was forced to discipline in the pre-independence days to placate the colonial interests. And in the post-independence period, the political elite and the organized working class confront each other as potential consumers of the economic surplus. To combat the growing dissatisfaction of the working class and the urban lumpenproletariat—which in Ghana was expressed both by the Ga Shifimo Kpee and the 1961 General Strike—the political elite is forced to turn more and more to mystification as a source of legitimacy. The cult of the leader is born—not from the nationalist hero's desire for flattery, but because, as Fanon points out, "the leader is all the more necessary now that there is no more party." But even this does not solve the economic problem.

Consequently, the political elite must turn more and more to foreign interests: taxes on the mines, the banks, the firms, small as they may be, provide the only solid source of revenue; suppliers' credits, onerous as the terms may be, remain the only hope for increasing the economic surplus as the population expands and the terms of trade decline. Eventually, however, the foreign investor demands his money back.

By the time the coup occurred, the CPP's relation to the masses had passed through three stages, similar to those experienced by political elites in oppressed countries elsewhere. During the first stage, the CPP derived its legitimacy from its ability to strike bargains with the colonial leaders. During the second stage, it derived legitimacy from its past successes in bargaining with the colonialists. During the final stage, the masses and the other competing elites—the army and the civil servants—began to realize that the bargains struck by the political elite were worthless to them. From this point on, it was only a matter of time before a new elite emerged which would resolve the contradiction either in favor of the masses or in favor of neo-colonialism. The effort to coordinate the interests of both had proved impossible.

The era of postwar colonial independence movements is over now. The political elites who mediated their way to power are giving way to new military/bureaucratic elites who function in the name of austerity and efficiency. But it must not be thought that, simply by acting in favor of the old colonial power, the new rulers have put an end to the contradictions which faced and defeated the departing political elites.

How can this "circulation of elites" be stopped? What is needed to put an end to the politics of mediation? How can political and economic independence be combined? The specific answers to these questions can only come from Africans, through the experience of their own revolutionary movements. Already, however, in "Portuguese" Guinea, where the *Partido Africano da Independencia da Guiné é Cabo Verde* (PAIGC) has liberated over half the country, a general outline of the solution appears to be developing. In "Portuguese" Guinea, starting with a movement very similar in class composition to that in Ghana during the early days of the CPP, the PAIGC has been able to develop a revolutionary movement through the process of anti-colonial war.

In the oppressed countries of the world, this process serves as the functional equivalent of the 19th-century industrial war between proletarians and capitalists. Not violence in itself, but the experience of serving in the militia and in the guerrilla army prepares the peasants and the urban workers for the post-liberation struggles of industrialization and national reconstruction. Peasants, proletarians, and revolutionary intellectuals develop into a homogeneous, disciplined force, learning at the same time the technical skills and the inventiveness needed for industrialization. The guerrilla army and the people's war reproduce the conditions of the proletarian army in countries where virtually no industry exists.

If, as the evidence of recent history suggests, this is the road forward for the exploited colonial and neo-colonial peoples of the world, then it will be in the forests and savannahs, where the roads turn into paths and the sun beats down on thatch-roofed shacks, that Ghana's working classes will join together to prepare the future.

MONTHLY REVIEW

an independent socialist magazine
edited by Paul M. Sweezy and Harry Magdoff

Business Week: ". . . a brand of socialism that is thorough-going and tough-minded, drastic enough to provide the sharp break with the past that many left-wingers in the underdeveloped countries see as essential. At the same time they maintain a sturdy independence of both Moscow and Peking that appeals to neutralists. And their skill in manipulating the abstruse concepts of modern economics impresses would-be intellectuals. . . . Their analysis of the troubles of capitalism is just plausible enough to be disturbing."

Bertrand Russell: "Your journal has been of the greatest interest to me over a period of time. I am not a Marxist by any means as I have sought to show in critiques published in several books, but I recognize the power of much of your own analysis and where I disagree I find your journal valuable and of stimulating importance. I want to thank you for your work and to tell you of my appreciation of it."

The Wellesley Department of Economics: " . . . the leading Marxist intellectual (not Communist) economic journal published anywhere in the world, and is on our subscription list at the College library for good reasons."

Albert Einstein: "Clarity about the aims and problems of socialism is of greatest significance in our age of transition. . . . I consider the founding of this magazine to be an important public service." (In his article, "Why Socialism" in Vol. I, No. 1.)

DOMESTIC: $7 for one year, $12 for two years, $5 for one-year student subscription.

FOREIGN: $8 for one year, $14 for two years, $6 for one-year student subscription. (Subscription rates subject to change.)

116 West 14th Street, New York, New York 10011

Selected Modern Reader Paperbacks